Dear Lorraine

Thank you for the

I hope you enjoy

(Please post a review if you—

DOMIN8

by

Stephen B. King

Domin8

Copyright

First printing 2016

ISBN: 978-1536988499

Stephen B. King

PO Box 416

Cannington, Western Australia, 6109

Australia.

www.stephen-b-king.com

Stephen B. King

Special Thanks

Domin8 has been a very long labour of love (I could write a book on writing this book!). It is the second book I wrote, but the fourth to see the light of day, which gives an idea of the work that's gone into it after that first draft. With each re-write and editing stage it has grown not only legs but extra feet and I would be very remiss if I didn't thank some people who helped me enormously along the long road that this has been.

My wife Jacqui puts up with a lot from me when I'm in the zone. She gets embarrassed when I complement her, but she is a woman by which other women should be measured. My daughter Tania has provided endless support and tireless patience and she was the first person to read that initial draft of Domin8, and while she gave great objective criticisms, she loved the story and pushed and cajoled me to write more.

I've worked in the motor trade for many years, and met lots of people who unknowingly gave inspiration for Dave and others in this book, far too many to thank individually. And while the central characters are amalgamations of people I've known and worked with, any direct similarities to people alive or dead, is purely coincidental, trust me – I'm a car salesman.

On the technical side of things, I must thank two amazing people: My editor Alex Moore for fixing up the manuscript and making it readable, and web site and book cover designer Katrina Wall for bring my imagination to life. Alex put body and soul into telling me all the things wrong I'd written, and made some incredible suggestions where things could be improved, and this book would not be what it is without her input. Thank you Alex.

Domin8

Any mistakes left are my own, email me, please if you find any I missed.

Also by Stephen B. King

Forever Night
Repo
The Vigilante Taxi
Burial Ground

Available at: http://www.stephen-b-king.com

Stephen B. King

Contents:

Domin8

Stephen B. King

Domin8

BOOK ONE

"Be sure your sin will find you out"
The Bible

Stephen B. King

Chapter 1 – Melanie – Starsky and Hutch

Day One of the Nightmare

When the doorbell rang for the third time Melanie was desperate for me to permit her to reach orgasm. She was on her knees, naked, and positioned directly in front of her webcam. She was in her late thirties, thin, with short straight blonde hair and and was a vision of pure eroticism.

Melanie was a deeply submissive woman that I had met online and this was our third meeting. She had been begging for two or three minutes. As much as I wanted to help her finish what we had started forty-five minutes ago, whoever was at the front door was clearly not going away.

Making a decision, I said, "Melanie, please stop. Turn the vibrator off. NOW! Melanie."

She could tell by the tone of my voice I was serious. Her need was strong, but her desire to submit was stronger. With a tiny whimper she obediently ceased and settled back on her knelt haunches. She bowed her head and breathlessly replied, "yes, Master."

"Kitten, there is someone at the door who isn't going to go away. I will call you back as soon as I can. In the meantime, you must wait for me. No more playing; do you understand?"

"Yes, Sir. I will wait. May I please get up until you call back?"

"You may. Be good." I broke the connection to the private chat room we used and closed the laptop, feeling very annoyed at the interruption. I stood up from my study desk and went to see who was at the door, just as the bell rang for the fourth time.

I opened the door. Two men stood there, both wearing suits and ties. One was holding a large folder. It was after 8:30 on a Tuesday night. *"Too late for Jehovah's Witnesses,"* I thought.

"Mr. David Barndon?" The older and darkhaired of the two held out an identity card at arm's length for me which I couldn't read by the rather dim light above their heads and added, "I'm Detective Sergeant Milanski. This is Detective Collins. May we come in?"

Probably because one was gruff-looking with brown but greying hair, and the younger and more fit looking one was blonde, I immediately thought of Starsky and Hutch. I never really liked the TV show back in the day, but Dianne, my wife of twenty-six years, used to suffer a serious case of fan love for David Soul, who played Hutch, so I used to watch the show with her.

I found myself smiling at the thought that two TV cops from the seventies were calling on me. In fact, I found it so humorous I had to stifle a laugh.

"Sure," I replied. "Don't tell me the dealership's been broken into again?"

I was General Manager of a large Toyota car sales dealership near the city, which did get burgled from time to time, but a personal visit from two detectives at night was unusual.

"No, sir. It's a bit more serious than that, I'm afraid," he replied as we walked through the passage to the living area. I stopped dead in my tracks and turned back to them.

"What's happened to my wife? Is she hurt? Or is it one of the kids?"

Stephen B. King

I was suddenly worried. Dianne, my wife, was at work. She worked as a nurse and did three night shifts a week, which she preferred to days. It was quieter then. Our three children had all left home. Police only visit if it's bad news: they never come around to deliver good news.

"No, sir. It's got nothing to do with your family, but it's perhaps a good thing your wife isn't here. We need to ask you some questions."

For some reason he winked at me conspiratorially, and I breathed a sigh of relief. I turned back around, continued walking and sat at the dining table while they seated themselves opposite me. Blondie placed the folder in front of him and took out a notebook and pen.

"My wife is a nurse and works nights. Tonight she is on shift. So, ok. You've got my attention. What's up?"

"Mr. Barndon, do you know a Patricia White?"

They both stared at me while I thought about the name without success. I shook my head as I couldn't ever remember meeting anyone by the rather old-fashioned name of Patricia. I am sure I would have remembered if I had.

"No. I'm sorry. The name doesn't ring a bell. Why?"

The man with the folder took out a small black and white picture and placed it on the table between us. With a slightly sarcastic tone, he asked, "does her picture ring any bells for you?"

I felt the colour drain from my face, and my heart suddenly pounded hard in my chest. I looked up from the picture to them, in total shock. The photo was a head shot of a woman with closed eyes and extremely pale skin. She looked dead. "*How could that be?*" I thought. But there was no mistaking who it was.

Domin8

"Oh, I think he knows her. Let's just arrest him now," Detective Collins said. As he started to stand, his boss stopped him, "settle down, Sam. Let's give Mr. Barndon a few seconds to gather his thoughts. He looks like he's had a bit of a shock. Do you mind if I call you Dave, Dave?" He asked. I nodded slowly, thinking, deep in shock. He then said "Forgive my colleague, Dave: the exuberance of youth."

He raised his eyes quite comically. I had seen enough TV to realize they were doing the good cop, bad cop routine on me. That in itself was worrying, but the picture staring up at me was even more so.

He went on, "Make no mistake, Dave. This is a very serious matter. How you answer these next questions could mean the difference between being arrested or us leaving you in peace. You see, we know quite a bit about what you've been doing, so if you are anything less than totally honest with us..."

He let the silence hang in the air like a dark cloud.

I realized I had been holding my breath and let it out with a whoosh. I shook my head to clear it and once again looked at the picture. This was bad. Very, very bad. It could mean the end of my life as I knew it. It was one of those times when your whole past flashed before your eyes. If this went south, Dianne, my wife, would be devastated. The woman in the picture must have made some sort of complaint against me, but that sounded bizarre. "*She couldn't possibly have said I raped her, surely?*" I thought.

"Do I need a lawyer here?" I asked quietly. I was still trying to marshal my thoughts and stay calm as I looked Milanski in the eyes.

"Well, Dave, that depends on whether you have something to hide, wouldn't you say? Certainly if you want one present, that is your right, of course. We can leave and give you time to arrange that, no worries whatsoever. In the meantime, we could probably get a search warrant and serve it while he is here. How does that sound? Or, maybe, if you prefer, you can be honest with us now and possibly we could leave you alone, if we think you can't help us further with our inquiries."

He stared back at me with eyebrows raised, waiting for my response. He had me, and he knew it. I had no choice but to tell the truth and find out what the fuck this was all about. I took a deep, very nervous breath and began.

"I only know her as Patsy. I didn't know her name was Patricia and I never knew her last name. She told me she was divorced, bi-sexual and seemed to be a very happy-go-lucky, free spirited woman. We met via an online sex dating site. She emailed me to make contact and said she wanted to try being submissive for a change. We hooked up twice—once at a bar in town for half an hour or so to see if we liked each other and wanted to take it to the next step. The second time was when we had sex in a motel in Redcliffe on Saturday night."

I admitted it all, feeling very much like a naughty schoolboy in front of the headmaster. I could feel my face glowing red.

"I see, thank you for being so candid. Can we assume your wife doesn't know of your secret life of online dating, Dave?"

I shook my head and wished he wouldn't call me Dave. It felt more intimidating than if he used my surname, but of course I didn't want to anger him by asking him to stop after giving him permission when he asked me before. My head was spinning, and it was hard to think straight. I could feel my face burning with embarrassment.

"No, she doesn't know about it, and obviously, I'd like to keep it that way, please, guys. We've been married 26 years, and this is just a bit of fun for me, really. It's just a distraction to pass the time while she works nights: nothing more serious than that. The kids have left home, and my wife works night shifts three, sometimes four, times a week, and let's say the spark went out of our sex life years ago. It's nothing serious, no long term affairs. It's just no strings attached sex, and I love my wife deeply. What has Patsy accused me of?"

"Well, Dave, she hasn't accused you of anything, as such. When did you last see her?"

"I left her in bed at the Great Eastern Lodge Motel on the highway about eight-thirty or so on Saturday night."

The younger blonde detective was writing everything down in his notebook, Milanski nodded. "Are you sure about the time, Dave? And also, how was she when you left her?"

"Umm, let me think about this for a mo. Yes, I'm pretty sure that was about right. I met my brother at the Crown Casino just before nine as we had arranged, in the sports bar. I got there in time for the start of the second half of the Eagles' game. As for Patsy, she was absolutely fine, glowing in fact, but she was tired." I gave a crooked smile because it was, after all, my fault she was tired. The men didn't smile back. My weak attempt at humour went over their heads, so I hurried on.

"She thanked me for an amazing time and said she would stay a bit longer and have a sleep. The room was paid for, and she had nothing else planned for the night, she said. We arranged to meet at the same motel, at the same time next week. Really, Sergeant, what's all this about? What am I supposed to have done? The last I heard adultery wasn't against the law."

He totally ignored my question, "Dave, we will try to be discreet, but we are going to have to confirm this with your brother, because the timing is important, and the matter is

14

extremely serious. What are his details? Also, can you think of anyone else who can verify what time you got to the Crown? It will help your cause a lot if you can."

My heart sank even deeper, which a few moments prior, I wouldn't have thought possible. My brother was a devout Eagles fan, but he was also one of the biggest prudes in the world. As Vice Principal for a Catholic School I suppose he had to be. He had always been the white sheep of the family. I had most definitely been the black one. I searched my memory for the night at the crown.

"I parked in the new multi-story car park so I assume they have CCTV that will prove I was there well before nine. Oh, hang on, I paid with my credit card so that should be time stamped, too. I went straight to the bar and bought my brother a Gin and Tonic. He prefers Bombay Sapphire, which the girl who served me might remember—it being such a girlie drink. I asked her what the score was, and she said she was more of a rugby girl and didn't have a clue. I ordered a beer for myself, an Asahi. The girl's name who served me was…Julie, Jackie, Justine, something like that. It definitely started with a 'J.' She had short blonde hair with a fringe: kind of a bob cut."

I felt relieved and thankful for being able to be so coherent, because I felt far from that.

"Well, Dave, here's how this is going to work. You are going to call in at the station tomorrow and make a recorded statement in line with what you've told us and answer some more questions we may have for you. We are going to do you a favour and not talk to your brother just yet and possibly, if you've told the truth, not at all. We will check the CCTV and this 'J' woman at the Crown. If we can prove that you were there before nine, you may be very, very lucky and escape this ordeal with your marriage intact. But, if you don't mind a tip from a personal point of view, from someone who has been married thirty-seven years: stop the secret life. If your marriage is not working for you, fine. That happens to people all the time, but then leave her and play around as much as you want. Do you think she deserves this?"

I hung my head in shame. He was right, of course. I know I am a self-centred prick and really, I always have been. There was no argument there. But I still didn't know why an officer was giving me marriage guidance in the first place.

"If she hasn't complained about me…and realistically, I don't think she would have, as she was the one who initiated contact…*she* was the one who wanted to try it out and from what I could tell she loved our time together…but if she hasn't complained, other than being a complete bastard to my wife of twenty-six years, what have I done wrong? Please tell me what's going on."

They looked at each other, and some signal passed between them. The younger one sighed. "I'm sorry, Mr. Barndon for my earlier aggression, that's just how we roll. We are investigating a very serious incident. For myself, I'm a man of the world—and what you are doing, well, is not necessarily my cup of tea—but I've also had the occasional stray affair when I was married. Some of us cops do, just like 'normal' people, and maybe that's why I'm no longer married now. So, I'm pretty cool with the whole online dating thing for married people, and according to the papers, everyone is at it these days. But the old man here..." He pointed at his partner. "Well, he is perhaps not quite as forgiving, but he has his own reasons for that. We know she initiated contact with you and we also know what kind of relationship she was looking for with you. We've read all of her emails, not just to you, and they are pretty hot, let me tell you, so I can understand why you might want to meet up with her for a bit of fun."

Stephen B. King

"Oh my God," I thought. "Will the embarrassment of tonight never end? They had read my emails?" I must have turned an even deeper shade of red, because he smiled and chuckled, "Oh, don't worry. You weren't the only one. Let's just say she enjoyed being single and had a very uninhibited lifestyle. Your emails were kind of tame compared to some of the other men, and women, she dated. But the fact is that on Saturday night, so far as we know, you were the last person to see her alive. She died sometime between nine and ten, so forensics tell us."

I sat there, open mouthed, and couldn't speak. After some time, which could have been seconds but may have been minutes, I became aware they had been watching me closely, obviously to watch my reaction. "But she was in her late thirties or early forties and pretty fit. What killed her? Was it a heart attack or something?"

"No, Mr. Barndon. Someone bashed her head in with a piece of scaffolding pipe in your motel room. There was a mess everywhere. I've never seen so much blood and brains splattered everywhere in my life."

The shock and the thought of what it must have looked like was too much. I threw up. I only just turned my head in time; otherwise, I would have hit them with the projectile vomit. My early dinner came up, and my stomach continued to empty until I was dry retching. Through the fog, I heard a voice asking, "Are you OK? Would you like me to call your wife, Mr. Barndon?"

Domin8

Chapter 2 – Dianne
1985

I first met my wife in the most unexpected of places just before Christmas in 1985. Back then, Roger Moore was James Bond, Clint Eastwood was a Pale Rider, and Michael J. Fox first went back to the future. All I was interested in as a twenty-one year old male was sex, as often as possible and with as many girls as I could convince to do it with me. Funny how life comes full circle, because that's all I think about in more recent times too.

Dianne was the sister of a fellow salesman at work, who I met by total chance. I was a used car salesman who earned great money and drove nice cars. I dressed sharp and looked cool.

It was a Christmas work function, and my girlfriend of the day had come down with the flu—or so she had said—so I went along by myself, intending to get pissed with the workshop staff. They were all known for their Jack Daniels' binge drinking habits, and the company had an open bar for the night, so it was set to be a big drink and a lot of fun. That was probably the real reason my girlfriend, who I think was getting close to dumping me, decided she would stay home. She had started to get fed up with me because I wasn't serious about her. A steady relationship was the last thing in the world I wanted—there were far too many other women I hadn't yet met.

Lyin' Ryan, as he was known at work, was a womanizer of the first degree. In fact, he could have majored in it and made me look like an apprentice. He was a fellow used car salesman, and we got along well. Sometimes we would go out together at night and pull girls together, a couple of times even ending up swapping and sharing them in the same bed in a motel. That was just how we rolled in those more enlightened days. It was the car business, after all.

He never had a girlfriend longer than five dates. It wouldn't even last that long, if she wouldn't sleep with him. He said that any more than five, and the girl wanted to get engaged. Ryan was never going to do that, as there were far too many women he had to fuck before he died young. "Leave a good looking corpse behind," he used to say in his best James Dean way.

He was typical of all the bad things about used car salesmen in that era. He talked quickly, was very sharply dressed, wore mega expensive shoes and reflective high end sunglasses, but he could "move metal" and was, not surprisingly, one of our best salesmen. With his longish but very thin white blonde hair and his steel grey eyes and slim build he was a good looking guy who wore his "bad boy" used car salesman image as a badge of honour, along with his tattoos. The number, and quality, of the women who would be drawn to him like a moth to a flame never ceased to amaze me. Sometimes they would literally almost climb over me in a bar to get to him. They knew he would dump them. They knew they would have to have sex with him whenever and however he wanted, and none of them minded at all. At least, until the relationship ended; then there were tears galore, but he never stuck around to soothe the girls. He just didn't care.

He was an arrogant, self-centred and egotistical narcissist, but he had an incredible sense of humour, and people couldn't help but love him. No matter how sexist or sarcastic he would be, people thought he was hilarious. I don't know of a single occasion Ryan would go anywhere and not pick up a good looking girl, and that was why he wouldn't take one to a work function as that was just another opportunity for a "fresh one." For him, and myself, it was all about variety.

He would mingle with friends, have a few drinks and check out any women who were available—and some who weren't. If he didn't do well there, he would be off with any of the guys who wanted to hang off his coattails to a bar, club or the casino where he would "meet" someone. When he walked into a bar it was as if a spotlight was over his head, and every woman saw him immediately, wanting to have his baby.

So, for the Christmas function, he took his sister, Dianne. When he saw I was flying solo, he took the opportunity to leave her with me so he could go and chat up one of the married admin women, Jenny, to ask for a quick head job in the car park. He was insatiable. Ten minutes later, I saw Ryan leading the woman out the back door and shook my head at his sheer good luck, or was it audacity? His favourite saying was always, "a faint heart never won a fair maiden," and he sure won a lot of fair maidens.

If ever there were a brother and sister who were complete opposites, it was Dianne and Ryan. Not just in their looks and build, but personality too. He couldn't care less about people's feelings, while she would go out of her way to be nice, never expecting anything in return. She was brunette and big-eyed, he was blonde with thin grey eyes, but she was cute, no doubt about that. In fact, she was a whole lot better than cute.

No sooner had Ryan left us did she say to me in a cheerful voice, "Well, there goes my brother. That's the last I will see him tonight. Don't feel like you have to babysit me, Dave. I knew he would hand me off to the first person he could find, and I'm sorry you drew the short straw. I brought my own car because I knew this would happen so please don't feel obligated to look after me. I'm fine." She smiled the nicest smile, showing her flawless teeth, and added, "It's fine, really. You go and have fun. Go on, off you go. I used to go to school with Tish so I will catch up with her when she arrives."

Tish was our receptionist, so that told me that Dianne was 19 if they had been in the same year together. I had never seen Dianne before that night. To me the word that summed her up the most was: lovely.

Sure, she wasn't the most beautiful, she didn't wear the most expensive clothes, she wasn't smothered in makeup, she sipped beer from a bottle—not a cocktail through a straw—and she oozed old-fashioned niceness. The more I looked at her, the more I realized just how gorgeous she was with her high cheekbones, Farrah Fawcett-styled big hair, same grey eyes as her brother but so much bigger. She did possess a body that would always attract attention.

She wore a fairly simple, thigh-length dress, which was white with tiny purple flowers on it, that hugged her in the right places without being slutty. She didn't have a Barbie Doll figure, she was full-bodied, but not overweight, with good tits and legs, but the thing that set her apart from most women was her smile. She radiated happiness.

"Do people call you Di, or do you prefer Dianne?" I asked, thinking that I would hang around with her at least until Tish arrived, just to be sociable. By then the Jack Daniels and the mechanics would be screaming my name.

"I don't mind either way, but my friends call me Di mostly, I guess." She took another sip of her Corona with a lemon twist in the neck.

"Well, Di, it's true your brother did dump you with me, we both know what he's like. You should know that I would only stay if I wanted to. I'm a big boy, so the fact that I'm still standing here means that—for the moment, anyway—I'm right where I prefer to be. That said, your rules should apply to you as well as me, so if you feel like I've got bad breath or B.O. then you can feel free to go and mingle with no hard feelings either."

She leant in close and put her face in the crook of my neck, smelling my Pierre Cardin after shave. "Mmmm, well you don't have B.O. You smell rather dishy, in fact, and you've intrigued me. When you say you are a big boy, just how 'big' are you?" She giggled, her gorgeous boobs jiggling as she did. "*A sense of humour as well*," I thought. Another point was scored. I leant in close and smelt her too: what's good for the goose. I'm not big on women's perfumes—one smells just like another to me—but she did smell very nice. While leaning in close I whispered in her ear, "there is a rumour going around that I have eight inches."

"A rumour going around, really? Wow, what a good rumour." She laughed. She had a nice laugh, and I smiled back at her.

"Yes, a very strong rumour at that. I should know. I started it." I nodded, keeping a very straight face, while she laughed again. "Damn, her jiggling tits," I thought and then added, aloud, "there is a second one going around. Would you like to hear that one, too?"

"Oh yes," she said. "I love a good rumour."

Her eyes twinkled and gleamed with mirth, and while she didn't seem sure about the eight inches, she did have a faraway look in her eye. "Probably trying to imagine it," I thought. She was also trying very hard not to look at my crotch to check for herself, but I knew sooner or later she would.

"Well, the other rumour is that I have a five-inch tongue and I can breathe through my ears." I stared back at her. It took about thirty seconds or so before she caught on to what I meant, but when she did she laughed loudly and bent over at the waist, one hand on her knee while the other held onto her beer, trying not to spill it. She really did have a beautiful, sexy laugh, and looking down at her in that position I could see straight down the neckline of her dress. I admired her amazing breasts she had encased in a plain lace white bra. She could make very simple clothes look stunning, I realised, and my estimation of her went up another few notches.

She stopped just as the music changed to Robert Palmer, and I grabbed her hand, "Come on. Let's dance. This is my theme song." And without waiting for her to protest I led her to the dance floor, and we made some fairly outrageous moves to 'Addicted to Love.' She couldn't help herself; she had to look south to see if the eight inches were obvious.

I didn't get drunk with the mechanics that night, and I didn't get to show Dianne if I was lying about the eight inches; that was to come a few weeks later at a drive-in movie. What I did do was have a really great, fun night dancing with her and enjoying her company. I introduced her to everyone I worked with: not as Ryan's sister but just as Dianne. Everyone assumed she was my girlfriend.

After we ate at the buffet and had another dance session we went for a walk outside in the warm evening air, two fresh Coronas in hand. She asked me the obvious question, "So where's your girlfriend tonight?"

The thought crossed my mind to lie to her and try to fuck her. After all, I reasoned, she had been flirtatious and made it pretty clear anything was possible, but something held me back. That something was the realization that I had had more fun with her that night than I had had with any of the girlfriends I had previously, and so she deserved my total honesty.

"She's at home in bed with the flu, but to be honest, I reckon that was an excuse. I think she is getting ready to move on

Domin8

for Christmas and trade me in. I think she thinks I'm not mature enough for her. We've been fighting a lot lately, and to be fair to her I'm always fucking up around her. And, you know what? I agree: she does deserve better than me." I smiled to let her know I wasn't suicidal about it.

"Hmm, you mean she learnt to resist your five-inch tongue and eight-inch penis?" She made the word "penis" sound like the height of eroticism.

"Yeah, well, three times a night makes her too sore, she says. Anyway, how about you? Where's the guy in your life tonight?" I continued the subject. After all, I wouldn't have knocked back a quickie with her, but at least I had been honest if it did end up happening. But I knew enough to know she wouldn't if she had a boyfriend—and probably wouldn't anyway now that she knew that I hadn't broken up yet either. Dianne had morals, unlike her brother, it seemed to me.

"Oh, he left me to go and join the army. I've been boyfriend-less about six weeks now. My loss is the army's gain, I suppose." She smiled to show she wasn't suicidal either, and I nodded sagely and said, "Ah, the army." I nodded some more as if that explained everything, when really it didn't, and she giggled some more, seeing right through me.

"Well, Dave, firstly I'm sorry for you—that you're breaking up, though you don't sound terribly cut up about it. Secondly, umm, would you do me a favour?"

"If I can, sure, what is it?" I hoped she would say "take me somewhere and show me your eight-inch weapon." But, of course, she was far too nice and honourable, to sleep around with a guy who already had a girlfriend, even if the relationship was waning. I knew that, and to my surprise, I wasn't really disappointed.

Stephen B. King

"If you do break up, and you'd like to go out sometime, would you give me a ring? I'd like to get to know you a bit better. I think your girlfriend can't see the real you." She smiled at me, nervously, clearly unused to asking guys out. She continued, "Now, I think it's time I went home, beauty sleep and all that stuff. Thanks for a really nice night. I enjoyed myself and am glad Ryan dragged me along."

She held out her hand. I took it and shook it gently, and held on to it for a few seconds. I remembered a movie, a Billy Crystal one if memory serves, where the word "nice" was described as being awful, but by the way she said it, I knew she meant it. She enjoyed my company as much as I had enjoyed hers.

"Yes, I will give you a call, Di. I've enjoyed tonight as well." She turned and left with me admiring her bum as she walked away, in that simple dress with the faintest outline of her panties beneath and something clicked inside me, other than horniness for her body. I wasn't sure what it was, but I knew I wanted to see her again.

I was twenty-one at the time, with no intention of having a serious relationship with anyone. Isn't that always the way? As a freshly unattached guy I took Di out for dinner and drinks on Christmas Eve, which I thought was pretty sophisticated. From that first date we became good friends who could laugh and joke about anything and everything. I realized she was something special, so much so that when I took her home, all I did was kiss her goodnight.

It was unusual for me, in that era, not to try to feel a girl up at the earliest opportunity. In those days I must admit I was nothing if not shallow and sex obsessed. With anyone else in that period in my life my hands would have been all over her as we kissed, testing the water to see how far I could go, watching the reaction to see if she got turned on. Even though he was next

Domin8

level, Ryan and I did have a lot in common. I was content, though, on that first date with a kiss. But boy, what a kiss it was.

At the end of our third date, Dianne and I were in the car, parked in the parklands after seeing the movie Witness, with Harrison Ford, and we were getting pretty hot and heavy. She was a fantastic kisser, and I could have happily spent hours just doing that. My hand was up her t-shirt—which she wouldn't yet allow to come off—and inside her bra. I knew if I could turn her on enough I could progress to the next base; either get her bra off or even better get inside her panties, and that was my goal that night.

She told me that she was a virgin. I stopped immediately, as in 1986, nineteen-year-old virgins were pretty hard to find, not that I ever tried to find one, of course. Truthfully, though, I don't think I had ever met one.

Now, I'm not saying she just came out with it like, "Oh, by the way, I've never had sex before." No, I had asked if she was on the pill, between very passionate tongue on tongue kissing and squeezing her breasts.

"Dave, I umm, haven't been all the way with a guy yet, so, I've not gone on the pill." She replied quietly.

To say I was shocked would be an understatement. I even think my mouth was open. She laughed and said, "don't look at me like I've just grown a second head. It's not a religious thing or anything like that. I just haven't met anyone yet who meant enough to me to go all the way with. Don't panic, I'm no prude, and you can keep touching me. I love the way you touch me. You make me so hot and horny."

I hadn't realized I was holding my breath in surprise until it all came out in a rush, which made her start laughing again, and I joined in with her.

Stephen B. King

We didn't go any further than that, that night, but I still had a really good time with her. When she looked at me, it was with a promise that she would want to go further, but I had to give her time.

I felt, in some ways, like possibly I had finally grown up, which was a milestone for me. I really did like her, and I had to respect her for being her own woman and not just doing it with a boy because she was expected too. I had been guilty of using emotional blackmail on girls to have sex with them and I knew how tough it could be for a girl, not that I ever gave a damn before then, but with Dianne, I did.

We both still lived with our parents, so it wasn't as if it could happen at home anytime soon, and I had to make a choice: either dump her or hang around with her and see where things headed. As we got along really well I opted to wait it out, and the weird thing was it didn't feel like a sacrifice. I was excited to be with her, and every day at work I thought of her constantly, when not with customers or talking bullshit with the other salesmen.

Over the next few dates we slowly progressed, always in the car, and every new milestone was fantastic. I still remember, over thirty years later, the first time she let me expose her breasts and kiss them as, if it were yesterday. If we had sex straight away it wouldn't have meant anything, and I would likely barely remember her now, just like all the ones before her.

That said, at the time, all I thought about was making love with her. I knew I would get to one day, and when it did happen finally, I thought it would be incredible and worth the sacrifice of waiting for her.

The next date was at a drive in movie. We were parked in the darkness of the back row, and her t-shirt and bra was on the seat beside her. I have no idea what the movie was about; I was feasting on her breasts, marvelling at how hard her nipples were

Domin8

and how she moaned with pleasure when I went from one to the other. I was thinking that they were just the best boobs in the world and I had been transported to heaven.

Suddenly, I felt her hand in my lap and for the first time she fondled my incredibly hard penis. God, it was heaven to feel her hand there. I was so hard I was tangled up in my underwear and pubic hair, and it was painful. Dianne sensed my discomfort and heard me moan, she pushed me back in the partly-reclined seat and, with an agonizingly slow speed, undid my jeans and unzipped them. She then pulled away my jockey underpants and reached in and took it out and held it in her hand slowly masturbating me up and down. I saw her eyes as she took me in. She licked her lips and seemed to like what she saw and felt. She kissed me hard, open mouthed, and we both moaned loudly. When the kiss ended, she said "Mmm, yes Dave, that does feel like eight inches to me."

She turned in her seat so her back was to my tummy, then she lay back against me so she could slip her left hand inside my underwear to cup and squeeze me while her right hand masturbated me slowly while the tip touched her nipple.

She took her left hand out of my underwear so she could cup her breast to stop my mess getting on either of our jeans as I experienced, without doubt, the biggest orgasm I had ever experienced in my life.

At that time of my life I had probably had sex with twenty-five or thirty girls, and I had never cum so hard or felt so good afterwards as I watched her clean herself up with tissues from her handbag. Afterwards, she cuddled into me and said, "Mmmm, Dave, that was nice. Next time I might use my mouth."

And, true to her word, the next date she did. That memorable occasion was immediately after the first time she allowed my hand to get inside her jeans and panties. We were once again parked in a dark area of King's Park after a night out. She had worn jeans, and after I had her top off and had been suckling her nipples my hand had moved between her legs to rub her. This time she didn't stop me and after a few minutes of alternating kissing her mouth and breasts while rubbing her I undid the button and tugged her zip down.

I looked into her eyes as I slipped my hand inside her jeans and panties and felt the soft curls of her hair. I had been dreaming of that moment for so long and I lingered there just enjoying the feeling and the effect it had on her. To this day so many years later, possibly because of that moment, I have always preferred women to have pubic hair rather than be shaved as has become fashionable.

She wriggled in her seat and parted her thighs, giving me access, and I felt her for the first time. It was at that moment that I realized I loved her. She buried her face in my shoulder, breathlessly moaning. It didn't take long; she must have gotten as worked up as I had been with her, and she orgasmed biting my shoulder hard as she did. It was a bite I loved feeling, as it proved how much she felt for me to have permitted it to happen.

The moment she recovered she pushed me back in the seat and, without hesitation, she went down on me and didn't stop sucking and moving her mouth up and down me until I lifted my hips up in the air and came.

It's true to say that was the first time I had any form of sex with someone that I knew I cared deeply for and I realized what a difference it made. I didn't dare tell Di I thought I loved her, as I was too scared, but I think she knew by then anyway.

That next Sunday I was invited to have dinner with her parents. I enjoyed a marvellous roast chicken meal while Ryan glared daggers at me every chance he got. This was a guy I had been out with meeting girls, even sharing the odd one or two, and

Domin8

he was thinking that I was treating his sister as badly as I treated girls in the past. I couldn't really blame him. He knew me well, after all. I had never spoken to anyone about personal things about her at work, because I didn't want it getting back to him. I knew he wouldn't like it, and we had not had a specific conversation about my dating her. He thought he knew me well enough to know if there was no sex there would be no relationship; ergo, we were fucking.

After dinner, he and I played pool in their games room while the women and Di's father cleaned up the table and dishes. He snarled at me, "You're fucking her, aren't you, *Dave*?"

For the first time ever I heard aggression in his voice, and he emphasised the word *Dave*, which is usually the kind of thing men do just before they punch you. I wondered about the hypocrisy of him wanting to fuck any woman who had a pulse and two legs, but his sister was off limits.

I very slowly put the pool cue down and calmly but menacingly said, "Ryan, I'm going to let you get away with that sort of remark only once, because you are Di's brother and you introduced us. But don't you ever speak disrespectfully towards her again to me. I really care for her, and what we do or don't do is none of your fucking business. Now take your shot or try and hit me, but let's stop fucking around."

He stared at me for a while, and as he could see I was sincere his anger dissipated. He nodded and said, "Fair point. Just don't treat her like a slag, ok? And don't hurt her." Then he picked up his cue and lined up a shot.

"Oh right. You mean don't treat her the way you treat the sluts you go out with, is that what you mean, Ryan?" We both laughed at that. The ice was broken, and we were ok about it from that point on.

Stephen B. King

Dianne and I didn't speak about it beforehand, and we certainly didn't plan it, but the following weekend she lost her virginity to me. That made me feel the proudest I had ever felt in my life.

I had taken a chance and booked a motel. I picked her up from home on time and went into town to go tenpin bowling and have a meal. During dinner—in fact, just before the dessert arrived we were going to share—I plucked up the courage and said, "If you feel like it, we could stay in town tonight. I've booked a room, but we don't have to use it if you don't want to."

I topped her wine glass up, and then mine, trying to look casual, but I felt like a nervous schoolboy. It was only a cheap wine—Moselle, as I recall—but it was working fine on both of us.

"You sound pretty sure of yourself. Do you think I'm an easy lay?" Her eyes sparkled in the candle light, and I knew it would be OK. She always joked when she was nervous.

I took her hand in mine and after taking a deep breath said "No, Di, I'm not sure about this at all. In fact, I've never felt less sure about anything in my life. All I do know is that I want to be your first, and I don't want that to be before you are ready for it. If tonight is too soon for you, then that's completely fine. I'm ready, willing and able to wait until it does feel right for you, no matter how long that takes."

She squeezed my hand and smiled at me, and I knew I had to tell her how I felt.

"I want to tell you this before we go any further—because I don't want you to think I'm saying it for any other reason than this is how I truly feel—but I've never been in love with anyone before, never ever wanted to, in fact, but I'm in so love with you, Di. You are all I ever think about. You are the last thing I think of before I go to sleep and the first thing I think of when I wake up. I

Domin8

love you." I felt so good to finally tell her how I felt; it was like a massive weight had been lifted from my shoulders.

She bit her lip silently for a moment while she thought about what I said, before almost whispering, "Well then, I better phone home and tell mum I won't be back till morning, hadn't I? I love you too, Dave. I have for quite a while but didn't want to say it in case it made you feel trapped."

She got up to go and use the phone, and I felt more nervous than at any time in my life. I actually felt panicked that she might not like making love with me. I was worried I might hurt her or that I would come too quickly. A hundred fears went through my mind but, in the end I worried for nothing.

We went to the motel and entered the room. She turned to me and put her hands on my shoulders and smiled. She kissed me deeply then in a half joking, half serious voice said, "Be gentle, won't you?"

I nodded, and we kissed again. It was one of the longest kisses ever as I was so nervous. Here I was, usually so self-assured, and I was trembling with nerves. I wondered if it showed. She turned her back to me and said "Unzip me, Dave, tonight you get all of me, anything and everything you want to do to me." She looked back over her shoulder and I never saw her look more beautiful when she added, "I love you."

My fingers were shaking as I unzipped her dress and saw her well-tanned back with the contrasting white bra straps in the dim light. That night I struggled to unclasp her bra, which was unusual for me. I had even become adept at doing it one handed in the past, and sometimes had even done it so softly a girl couldn't feel it happening.

Stephen B. King

Eventually, I got it unclasped, and she let it and her dress fall to the floor. She stepped out of her dress and turned back to face me, wearing only her white panties. How I ached for her.

Then it was her turn as she unbuttoned my shirt. With dismay I noticed that, unlike me, she wasn't trembling at all. She opened my shirt, kissed my chest and then tugged it out, pushing it down my arms. She knelt down and undid my jeans and pulled them and my underwear off as one.

She sucked me on her knees, head tilted back and looking up at me, her hands on my hips as she pulled me deep into her mouth. I closed my eyes and concentrated hard not to come too soon. I told her how much I loved her and helped her to her feet.

Then it was my turn to kneel and kiss each breast, in turn, then move down her tummy and lick her belly button as my fingers slipped inside her panties, gently working them down. She put her hands on my shoulders to steady herself as she stepped out of them and for the first time I could see her fully nude body. I scrunched back on my ankles and pulled her forward so she lined up with my mouth and for the first time she felt my lips and tongue licking her.

She tasted incredible, and I couldn't get enough of her. Suddenly my nerves were gone, replaced with a lustful want and need. I needed to make this as memorable as I could for her, knowing what a sacrifice it was for her to wait that long. I felt so proud that she chose me to be her first lover.

My hands were on her bottom, and I held her against my mouth. I put my tongue inside her and I licked and sucked her as her hairs tickled my nose. She had never looked more beautiful than from that angle, her face looking down at me from above her breasts, loving the sensations I was giving her. Her hips started an involuntary rocking as she rode my mouth and within a very short time she called my name over and over again as she climaxed hard. Her head was thrown back and shook from side to side, as her orgasm went on and on.

"Oh my God," she said, as she came down from her high, and I held her tightly. "Lay me down before I fall over."

I stood up, and we walked arm in arm to the bed, pulled back the covers and climbed in. Our arms and legs wrapped around each other, as we kissed, holding each other and cuddling. I was in no hurry. There was all the time in the world. I was enjoying the breather knowing it would help me last longer, as I had come very close earlier.

I kissed her deeply, and my hands wandered all over her: touching, feeling, exploring and enjoying the moment. I felt her hand on me, as she gently but firmly used it to guide me on top of her and between her legs.

She had me positioned perfectly, and I broke the kiss so I could look into her eyes, as I slowly entered her for the first time, gently rocking forward and back ever so gently so as not to hurt her. Her eyes were bright and wide open; she was biting her lower lip and moaning. My weight was on my elbows and knees while she lifted her hips to meet me. She removed her hand and held me tightly. She whispered, "God, I love you, Dave."

I had tears in my eyes as I realized how much I loved her for waiting for me to share this moment with her.

Many years later, Dianne said something during an argument we had about the lack of sex in our lives that haunted me. Over the years, her desire and want for making love with me had diminished, but my need for her hadn't. What she said that was that I was the only man she had ever been with in her life and that I was enough to last her until the day she died.

With all that happened later I never stopped wondering why she couldn't have been enough for me.

Stephen B. King

Chapter 3 – Tracy, Tamika & Judith

The Intervening Years

I consider myself to have been, up to a certain time in my life anyway, just about as normal a man as any other fifty-year-old Australian alpha male. By that, I mean I loved looking at, and thinking about, women.

When Starsky and Hutch came calling I had been working for eleven years as a General Manager, running an ever changing team of four used and six new car salespeople for a large dealership group. I was successful, drove a nice car, owned a nice house and had three fantastic children, the youngest of which at that time was 19. Yes, she was a bit of a handful, but none of our children had gotten into drugs, violence or wild parties. They had never been brought home by police, thankfully.

Having been in sales all of my adult life, it has to be said I was good with people and was good at my job. In all honesty, I'm a bit of a chameleon. I have oodles of self-confidence and a good, though some would say whacky, sense of humour. In general, most people who meet me like me.

I've always been a flirt with women, and loved the sexual banter between two people who find each other attractive. Most of my friends throughout my life have been women – I just get on much better with them than men. Perhaps it's the 'hunter, gatherer' in me but I think the hunt can be more fun than the capture. On many occasions, when I've met a woman, I found it incredible fun to see if I could get them into bed, without actually wanting to get them there.

Domin8

And, I have to admit, most women who meet me like me, too. Now, I'm not saying every one of them wants to jump into bed with me. That would be a ridiculous thing to suggest. But, when I was single, finding someone to have sex with was never very difficult, and since I married Dianne I had plenty of chances, over the years, to fool around on the side. Mostly I didn't and was true to my wedding vows, but on three occasions (prior to my descent into a life of wild no-strings online sex), I did have three short-term affairs–just for fun, nothing more. That old hackneyed and well-worn cliché, "they didn't mean anything to me" was never truer than in my case.

My 'dalliances' were nothing serious, or so I thought at the time. In retelling the stories here, I am not exaggerating, understating or making them out to be anything that they weren't. They were for sex only, when Dianne and I were very rarely doing it ourselves. Her desire for me became, sadly, virtually non-existent.

As I'm being honest here, let me say how sorry I was that they happened. How I wished that they had not. But in retelling my story, as I must now, here are the details of my three illicit dalliances, with nothing withheld. I never did it to hurt Dianne. I did it for my own pleasure and gratification. And yes, I fully know this makes me a self-absorbed, selfish bastard. I know that is exactly what I am.

Tracy

Stephen B. King

The first occasion was when my wife was away for a few days on a nursing training course, and I was a little bored and met a woman at a bar I had stopped at after work, rather than go home to an empty house.

Her name, as I was to find out, was Tracy, and she happened to walk past me as I leant on the bar chatting with the barman, who I knew well and had sold him and his family numerous cars over the years. She seemed nice. She had bleach blonde hair, was reasonably tall and was wearing black jeans, heels and the brightest yellow, low cut, top I'd ever seen. To me, after a couple of beers, it seemed like she was commanding men to look at her boobs wearing that colour top and showing that much cleavage. She had long, mousey brown hair, looked to be in her mid to late thirties, and since I'm being honest, wore a bit too much eye makeup: like she was trying just a bit too hard. But she was attractive, with a bright smile, and as she walked past me on her way to the toilet I complemented her on having amazing breasts.

Some women might have been angry and some might have slapped me, but thankfully not Tracy. She laughed a nice laugh, but with just a little snort at the end of it, which was quite unattractive. She stopped in her tracks and in a very Australian accent, asked me, "What did you say?" I was certain she had heard me perfectly well the first time.

I leant in close so she could smell my recently applied David Beckham Cologne. I'd moved on from Pierre Cardin. I replied, "I said you have amazing breasts. I could play with them for hours." Then I stood back up smiled and winked at her.

"Jesus, man. That's an original pickup line," She giggled again, with her signature little snort, and I felt sure that within an hour I could have both of those amazing breasts in my hands: if I wanted to, of course. So far it had just been a bit of harmless

Domin8

flirtatious, banter. The question was: did I want it to go further or just have some fun flirting? I held both hands up in surrender to show my wedding ring. "Sorry Ma'am, I don't do pickup lines. I'm a happily married man,"

I pointed directly to my ring so there could be no mistake and said, "I'm just telling you the truth, which you already know, don't you? They are spectacular." I was openly staring down at her chest. She said nothing, just stared back nervously smiling, so I pressed on. "Let me buy you a drink so I can ask you all about them, And about you too, of course. What will you have?"

She had a choice, to stay or go. She knew I was married and could walk away, or she could stay and have a drink, but if she stayed she knew we would be discussing her breasts. She thought about it just for thirty seconds, "Ok, this is something new for me. I'll have a cider in a long glass with lots of ice, but I'm not really comfortable talking about these, if you don't mind."

She pointed to her breasts and she had a slight blush to her face and upper chest. The reddening of her chest told me she was just a little bit turned on and I thought: *this will be fun.*

She was hooked. I knew it. Women do not talk to strange men in bars about their breasts unless they are interested. If nothing else, I thought it would be a bit of sexy banter, still with no clear intention to do anything more than a little flirting.

She still had to go to the toilet, and I got her drink while she did. She returned shortly, sat on a vacant bar stool beside me, held out her hand and told me her name. I took it in mine but didn't shake it. I just held it and noticed the wedding and engagement rings on her other hand. "I'm Dave, Dave Barndon. First question has to be what size are they? I would guess 36C?"

"You'd be close. I'm a D cup. Do we really have to talk about these? I thought you were just kidding. I'm Tracy, by the way." She still hadn't taken her hand out of mine, choosing instead to pick up her frosty glass and sip from it in her left hand.

"We most definitely do. Breasts as magnificent as yours deserve to be talked about. They also deserve to be caressed, squeezed, licked and sucked. Do you like to have them sucked, licked or bitten, or all three?" I asked, not so innocently.

"Look, Dave. I'm not answering that. I don't even know you. Jesus, ease up turbo." Her Australian accent got broader, and now she really was blushing. Her nipples were hard. I could clearly see them poking out through her bra and top. She couldn't help herself; I was getting to her, and she loved the attention, despite the fake complaining.

"Sure you know me. I'm the kind of guy you fantasize about sometimes, don't you? Like when your husband has left for work, and you feel horny because he didn't fuck you properly the night before and left you high and dry. You use your vibrator then, don't you? It's red, I know it's red, don't deny it. You hold it with one hand and the other is squeezing one of your fantastic tits. Do you play with the left or the right one or do you treat them the same and play with both?

"Oh my God, what are you doing to me? Stop it right now. For your information I'm separated. He left me. And also for your information it's black, not red. See? You don't know everything, Mr. Smarty Pants."

She took a large drink. She was really quite flustered. She took her hand out of mine and squirmed on her stool a little. I looked at her and thought to that she was really turned on, which was why she was squirming. Her throat was now really red, as if she had a rash.

Domin8

"Ah, it's black, is it? I imagine it's big. Do you like the thought of a big one, Tracy. Is that why you use a supersize vibrator?"

"Will you please stop talking like that, but yes, if you must know, I have wondered what a big one would be like. Now change the subject, please."

"I'm really sorry to hear he left you, Tracy. Did he make love to your breasts though; did he really play with them for a long time to get you turned on? Did he spend minutes on end just squeezing them while he went from one to the other sucking and biting your nipples? Could he make you orgasm just by playing with your tits, tell me that at least?" I was really enjoying myself, and I realised I hadn't had this much fun with a woman for a long, long time. Why was I treating her that way? I don't know, months of pent up frustration, perhaps, but its important to understand I had made no clear-cut decision to have sex with her. I was just having a ball, flirting away and watching the effect I was having on her.

I was sure this woman had never truly had a really massive orgasm with a man, and it showed.

"What is wrong with you? Are you sex mad? No, he never did all that kind of stuff if you must know—well, not towards the end anyway. He barely touched me at all."

She looked a little bit sad, but still red in the face, and her voice had the tiniest quiver to it.

"His idea of foreplay was to ask if I wanted sex, then he would get off very quickly and would make me sleep on the wet spot. Useless bugger: everyone says I'm better off without him." She finished her drink and looked at me, licking her lips for just a moment longer than she needed to.

Stephen B. King

I placed my hand high up on her thigh, while staring into her eyes, barely a couple inches from her crotch. She flinched monetarily at my touch, but then recovered before parting her legs just enough so I could slide all of the way up. I rubbed her and could feel her arousal through her knickers and jeans.

"When was the last time you had a really big orgasm on the backseat of a car, Tracy? I think you want me to play with your tits, don't you? I can make you come like you haven't in years. You do know that, right?"

So that was how we ended up in the backseat of my car, parked at the darkest end of the car park, with her stripped completely naked. I was right; she did have fantastic breasts and she did go wild with the attention I lavished on them. I could tell we had the kind of sex she hadn't had in a long time, if ever.

Both of us were unused to such an impulsive act. Neither of us had a condom, and I had to promise to pull out. Always good to my word, of course I did.

I saw her twice more: once in a motel, where we both got tipsy on wine and had sex three times, including once on the balcony, as it was a warm night, and then once again in the morning before I left to go to work. That time we were prepared; I paid for the room and the wine, and she brought the condoms.

The last time was at her place, as her children were with their father for the night.

Tracy was a nice woman, but as my wife was due back from her trip the next day, I thought it best to end it then. She understood perfectly; she knew I was married from the start and that we had no future together. We parted on good terms. It also made sense to end it before she developed any feelings for me. I could never develop feelings for her; her snort when she laughed and disdain for oral sex saw to that. Of course, I was married too

Domin8

and would never have swapped Dianne, even without sex, for Tracy with it. She had been a bit of fun and a break from the normalcy of life—and nothing more.

She even thanked me as I left and told me that I had helped her realize she could move on from her broken marriage. "*No harm, no foul,*" I thought. No one had gotten hurt. In fact, she had said she benefitted, and we both had made some nice memories. I even wondered what she thought when she read about me in the papers years later.

Tamika

The group of companies I worked for had put on an incentive-based target for its managers. Across all the dealerships in our group I was one of five who won a seven-day trip to Macau. No partners were allowed; it was a staff-only trip.

It was the third week of November, and the five of us, along with the Managing Director and his personal assistant Christine, flew out at 4 a.m. on a Monday morning. After a brief stopover in Singapore we were having our first beers in the bar of the Venetian Casino and Resort around 3 p.m.

The Venetian is an incredible resort, complete with canals, gondola, opera and a replica of St. Mark's Square in a suitable massive building complex, with hundreds of high-end fashion stores, restaurants, bars and even a permanent Cirque du Soleil show.

Stephen B. King

Christine is a beautiful woman and a lovely person, who every staff member lusted after and failed to bed, because she was a happily married woman. I liked her far too much as a person, and respected her for her work ethic, to ever make a move on her. I never had tried anything with anyone I worked with – far too complicated, and dangerous, for me. I am 100% sure that even if I had made a pass at Christine I would have been rebuked with a genuine smile, so as not to have felt let down, such was her grace and charm.

She was completely dedicated to her career: especially workplace safety and company liability. She was fanatical about it. After two days we knew we had to get away from her because she advised against doing anything we wanted to do, to avoid being hurt, put in jail or end up in any one of the hundred or so dire situations that posed a liability to her and the company.

The five of us began feigning early nights to bed after dinner, but instead, we would meet in the lobby, grab a cab and head off to one of the casinos on the island. While she watched movies in her room or studied workplace health and safety documents, she never knew what we men got up to. That said, I am sure that she knew something was going on by the state of some of us at breakfast. But, if she did, she never said a word, and we operated on the basis that what she didn't know couldn't hurt her.

I'm not much of a gambler, but I am a fairly decent drinker and did have a play on the tables, even winning a few times. What stunned me about every casino we went to in Macau were the unbelievably beautiful women walking around, smiling at every man who walked past them. They wore stunning ball gowns and make up done by L'Oreal or some other exclusive products. Everywhere you looked there were "10s" meandering around the

Domin8

tables. It was a very horny situation for us to find ourselves in, thousands of kilometres away from home and our wives.

I had been playing Casino War with Stuart and Paul and I got up to go to the bar. I could have stayed there as the waitress was pretty quick in bringing us refills, but I wanted to stretch my legs. I also thought I would visit the toilet and make room for the additional drinks we intended to inhale throughout that night. That was to be our second last night before heading home, and we thought we would make it a good one.

I was walking down the main aisle between tables and saw a vision of pure beauty and female sexuality walking towards me. She was of Asian origin, perhaps Japanese, and had long, silky black hair tied with a ribbon, which draped over her shoulder down over her right breast. Her gown was superb. It was floor length, black and sequined, with a long slit up the side and slightly to the front so, as she walked, her upper right thigh was exposed with just a hint of stocking top. She wore ridiculously high heels that just made her legs look like she was a supermodel, though without the heels she would have been quite short. Her body would have looked at home in a Hollywood movie or fashion magazine. She was, quite simply, one of the most beautiful women I had ever seen.

When we were five or six meters apart she smiled at me. When a woman that beautiful smiles at a man there is only two things he can do. He can smile back or stare, mouth agape, tongue hanging out the side and dribble. Thankfully, I chose the former option. She stopped to wait for me, still smiling and slightly tilted her head to one side, and almost coquettish look, standing so the slit in her gown opened. "My God," I thought, "she wants to talk to me."

Such is a male ego that a man rapidly approaching fifty, with greying hair, thinks the most incredibly beautiful woman on the planet, certainly that he has ever seen in his life immediately wants him at first sight. Yes, I know it's laughable, really, and I can only blame the alcohol I had consumed.

I stopped in front of her, tried to sober up, sucked in my stomach, put on my best Brad Pitt smile and said, "Hi." I immediately thought of myself as an idiot for not saying anything more original than that.

"Hi, I am Tamika." She actually batted her eyelids, and her voice was as sexy as her looks, while her accent made every single drop of blood in my entire six foot two frame go immediately to my penis.

With all the sparkling wit and intellectual banter at my disposal, what did I come up with? I gulped and countered with, "I'm Dave. I'm from Australia."

"Well," I thought, "that's done it. Telling her I'm an Aussie is sure to get her to want me." I could feel myself blushing at how dorky I must sound to a sophisticated woman like this. Usually I like to think I'm Mr. Joe Cool, but not that night. "*Take me out and shoot me now*," I thought.

This was a woman of the world. She was intelligent, glamorous and sexy. She probably quoted Shakespeare on quiet nights when not reading War and Peace, just for fun. Tamika could see the effect she had on me and laughed a genuine, husky laugh at my discomfort. She was enjoying this, and the throaty laugh only made her sound sexier.

"Well, Dave from Australia, would you like a massage?" She tilted her head to the other side, flicking her hair as she did, and licked her full lips. I couldn't help but think, "*all the better to devour me with*." Her eyes were diamonds on fire. No red blooded man could have said no. There was no amount of money that would be too much to pay.

Domin8

Brad Pitt would probably have said something like "Yeah, babe. Let's go do it," but all I could manage was, "Who, me? A massage?"

No sooner had the words left my stupid mouth than I realized that "massage," of course, is hooker-speak for fucking for a money. She just smiled that sexy smile, stared right back at me and nodded.

Being a true Aussie—and a salesman at heart—I asked the obvious question, "How much?"

"Not much, Dave from Australia, and I worth every dollar."

I was so stunned I couldn't speak, and she took my silence as agreement. She winked at me, again, entwined her arm in mine and started leading me towards the exit. "At last," I thought, "she has an imperfection: she spoke in broken English!"

"You have room in hotel?" she asked.

"I'm at the Venetian. Can we go there?" As soon as I said that I realized my mistake. I was sharing a room with Stuart, and there was no way I wanted a reputation in the company for screwing prostitutes while on a trip. Even one as beautiful as Tamika could ruin my good name, so that wasn't going to happen, but I needn't have worried.

"No, I can't leave hotel when I working. We have rooms here we use. Don't worry. I give you special price. I worth it. Two fifty Macau dollars for hour, but for you six hundred and you have me all night. You very lucky man. You have enough chips there to pay for me. I make you come lots for six hundred."

I had never been with a prostitute. To be honest, I never saw the point. For me, to enjoy sex there had to be some sort of two-way attraction or at least a perceived attraction. And the thought of someone screwing me just for my money is a complete

46

turn off. I'm not criticizing men who use them, but it was never my thing: that is, not before meeting Tamika.

And she did. To use her words, "make me come lots." And either I'm pretty good at making a woman orgasm or she deserves an Oscar for her acting. On balance of thought, the Oscar is most likely.

That night changed my beliefs about prostitutes. Man, that woman was unbelievable. It seemed as if her whole purpose in life was to please men, and she most definitely pleased me.

I had left the Casino with Tamika with nine hundred Macau dollars in chips. I left her room in the morning with none, but she was absolutely correct she had been worth every cent. I had never had such a time with a woman. Yes, it went against everything I had believed in the past about hookers, but I had no idea that sex for the sake of sex (and money) could be that good. I guess like when painting and decorating, it proves to always use a professional for a better quality job, and boy was she professional.

Of the nine hundred dollars, I had given her three hundred as a deposit to book her for later the next night after our farewell dinner. She had promised to wait for me at ten o'clock for round two. The next day all I I thought to myself was, *"well, that's three hundred bucks I won't see again."* But at the bar, there she was waiting for me. She was sipping from a long stemmed champagne flute, which seemed perfectly fitting. You could say she was a fantastic actress, and she probably was, but I thought she was genuinely pleased to see me—and not just for the other four hundred in cash I brought that second night (including her tip).

She was exquisite. She was the first woman I had ever been with who not only shaved her pubic hair off; Tamika was waxed to the point I wondered if she ever had possessed pubic hair at all. I will never forget, among other things, her being knelt

Domin8

over my mouth, holding onto the headboard of the bed, screaming in a very well-acted, or was is genuine, orgasm.

So that was my second foray into extramarital sex. Once again, I just saw it as a bit of fun and nothing more. Dianne didn't know, and there was no way she could find out. Again, no harm, no foul. I returned home to the arms of my loving wife and settled back down to a "normal" life once more: consisting of work, more work, a happy home and a sex life that was as infrequent as it was unsatisfactory—probably just like most other men who had been married twenty-odd years.

Judith

In my mind, Judith could be excluded from this list, as it was very much a situation where she seduced me and not the other way round. That sounds ridiculous, I know. I had sex with her while I was married to Dianne, so I'm guilty as charged, but. I didn't seek it from her; it was nice, for once, to have the shoe on the other foot and for someone to lust after me for a change. It is true to say, had she not made a very open and obvious pass at me, we would never had had sex. That was very flattering, and as any fifty year old man will tell you, it almost never happens, at least not like it does in your earlier years.

Judith had come into the dealership with her nineteen-year-old daughter to help her pick out a new car, and being "mum" she bargained on her daughter's behalf pretty well. In fact, she drove such a hard bargain that the salesman, Jules, got me to come and talk to them as he was close to pulling his hair out and needed the world famous "General Manager's Close."

It was an instant attraction—or to be more precise, it was instant lust. Judith was into her forties but she took pride in her appearance. From the moment I walked up and sat down at the desk with her and her daughter, her whole demeanour changed. It was almost as if she was wearing a sign saying, '*please fuck me, Dave.*'

She had short hair, which was very well cut, coloured and styled. She wore a lot of gold jewellery, so much so that I was surprised she could lift her hand to sign a contract with the weight on her wrist and fingers. She wore an opaque, crisp white silk shirt with a lace slip and bra underneath so she looked sexy and classy. Maybe I am old fashioned, but I love to see see a slip under a see through top. And, naturally, the sight of her bra strap was such a turn on for me too. I've always thought it was like a word association test a psychologist might use; he says bra, I think breasts.

She wasn't overly adorned with makeup, but just enough to highlight her features. She didn't mind looking her age and she had a body that clearly showed that she had spent lots of hours a week in a gym, with a personal trainer whose name would have been something like Brandon, or Rock. Her muscular build was a little on the heavier side, but somehow it made the whole package that much more appealing.

I introduced myself, and she held on to my hand for three seconds longer than she needed to when we shook. I asked the salesman, Jules, to make us all a coffee and then we spent a very pleasant ten minutes during which the only thing we didn't talk about was the purchase, much to her daughter's dismay.

Judith looked into my eyes while telling me that her husband worked in the mines and was away two weeks out of every three. She also mentioned that she frequently got bored, as she was alone in the big family house that they still owned, even though her children all had moved out. She called herself an empty nester, and I said I was too, and that my wife was a nurse.

Once the deal was agreed to, Jules took her daughter through to the aftercare department and settlement manager. Meanwhile, Judith asked if I would walk her around outside to look at some of the cars in the fresh air while she waited. I agreed, as for some strange reason, I have always preferred the company of an attractive woman to preparing the next financial year's budget for the Board of Directors.

No sooner were we out of earshot of anyone else did she say, "I don't want you think I'm forward or that I do this sort of thing a lot, because I don't, but I'd like you to come around during the day sometime to my place, if you can get away, that is? It's OK. I can see you are married. So am I and I don't want complications any more than you do. I just want some good sex. I like the look of you. If you like the look of me, why don't we have some fun?"

This was not something that happened to me every day. I had heard of it happening to salesmen, this was the first time I had been so openly propositioned at work. She was a bit of a Jekyll and Hyde; in front of her daughter she was so prim and proper, yet alone with me she was like a bitch in heat. And there was no denying it; she was a very desirable, sexy woman.

I was just a little bit shocked into silence, momentarily, which she took as positive affirmation and continued, "You can do anything you like to me." She let out a very nervous laugh, "God will you listen to me? I promise I don't do this often, Dave."

I was still in a bit of a daze, but almost unconsciously I replied. "When is good for you? I can slip out during the day for an hour or so fairly easily and often. I am the manager, after all, and rank does come with some privilege."

At eleven the next morning she opened the door to me wearing a bright red silk kimono style robe. As soon as the door was shut behind me she yanked on the belt and let it fall to the floor, showing off her body. She was wearing a black, see-through bra and matching panties, a suspender belt and black stockings. "*My god, she looks hot*," I thought to myself. The day before she had been so well dressed, and now she looked like a very expensive whore.

"I thought I would dress like a slut for you so you would know to treat me like one."

We kissed with a hunger and passion born of our imaginations thinking of this moment since the day before. She moaned loudly, broke the kiss and breathed, "Do whatever you want to me. Just don't mark me where it shows."

The first time we had sex it was like two frantic school kids, in a hurry to get done before parents got home. It was hot, it was loud, and we were both partially clothed as I took her standing up in the hall. The second time was much slower. We joked afterwards, lying in her huge king-sized bed, that the first time was for me, and the second was for her. Both were very deeply satisfying.

Judith was a very sexual woman who knew what she wanted and how to get it. She loved her husband and he knew there was always the possibility she would take lovers. He had told her he approved so long as she never kept secrets from him. Apparently he felt confident in knowing that she would always be his on his week back home and she was free to have fun when he wasn't. He even looked forward to hearing of her exploits, and Judith told me he got off on her telling him all the intimate details.

Domin8

She never made any demands of me. If her hubby was away, and I was free, she would welcome me with open arms. She loved every kind of sex. I have never known a woman who loved the taste of sperm as she did. This was a woman for whom too much sex was never enough. Nymphomania was just a word, so far as I was concerned, but I actually think there were times Judith was one.

She was voracious, and I could barely keep up with her when I visited her. It seemed that the more we did it, and the harder she orgasmed, the more she would want to orgasm again. It was as if she was addicted to it.

Things were amazingly good for a few weeks, and I was never sure why they changed, but change they did. The more I got to know her, the more I began to think she suffered from bi-polar disorder or something very similar. Maybe that explained her high sex drive whenever she was happy. It certainly explained her low moods and depression, which came on out of nowhere. She could change from screaming *"fuck me, Dave"* nymphomania to self-loathing tears in an instant.

She would never discuss her moodiness with me. To her it was how it was. Really, it was none of my business, which she told me on more than one occasion. My main function when her mood was good was to fuck her, as often and as hard as I could. On the other hand, she usually wanted me to leave if I had arrived during one of her dark times. I would get there as arranged, and we would either do it like rabbits with no tomorrow or she would be too upset. At times she opened the door in tears and, despite my best efforts to either help her, cheer up, provide a shoulder for her or an ear to listen to her woes, nothing seemed to work when she was in one of those moods.

For me, for a while at least, it was. But in the same way shooting stars burn brightest the really fantastic times seemed to dry up and her darker moods won out and became more frequent. I never knew which version of Judith would be waiting for me. When she was down, she was terrible, and when she was up she was fantastic. There was rarely any in between, but to be brutally honest, towards the end the great times were so few and far between I couldn't be bothered going.

One day not long before the end, a man was there when I arrived. He had furtive eyes that never kept still, and talking to him was a challenge as you felt you wanted to grab his head and hold it still. I tried to talk to him but one moment he would be looking in my eyes, then above my head, then to the left, then down at my crotch.

Judith seemed a little embarrassed and hesitant. "Dave, this is my brother Neville." She then left for the kitchen to get something that he had come round to pick up.

He looked at my hands and said, "So you're the one fucking her, aye mate?" He looked out the window before sniffing loudly and stared at my crotch before staring at his own hands.

He had oily, straggly hair and was as skinny as a rake with the merest hint of a thin moustache. I just nodded as there seemed no point in denying it. He looked at my chin and said "How 'bout you guys let me join you some time, aye mate? Bit of fun, mate. What do you say?"

He sniffed and looked down at his rather grubby trainers as he shifted from foot to foot. I exploded with shock, horror and sarcasm.

"You mean you want to join me in fucking your sister? What are you, sick? That's never going to happen, *mate*."

His eyes were even more all over the place and I could hardly keep up. While I am not, and never have been, a violent person I would have quite gladly hit him; he was without doubt

Domin8

the most obnoxious person I'd ever met. I just wanted to punch his furtive little rat-like face over, and over again, and *that* is not like me at all.

"You think you're tough, mate? Think you can handle me, mate, do ya? I might be a bit tricky, mate, maybe more than you give me credit for, mate."

Just then Judith came back from the kitchen with a beer for me and an envelope for Neville. She heard the last of the conversation and yelled, "Neville, what are you on about? Why are you trying to spoil things for me? You better leave right now."

"Yeah, *Neville*, run along now, *mate*," I chimed in, still hoping I could punch him. This time I winked, hoping he would say something back. If he did, I swear I would have lost it, but alas he left in a sulk.

The sexual energy was gone, despite Judith's best efforts. She was trying to give me a head job on her knees wearing nothing but a bright orange bra, but I just couldn't get the mental image out of my head of that snivelling little rat in bed with us.

I think I'm generally pretty open minded about most things, but a brother having sex with his sister and her boyfriend? I completely lost my erection and inclination. Though she tried it wouldn't come back, and she ended up in tears again. One moment she blamed me and the next it was that "*fucking Neville*" spoiling her life again.

I asked her what had he done before that had spoilt her life, but she just shrugged and told me not to worry about it. Then I told her he wanted a threesome with us. She turned bright red and said "No, no, no. Not that again."

"Again? You mean you *have* had sex with him?" I yelled.

"You don't understand, Dave. It wasn't like that, lets just drop it." Then she started crying and wouldn't talk about it
54

anymore. I assumed it was either in his imagination or something that occurred when they were kids: maybe something quite innocent. But I simply couldn't accept she would want to, not with him, no matter how much she loved sex. We never spoke of it again. Neither of us wanted to bring it up because clearly it was a 'no-go-zone.' I thought about him once or twice, but shuddered every time I did, and fortunately I didn't see him there again.

I called around the next day to see her, she seemed to be much better. Mission control launched successfully, twice. She was fine two days later, too, but then on the following occasion she was so deeply depressed she wouldn't even let me in through the door. Instead, she just told me to leave. The next occasion was the same. She was inside, crying, but wouldn't let me in. She just told me to go away, and that was very definitely the beginning of the end.

I found myself calling her less and less, and she didn't call me, until it petered out altogether. Though we never formally broke it off I just stopped calling her, and she never bothered to follow me up to ask why. The last time we had successfully hooked up was probably around four months before the TV show that changed everything—and I first heard the name Domin8.

Domin8

Chapter 4 – Patsy

Day Two of the Nightmare

Every time I thought of the two police officers who visited me on that fateful night I couldn't help but think of them as Starsky and Hutch. It was just one of those stupid things that got stuck in my head: like hearing a song out of the blue on the radio you can't stand but then can't help but whistle it all day long afterwards.

They had left me feeling very ill, but recovering and with a mess to clean up. I had an appointment for me to go in and make a statement the next day. I spent the rest of the night worrying about it.

Being the selfish person I am, I was more petrified Dianne would find out what I had been doing with the women I had been seeing than feel sorry for Patsy being murdered, I'm ashamed to admit. Mostly, my proclivities had been pursued while Di was working, but there were some other times too: like when I had invented meetings or nights out with the boss, or something similar.

I couldn't sleep a wink that night thinking that in a murder inquiry, where I was the last person to see the victim alive, that information would come out in the media. I was sure it had to. I clung to the hope that maybe, just maybe, there was a way it wouldn't leak: if I was very lucky.

I was also upset for Patsy, though in reality I hardly knew her. She seemed like a really well adjusted, sexually active woman who loved to experiment and who was proud of being openly bisexual. When we were together, she loved everything we did, or so I thought. She was a woman who could enjoy multiple orgasms, with each successive one gaining in intensity. I thought she would go on to become more of a Dominatrix than a submissive, as that seemed to be her true nature. She was a woman who was high on life, and trying to get the most out of every minute of every day.

The only thing that made sense to me, with her killing, was that someone from her past—a jealous ex or someone like that—had followed her to the motel. He must have waited for me to leave and then entered and murdered her. If I could make the police believe that, maybe I could get off the hook; the information might not leak and I could stay married. I truly loved Dianne, in my own selfish way and I couldn't imagine life without her in it. All I could do was hope.

At 11 a.m. the next morning I was at Police Headquarters waiting for Starsky and Hutch to take me through for my recorded interview, hoping no one who knew me would see me at the station. I was also wishing I was still a smoker while sitting in the waiting area for them to appear, as to be blunt I was nearly crapping myself with fear. Not, of course, that I'd have been permitted to smoke inside, but you know what I mean.

Detective Collins appeared through the door in the waiting room and held out his hand to shake. I stood up and shook it firmly.

"Thanks for coming in, Mr. Barndon. Come with me, please. Let's get this done as quickly as we can so you can get back to work—or are you catching up with one of your women on the side, as you are in the city?"

I couldn't figure out if he was being funny or genuine: probably the former I decided.

Domin8

"I will be going back to work, Detective. I've sworn off women on the side for now, thanks," I replied, trying not to let him get under my skin.

We walked in silence, until he opened a door marked "INTERVIEW ROOM 3" and said, "Please take a seat, Mr. Barndon. Detective Sergeant Milanski will join us shortly. Can I get you a coffee or a glass of water?"

"Water would be good, thanks," I said as I sat in the indicated chair, crossed my left leg over my right, trying to not look as nervous as I felt.

Four or five minutes later they walked back in, Collins was carrying two glasses of water, while Milanski had a paper cup of steaming coffee balanced on top of a folder. They sat down, and Collins hit a red switch on the wall between us marked "Recorder ON." Milanski put his coffee down on the desk and said, "This is a record of interview with Mr. David Barndon, in connection with the murder of Ms. Patricia White. Mr. Barndon, for the benefit of the recording, can you please state your name, date of birth and address. Also, can you state that you have been informed this interview is being recorded and that you have declined to have legal representation at this time?"

In a voice I recognised had a quiver of fear in it I gave them the information they wanted and then took a sip of the water to try to calm down.

"Thank you, Mr. Barndon, and thank you for coming voluntarily to answer questions. Can we start by telling us the background of how you came to meet Ms. White?"

"*Here goes*," I thought, and started aloud, "She contacted me about two weeks ago through the *After Dark dot com* web site. That is an online meeting place for adults, including married people, who want to get together and try alternate sexual lifestyles. I have had a profile there for some time, advertising for women who want to try being submissive."

"Thank you for being so open, Mr. Barndon, I know this is difficult for you. We have read your profile on that site, and it's very interesting. Since we put it up on the evidence white board here one or two of the female police officers seem to have taken an interest in it." Milanski winked at me and smiled, while I just cringed lower in my seat. "You openly admit to being married, but it is true, is it not, that your wife does not know of these women you meet?"

Again, I felt the stab of guilt through my heart, knowing I had been betraying Dianne. "That is true. But, in my limited experience, most of the people on *After Dark* are in relationships. They are just looking for an outlet for their fantasies or a bit of fun with no hassles or strings attached."

"Hmm, yes I see. But hypothetically, if Ms. White had, shall we say, threatened to tell your wife, you wouldn't be best pleased, would you?" He just stared at me. I hated this more and more as every minute passed.

"No, I would not be best pleased, as you put it, obviously. However, I wouldn't commit murder to stop it."

He nodded and replied, "People have committed murder so for much less, Mr. Barndon."

"I'm sure that perhaps some people have, but you are missing the obvious point, Sergeant. *After Dark* is anonymous. That's the whole point. Yes, Patsy knew I was married because I made no secret of it, it even says that on my profile. She didn't even know my first name until I told her, let alone my last. How would she know who my wife was to be able to tell her? She was a wild free spirit who loved life, and particularly sex, and she would no more want to tell Dianne than fly to the moon. Besides, why would she? Do you really think she would do that because she wanted me for herself? After only just one night that was of less than two hours' duration? Jesus, I'm good, but not that good."

"That's as may be, but we have to explore all avenues. This is a murder investigation, Mr. Barndon, and you admit to being the last person to see her alive. Please go on with how you came to meet her."

I nodded, accepting the seriousness of the matter. "She contacted me out of the blue about two weeks ago in response to my profile. We swapped a few emails about what we both liked and didn't like and how we might 'fit' together. We then spoke on the phone once and swapped pictures by text. I met her in Harvey's bar in town on my way home one evening after work. We chatted face to face. I had a beer, she had a white wine and we made a date for Saturday at the motel. She booked the motel, and I gave her the cash because I didn't want it to appear on my credit card statement."

"Very wise, Mr. Barndon. You are obviously very experienced at deception."

"I'm a car dealer. What can I say?" I tried to smile to show I was joking, but I think it may have looked more like a pathetic grin. Either way the joke went unnoticed.

"Tell us what happened Saturday night. Did you hit Ms. White at all?"

I couldn't help myself. I stood up, angry, and said "NO! I did not. Why the hell would you think I hit her?"

They calmly stared at me before Detective Collins spoke for the first time, "You mean, apart from the fact she was beaten to death with a steel pipe? Sit down and try to stay calm, Mr. Brandon. Please understand we have to ask these questions. We don't know anything about you other than you have a habit of telling lies to your wife and you enjoy dominating women who you meet on the internet. What would you think if you were us?" He stared at me with wide open eyes and hands on the desk, perfectly calm.

Slowly I relaxed a bit and tried to see how I looked to them. I shook my head and sat down, then took a deep breath and began again, "I apologise. Please let me try to explain this. There is a world of difference between Dominance and Submission and Sadomasochism. In SM the sadist derives pleasure from inflicting pain while the masochist enjoys that pain as his or her pleasure that they receive. But a Dominant enjoys exerting control over his or her partner, and a submissive enjoys giving that control to her Master or Mistress. The thing that most people don't get is that, ultimately, though you might not realize it, the submissive has all the control by what they will allow or not allow to happen to them. This is done by the use of safe words. Nothing goes further than their limits which they impose themselves. There may be spanking, minor pain and the like, but it's more about the reciprocal giving and receiving of sexual control than actually causing or receiving pain."

I continued after another sip of my water, to give me time to gather my thoughts. "I enjoy and am fascinated by submissive women but I don't get off on hurting them. Far from it. I enjoy making them orgasm as hard and as often as they possibly can, and even more than they think possible. The submissive woman enters this world, because by giving up control, she is free to enjoy sex without restraint or guilt. She may have a desire for something different but is too hung up to suggest it, but if her Master commands her to, she can be free to enjoy it. I am not, never have been, and never will be into hurting women. You could ask any of the women I've met through *After Dark,* they would all tell you the same. So, to answer your question: no, I did not hit Patsy."

Domin8

"Well, that's all very enlightening, Mr. Barndon. Thank you for explaining that to us. We didn't have a clue, did we, Sam? For your information, Ms. White had a bruise on her chin as if she had been punched before being beaten to death, so we had to know if you were responsible for the bruise. Now tell us about Saturday night, please."

"She booked the room, as I said, and emailed me the room number that afternoon after she went, paid and picked up the key. I got there between five-thirty and six. I had picked up a bottle of wine and umm, well, we had sex: quite a lot of it, actually. Around eight I had a shower and dressed, then I sat on the bed, and we chatted for ten minutes or so. I was out the door about eight-thirty because I had arranged to meet my brother at the casino at nine. Otherwise, believe me, I would have stayed longer. She was incredible."

"Mr. Barndon, I hope you don't mind me asking but did you have sex for the whole two hours or did you actually talk about anything? Did she seem troubled or upset about anything? Did she mention any problems of any kind?"

I thought for a few minutes and shook my head. "Honestly, she was in a very happy, even contented, mood when I left. It didn't seem like she had a care in the world. Her ex had left her pretty well provided for, she had told me, and so far as I know they were pretty amicable from the one or two remarks she made about him. I know she was a player and that she enjoyed her sexuality and freedom. She told me she was bi but she didn't mention any problems she was having in her life. She was very open with me and told me up front she had no intention of being faithful to me in any way, which I completely accepted, and I assume she was that open with her other lovers."

Stephen B. King

"And where was your wife while this was going on?" Sam Collins chipped in with one from left field, no doubt to catch me off guard.

"She works three nights a week, sometimes four, from 7 p.m. to 7 a.m. She doesn't need to. She does it because she loves her work. She is totally dedicated to it. She got home at her usual time—about seven thirty—and woke me up with a coffee, as she always does."

"So, to your knowledge, she doesn't know about you meeting women and having sex with them: in particular Ms. White?"

I could see where this was heading. What they were suggesting was ridiculous, but I wondered how I could possibly convince them of that without them interviewing her. "My wife was a virgin when we met, and we have been married twenty-six years, after being engaged for three. So far as I know she has never thought about another man, because that's just not her to do that. If she discovered I was meeting Patsy in a motel, she might want to kill me, but not her. She is a nurse. She is all about healing people, not hurting them. She would certainly have it out with me. She wouldn't be able to help herself. What she wouldn't do is kill my lover and then calmly bring me a coffee in the morning. And, let's not forget; she had no way of knowing about her as I only found out the motel and room number myself that afternoon by email."

Milanski nodded to show he understood that made sense, then asked, "When you left the motel—think carefully, Mr. Barndon—did you see anyone hanging around? Was anyone watching the room or did you see anyone in the car park?"

I closed my eyes and thought back, mentally retracing my steps. I had stood at the door and looked back at Patsy curled up in the bed. The covers had been over her hips with one leg covered and one out. Her smallish breasts with proud nipples were exposed, I think, as a tease to me to get me to stay longer. I remember thinking at the time, "Damn my brother."

Had I not arranged to meet him I would have gone back for seconds and possibly even thirds. I had waved at her. She waved back and smiled tiredly. Her hair was messy, and she looked gorgeous. I had closed the door behind me, turned and walked down the external passageway to the stairs, then down into the car park. My car was parked in front of the hotel room but on the lower level. I had gotten in the car and had one last look up at the door regretting that time was so short before starting the engine and driving away. I remember thinking there were an awful lot more cars around than when I had arrived, but I didn't remember seeing anyone lurking around.

"I'm sorry. I don't remember seeing anyone at all, but the car park was pretty full. If someone was watching there would have been fifty places to hide."

"Interview with Mr. Barndon terminated at 10:47," Collins said and switched off the recorder. Milanski then said, "Dave—I can call you Dave now the recorder is off—I want to ask you something off the record. We are all guys here, so please be honest. Did anything, anything at all, happen in that hotel room that you might not want to be recorded? If so, now is the time to tell us."

"Guys, the only thing I am guilty of is screwing around behind my wife's back. I've never even been untruthful to the women I've hooked up with. I made sure they all knew the rules. It's just a bit of fun and a chance to live out a few fantasies before I get too old, and while I can still attract someone to do it with. Call it a bit of a midlife crisis if you like, but you would be amazed at the number of women out there who are unhappy with their lives or sexually bored and frustrated like I am with mine.

Stephen B. King

They want to fool around with no strings attached and be the kind of slut they can never be in their real lives. Some have husbands and kids they can't walk away from, some, like Patsy, have let go of their inhibitions, while others have secret fantasies that they want to explore in safety and secrecy. It's just sex—pretty wild sex, for sure, but that's the attraction. I have no shortage of women who contact me through the website who want to lose themselves for a while, have fun and be dominated. You would be amazed."

Sam looked like he was interested in pointers for himself, while his older, senior partner just shook his head and scowled, "That's as maybe, Dave, and I suppose while you can get away with it, good luck to you, but this woman got murdered and so far you are the only suspect we have."

I held my hands far apart and open, my body language showing total honesty, and replied, "It's not me, guys. Yes, I was there, but I had no reason to do it. Did you check the time I arrived at the Casino? And was I covered in blood on the CCTV; I assume the guy who did it got covered in it by the way you spoke of her injuries?"

Detective Collins leant forward and asked, "Do you mind if I call you Dave, too?"

I nodded and he added, "We don't think you did it."

I let out a massive sigh of relief, but he went on, "Wait a sec, Dave. While we don't think you did it, you are still our only suspect. It's just that we can't see how you could have done it and got to the casino in time, as you say, not covered in blood. We also can't see why you would do it. Patsy White, we know, had a lot of men and women she played around with, so why would you kill her? It makes no sense, but it also makes no sense that anyone else she knew would kill her either. As you pointed out the arrangement was only made that afternoon, so unless one of you

Domin8

was followed, who even knew she would be there? We've spoken to her other lovers and ex-husband and they, like you, knew her rules and accepted them. She was very promiscuous, but that only seems to make her lovers innocent because they knew she was promiscuous."

"Was it a robbery?" I asked.

Milanski shook his head and looked at me. "You're a generous man, aren't you, Dave? You gave her a hundred and fifty dollars towards the room which was only one twenty and you put it on the bedside cabinet alongside her handbag, didn't you? It was still there, untouched. No, this wasn't a robbery gone wrong."

Collins nodded and added, "We have had a profile done, Dave, from a psychologist. She tells us this isn't a crime of robbery or opportunity. This is a crime of passion. The murderer was angry and acted in a rage. What we think happened is that, after you left, there was a knock on the door. She wrapped a sheet around her and, probably thinking it was you coming back for more, she opened it. Someone punched her on the chin, which knocked her to the floor. The assailant then closed the door. She was dazed and on her hands and knees trying to crawl away, when she was hit on the back of the head three times. Once would have been enough, Dave. The back of her head was caved in. But our killer didn't stop there. He—or she—hit her body another thirty-six times. Both arms and legs were broken, as was her spine in three places. To be fair to you, you don't seem the type."

"Oh my God! That's horrible. Poor Patsy. Thank you for believing me. It's been a very worrying time. I wish I could help, I really do. She was a beautiful woman, and she didn't deserve to die like that," I said, shaking my head sadly.

Sergeant Milanski then gave me the good news, "Dave, we see no reason to fuck up your life by telling your wife right now, but you should consider telling her anyway. We cannot guarantee you may not be a witness in any future trial once we do catch the maniac responsible, so it may well come out. I can tell you that we will do our best to keep it discreet, though, but there are no promises."

"I appreciate that catching your murderer is far more important than my marriage. I made my bed now I have to lie in it. I won't tell her for now, but if you wouldn't mind keeping me informed and if it looks like it's going to come out, I will tell her and face the music. Who knows, she may forgive me," I said, with absolutely no conviction at all. "You guys have to do what you have to do. My marriage is my problem."

"We will stay in touch Dave. We have to, as you are still very much a suspect, no matter how unlikely. Thank you for coming in today. Sam will see you out," Milanski said, but he winked as he said it. I couldn't tell if it was a wink or a tic.

Domin8

Chapter 5 – Starsky and Hutch (2)

Day Three. Things Get Worse.

"What do you think?" Sam Collins asked his boss as he sat down at his desk after getting back from seeing their suspect out of the building.

"About him? I think he is a lying scumbag car dealer who doesn't deserve the wife he has. That's what I think," Milanski offered.

"Is he our man though? What do you think? I believe him. He seems like a decent guy to me."

Milanski raised his eyebrows, "Clearly, our definitions of 'a decent guy' are very different." He shook his head at Sam before he went on, "I wish he were our man. No one his age should have that much sex. It's undignified at best and downright wrong at worst. But I can't see how he did it, or even why. It just makes no sense to me at all, no matter what I think of his personal life. The timing just doesn't work. Luckily for him, there is no way he could have done it, cleaned up, changed clothes, got to the casino when he did and be as cool as a cucumber ordering a drink. We know he didn't clean up in the room because there was no blood in the drains, so if he cleaned up before going to the casino, where did he do it? Jesus Christ, even the barmaid fancied him at the Crown, for fuck's sake. What is it about him that makes younger women want to fuck him?"

"I think he's one lucky bastard, in more ways than one. He could have been killed if he was still there when the murderer got there. Plus, this woman threw herself at him and let him do what he wanted to her. How many others is he doing it to? Do you think he would give me some pointers?" Sam laughed.

"You need them with your looks, Sam. Less of the hero worship, if you don't mind. We've got a murderer to catch. What do we know about the wife? Could she have done it to spite him?"

"How could she? I made a discrete inquiry at the hospital regarding staffing that night. Yes, it's theoretically possible; she could have slipped out, gone to the motel, waited for him to leave, killed her, cleaned up and gotten back to work without being noticed. Seriously and realistically, though, it's impossible. And again, if she did do it we come back to the question of where did she clean up? And then she drove back and got onto the ward without being noticed? Nah, no way could she get out of the hospital, do all that, including change clothes, then get back to the hospital and carry on as if nothing had happened. It just won't fly for me, and that's assuming she knew it was going on in the first place and that they were meeting at the motel. And how did she know it was that motel and room number unless she followed him? And if she did follow him then that would mean she was away from the hospital for hours, and she wasn't."

"How is the alibi for the ex-husband stacking up?"

"Fishing trip two hours up the coast. He is in the clear. For my money it has to be one of the guys she has met through this *After Hours* dating site, but they won't give us a list of her contacts without a warrant, and as they are an American-owned company that could take months, if we get the information at all."

"So, all we have is the picture from the car park CCTV, which is about as useful as tits on a bull," Milanski moaned, referring to a grainy single shot of the rear view of a tall man wearing a dark hooded jacket taken in very poor light. That picture, assuming it was the murderer because the camera did not show him near the room, was further proof that Barndon was not their man. The emails and meeting for illicit sex in the motel still seemed like he was the perfect suspect, were it not for the timing of meeting the brother.

They both sat in silence thinking very similar thoughts. The victim was an extremely promiscuous woman, who by her emails had enjoyed numerous partners of both sexes. Those emails showed no relationship problems, and everyone seemed to be perfectly happy sharing her around and having casual meetings. Her phone records and text history showed the same pattern with all of her male and female contacts except one particular male who seemed to want more. That was over a month prior to her death, and that suspect was in Melbourne on business, so he couldn't have done it.

They were at a dead end now that Barndon appeared to be just one of her many lovers with a near perfect alibi. True, it was just possible that he could have done it, but they couldn't figure out how, or why, especially considering the murder weapon was a piece of steel pipe. It's not the sort of thing he would have found in the car park so theoretically brought it with him if he were the killer. If that were the case it would show premeditation, yet they had sex for over two hours which the medical examiner had proved.

Forensics hadn't turned up anything of value. The killer seemed to be in and out within minutes—just as long as it took to beat her to death with the pipe, which was dropped, alongside the body. There were no prints on it. It had been wiped clean before use, and gloves were used during the beating. The blood spatter had left the imprint of a perfectly discernible, gloved handprint.

Her car and home were clean, her work colleagues at the school where she held her part-time teaching assistant and admin position were all complimentary of her and none of them knew of the varied and wild sex life she held outside of work. She was everything you would expect a teaching assistant to be, or at least so her colleagues thought. They had exhausted all of the avenues, there was nothing left but to go back through everyone again and see if something was missed. If that failed, then they were left with no other conclusion than it was a random, motiveless, thrill kill.

"Just a thought here, Boss, but what if she wasn't the intended victim? What if he was, but the killer was too late?"

Milanski looked across at him, while he mulled that idea over. He stood up and crossed to the white board, picked up a pen and wrote:

How did the killer know of the motel?

If Barndon was the victim and he was followed why wait till he left? Motive?

If White was the victim what was the motive? Jealousy?

Is it a random killing?

He underlined the word random in three or four strokes and said, "No matter how I think about this, that's what I come back to: a psycho on the prowl. Maybe it's just someone who saw Barndon leave. He knocked on the door, she answered it and he killed her. When he calmed down he then hi-tailed it out of there in a panic. Let's check records and see if there are any robberies which resemble this MO. Maybe it started out an intended robbery and progressed; we know there are no similar murders with this MO, but we haven't checked robberies."

Collins nodded, not bothering to bring up the myriad of questions he could ask to shoot that suggestion down in flames, because he had nothing better himself. The number 2 point on the board realistically shot his one and only theory down. Another possibility was that someone was trying to make it look like Dave was a killer. But that bordered so far on the ridiculous it wasn't worth contemplating. He shrugged to himself, and thought, *"maybe this is just a random killing after all."*

Stephen B. King

Chapter 6 - Domin8

The Very Beginning of the End

I could fill a series of books with the intervening years of my marriage to Dianne, but there would be no point. This story is not about the ups and downs of an otherwise normal married couple. We are pretty much like any other fifty-something heterosexual couple, anywhere in the world—save for my extramarital affairs. Although I'm quite certain we're not completely atypical in that regard, either.

I loved Di, and she loved me. It was that simple. But sometimes love is not enough. It needs affection, and yes, it needs sex. Perhaps not as much, or as often, in later years, but it needs some. Sadly, for Di and me, somewhere along the way it just dried up, and of course it was never my choice that that happened.

We had become engaged after eleven months of dating. Both sets of parents thought we were made for each other, and to this day I agree. We were. We married just before our third year anniversary, in early December. In those days I never, not once missed my single life I had before Di, she was more than enough for me back then.

At work I slowly worked my way up the promotion ladder in the motor trade, and Di finished her studies and became a qualified nurse, before having to give it away when she gave birth to our son, Jason. He was followed by another son, Bryan, and a daughter, Missy and nickname Bryan came up with. We stopped at three, deciding that was enough. I had the "snip," as long term birth control was in the news at that time because of possible problems with women's health. Di being a nurse was particularly

Domin8

worried about it, so I went under the knife. It was the right thing to do and I never regretted it.

Life was good for us. We worked hard to get our first home, which was a rundown renovator, and we spent months making it nice before moving on and doing it again and again. We made a few thousand dollars with each renovation, and we enjoyed doing it.

Sure, we had our ups and downs over the years, but it would be fair to say we had many, many more good times than bad. We were happy together, and nothing that happened later was because of anything that Dianne did wrong or specific problems in the way we got along together.

I don't blame my wife for anything that happened. She was an amazing woman: kind, loyal and loving. And in the final analysis she deserved a whole lot better of a man than me. It's just that somewhere along the way she lost her interest in making love with me, even though I didn't lose my interest for her. I'd like to think that it wasn't because I wasn't considerate of her needs, on the rare occasion we did make love I always ensure Di orgasmed.

Yes, you could say we just got into a rut but what long term marriage doesn't? Every man I know my age says pretty much the same things about their wives as I did about mine. Yes, the sex dwindled away over the years—Dianne stopped me coming in her mouth, for example. That became distasteful to her, yet that was so enjoyable to her when we had been dating.

Then, further down the track, she almost never went down on me at all. Interestingly, I never tired of licking her but that is not meant as a criticism. I've always loved doing that to a woman and always will.

The quality and quantity of sex did drop off with children around the house, naturally, especially when they got older, but I

Stephen B. King

understood that. I wasn't consciously bored with her. I still wanted to make love with Di, and more often than not, she didn't want to with me. We fought quite a lot over that subject for a long while, which didn't help, of course, but I was only human.

Like most men, I suppose, there was always pornography to fill the gap, which I discovered after a period of us arguing more and more about not having sex. We fought about it far less as I amused myself with video tapes, later replaced with DVDs and then came the internet. The question I would ask is: if other men weren't like me, how come sex on the internet is so big?

When the kids were younger Di was tired all of the time, especially because we had the three of them reasonably close together, and she was always busy. Di kept the house neat and clean. The washing and ironing was always done, and the kids were loved and cared for and they all played a heap of sport. Di fit into the housewife role perfectly, and I loved her for it. When the kids went to bed at seven or seven-thirty she would be exhausted. And the idea of sex after a day of housework was just not appealing to her. No way. She was far too tired, and mostly I understood.

Then when they got older, they were up later at night, and in their teens they could even be up after we went to bed. If sex before was rare, when they got older it was almost non-existent. Dianne was always worried that we could be heard by them, and they could be traumatised by it. The times we were in the house actually alone was almost unheard of. If one was at a sleep over, another had someone stay with us. It never ended, so sex became even less frequent than before.

I accepted it was the nature of our circumstances—and not because she didn't want to—that caused the beginning of the drought. She hadn't fallen out of love with me. It was just that the opportunities to make love with each other became fewer and

Domin8

fewer. And before you know it our address changed to number 1 Rut Street, Rutsville County.

It became a habit not to make love at night at all. Even kissing became even less frequent because I found kissing my wife a turn on, and if I got turned on, I wanted to make love to her. If she didn't want to, we would fight about it. So it was simpler not to kiss at all and avoid the inevitable fight.

Over the years I can truthfully say I never once consciously thought that I was bored sexually, but it's true that if we had made love more regularly I probably wouldn't have strayed with Tracy, Judith and Tamika. Maybe not, though. I might just be so obsessed with sex I'd have done it anyway. It's hard to look back on your life and wonder if different choices would have been made if circumstances had been different. All I know is that, when those chances came along, I took them.

Dianne and I were more like really good friends who shared a house than a sexually active couple. The rut was deep and wide, and I think in the end even if either of us wanted it we were so frightened of rejection we just didn't bother.

The die had been cast and old habits were hard to break. That is not to say we never did it. Some Sunday mornings or, even rarer, late at night we managed to stir some interest, but it tended to be times when Di was in the mood. Whereas, if I was horny it may or may not have prompted something to happen, but more likely not.

For all of that I still loved Dianne. I adored her. I don't relate my unfaithfulness to not loving her. It's true that if she had sex with other people the way I had, I daresay I would have left her. That's just the type of person I am. But I would like to think I would never had given her cause to find it elsewhere, whereas it seemed as if Di didn't care if I did, just so long as she never knew. Sometimes, from comments she made, I thought she

Stephen B. King

actually wanted me to have sex outside the marriage because that would mean I would leave her alone. I will never ever forget that one night, during a fight about – you guessed it, no sex- Di said that her idea of the perfect marriage was one without sex! How can that be the perfect marriage?

So the years passed by, life was good and pretty normal, except for me having those three short term affairs, which meant nothing to me emotionally at the time. It had been purely sexual, a fun release of tension, if you will.

But then, a few random things happened within a short space of time that started me thinking about submissive women. Once that taper was lit, it was only a matter of time before I needed to know more and experiment with the subject. I didn't plan Domin8 to happen. But when that snowball started down the mountain, it picked up speed and got bigger until it crashed at the bottom.

Di really enjoyed crime movies and TV shows. One of her favourites was a show called "Wire in the Blood," where the lead character, a psychologist named Tony Hill, works with the British police to help them get inside the minds of serial killers. We both thought this show was great drama. It was incredibly well written and acted.

I don't remember the name of the particular episode that started me off, but it was one we watched together and featured a killer who met his female victims via an online chat room. He used the screen name Domin8. He lured incredibly beautiful women, who were attracted to his Dominant male persona, to a location where he would lock them up and treat them like sexual slaves until he tired of them and murdered them. Then he would go back and find another one.

The concept intrigued me. I wondered why gorgeous women would crave that kind of sex, and why they wouldn't be

Domin8

turned off by the username Domin8. Of all the women I had been with, I had never met one who liked being a kind of sexual slave—at least not that I knew. I spoke to Di about it and said I thought it was a bit far-fetched that the women would put themselves in harm's way like that because they needed to be controlled sexually. I asked her what she thought might be the attraction from a woman's point of view.

She had gone back to nursing some years before, when the kids were old enough, and she said that she had met one or two female co-workers who admitted they liked it. She said they were both women in authority at work and that, somehow, because they controlled others in their work life, when it came to their home and sex life, they didn't want to be in charge. Sexually, they wanted to be taken charge of and have all the decisions made for them. Then also, she pointed out, it was also the 'bad boy' syndrome; women were often attracted to someone they thought were bad. Even she admitted to an occasional fantasy of a strong male taking charge of her, though she was quick to add that wasn't rape, far from it. I still didn't get it, but she insisted there were plenty of women who liked that kind of sex, though she insisted she couldn't see herself enjoying it in the real world.

I was stunned. She was telling me, in all seriousness, that there were women liked to be dominated in real life, and that she knew some. In fact, she thought it was more commonplace than people thought. To say I was amazed would be an understatement, and over the next week or two I couldn't stop thinking about it. My tastes in pornography changed, and I started researching submissive wives who liked to be shared and used, and—surprise, surprise—if the internet can be believed, there were thousands (scratch that), *millions* of them out there.

Around about the same time, the books *50 Shades of Grey* became massively popular, and women everywhere seemed to love the fantasy of being submissive, and bought the books in droves. We had a book display on the reception counter at work from a charity book reseller, and when the three "Grey" books were featured, the poor bookseller couldn't keep up with the demand. Every woman at work had read it. I could not imagine any of them being in the slightest way submissive in their real life, which, of course, made me even more fascinated with this concept.

I was coming to learn that some women were submissive by nature and hid it from the public, or they were more dominant in real life, but fantasised about being a submissive in the bedroom. I wondered about those women who fantasised about the subject and what it would take for them to actually try it.

In the lunchroom I asked a couple of the younger women about it, and they were pretty non-committal about their sex lives—as they should be to the general manager. But, they weren't embarrassed by people knowing they read the books. Then there were the "50 Shades" themed parties and the like, and suddenly it seemed to me that being a submissive woman was now, somehow, cool and fashionable.

While life went on in its normal way, two things were percolating in my brain. With the episode on "Wire in the Blood," I couldn't stop but wondering why would a beautiful and otherwise "normal" woman want to submit herself to a Dominant Male, especially a man she met on the internet?

Purely by chance, someone recently divorced at work mentioned the swag of free online dating sites that had cropped up. Then one night watching a movie that ran well past midnight I saw a TV ad for a website that specialising in married people looking for sex behind their partners back.

I don't really know why this subject matter was nibbling away at the cheese of my brain, but it was. One day, on my work computer, in my office I googled the subject and looked into it,

Domin8

because it was a quiet day and I was bored. At that time, the website I'd seen on TV for married people looking for affairs advertised they had millions, of members worldwide. It seemed like it was going on everywhere, and the number of results for my Google searches for D/s web sites, chat rooms and dating sites was staggering.

I found a site that specialized in erotic stories, reader's wife's pics, webcams and chat rooms that was completely free and didn't require a credit card to join. It seemed all you needed was an anonymous email address, so I created a Hotmail account, domin8@ and then thought about a profile. I kept telling myself that it was purely for the intent to research this perplexing and interesting subject.

I had absolutely no intention of "doing" anything or meeting anyone, quite honestly I still didn't think there were many out there. Really, the main reason for doing this was to find out if there were such women if so what their motivation was. I was not then, nor any time since, a truly dominant man, but I thought about acting like one, to see what would happen. I had to know if I could attract a submissive woman, at least online. I had no idea I would actually play out this fantasy in real life.

I used real facts about myself in terms of my looks, build and personality. I told the truth about my age. But for a screen name used Domin8, borrowing it from the TV show that started it all. In the comments section I said I was well dressed with a good appearance, not overweight was well-endowed and wanted to meet submissive younger woman who were interested in being controlled in a firm, but caring way. I wrote a long and (I hoped appealing) sexy story about myself but said I would only talk with submissive women and finished by saying to contact me if they dared, as a challenge. Then I sat back and waited. I thought I wouldn't get any interest.

Stephen B. King

In the erotic story section of the site, I read some tales along the lines of the D/s theme so I would have some idea of how to act and what to say if I could possibly attract such a woman to talk with me. The stories, I admit, were a massive turn on for me and, as unbelievable as some of them seemed, they only stirred my interest more.

In particular, I found stories written by the women themselves about their submissive wants and needs to be a huge turn on. I voraciously read anything like this I could find.

And thus, I entered the chat room world at the story site as Domin8, and started my slow downward spiral into a world of sex, submission and murder.

Domin8

Chapter 7 – Melanie (2) Dianne (2)
Day Three (continued) into Day Four.

I arrived back at work after the police interview, thinking and hoping that I had dodged a bullet. If I was lucky there was a good chance I wouldn't have to confront Dianne and admit my sins, I really thought I had got away with it.

Joy, our receptionist, greeted me with a smile as she always did and told me that a friend of mine had called in to see me earlier but didn't hang around or leave a name. She then told me that he had said he would leave a note on my desk for me. I thanked her. When I got there I couldn't find any note. I didn't worry about it. I thought that whoever it was would call me sooner or later and got on with some work.

It was about an hour later that I realized my brushed gold Mont Blanc pen was missing. I searched around and shrugged, as I assumed I had left it on one of the other guy's desks and that it would turn up. Unfortunately, when it did turn up, it spelt disaster.

During the afternoon, from out of nowhere came the realisation that I had never gotten back to Melanie—the woman from the night before on webcam. "*The poor girl*," I thought. I had left her dangling for an orgasm when the police had arrived with the promise I would get back to her. If she was a true submissive she would have been good and done as I had asked and not relieved herself. I smiled to myself at the thought. It really was quite funny. More likely though, she would have waited as long as she could and sorted herself out, but, I mused, perhaps she didn't.

I took my phone out and sent her a text message.

Stephen B. King

Dave: Melanie, I am sorry for last night. Something came up.

Two minutes later she replied.

Melanie: Your wife, Master? LOL

Dave: No, kitten, not my wife. Are you OK?

Melanie: I was a good girl, Master. I didn't play.

Dave: Not even with your husband? Tell me the truth, kitten.

Melanie: He is on night shift, Master. So no, he hasn't touched me. He hasn't for weeks. I will be ALONE tonight too. HINT, HINT. ☺

I had been given a warning and knew I should stop all the nonsense and grow old gracefully without screwing around anymore. Melanie was a cutie, a natural sub and had a husband who wouldn't listen or care about her needs, but that should not be my concern. My concern should be trying to save my marriage.

She was a sexual dynamo, stuck in a boring marriage. She was very much like myself, I realized. While I knew logic decreed to tell her "sorry, no can do," I felt like I did owe her something for teasing her and taking her to the precipice of an orgasm only to whisk it away. "*I could*," I mused, "*leave work just a little bit early and call in on the way home.*" It was a Wednesday, which was late night trading night for the motor trade, and Dianne wouldn't expect me home until ten. It was tempting. Perhaps one last fling, just for old time's sake?

Dianne would be tired anyway, having done a night shift the night before. She could possibly even be in bed by the time I got home. She often was on a Wednesday night.

I revolved the questions around in my head, "*Should I? Or shouldn't I?*" A mini civil war was being fought inside my head

Domin8

between the union side of common sense and finally being faithful to my wife for ever more and the much more heavily armed confederate side of pure sex drive.

Dave: I could be there about eight-thirty and stay for an hour only, kitten.

Melanie: MMMM Perfect Master. How should I dress?

She had made a perfect response. She was so gorgeous and would wear whatever I told her to. She had dark hair and very olive skin; she looked so perfect in white.

Dave: I think the white bra and pantie set I bought for you, and a nice perfume.

The underwear was a Bendon set in the whitest of white lace. It was totally see through and helped her feel like the beautiful woman she was—and the slut she longed to be for her husband, who just didn't see her for what she was.

Melanie: Yes, Master.

Dave: I will see you then.

Melanie: Yes, Master. Thank you (can't wait –I'm so turned on I'm climbing the walls here).

I sat back in my chair and tossed my phone onto the desk. *"Seriously,"* I asked myself, *"could any normal man resist?"* In the short space of time since I had discovered this alter ego, it never ceased to amaze me how many women wanted to experiment with their fantasies—and just how sexual they could be, when they let themselves—while others, like my own wife, had almost no desire whatsoever. I knew I would miss Melanie, and the others, but this lifestyle had to stop. I had decided tonight would be the last time, definitely, no ifs or buts, done, finite, end of 'Dominant Dave, or as he was known on line, Domin8.

Stephen B. King

I got on with my work, and the day passed uneventfully. Just before eight-thirty I stopped the car and parked down the street from Melanie's three-bedroom house. She had left the outside light on as a sign that her husband was not there as a signal for me. As discretely as possible I locked the car and used the shadows as much as possible as I crossed to her front door and knocked. It opened almost immediately, and there was a vision of sheer beauty and slutty sexuality. She wore nothing but her white lace underwear, as I had specified and held her head slightly bowed.

She opened the door wide, stepped back and knelt for me, head bowed with chin resting on her chest, placed her hands with palms facing upwards on her thighs and held her knees wide apart. She said in a very quiet voice, "Welcome Master. Please enter. Your slave awaits your command."

I closed the door behind me and unzipped my pants.

XXX

I arrived home, only just after the time I would have on any other normal Wednesday night, feeling pretty good. Well, if I am honest, I felt considerably better than good, more sensational, really. The time spent with Melanie had been the perfect antidote to the last twenty-four hours. I felt de-stressed, calm, and very, very satisfied. Deep down I knew Melanie would be feeling the same. I had told her that that was to be our last time, and while she was disappointed, I think she understood. Everything comes to an end, sooner or later. We went out on a high note. Her last words to me, and showed her true submissive nature, was to ask my permission for her to be able to go back to *After Dark* to make

Domin8

herself available for another Master to take care of her. Of course I agreed she should, and wished her nothing but happiness.

I was whistling a tune, a Deep Purple song as I recall, when I parked in the garage and entered the house. I walked through to the rear, where the family room was located, to the sound of the TV playing, which told me Di was still awake.

There was a time when I had felt guilty about the affairs I had, when I could barely look Di in the eye after having been with someone else, but that time had passed with the frequency with which it had happened over the preceding few months. I'm not proud of that, but it is what it is. There were many, many nights before when I had lain awake in bed, angry and frustrated because, once again, Di had been too tired, or had a headache so denied any form of sex. Since then, I had vowed to myself to think of my needs, and not just Dianne's, from time to time and to not feel guilty because of it.

"Hey babe, how was your day?" I asked cheerfully.

"Only so-so. Mr. Johnson died today." She sounded very sad.

I knew he had been one of her favourite patients at that time. He had come in for a routine hernia operation, and they had discovered he was riddled with cancer. All they could do was to sew him back up and give him the news. He never left the hospital, as they knew he had very little time left. They had tried chemotherapy, but it wasn't going to cure anything, and once he experienced the side effects he stopped all treatment and accepted his allotted time was up, gracefully.

But, even with the terrible news, he was apparently always in good spirits. He and Di shared some long, in depth conversations about his life's history. He was sadly lacking in family that would visit and keep him company during his wait for death to come calling, so Di had befriended him: such was her caring nature. During quiet periods on night shift they would play cribbage together and he wold regale her with tales of his merchant navy days travelling the world.

"I'm sorry to hear that, hon. Are you OK?" I asked.

I crossed over to her and sat by her side on the couch, placing my hand on her brightly coloured track pant covered thigh. She turned into me and put her face into the crook of my shoulder and cried. I held her, knowing she was a wonderful woman with a massive heart, who cared for everyone more than herself. Then, suddenly, I *did* felt very guilty for what I had been selfishly doing an hour before, while my wife had sat home alone and cried.

"He was such a nice man. He had no family there with him on the last day of his life. Don't you think that is so sad?"

"Yes, babe, that is sad, but at least he had you there with him last night. There would be no one I'd rather spend my last night on Earth with than you."

She hugged me tighter, appreciating the compliment, and sobbed into my neck.

A little later I made her a coffee, and we watched a Law and Order episode together holding hands on the couch before going to bed. There were a couple of times that night that I almost told her of the police visit and bared my soul to her. Quite possibly I would have, were she not already so upset.

I think that I had reached that point where I had stopped caring about whatever might befall me, but I was still very concerned that telling her would hurt her deeply. If that sounds hypocritical then it is. But I was more concerned about her not being hurt, than her leaving me. While I freely admit am a

Domin8

complete bastard for being unfaithful, I still hated the thought that she would be devastated if everything came out.

Dianne was the only person I had ever loved. I thought she was the only woman I was capable of loving. If we did split up over my affairs, which I thought we would, if and when, it came out, there would never be another woman for me who I would want to share my life with. Yes, I would carry on screwing everyone that I could, because I had always loved sex, and wanted it as much then as I had in my younger days – I hadn't changed in that regard. But, I would never let anyone get close to me again. I had come to realise it would be impossible for me to give anyone the exclusivity they might want from me.

We went to bed, neither of us wanting anything more than to cuddle until sleep came. She was still upset over her patient dying, and I was satisfied after my time with Melanie. In some senses of the word, that night in bed, I had the perfect marriage.

In the shower in the morning I thought about Di and my feelings for her. Life would be perfect if she just wanted sex with me, even if it was only occasionally. That way, I wouldn't need to find it elsewhere. But, the fact was that she didn't want it with me. I let my mind wander to ask the same questions I had been asking myself for years, "*Didn't her disinterest in me not allow me to find it where I could? Did marriage have to mean that one of the players had to virtually give up sex of any kind just because the other had tired of it? How could that be fair?*"

When I entered the kitchen she was at the sink, wearing a thin white opaque robe. The sun was shining through the window which overlooked out onto the pool. It looked like another beautiful day in paradise. The sunlight was making her gown look less opaque and more see-through. I could see she only wore white panties underneath. The lacy pattern clearly showed through. Suddenly I wanted her, I mean *really* wanted her, and I decided to take a chance and try. I walked up behind her and put my arms around her and cuddled into her body. She relaxed back into me and softly sighed. 'I love you, Dave," She moaned softly as I cupped her ample breasts in my hands. I kissed her neck softly and gently licked her skin. In my heart of hearts, I didn't expect her to respond, but surprisingly she did. Di leaned back into me harder, tilting her head to the side, giving me access to her neck and throat. That had always been an erogenous zone for her, and this was no exception, 'Yes, Dave." She said, giving me permission to go further.

I felt her nipples stiffen and elongate in my hands and I ground my hardness against her bottom. She moaned softly but louder than before. I tugged open the belt of her robe and opened it, tucking the end around her hips between us so it stayed that way. If someone was in the back garden they would see her naked breasts through the window as I pinched and pulled her nipples the way that I knew turned her on.

I bit her neck and felt her hand reach around behind her and grip me. The feel of me made her moan louder. I lowered my right hand down her front and into her panties, once more loving the feel of her thick pubic hair before curling my fingers and slipping my middle one inside her. She must have been harbouring some sexy thoughts herself.

"Oh my God," she said and started rocking her hips so she increased the friction against my hand, becoming wetter by the moment. This was not like her. This was not my Dianne of recent years, but I wasn't about to question why. I felt her need and wondered momentarily if perhaps the death of her patient the day before had affected her in some way. Her next words both shocked and excited me even more, "Take me Dave, right here and now. Just fuck me."

Domin8

I pushed her so she was bent over the sink and pulled the robe to one side. I yanked her panties down then squatted behind her before parting her cheeks, exposing her so I could lick her up and down. She pushed herself back further and spread her legs wider, giving me access. She was moaning louder, becoming quite frantic as I pushed my tongue into her, loving the tangy taste of her and the noises she made.

Knowing these days, she was only good for one orgasm at a time and sometimes that would last her for a month or more, I stopped before she could climax and stood up, dropping my pants and underwear in one fluid motion. I pushed inside her as she moaned loudly yet again, while her hands gripped the sink tightly, and she pushed back against me, urging me in deeper. I held her hips in my hands and loved her with long deep strokes. Her breasts crushed against the cold, wet draining board of the sink, but neither of us cared. We were living in that moment of true togetherness.

That was the last time I ever made love with my wife.

Stephen B. King

Chapter 8 – Melanie (3) Starsky and Hutch (3)

Day Four. The Calm Before the Storm.

I was at work later in the day, still trying to finish the budget reports for the Board of Directors, when my phone intercom buzzed.

"Yes, Joy," I answered. It was just after twelve.

"Two policemen are here and asking to see you, Dave."

I looked up through the glass door. My first thought, yet again, was that it was Starsky and Hutch come calling. Why they reminded me of those seventies TV icons was beyond me. I got up and went to meet them, thinking it was a follow up from the day before.

"Hi guys. Come in," I said cheerfully as I led them into my office and closed the door after them. "Have a seat. Would you like a coffee? How can I help?"

"Do you recognize this, Mister Barndon?" Sam Collins said, without any acknowledgement of my cheerful greeting. He took out a plastic evidence bag and held up what looked very much like my brushed gold pen.

"Well, from here it looks like my missing Mont Blanc. Does it say 'Dave, Happy 25th' on it?" I said, still with no idea what was about to come.

"Yes, it does, Mister Barndon. It also has your fingerprints on it. Well, that is to say it has the same partial prints on it we recovered from the motel room. We haven't taken your prints yet

Domin8

officially, although, we didn't really need to as you left us a nice set yesterday on the glass of water you had at the station."

I nodded, intrigued, and wondered where in the hell they had gotten my pen, as I knew it wasn't left at the motel. "Well, I suppose that shows what a useless criminal I would make doesn't it?"

"Do you know a Melanie Brewster?" Milanski asked as the earth opened up and swallowed me. Suddenly I knew. I just knew. I felt the blood in my veins turn ice cold and I sat up straight in my chair.

"Don't tell me, please don't tell me she is dead, too?"

He nodded, while watching my every move.

I collapsed back into my chair, shocked and stunned into silence, knowing I was being watched and judged, not that I cared right at that moment—and by the look on their faces—harshly.

"Yes, I know Melanie. I saw her last night, and we had sex. I was actually online with her when you visited me at home the night before. I caught up with her on my way home from work last night because our, shall we say, session together had been cut short. I was also visiting her to tell her I was ceasing that lifestyle and would no longer be seeing her."

Sam broke in incredulously, "Dave, just how many women are you seeing? Seriously, how the fuck do you do it?"

I ignored the question, and instead asked my own, "Please don't tell me she has been murdered, too."

Milanski just nodded before continuing. "That's where we found your pen. Right by her body, careless that. What time did you leave this particular victim?"

It took a long time to answer. My head was spinning with thoughts, "Why would someone be killing women I was seeing?

92

Stephen B. King

And how did my pen get there?" It made no sense at all. They were both lovely women, who had so much to live for and neither would hurt a fly.

"I was home by 9:45 or so. I had left her place between 9:20 and 9:30, and before you ask, she was breathing when I left. How was she killed?"

"Was your wife home when you arrived?" He asked ignoring my question completely.

It dawned on me suddenly. They still thought either Dianne or I was the killer. "Yes, she was. She was sitting on the couch, upset because a favourite patient of hers had died that day, Alec Johnson, from cancer. He had no family, so Dianne had spent a lot of time with him because she couldn't bear the thought of someone dying alone. She is *so* not a murderer. I wish you knew her. You wouldn't have to ask." I was becoming exasperated with the direction things were taking.

"Look here, Dave. Stop getting stroppy with us and think about things from our side. Two women you've banged are both dead, murdered. The time of death in both cases means you most definitely *could* have done it. True, it appears unlikely, but if it's not you who else would have a motive? So far as we can see *you* are the only link between these women."

He stared at me, and the silence continued while I thought, "*who would do this?*" Something he said though was wrong, wasn't it? "And, *After Dark* of course. I met them both through that website. Suddenly, an idea hit me. I jumped up and opened the door and yelled out across the showroom.

"Joy, get in her now please, and bring Brad with you!"

Then I sat back down and said "Let me ask these guys a couple of questions in front of you, ok? I think the answers will help clear things up."

Domin8

They both nodded as Brad, my used car manager, and Joy entered. They both looked very nervous, knowing the police were there.

"Joy, these officers may want to talk to you in a few minutes. Don't be nervous. I am being questioned about a very serious matter and I need you to tell the truth. Now, when I got to work yesterday, please tell these officers what you told me."

She looked blankly at me, not really understanding what I was talking about.

"Joy, it's all right. You've done nothing wrong but you told me someone came to see me while I was out yesterday?"

"Ah, yes. Sorry, Dave. Now I know what you mean. Yes, a man was here and asked for you, and I told him you wouldn't be in until after lunchtime, which was when you had told me you would be here."

I nodded for her to continue.

"He said he was an old friend of yours and said he would write a note for you and leave it on your desk. He seemed OK. Dave, that was OK, wasn't it?"

"Yes, it's fine, Joy. No problems at all. What did he look like?"

She looked blankly at me, not understanding, and I thought, "Oh my God, in the lunchroom one day, she had made a point of saying we, meaning Caucasians, all looked the same to her." As she was Asian, I thought it was a joke, but clearly it wasn't. She screwed up her eyes as she struggled to remember, "Dave, all I can really remember was the black hoody her wore, it was an Everlast and sunglasses, the ones that reflect back.

I turned to Brad and said, "Don't worry, Joy. These officers may talk to you later about it. Please have a good think about it and see what else you can remember. Now, Brad, I came to your office in the early afternoon. Other than business, what did I ask you?"

It was his turn to look blank until he remembered.

"You asked me if you had left your pen on my desk, the gold one, you said it had gone missing."

"Thanks, guys. That will be all. Brad, these guys may or may not need to talk to you later, too, about that pen."

They both left looking confused. Once the door was shut I said, "I have no idea who is doing this, but I promise you it's not me and it's most definitely not Dianne. There was no note on my desk when I got in here yesterday, so whoever it was came into my office, and it was that man who stole my pen. When I got here it was missing, so I went looking for it and—surprise, surprise— you found it at Melanie's. Trust me, I was with Mel for a bit over an hour, maybe an hour and fifteen minutes max. I didn't bring along my biro to take notes. I was too busy with other things. We had sex and that's all, other than talk about it being our last time. Guys, I'm just not that dumb. If I was going to kill her I wouldn't leave my pen behind. Whoever was here in my office and stole my pen is the killer."

"Dave, I've been a copper over twenty years, and that is the dumbest thing I've ever heard. Let's say you're right, though. Who would hate your guts enough to go to this much trouble to frame you for two murders? Have you any upset customers lately?"

He was sneering at me, and thinking about it I couldn't say I blamed him. "Ok, I know it sounds stupid, but what makes more sense to you? That I kill women I meet online? But I'm so stupid I use my own phone to text them; I'm guessing that how you got onto me?"

Domin8

He nodded, watching me put the noose around my own neck and kick the chair away.

"So let's run with the fact that I'm the world's stupidest murderer. I pick them up online—and let's just think about that for a minute or two. I use my own phone and an email address Maxwell Smart could track down. But wait, that's not dumb enough so I leave a biro there with my name and finger prints on it. Why would I set up it was missing earlier in the day? I don't bother cleaning my finger prints off anything, so you can come and arrest me. Does any of that sound logical? And, as for Di; she was home when I got there, crying over a bereavement. I comforted her. She couldn't possibly have done it even if she knew about the women in the first place, which she didn't."

"Is she home now, Dave?" Sam Collins asked.

Fearing the sky was about to fall in, I just nodded.

"Trust me, OK?" He said, then took out his mobile phone and dialled my home number, which he checked from his notes in his folder. He looked at his boss, who looked back approvingly.

"Hello, is that Mrs. Barndon, wife of David? Hi, Mrs. Barndon. It's Detective Sam Collins here from the WA Police. Please don't be alarmed. There is nothing to worry about. We are looking into a traffic incident which occurred late last night. Could you please tell me approximately what time your husband got home?"

He sat silently, nodding now and again. "Thank you so much for that Mrs. Barndon. I'm sure this is just a case of mistaken identity of your husband's registration number, which was what we thought all along. There is nothing to worry about. He is in the clear. Thank you for helping out as you have."

He hung up his phone and said to his boss, "Dave is right. She confirmed that he got home quite a bit before ten, which, she said, was his normal time. He seemed fine, and in fact was a great comfort to her as someone she knew had passed away. I didn't ask, but I am sure she would have noticed if he was covered in blood."

I hadn't realized how tensely I was sitting until that moment, when I relaxed back into the chair. I looked down at my hands and noticed they were shaking.

"Good work, Sam. Now, Dave, lets say we go along with your theory, we still have to come back to who? And why? Who would risk coming here to steal a pen to implicate you in a second murder, and why?"

I was lost on that point. To my knowledge I didn't have any enemies. I was just a normal guy doing a normal job with a normal family. The only non-normal thing I did was find submissive women via the internet and have sex with them. I had to admit that probably wasn't normal, although possibly more common than one might think. But somehow, I thought, that must be the key because, in my humdrum life outside sex chat rooms and online dating, I couldn't think of anyone who disliked me, let alone want to frame me for two murders.

"I don't know, guys. The only thing that makes any kind of sense is someone who knew Patsy and Melanie that was jealous. Maybe one of their previous lovers followed them. At the motel, they saw me arrive and waited till I left then killed her. But then how did they know where I worked to come and steal my pen, unless they then followed me here? I'm lost. I just don't know who would do this."

Then it struck me. "I just got an idea. It sounds crazy but...what if the second murder occurred *because* you didn't arrest me for the first?"

Domin8

They both looked at me, blankly. I explained, speeding up my speech as I gained momentum with this train of thought, "If someone really did have it in for me and framed me for Patsy's death, they would have been annoyed it didn't work. So maybe he followed me, and I led him to Melanie."

"You are a car dealer, they say that's one rung above child molesters and lawyers. Have you had any irate customers lately? One who might be angry and mad enough to do this to the big boss?"

"Look around you. This is a multi-million-dollar business. Aftersales service is vital these days. If we had a customer with a problem, we would fix it. The days of the big, bad car dealer taking advantage of a customer are long since gone."

That wasn't the right answer, I was sure of it, not that I knew what the right answer was, it just didn't feel like an angry customer.

"Dave, do you realise we have enough evidence to arrest you?" Milanski asked.

I spread my hands and arms. I couldn't have been more honest with them. I also knew how this looked; it looked like somehow I had murdered two women, which was the easiest thing to believe, because anything else was ridiculous to the point of being mad.

"I can only tell you that if I wanted to kill these two women, who I enjoyed immensely and could have carried on seeing for sex, I would have done it in a way that wouldn't make it look like I'm the prime suspect. I'm not dumb. Do you really think I could have done this, seriously? They pay me a lot of money because of my management skills. Don't you think I could have done a better job than this? Why would I implicate myself? I am successful, married and have three children, for God's sake." I pleaded.

Sam leant forward and asked, "I can't see anywhere around here or near where you live where you could get convenient lengths of scaffolding pipe. Boss, can you?"

I pounced on this, grateful for anything, no matter how small that would help show I was innocent. "So, he used the same kind of weapon again? Do you have a time of death? Guys, how about you tell me what you do have. You never know; it may help me to think who could be responsible."

Milanski thought for a minute before he said, "Time of death is always difficult. It's not an exact science despite what TV shows would have you believe. Sometimes there are things which can help tie it down. In this case we may know more when we get the full post-mortem results. For now, we only have an estimate. Her husband discovered her when he got home from work around seven-thirty in the morning and the M.E. got there after eight, so rigour and lividity would indicate time of death was ten to twelve hours prior, but that's always plus or minus an hour, you could be in the frame time, just as you could be for Ms. White, Dave."

"Yes, I see. I suppose as a frame up, the times would have to be close though, wouldn't they?"

They both chose to ignore that, Milanski carried on. "She was beaten to death with scaffolding pipe the same length as before. Again there were no fingerprints but this time he, or she, was even angrier. There were forty-seven blows to her body, which was located inside the entry hallway just inside her front door. Once again there was a bruise to her chin, from a punch which may have dazed her as she opened the front door to her attacker. It's like she was pulverised, and if we believe it wasn't you, then we are faced with someone who followed you to her home, waiting until you left, then knocked on the door. Perhaps he hoped she would think it was her wonderful lover—that's you, Dave—returning for dessert."

"Do I detect a note of jealousy there, Sergeant?"

"No, I leave my detective to be jealous of your sexual conquests. Let me ask you this. Think carefully, Dave. Is there a lover who you think might want more from you than you wanted to give, and this is her way of getting back at you? Or have any of them said they had a very jealous and dangerous husband or ex-lover? Just how many women have you met through this dating site?"

That stopped me in my tracks. My mind reeled, as on the face of it, it made sense. Though I wasn't sure it fit with the women I'd been with. "*Jesus, how many have there been in the six or seven months since I started my journey of self-discovery?*" I wondered to myself, never having counted them specifically. They could both tell they had hit a nerve and waited for my response.

"I'm only hesitating while I think about that because it's not something that I contemplated before. When I started this it was because a few coincidental things happened in my life at the same time, and well, for want of a better word, I was *tempted* to look into it, more for interest or research than to actually try to have sex with anyone. Then when I began, the first few people I played with were online only, in chat rooms and it was more…Look, if I tell you, you aren't going to take the piss are you?"

Milanski looked weary and interested at the same time said, "Look at us. Are these the faces of two men who are going to take the piss? My young off sider is jealous of you and wants some tips while I want to catch a scumbag who is killing off your lovers one by one. If there are any others we may need to arrange protection for them and won't my boss love that overtime. I can just imagine me explaining this to him, so you better make this damn good, Dave if I am to have any success at all, and stop him sending me back to traffic duty."

"OK, here goes. Firstly, while I do, I promise, adore my wife, we almost never have sex anymore, and that frustrates me, because I want it as much as I ever did, preferably with her. I still fancy her like mad. She is a very attractive and sexy woman, but she either doesn't think she is or doesn't want to be sexy anymore. Her life is complete. Either way, it's the same result for me. I'm expected to live like a monk, and damn it, that's not fair. I didn't want to use hookers, and I didn't want to have an affair with someone I know in case emotions might have come into it and someone would be hurt. It's a shithouse situation if you are as "highly sexed," as I am, although often I wonder if I am unusual or normal. I mean, don't you think about having sex with other women or are you one of the lucky ones with a wife who wants it as much as she did in her younger days?"

I looked at Milanski. I waited for a response I knew would never come.

"Don't worry about my sex life. This is all about yours. Go on."

"So, I wont bore you with my own personal journey as to why and how this all happened, but take my word for it it was due to a series of circumstances that just happened and perked my interest six months or more ago. I've discovered for myself now there *are* lots of women—some married, some not—who crave submission to a strong, dominant man they trust. So where does such a woman find such a man these days? The internet, of course. For me, I started in chatrooms and had some fun. It opened my eyes to what some—in fact, lots—of women all over the world want."

Domin8

Sam broke in, "From what I hear, though, a lot of those women in chat rooms are men pretending to be women. Did you find that anyone you thought was a woman was in fact a guy just fooling around?"

"Yeah, I heard that was often the case too, but I went to places that had webcam rooms. I could see them and they could see me, so I never came across it myself. The chatrooms are places where people play around and act out fantasies. It's just role play really that they call "cybersex", but you know what a woman named Helen said to me once in one of those rooms?"

"No, what did she say, Dave?" Sam asked. He was hooked, while Milanski still had a bored look to him. I could tell he had that same fascination as I had felt months before.

"She was one hell of a sexy, mature New Yorker. She was bi and leaning towards being gay. We played only once, but it was pretty awesome and interesting as well as fun. She worked, so she said, for Madison Square Garden in the administration department. Anyway, what she said was that 'the biggest sexual organ we have is our brain, by which she meant our imagination.' I've found out that is true. There are lots of women out there who want to play around with their fantasies. A lot of them are, deep down, truly submissive, though they hide it in the real world.

"Don't ask me why that is. Maybe their subconscious can't get past the days gone by when they didn't have equality. Or maybe they are powerful women in their day-to-day lives, so when it comes to sex, they don't want power or to have to make any decision at all. Some just crave that kind of sex and want it kept in a different compartment to their day to day lives. Ones that I tend to play around with are those who have fantasies of being sexual slaves. I don't mean being whipped or beaten. They don't want to be hurt; they want to be titillated, teased if you like. They want to know it's OK for them to climax over and over

102

again; they want to be used and controlled. One of the most incredible ones I have ever met was Melanie. She was truly amazing, an absolute submissive, but her husband thought that way of life was 'dirty' and wouldn't let her experiment with him. Funny isn't it? He should have married my wife and me, his.

"Sorry, I got carried away there. Anyway, the point is that someone like me, of a certain age and maturity—who is successful, confidant and has decent looks—who advertises to women who want to explore their submissive side in a safe way, is not exactly short of takers. I get as much pleasure from making a woman orgasm as I do myself, and a lot of women find that unusual. Their men generally don't care if they enjoy it or not. They just care about themselves."

"For those women online sex is discrete and safe; they can escape their normal lives and come with me and just have good sex. There are no commitments and no strings: just enjoyment. I started in chatrooms and met women from all over the world. Once I learnt more about the D/s scene I put my profile on places like *AfterDark.com*, because fantasy and webcam rooms are OK and a lot of fun, but it's still not real, is it?"

"None of this seems real to me," Milanski said, shaking his head.

I took a breath after a pause and mumbled, "Locally, I've been with fourteen women, most from *After Dark*, in the last six months or so."

"Fourteen? In six months?" Sam replied, incredulously, while Milanski was shocked beyond commenting, but for some reason he was mad at me.

"I know that sounds like a lot, but you see, *After Dark* has a ratings system, so when I meet someone I score them so others can know if she is good, bad or indifferent. What can I say? The ball started rolling and they rated me highly, which made me more attractive to other women, so once it started, well, lets just say I'm in demand."

"So, there are twelve more potential victims? This is just bizarre. There is no way I can get twelve women into protection just because they let you fuck them." The senior detective almost shouted.

He was getting *really* angry, and I didn't blame him. It sounded ridiculous to me, too. "Sergeant, I agree. It is stupid. Some of those were only once; either they or I didn't want to continue it because we didn't '*fit*' well enough. My main interest is in genuinely submissive women, not women who play act—which, by the way, is what I do. I'm play acting I don't really have a dominant bone in my body. Most I've met were just casual, because that's how we all wanted it. Sometimes we met online and it progressed to play around IRL—that's internet speak for 'in real life,' by the way. Sometimes, we got together more than once, and a few, like Melanie, became regular, but I wouldn't pick any of them as murderers."

"Give us their names and contact details. We have to talk to them and let them know. Who knows: they may have a jealous husband who doesn't approve of you giving his wife multiple orgasms while he is at work. Yeah, I know, strange concept. Go figure, huh?"

I grabbed a notepad and started writing names, addresses or at least contact details from my phone that I had. It took a few minutes and they sat silently in their own thoughts until I handed the list over to Milanski.

"Tell you what we are going to do, Dave. We are going to be policemen and go off and do what we do. That is to investigate. We are going to take your receptionist with us. Don't worry. I will arrange for a police car to drop her back when she has finished with the artist. We are, in particular, going to look into Melanie Brewster's life and past, including her husband. We are also going to look at these women you've given us. What you are going to do is come in tomorrow at eleven and once again make a record of interview along the lines of what we've discussed today. In the meantime, have a good think about all of your conquests and we will go into more depth about them tomorrow."

They stood up as one, Sam held out his hand to shake and I gladly took it. I then offered it to Milanski, who reluctantly shook it back. He didn't like me, or perhaps to be more specific, he didn't like what I'd been doing. That was obvious. They left, leaving me to think long and hard about who would set me up like this? After a couple of minutes. My door opened, and it was Sam Collins, again.

"Dave, I think it's time you came clean with your wife. There is no way this can be kept secret. We are going to need to speak to her, there is just no way around that now there's a second victim. Better it comes from you rather than us, don't you think?"

I stared at him, realising he was right. I was going to have to face the music. "Thanks Sam, I will talk to her tonight. I may be in a motel if I get kicked out; you have my mobile if you need me?"

"I do, and one other thing? Best you keep your cock in your pants till we get to the bottom of this don't you think? We don't want any more victims." He said, smiling, but at the same time he was deadly serious.

"Don't worry. I'm sworn off of sex for life." And I honestly thought that I was.

Domin8

Chapter 9 – Starsky and Hutch (4) – Joy

Behind the Scenes

Once they had delivered Joy to the artist, who was a portly balding man with a grey poncho moustache named Willie, they both went to the canteen for lunch. The special of the day was a pasta dish which they both opted for. Milanski had it with garlic bread and tea. Collins had a sparkling mineral water. After two mouthfuls each they both decided the pasta was edible, which was never a given with the police canteen daily special. It could be very hit and miss.

Milanski started the inevitable conversation, "This fucking case is giving me the heebie-jeebies, and absolutely fuck all makes sense. We have a prime suspect who is a dead certainty for it, but I don't think he could have done it. The pen makes it fairly probable It's a frame up, but if it's not the wife who the fuck would go to that much trouble? It's doing my head in, Sam."

Sam nodded. He shared exactly the same thoughts, "As you know, when I went back in I told him he had to tell his wife, that it couldn't stay a secret any more. He agreed, he had to, and his attitude would suggest he's not a murderer, and neither is she. I think we need to talk to her tomorrow, but you know what, boss?"

"What?"

"She isn't going to be able to help us. It just doesn't feel like she would, or could, know anything. Unfortunately, her world is going to get turned upside down because of it, and I feel sorry for her. We have the pic of the guy in the car park at the motel, and now some guy stealing his pen of the desk also wearing a hoody, just to frame him. So that means the second killing was premeditated even if we accepted that the first one wasn't. Who does that? Who could be calm enough to risk identification by stealing his pen, but mad enough to beat two women to death in a fit of rage?"

"So you are assuming too that the pen thief is the killer, and he's the same guy in the car park? You like him, don't you, Sam? Is that a bit of hero worship there?"

"I wouldn't say I like him, no. I wouldn't mind his lifestyle, though. He probably earns more than you and I combined and he has this way of attracting women who will do anything for him. I actually think he has been totally honest with us and is blameless for the murders. A, I don't think he is the type to kill women. B, why would he? No motive that I can see. C, the timing, though theoretically possible just doesn't seem to work on closer inspection."

Milanski nodded while taking another mouthful.

"So, if he is innocent, as we believe him to be, what's not to like about him? Other than the fact that you have to feel sorry for his wife. She seems very nice. But, maybe, she is the root cause of his fooling around as he says. I can't help wondering if I had been married over twenty-five years, and my wife hardly ever wanted sex with me, would I do the same? One thing is for sure, I wouldn't want to be a fly on the wall tonight when he tells her what he has been doing."

Felix nodded as he took a bite, "She will leave him for sure. There is no way any self-respecting woman would put up with what he has been doing. And rightly so. In my book, he deserves all he gets. I don't blame him for fucking around, but he should have left her first. That old saying about having cake *and* eating it comes to mind."

Domin8

"*He is so old school,*" Sam thought. "*He's been married to the same woman over thirty years!*" That thought alone was frightening for the much younger, and recently single, subordinate. "You never, not once, were tempted to have a play on the side, Boss?"

"Of course I've been tempted, and had chances too—as most of us do—but I never took them. That was a choice I made. He could have made that choice, too. To me when you love and marry someone, being faithful is a major part of that commitment. Otherwise, what's the point?"

"Children, I suppose, Boss. But it seems like she changed over the years and he didn't. Is that fair, either? If it weren't for some lunatic targeting his lovers, he would have got away with this forever, in which case his wife wouldn't have to be hurt. Maybe, in some way, that's the motive here. Could it be someone wants to hurt her, and this is an elaborate way of doing that?

"Stop that right now. Don't let this spiral out of control with a whole lot of what-ifs and even more ridiculous scenarios than we have already. We will talk to the poor Mrs. Barndon tomorrow morning after he has told her the bad news tonight. Let's see what light she can shed on things then. When we have the picture from the artist, you take the receptionist back yourself and take a copy with you. See if anyone else can verify the guy was there. And see if Dave recognises him, too. Maybe it was just a mate who changed his mind about leaving a message, and maybe Barndon is smart enough to set up the missing pen before leaving it behind deliberately to throw us off the scent."

He held up his hand to stop Sam for interrupting, "I know what you are going to say, that it's just stupid. Why set up a story about the pen and then deliberately leave it behind when you murder someone? I know, but nothing about this case makes sense, so that's as feasible as anything else."

Stephen B. King

Once he finished, Sam summed it up. "I agree with you, boss. Everything about this is screwy, so taking that as a given, the least screwy scenario is that somehow Dave has upset some nut who is trying to frame him for murder. The scary thing to me is what happens if we don't arrest him? What will this guy's next move be?"

His boss simply stared back, thinking that thought through before sighing. "So we are back with his other twelve lovers. Is that what you are saying?"

"I think we need to talk to them ASAP. I've given the email addresses to IT to identify the owners. The phone numbers he has given are easy, as are the physical addresses. You realise at least seven of them appear to be married? So that could give us seven suspects in the husbands, but even if one of them *is* our man, we are going to ruin another six marriages."

Milanski pushed his plate away, suddenly losing his appetite. "That's not our problem, Sam. It's not pleasant, I know, but they made a choice, too, and they have to pay the consequences. More importantly, though, if you are right, they could be in danger themselves. We better get going; this could be a long day."

They had no idea just how long of a day it was going to be.

XXX

The police artist, Willie was trying to keep his temper and not doing terrible well at it. "*The bloody woman is exasperating,*" he thought over and over. She was all over the place and was, to all intents and purposes, next to useless as a witness. He tried to guide her through the possibilities of every facet of the human face as one step at a time; she would make a decision and then later say that was wrong and try to change it. It was true; as he and every other cop knew, that a single witness was the most dangerous method of identification there was. And often when there were several witnesses, their descriptions often conflicted with each other. It was a sad but true fact; people are naturally unobservant and unreliable.

He knew that the problem in Joy's case was twofold. Firstly, in her job she would meet a hundred people a day, so faces tended to blend into one twenty-four hours later. This would be especially true for someone so young, who would be twittering or Facebooking away every chance she got, so would be distracted. Secondly she had no reason to notice this man, and therefore she didn't, the hooded top and sunglasses wouldn't help either. Maybe her phone was ringing at the same time. She had said that the phone never stopped ringing at reception, being a big Toyota dealership.

They also had the same issue with Caucasians trying to describe Asians. It was very difficult to see the differences, and nuances of the human face, as it was for Joy. She tried her best. It wasn't that she was being deliberately unhelpful, but after two hours they still didn't have a useable drawing, and he didn't think they were going to.

All they had from her description was a reasonably tallish man, who was quite thin, who was Caucasian, which at least ruled out the other skin colours. She couldn't remember anything that stood out, like a crooked nose, missing teeth, scars or tattoos. Just a normal looking guy. She was also hopeless at guessing an age range; he could have been a young man all the way up to middle age. And as for his accent? She looked at him blankly when he asked her that. "Normal Australian," she replied.

He reported back to Milanski and Collins. He knew Sam was taking her back to work, but now had no sketch to take with him, but Sam was going to ask to see if anyone else had seen this man go into the boss's office anyway. Possibly, if there was another witness, they would be more help than Joy had been.

Milanski thanked him for his efforts and apologised for wasting his time, wondering to himself as he looked at Willie's retreating back, *"Why am I not surprised? Of course, there's no sketch. That's perfectly in line with how this whole investigation is going."*

He thought he had time to visit and interview a few of the twelve women to have crossed the path of Dave Barndon, knowing Sam had his list to see as well once he finished at the Toyota yard. Milanski was very aware that the time was ticking away. He also harboured a very bad feeling that they hadn't seen the last victim, yet, and he was correct.

Domin8

Chapter 10 – Dianne (3)

The Very Depths of Despair

I knew that I had to tell her and tell her that night, but when was the right time? I felt miserable for the rest of the afternoon knowing the scope of what I had to reveal about myself. Firstly, of course, I was responsible for two women's deaths, and that burden weighed heavily on me. Secondly, for knowing I was about to break Dianne's heart. True, she had lost most of her desire for sex with me, but I had no doubt she loved me. I knew that when I told her I had been unfaithful, not just once, but on numerous occasions, and with several women, there would be no way she could possibly believe that I loved her. I couldn't possibly believe that if I were in her position.

I hadn't experienced butterflies in my stomach since childhood, that I could remember, but I had them that day. The longer the day dragged on, the more the butterflies bred and multiplied inside me so by the time I got home, they had grown themselves into a full infestation.

When I arrived home, Dianne was in the kitchen preparing dinner. She greeted me with a big smile and a kiss that was, in itself, unusual. Perhaps making love at the kitchen sink that morning had brought about a change in her. The kiss hello only served to make me feel sadder and guiltier for what I knew was to come.

I went to grab a beer, but changed my mind and poured a scotch instead; I needed it to steady my nerves. "Babe, I'm going to grab a shower and change, and then there is something I need to talk to you about, OK?"

Stephen B. King

"Sure, no worries. Dinner will be a while anyway."

I didn't think either of us would feel like eating once I had finished talking with her.

I grabbed a change of clothes and fresh underwear and carried it all including my scotch through to the bathroom. I shut the door and stripped off. I looked into the mirror at my body, which I had to admit wasn't too bad for my age. I couldn't help but look at the reflection of my penis. It had gotten me into a lot of trouble. I realised then that the old cliché about the little head thinking for the big head had never rung truer for me. I sighed and reached in the cubicle to turn on the water.

Just as I turned it on I thought I heard the doorbell in the distance. I contemplated re-dressing, but thought, *"No, fuck it,"* and stepped under the now steaming water and waited for Dianne to come and tell me who it was, if it was a caller for me.

She didn't interrupt me so I enjoyed the hot shower and took my time washing my hair and body, fully realising I was putting off the inevitable confrontation with Di. When I knew I couldn't delay any more I turned off the water and dried off.

I put on my favourite comfy jeans and polo shirt. *"All the better to wear to the motel,"* I thought, *"once I'd been kicked out of the house."* Still in bare feet, I finished the scotch and enjoyed the burning sensation as it went down. I picked up my dirty clothes and put them in the hamper. Di hated it if I didn't do that and I may as well get it right for the last time. I'd put it off long enough, it was time to go and face the firing squad.

She wasn't in the kitchen, and I called out to her, but there was no reply. Maybe she was in the toilet, I thought, and went to replenish my scotch. I sat down at the breakfast bar and started rehearsing in my mind how I would start this and several permutations came to mind. *"Di, I'm really sorry but I've been*

Domin8

unfaithful to you." No, too blunt. "*Di I love you more than life itself but I've been stupid and done some things you're going to hate me for.*" Better. That one had possibilities.

I got up, unable to sit still, and began to pace up and down, feeling like I needed to vomit with worry. I made another drink and still heard no sound from the rest of the house.

"Di, where are you?" I yelled out, but no reply came back. "*Where the hell is she?*" I thought. Maybe she was still at the front door with some survey people or Jehovah's Witnesses. "*Shit, that's been going on a while,*" I thought. Then another thought followed, and my heart sank, "*Oh God, what if it's Starsky and Hutch, and they've been questioning her?*" I went to check it out as the butterflies had, by then, gnawed great big holes in my stomach.

The first think I saw was the bloody, steel length of pipe. It had rolled across the hallway to where it turned left into the passage. I was halfway along when I saw it laying there on the floor, caked in blood and what looked like matted hair.

My heart sank like a stone, and I ran the rest of the way. I turned the corner to see my wife, battered and beaten. She was a broken, bloody mess, her head gaped open and grey matter oozed out. It was a scene from a nightmare and I was rooted to the spot in shock. I knelt, cried out her name and turned her over, hoping upon hope for some sign of life. But, of course, there was none. No one could have survived such a beating.

I howled, distraught. She should never have been put through this. Everything was my fault. At that moment of loss, I realised the depth of love I had for her and hugged her broken body to me and cried and cried.

XXX

Stephen B. King

They arrested me for three counts of murder. They had to, really.

I had called Milanski directly once I could bring myself to do it, using the mobile number on the card he had given me. He and Sam Collins arrived a few minutes after a marked car with flashing lights pulled into the driveway. An ambulance arrived shortly after that.

They found me sitting on the floor in the hall, my back to the wall, staring at Di's body. I was covered in blood from head to foot, tears streaming down my face. I didn't want to leave her, but they half-dragged, half-carried me into the family room, where I sat on the couch, elbows on thighs, head in my hands and wept.

Milanski's voice broke through the fog, telling me I was being arrested for murdering my wife and two other women. He said I didn't need to say anything and that things I said would be used in evidence, blah, blah, blah. The nightmare went on and on. I no longer cared about anything.

I was handcuffed and led out to the police car still bare footed and dressed in blood-stained cloths. They bundled me into the backseat, and I sat there just wanting to die. I was lost in the thickest fog imaginable, and I would have been happy if they shot me dead right there and then.

The next hour passed in a daze. I was stripped naked and given what felt like a paper set of overalls to put on, photographed, fingerprinted and led into a cell. It had white walls, a single bunk and toilet with no seat. If I had been given the means to kill myself I would have.

I lay on the bunk, cold and shivering, in the foetal position. The image of Di's body was in my head, and I was wracked with guilt and grief while time slowly dragged its heels and passed. All

Domin8

I could think was, "How could things have possibly come to this? How?"

BOOK TWO

"In just a few seconds a computer can make a mistake it would take a man many months to make" - Author unknown.

Domin8

Chapter 11 – Sexy Lexy

Into the Void: The Early Days of Domin8

When I logged in to the chatroom for the very first time as Domin8, it was a surreal experience. I had no idea what to expect. I had stayed back at work after everyone else had gone, and in the privacy of my office I logged into the chatroom world and began my descent down the slippery slope that ended up in a total catastrophe. The screen opened up. I was in the "Lobby" area, and the top line, which was in bright blue, said:

Domin8 has entered the Lobby

As I looked, the line was scrolling quite quickly as other screen names entered and some left to exit altogether or go to other rooms. There were people talking openly. It was mainly welcomes, but there was so much activity that it was difficult to read the lines before they scrolled and new lines were added. The names themselves were as diverse as I could ever have imagined, and I looked to the left-hand panel and saw that there were currently 518 visitors in 8 "Rooms" and 87 in *"Private Rooms."* The amazing thing was that as I saw the numbers, they too were changing quickly, again I assumed from people logging on and off.

It listed the names of the rooms in bold black. They were underlined so I assumed from that each was a link, and if you clicked on them you would be transported to that room.

The "public" rooms were:

Stephen B. King

First Timers

One on One

Gay and Lesbian

Bis and Triers

Bondage and Discipline

Dominant – submissive

Threesomes

Group Gropes

I sat there stunned for minutes on end. These were real people, over 600 of them at that same time, all looking to hook-up and talk to others about sex. And this was only one site! My Google search showed me there were hundreds, if not thousands, of similar sites out there in cyber land. Clearly, I had led a very sheltered life. I don't know what I expected to see—maybe a handful of deviant people at best—but this number of people was mind-blowing.

I was so shocked I hadn't noticed a smaller window had opened on the bottom right of the screen, until it flashed a second time. Someone by the unlikely name of "Sexy Lexy" had said "**hello**" on the first line and "**hello ?????????**" on the second. Her words were coloured red, looking back I should have taken that as an omen of things to come as the colour of danger, and left immediately. The window was entitled "Private Chat," and my cursor was flashing on the reply line, so I typed back.

Domin8: Hi, sorry I was a bit slow, I'm a bit overwhelmed. This is my first time here.

Sexy Lexy: Hey that's cool. I've never spoken to a newbie. where are you from?

Domin8

Domin8: Perth in Western Australia, you?

Sexy Lexy: Phoenix Arizona, safe to assume we aren't gonna meet any time soon then. ☺

We spent the next ten minutes or so playing twenty questions with each other, and I have to say she seemed like a nice person, though I was a bit taken aback when she admitted to only being 19, nearly twenty, and a Freshman at Arizona State University.

It's possible that, were it not for Lex—as I called her—meeting me that first time and being so openly friendly and downright sexy, my foray into cybersex may have died there and then as it all seemed so overwhelming and confusing.

She offered to make a "private room" for us, so we could talk in a big window, not a small one, because she said her favourite fantasy was to be taken and forced to submit by one of her lecturers, and my age and profile turned her on. She also said that in a private room we could swap pictures, as links would work.

I followed her into a room she created called "**Submitting to my Teacher**," using the password she had given me. Then by following her instructions she then listed some links for me to look at. I opened the first one, and it showed her—at least I had to assume it was her—sitting topless on a beach poking her tongue out at the camera. She said that that picture was, as were the next few she sent shortly after, taken by her boyfriend at that time. She was attractive, slim with brown hair and small breasts. She was wearing tiny bikini bottoms, but it wasn't a "sexual" pose, unlike the rest that were to come.

I stopped in my tracks and almost did a double take as I opened the second link, which was taken on the same beach and was a close up of her with her boyfriend's penis in her mouth. Her cheeks looked hollow with suction, her eyes were closed and there was a look of total happiness on her face.

This was a nineteen-year-old girl, and I was rapidly approaching fifty. Part of me was in total shock, as I had children her age. But I must ashamedly admit, I was extremely turned looking at the image of raw sex on my screen, so I was torn. In a way, for me it was bizarre, talking to a woman who would willingly show off such pornographic pictures of herself to a total stranger. I could never imagine Di allowing pictures to be taken of her, let alone be shown to others. I nearly logged off, but just before I could she typed back.

Sexy Lexy: Sir, did you make me stay back in detention to punish me? I'm sorry my assignment was late.

This was the sexiest thing that had happened to me in a long while. A young, beautiful woman wanted me to help her fantasize while she masturbated herself. For her to call me Sir struck a chord somewhere deep down inside too. I was so horny my immediate need won out over my common sense. Guilty as charged, Your Honour.

I was new to typing cybersex and creating fantasies in the chat world, and she was young and inexperienced too, but, she was very, very willing. One by one I opened her pictures as we talked about her fantasy, which got more and more graphic, to such an extent it made me wonder if all American college girls were like that.

We acted out a story of me spanking her rafter stripping her naked and putting her over my lap. It continued with me using her and ended as I opened her last picture, which was of her sitting on the beach, her legs spread wide after she had been used by her boyfriend.

Domin8

I finished, typing with one hand. That was the first time I had ever had any form of sex at work and I had extremely mixed feelings of shame, embarrassment but also gratification, all at the same time. Lex had told me she had orgasmed twice with her vibrator as I was talking to her, and she loved the mental image of me being one of her older profs at University. She even asked to see me again!

When I checked my watch, an hour and a quarter had flown by when I said goodbye to her. Before I left she asked if I had a webcam, which I didn't on my work computer but had on my laptop and iPad at home. She suggested next time we caught up I should have that ready, and we could meet in a webcam room. That way, she explained, I could see her body in real time as she played with herself for me, and she could watch me too.

I don't think I can easily explain how shocked, yet intrigued I felt, that this very attractive girl was inviting me to see her nude as she played with herself and I helped with a fantasy. I was staggered that she was suggesting ways for us to have more sex, and more graphic sex at that. As a nineteen-year-old she seemed way more mature than she should be. On that note I said, "yes," I would see her again and logged off to escape, as the guilt was setting in. I never intended to return.

I drove home still in a state of shock and was so guilt ridden to the point of feeling ill; both for being unfaithful to Dianne, albeit mentally rather than physically, but also with someone so young. That, for me, was the worst. I made a decision there and then that I wouldn't meet up with her again, and decided that would be first and last time in a sex chat room. The guilt afterwards far outweighed the fun I had enjoyed at the time, and that was final. I promised myself: no more.

I honestly meant it at that moment in time. I fully intended to keep that promise I made to myself and I felt better about the whole situation for making that pledge. It was, I imagine, rather much like an alcoholic, or drug addict saying they were going cold turkey, knowing that deep down they wouldn't be unable to resist the urge. As I pulled into my driveway my mind was made up. It had been a one-off fun thing, which would never, ever happen again.

I believe the lies that we tell ourselves are the worst lies of all.

Domin8

Chapter 12 – Good Girl - Sexy Lexy (2)
Domin8. The Second Coming.

I was good. I was really, really good for ages, or so it felt to me. And it wasn't my fault I strayed again, not really, said the alcoholic. Well, ok, yes of course it was.

Five days had gone by when I noticed a red number 1 on the email icon on my iPhone. My work email is not linked to my phone, so it could only mean one thing: I had an email in my Hotmail account. I didn't want to open it at all, but the sender's name, "Good Girl," intrigued me, and it preyed on my mind for the rest of the day, so eventually I opened it. I was only going to read it and delete it. That was my intention. I swear. But, as it opened, I saw a picture of an attractive, middle-aged woman smiling for the camera so decided to read further.

It was a perfectly normal picture. She was fully clothed and the sort of woman you would see at any suburban shopping centre, without being a stunner. She had a nice smile. Her clothes were fashionable without being revealing, and the photo did show she wasn't overweight. Her e-mail read:

Dear Domin8,

I am a married woman whose husband lost all desire for sex a long time ago after a car accident. I have never written to anyone from a dating site before and have only been a member for two days. To be honest I'm so shy I almost didn't write at all but your ad really sparked my interest and I can see we live quite close to each other.

I have had a secret fantasy for many years to submit to a big, strong man and do whatever I am told to do to please him. Even when I was having sex with my husband, he never took charge of me. Instead, he wanted me to be the strong one, which I wasn't terribly good at, and so our sex life was never great.

If you would like to know more about me, you only have to ask. I will do anything you tell me to, within reason. I have never submitted to anyone and given total control of my body to another person and I hope you find me attractive enough to make me your slave. I yearn to have a Master. Please sir, make me yours, and I promise to be a "good girl."

Melody

I sat for a full five minutes, absolutely stunned. I really had thought something like this wouldn't happen. I was still unconvinced that such women existed outside of pornography. But there, right in front of me, was the proof that they were out there. My mind went back to the TV show and I realised that were I a murderer, here was a willing victim. That thought chilled me to the bone, yet excited me too.

I didn't reply that night. I had to think about it and didn't trust myself so stay in character. I hoped that after sleeping on it I would decide against taking it further: honestly, I did. I wanted to give myself time to think it through, rather than being a fool and rush in where angels feared to tread.

Naturally, I was fooling myself. After dinner that night, I excused myself after we did the dishes and went into our study. I said I had some things to do on the computer. I think by then

Domin8

Dianne knew that was "Dave speak" for some "quality alone time.". She never disturbed me; it was one of those things we both knew I did but never discussed. We hadn't had a fight over sex in years so we both accepted that it solved my needs and kept the pressure off of her.

I opened up the email from her and started to write back. I wanted to test her willingness and see just how real she was. I think I still harboured doubts that she was genuine. After all, I reasoned, this was why I did all of this in the first place: just to learn about the why's and wherefores of submissive women for *research purposes*. I replied:

Dear Good Girl,

Thanks for plucking up the courage to write. You seem a very nice woman and I wonder if you have thought this through? It is a big step to take and one you should think carefully about. I know you say there would be no limits, within reason, so what I want you to do is be more specific for me.

I want you to think of a list of ten things you would willingly submit to, let your imagination and dreams run free, impress me. Then, I want you to tell me three things that you would not want to do. If we were to meet I would want to know where your boundaries lay.

If I permitted you to be my submissive I would control your orgasms. You could only orgasm if and when I permitted it despite what I may choose to do to your body. I would require your commitment and promise you would give that vow.

Think carefully, and remember the old saying…be careful what you wish for.

D8

Stephen B. King

I sat staring at the screen, fingers interlaced behind my head, debating whether to send or forget the whole thing and wondered if I really wanted to play with her. Already, even from that one e-mail, it was an incredible feeling of power to have over another person. All I wanted was a bit of fun and excitement without physically hurting anyone. I hit "send," thinking she probably wouldn't reply. Even if she did that still didn't mean I had to do anything more.

I closed down Hotmail and switched over to the chat room site so see if Lexy was there, forgetting my earlier pledge not to. She wasn't. The time difference between us would make it difficult, and I actually felt relieved she wasn't there. Out of curiosity, I entered the D/s room.

Of the seventeen people there chatting, six were submissive women, one was a sub male, seven were Dom guys and three were Mistresses. I made those discoveries by firstly their screen name, and if that wasn't obvious clicking on each of their profiles in turn. I was welcomed by a few people openly and was polite back. It was all very civilized but the conversations were a bit weird, such as:

Sub chrissy: *enters quietly and kneels by her Master's feet, legs apart, hands on thighs, palms up and says, Good evening, Master.

Dom Marcus: Welcome Chrissy, *ruffles his slave's hair lovingly.

I immediately noticed two things. Doms had a capital letter to start their name, subs didn't. Also typing an asterisk designated an action. I hung around for a while, got into a couple of friendly conversations. Nothing sexual. After a while, I said my good nights and left. I was taken with the seeming normalcy of those in the room, as if what they were doing was how they lived their lives and those who weren't D or s were the abnormal ones. It was

127

Domin8

all very interesting, but honestly, I found it just a bit boring after a while: watching but not participating. I suppose I've never been much of a voyeur.

I watched TV with Di for the rest of the night and we went to bed cuddling each other, I thought of trying to make love to her but I just wasn't in the mood for rejection, yet again, so I didn't bother and fell asleep thinking of Doms and subs and everything in between.

The next morning at work I checked my email. Nothing from GG, but there was one from SL saying she had logged on and saw me just as I was leaving. She left a sad face emoji. She was sorry she missed me and hoped I had fun without her. She hoped to catch up soon on webcam as she wanted me to watch her playing with herself. I wondered—not for the first time—why I hadn't met girls like that when I was nineteen. Maybe it was because she was American, or maybe this was just a different era.

While I hadn't done it consciously, I thought, I had taken my laptop bag to work. That was not entirely unusual, but not common either, and as the day wore on I thought more and more about seeing Lex. I thought to myself, "*maybe just once more, just for fun.*" There was no harm, the addict in me rationalised to myself.

Like a mouse eating cheese, the thought niggled away at me, and slowly my conscience fell away and my selfish sexual wants took over. My vow to myself to never contact Lex again disappeared. At six-thirty that evening, once everyone had left work, I closed my office door and fired up the laptop. It was as if she was waiting for me. The moment I entered the reception she sent a message in the open for everyone to see and read.

Stephen B. King

Sexy Lexy: *Runs over to her sexy teacher and jumps into his arms and kisses him deeply. Are you on your laptop Master? Do I get to see your cock today?

I've often thought since that no-strings-attached sex is a bit like trying to leave the mafia. Every time you think you're out, you get drawn back in. From that point on, going to the chat rooms became a semi-regular thing, and I reasoned to myself that sharing fantasies with other women wasn't really being unfaithful.

Interestingly, on a talk back radio show on one occasion, as I was driving home late at night I listened to a debate on that very thing: is playing around in chat rooms being unfaithful if it's not physical? There was a panel of so called experts and they threw the lines open for people to call in and give their opinions.

As you would guess the callers were split pretty much fifty-fifty. One man said he had lost his wife when she suddenly took off to be with a man in America who she had been having a cyber affair for months with. Another said that he met his current wife in a chat room and that they had really been able to *connect* mentally, sexually and emotionally before they met physically. Others said that it allowed them to be the real them! Because chat rooms are anonymous, they felt they were not constrained by morals and being who and what people thought they should be.

It was fascinating, and by the number and passion of the calls it was further validation that online sex was not only thriving, but almost healthy.

Domin8

Chapter 13 – Lady Melissa – Chloe – After Dark
Domin8. Learning to Fly.

I was in the D/s room one day, killing time, some weeks after becoming a regular in the chat rooms, when I received a private message from Lady Melissa asking if I was free to talk.

Its relevant to point out that Lex and I had both moved on with no angst whatsoever and we still said hi whenever our paths crossed. But sex…. well, as you can imagine, a fifty-year-old man losses interest in a nineteen-year-old girl as quickly as she looses interest in him. I had fooled around quite a bit, honing my Dominant persona and had some women who were willing to be my exclusive on line slaves and were more than willing to meet face to face if only we had lived in the same country. It was really still amazing to me the extent of this lifestyle that had hitherto been unknown to me.

I had also met up with *Good Girl* on a couple of occasions, during the day time in a motel. We both had a lot to learn, me in particular, and we practiced on each other. She loved being controlled and I teased her ruthlessly for over an hour forcing her to hold off orgasming. When I finally permitted it she erupted in bliss and she said it had been the single biggest climax of her life. She was the kind of woman that I could never fall for, and as we went on I felt as if she was unsure herself if it was really for her because deep down she suffered guilt over her husband. It was never going to last, but we had some good times together.

I had seen Lady Melissa around. We had chatted briefly in the open a couple of times, but it had been just friendly talk. Her icon was a beautiful pink butterfly, and I clicked on her profile out of interest that day she asked to chat with me. *"Why,"* I wondered, *"would a Domme PM me?"*

Her profile read like this:

I am an Australian Domme. I live in Melbourne, and was led to this lifestyle by my former boss, a wonderful woman who I adored. She took me when I was quite young in real life, and trained me to be her sub. We were together, exclusively for three years. Sadly, she left me to nurse her ailing mother. Before she left me she told me I was more suited to being a Mistress than a sub, and she still gives me pointers to this day. I am a Lesbian, so guys, please don't PM me. The only men in my life are good friends or work colleagues.

I demand total loyalty from my subs. I respect boundaries but do want to help broaden the horizons of someone I care for. If you think you could suit me, say "hi, and let's chat," but be warned, I don't "cyber" with just anyone, only someone I think is special.

I couldn't resist talking to such a woman! I had seen her a few times in the D/s room, chatting away in the open and occasionally disappearing into a private room with a sub. She always struck me as being a very nice person, who respected others.

Domin8: Hi LM, thanks for saying g'day, I love the honesty in your profile, how can I help you?

Lady Melissa: Well firstly, it's nice to see a fellow Aussie, and like you I respect the truthfulness you show in your profile. Honesty in here sometimes can be sadly lacking.

Domin8: How true that is. It is nice to see a fellow Aussie. I agree, there are not too many of us.

Domin8

Lady Melissa: Maybe we need to start our own site? Mostly the ones out there are American, I guess they have the population to justify it. Would you mind if I ask you some questions? I do have my reasons I assure you. Oh, and just so you know, I am gay and not interested in anything other than friendships with men. Is that OK with you?

Domin8: Sure, fire away. I value friendship above everything else, and TBH I'm pretty new to this lifestyle and still very much learning my way, so any help you can give would be really appreciated.

Lady Melissa: That's great, thanks. Forgive me for asking, but is your profile the full truth? It doesn't matter to me if it's not, as you and I will never 'play' with each other, so if you are hiding something, you can tell me. I promise it will go no further, and again I have a very good reason for asking.

Domin8: It's all true I'm afraid. I'm married to wonderful woman who isn't interested in sex anymore, but who I adore and would never leave. I'm nearly 50 years old, I manage a large car yard in Perth, and currently I think of myself as a Dom with 'L' plates ☺

Lady Melissa: LOL, that's good. I like that, Dom with 'L' plates. So you have a sense of humour and you are honest. You will go far in the chat world. I've just sent you an email with a pic. It's not of me, but have a look. See what you think.

Very intrigued, I opened a separate window and went to my mail, and there was one from ladymelissa101. I opened it to see a picture of a young woman. She had very short blonde hair and was exceptionally good looking. She was nude and wearing a velvet collar around her neck, which contrasted with her snow white skin and white blonde hair. She was kneeling, her knees spread, with her hands on the thighs with palms facing upwards. This was a classic pose of subjugation, one taken by a sub to her

Master or Mistress and showed respect and willingness to be controlled. Her body was near flawless, her breasts in perfect proportion to the rest of her body.

Domin8: She is stunningly beautiful, LM. I congratulate you, and envy you. Is she your IRL sub or online only?

Lady Melissa: I like you, D8. You are correct. She is my IRL sub and life partner here in Melbourne. Her name is Chloe. She is bisexual and thirty- three years old. She is a wonderful human being and she has been promoted. She is heading off to Perth to be State Manager. I am the CEO for large chain of clothing stores. Chloe has been a store manager here for me, and we have been together for nearly a year as a couple, but she is about to move on in her career, and I would never stand in her way of that happening.

I was unsure how to react to this news and I couldn't understand why she was telling me about her, and Chloe's personal life.

Domin8: LM, she looks and sounds wonderful. You are very lucky to have found each other. How can I help?

Lady Melissa: Again, that was the perfect answer, thank you☺. I assume, you being married, you don't feel jealousy? If you had a real life sub that saw others under 'special circumstances', and with your permission, would you be upset?

Domin8: LM, one of the things I hate above all else is hypocrisy. No, I would not be hypocritical enough to object to someone I see casually seeing others when I couldn't be with them myself. I only want part-time 'dalliances' so would be totally understanding of my sub's husband, boyfriends, partners or online playmates. That's just me.

Domin8

Lady Melissa: Would you like to share Chloe with me? Or at the very least just look after her over there in Perth? As I said she is moving there, and she is bi. She has been honest enough to tell me that she loves men as much as women. While we have been together she has been faithful, but is interested in playing with a Dom male from time to time.

Domin8: I assume you mean IRL here in Perth?

Lady Melissa: Yes, she will still be my part time online sub because her transfer to Perth is only temporary. As soon as I can get her back to Victoria I will, as State Manager here. In the meantime, I would like her to be looked after by someone who will care for her. She will make an ideal real life playmate for you, I assure you. She is very experienced, and a very obedient slave. She is multi-orgasmic and really she is one of the most special women I've ever known. Naturally I wouldn't hand her over to just anyone, and I am primarily concerned for her safety, so I would need to know your IRL details, just to be safe you understand. A woman like her in a strange city...there's no telling who she might meet, and I don't want to see her hurt. But I've made some discreet inquiries in here from people who know you; Sexy Lexy in particular, speaks very highly of you.

Domin8: I'm flattered and of course would love to meet Chloe. I have just sent you a pic of me. You are aware I am 50, albeit a reasonable young looking 50?

Lady Melissa: LOL, do you mind if I call you Dave? I already have a pic of you. I played with SL a few days ago. She wanted to be seduced by a female mature gym teacher, and I think I played that part very well LOL. Once I got her worked up I asked her to send me your picture, and all about you. She resisted for a while, but only a while. I know what you look like, and I know you are a manager for a car yard in

Perth. I don't know which one, but it wouldn't be hard to find out would it? I'm only doing this because I don't want to hand over someone I love to someone who might hurt her. You understand that don't you? I have no desire to pose any threat to your privacy.

Domin8: I think I understand; you can't be too careful. Can I ask what Chloe thinks of all this?

Lady Melissa: Another good question, Dave. Well a couple of things to consider. Firstly, she is my sub, as well as my partner, so if I told her to have sex with you she would willingly to please me. And she would love it, because she loves sex in all forms. In this case, though, we have talked about it, and she knows I am doing this out of love and caring for her, and her needs. I would like someone I trust to care for her and look after her until I can get her back to me in Melbourne. Not that I think she will go off the rails by herself, but I worry she may meet someone who will hurt her if I don't help her out. Does that make sense?

Domin8: Yes, is does, Melissa. Do you mind if I tell you I think you are a wonderful caring woman? I would be proud to keep an eye on her for you.

Lady Melissa: Thank you, I will worry a bit less if I know she is being looked after. I had a previous partner, long ago, and she went to a club one night alone, she was sub and her drink was spiked. She was hurt very badly; I couldn't bear for that to happen again. Please email me your phone and contact details, along with times that she cannot contact you. She arrives in Perth on Sunday, she will be in touch next week once she is settled. Now if you don't mind I am going to go and have a little cry.

And, with that, she was gone. I was left in a state of wonder. I had so much to learn about this Dominant/submissive

Domin8

lifestyle and realised the more I learnt the more I wanted to learn. Now I was about to meet my second real life submissive woman who was handed to me by her Mistress, and all as if it was perfectly normal.

XXX

A few days later Chloe sent me a text, which read:

Chloe: Dear Sir, my Mistress Melissa asked me to make contact. I am in Perth now and am available whenever it suits you to meet. Chloe

I phoned her, and we chatted for a few minutes. I asked her how she was enjoying Perth and where she was living.

"I am enjoying the promotion, sir; it's a big step up for me. I haven't had time to see much of the city, but I hope to over the next weekend. I miss my Mistress, but I'm trying to make her proud. I am in a furnished apartment in South Perth provided by the company. It's small but quite nice, and I do have a bit of a view of the river from my balcony." She had a softly-spoken voice.

"Well, how about I take you out for dinner tomorrow night as a welcome to Perth; I will take you somewhere nice."

"That would be wonderful, Master. What should I wear?"

She was delightful. "Well, I haven't seen your wardrobe, Chloe, but I trust you to wear something appropriate, plus you work in fashion, I have every confidence you won't let me down."

"Yes, Master, thank you. I will try to make you proud. Should I wear underwear?"

Stephen B. King

That question brought home to me, for the first time, the extent to which her submission went, and I was fascinated and very turned on by it. I could decide if she wore underwear or not, what colour, what style. This was a new world for me.

"Chloe, for our first meeting, I want you to feel comfortable. It would be my choice for you not to wear any as it's a sexy thought to take a beautiful woman to a good restaurant knowing she are not wearing a bra or panties. But as it's our first meeting the most important thing to me is that you feel at ease, and we get to know each other to see if we both want to take this further."

"Thank you, Master. I feel most comfortable doing what my Master or Mistress wants me to do, and if you feel it would be sexy I would be happy not to wear anything. I will be naked for you under my dress. Would you prefer your sub to be shaved, Master?"

"Do you shave for your Mistress, Chloe?"

"Yes, Master, she prefers me to be hairless, for when she chooses to please me with her mouth."

"Then I think you should stay that way for her. I know Melissa will be seeing you on some weekends here in Perth. I think it's important for you to stay ready for her, don't you?"

"Yes, Master. Thank you for your understanding."

"I will pick you up from your apartment at seven, Chloe. Text me your address, please."

"Yes, Master. May I ask a question, please?"

"Yes, of course. What is it?"

Domin8

"Master, I am collared to my Mistress. Would it be disrespectful to you if I wore my Mistresses' collar out to dinner with you as my new Master?"

I had heard of this collar thing and was intrigued by it. I read that a "collaring ceremony" is where the slave is given her collar by her owner, and vows are exchanged in front of family and or friends, very much like a wedding ceremony. It is a very serious thing and only done when a deep commitment by the slave to her Master or Mistress is wanted by both parties. While, apparently, it didn't mean the owner was required to remain faithful to the slave, they were, after all, in control; it did require the slave to stay completely monogamous, unless given permission, or ordered to please others.

"Chloe, I think your Mistress would be very proud of you for asking that, and I think it's a beautiful thing. Yes, you should wear your collar out of respect for her."

"Thank you, Master. I will try to make you proud of me, too. I will be ready at seven for you."

XXX

She was ready on time. I think she had been watching out for me through the window because as I got to her front door I found it open. She was kneeling as she had been in her picture, dressed in a long white dress with a slit up to her upper thigh showing the top of a white stay-up stocking. She wore her black velvet and gold choker collar and thick gold chain belt around her waist. She was simply stunning. Any man, or woman, would be proud to be with her.

Stephen B. King

Her head was bowed, her hands facing up. The moment I arrived, she said, "Welcome Master."

I stood in silence, before gathering my thoughts and realising I had to take charge of her or she would tire of me very quickly. Clearly this woman was deeply subservient, and in the most beautiful way. I now had to put all of my online practising to use. IRL.

"Thank you, Chloe, you look absolutely beautiful. You may stand."

She lifted her head to look at me and stood up with a grace I had never seen before. She was lithe and very fit. She stood with her hands clasped behind her back and head slightly bowed but only slightly. She said, "Would you like a drink before we go, Master? I wasn't sure what you liked to drink so I have red and white wine, beer and scotch. I would be happy to make one for you."

I crossed over to her and placed my hand under her chin. I lifted it so we looked into each other's eyes. Hers were the deepest blue. She was staggeringly beautiful, with only just enough eye makeup on to highlight what were one of her best features. I leant in and kissed her soft, moist lips very gently, "I will call you angel, because you look just like one. I am very, very pleased, angel. And no, thank you. I won't have a drink just now. I may have one with you when we get home, but I will let you decide that."

She looked confused and said, "Master?"

"Listen, angel. Tonight only I give you free will."

She tried to interrupt but I stopped her. "Shush, angel. I know your Mistress has given you to me to look after for a while when you both are apart, and I will treasure that and respect you both. But, I only want you if you are attracted to me. I value you and your feelings and do not want you to submit to me if you don't feel I am worthy. Now, let's go and have dinner and get to know each other. I will bring you home, and if you invite me in and offer a wine I will take it and know that you have decided I am worthy of you. If you don't I will leave with no hard feelings."

I knew by the look on her face she was pleased. She nodded, her eyes were sparkling and she said, slightly breathlessly, "Yes, Master. My Mistress assured me you were a good man and would take good care of me. I will do as you've asked but I can give you my answer now. The answer is that your subbie would be pleased if you would permit me to pour you a wine when we return."

She smiled and bowed her head again. That was how I got my first real life truly submissive woman. While Good Girl aspired to be submissive, Chloe most definitely was, and the difference was enormous.

Chloe and I had a wonderful dinner; she was beautiful in appearance and nature and very good company. I took her to a small French place I knew in East Perth on the river bank that was quiet and discreet. I had never had a dinner companion quite like her. She wouldn't speak in front of others unless I asked her a direct question. When I did she didn't call me Master, but if we were alone, she used the title in every single sentence.

Dinner was amazing, and I felt proud to be with her. If circumstances had been different—if I had been single, and she wasn't committed to Melissa—this was a woman I could lose my head and heart for. She was also my first truly submissive, though far from my last, and that meant it was all the more of a wonderful experience for being that. While I could own up to the fact that I wasn't a dominant (I was just playing at being one) this wonderful woman was a born sub.

Stephen B. King

After dinner I took her for a walk along the river as it was a warm night. I held her hand and asked her how she became the way she was, did she become sub or did she feel she was born that way?

"I've always felt this way, Master. My recollections of my mother with my father were of him being very strong, and she obeyed him in everything. Of course I don't know about their sex life, but I imagine it was the same. At school I was always timid and seemed to attract stronger guys. I just felt more comfortable if I succumbed to whatever my boyfriend wanted. There was one in particular, his name was Jonty and he was from South Africa. At a party one night he told me to give his best mate a head job, and I did, without question. I enjoyed the fact that I had been told to do it to please him.

"That was the start of it. After that he would tell me which of his mates I had to please, and I loved every minute of it. For me it wasn't about being a slut. It was that someone I cared for was controlling me, helping me to be one. He tired of me pretty quickly and was rather immature, to be honest. Then, one of his friends who had used me a few times, took over. He was much stronger, and he made me seduce a girl who he knew was bisexual, while he watched us. She was my first woman, and it was awesome which helped me realise I too was bi. After that they took turns controlling me, sharing me with whoever they wanted, and spanking me if I didn't please them to their complete satisfaction, and I learnt to love being punished. After school we drifted apart, and I started working in retail fashion.

"I was bored and couldn't find anyone who would treat me how I wanted to be. It was boring on normal dates. One of the women at work mention the dating site *After Dark*, and I met a couple of Doms before meeting my Mistress. It was love. I absolutely adore her, Master, and I have been with her ever since.

Domin8

You should try *After Dark* Master. It is a good site. And you will meet women like me."

That was the longest statement she made the entire night. Normally she only preferred to speak when she was spoken to. "I've never heard of it, angel. Tell me more."

"It is a dating site for people who may be married or not, but that are looking for a partner to experience different lifestyles. They may be bi, or gay, sadists, masochists, Doms, subs or people into pee games or really whatever turns some people on. The good thing is that once you meet someone through the site you have to go back in and rate them, so that others can have a guide as to what you are like. I can tell that you will be a great Master, and I am sure in time you would have a lot of women who would want to serve you."

Chloe was full of good information and she told me all about the site which was to show change my life.

We went back to her place, where Chloe offered wine and I got to undress the beautiful woman that she was. We made the most exquisite love: several times. She was superb, revelling in every command I gave her and seeming to enjoy herself the more she submitted. I had never had sex quite like it. It was a new experience for me, to have someone so willing to please and perform anything I asked. I got home before three, showered and went to bed, but couldn't sleep because I was thinking about the night. I was in total awe of her.

When Di got home in the morning she remarked that I looked tired. I blamed an upset tummy. Being a nurse she was concerned, and I told her it was just a bug going around. Naturally I felt guilty and hated myself for the lying I was doing to her, but she was fine. If she suspected anything at all it was as if she didn't want to ask anymore, in case she found out something she didn't like. That was genuinely what I thought at the time.

I had that feeling with Dianne several times over the next few months. Perhaps she was perceptive, or had an inkling of my infidelity, perhaps not. I don't know for sure. But there were times when I thought she suspected, but that she didn't want to know the details. I suppose if she suspected she could convince herself things were fine; her cosy life would stay the same.

Perhaps I am deluding myself in thinking that, but over time, the more I thought about it, the more that theory made sense, it helped somewhat with the ultimate guilt that was to come. Its hard, in light of what did happen to look back now and be totally objective and unemotional. In that time, I had no idea how bad things would turn out, so blindly carried on enjoying my selfish hedonistic lifestyle because I had been spurned by the woman I had chosen to spend my life with. Did I over rationalise it and think she knew? I can't honestly say. I wish I knew for a fact, but I never will now.

Dianne herself didn't have make up to play around. Sex wasn't something that was important to her, but it was me. I know she loved me, and that she didn't want to spend her life with anyone else, or alone. It's comforting to think now that she did suspect me, but made a conscious decision not to pursue it further.

I will take that grain of comfort to my grave.

Domin8

Chapter 14 – Chloe (2) – Lady Melissa (2) After Dark (2)
Addicted to Love

I emailed Lady Melissa the next morning and thanked her for the introduction and trust she placed in me with Chloe. She in turn thanked me for looking after her, Chloe had been on the phone to her to report back how much she had enjoyed being with me. It was a strange world: that making love to someone meant looking after them. But the theory was that, with me seeing Chloe when I could, it would keep her from temptation and straying with a stranger, keeping her safe from someone who could take advantage of her and possibly physically hurt her.

Over the next two months I saw Chloe never less than twice a week, and every time was a delight. I had gained confidence in myself and, in particular, had one amazing night when I arranged for Good Girl to join us for a threesome. She had never been with a woman before but wanted so badly to experience her new chosen submissive lifestyle that when I told her what she would have to do, she immediately agreed. That was a memorable night, with both of them vying to please me the most, and me being able to watch them please each other.

I had no idea such people existed—a woman who was only happy serving her Master. And the more I made her serve the happier she was. It wasn't just that Chloe liked sex, which she did—she loved it—but for her to feel complete she needed to serve.

Sometimes I knew she wanted to be punished, she loved to be spanked, and she would do naughty things to which I was expected to be angry at. For myself, I was so enamoured with her and so in awe of her beauty and nature, I feigned anger to give her what she wanted and needed.

I also should admit that having this beautiful woman across my lap spanking her bottom until it turned red was a turn on for me, too. And I am not talking tiny little play slaps, no. For Chloe a spanking was exactly that.

I had stumbled into this world as if by accident, but the more I thought about it at the time the more I thought it was fate, because while I loved my wife with every part of my being, I was only at my happiest sexually with Chloe and the others that were to follow.

It was about four weeks into knowing Chloe when I got to meet Lady Melissa in the flesh. She was the CEO, and Chloe was her State Manager, it was natural that she would visit WA. But this time, as I was to find out, it was to deliver the promotion to Chloe that would take her back to the Eastern States.

Chloe sent me a text asking permission to phone me. As I was at work, I agreed.

"Master, my Lady just phoned. She is coming to see me. She arrives this evening. I am so happy I could burst. Do you mind if I do not see you while she is in town?" The enthusiasm in her voice was infectious, and I was delighted that she was so happy.

"Of course, angel. Please pass on my deepest regards to your Mistress. I am happy to step aside."

"Thank you Master, but she has asked me to arrange a dinner for the three of us. She wants to thank you personally, as I have told her what good care you have taken of me. She is in Perth for three nights, and she asked me to ask you when it would be convenient."

Domin8

I knew this would be dinner only; therefore, I didn't need it to be a night when Di was working. I could make an excuse for a business dinner, as this happened frequently.

"Angel, I will book a table at Arturo's for tomorrow night at eight. I know you will be too busy tonight, getting re-acquainted." She giggled delightfully, "I am really looking forward to meeting her in person. If that doesn't suit her, let me know, and I will change it."

The next night I got to the restaurant early. They had given me a table with a spectacular view over the river looking out onto the city: one of the best restaurant views in the country. The food and wine menu is superb as well as the service. I waited at the bar for them to arrive with a chilled bottle of Champagne and three glasses ready.

I saw the cab pull up out front, and Chloe followed by LM got out of the back door. Chloe looked spectacular dressed in a sparkling red top and black skirt, but she was dwarfed by Melissa, both in stature and looks.

Lady Melissa stood a full six feet tall, with long thick flowing brunette hair and red highlights. She had the perfect body for her height and dressed to kill in black lace top, black long skirt and knee high boots. She looked like an Amazonian goddess, and I could see why Chloe was drawn to her. With Chloe being small and blonde and Melissa tall and dark they looked the perfect couple to me.

They walked into the restaurant, and every single person stared. I stood up from my bar stool and welcomed them both. I kissed Chloe on her cheek. She looked radiant with happiness.

"Thank you, Master," she whispered softly.

I turned to her Mistress, smiled and bowed. I reached for her hand and raised it to my lips, kissing it softly.

146

Stephen B. King

"Oh, you are a charmer." She said in a deep, but far from masculine, voice and smiled.

I poured the champagne and we toasted to their happiness. We had a fantastic night, as if we were old friends. The purpose of her visit to Perth was to inform Chloe she would be moving the following month. Chloe has been promoted to be the state manager of New South Wales, which was closer to her home, and Melissa.

I only met Melissa the one time, but it was a memorable night. We discussed *After Dark* at length, and while I had the pleasure of being with Chloe on seven more occasions my profile was already up and had attracted some new interest.

As a newcomer to *AD* the women were cautious of me. I joined their community, taking it slow, getting involved in some of the chatrooms, talking to other Masters and Mistresses and, slowly, the available subs. Both Melissa and Chloe had put up reviews about me in very glowing terms, which no doubt helped in others feeling comfortable in talking to me.

Through *After Dark*, I met Amy first but we didn't really click. She was far too young and flighty, and her signature trait was an annoying giggle. Perhaps it was a nervous thing, but she just giggled at everything – even serious discussions. But even knowing that, we had sex, which was good, and she gave me a good rating, which led to Ruth.

Ruth and I had more in common; she was married to a man who hadn't made love to her in three years since he found religion. I saw Ruth three or four times, but before long I had several women chasing me, and I played with them all: some online only if schedules didn't work, while others at their place or motels when Di was on night shift.

Domin8

Life was good. I felt happy being able to have as much good sex with submissive women as I wanted, with another bonus of sub women being that they never argued. And if I wasn't in the mood to talk endlessly about boring subjects, we didn't! The weeks quickly turned into months, and the great times continued right up until the murders occurred, leading to my arrest.

That first night in the cell I relived my memories of my encounters and could not see any possible reason for any of them to have murdered Melanie, Patsy or Dianne. I was lost in grief, confused and wanted to die.

Stephen B. King

BOOK THREE

"Fools rush in where other fools before made the same mistakes."

Domin8

Chapter 15 – Jason – Tom - Starsky and Hutch (5)

Day Five. Fighting for Freedom.

In the morning they let me shower and gave me breakfast, but I couldn't eat more than half a slice of toast without wanting to be sick. The policeman in charge led me to a cubicle with a phone after telling me my formal interview would be at 9 a.m., and that I should contact a lawyer. I asked him if my children had been informed, and he said he didn't know, but assumed they would have. I dialled my son Jason's home number, and it was answered on the second ring.

"Jase, it's Dad. Are you OK?"

"Dad, what the hell is happening? The three of us are here; we've been waiting all night for word from you. Are you alright?" His usually strong voice was quivering. He had always been particularly close to his mother.

"They've arrested me for killing your Mum, but I swear to you all I didn't do it. Somehow I've been caught up in something horrible. Someone is killing people I know and trying to frame me for it, please believe that." My voice broke and I cried, for my loss, my shame, guilt and for my children.

"Dad, I've never even heard you shout at Mum, let alone hurt her. There is no way you could have killed her. We all told the cops that. You guys were made for each other. Don't worry; we are on your side."

"Thanks, son. You've no idea what a comfort it is to hear you say that. I'm not perfect, far from it, and you are going to hear I had been seeing other women, and I am so, so very sorry for that. I adored your Mother; it's just that in one area, we had drifted apart over the years."

"They told us you had a secret internet life going on, but we know you wouldn't hurt Mum. It's 2015; if things were that bad you would divorce her—everyone does these days—not resort to murder. We don't understand why you would play around behind Mum's back. Missy is particularly angry with you about that, but we are on your side, Dad, don't worry. We need to know, though, what happened?"

"God, I wish I knew. Somehow, I must have upset some lunatic, and he has been stalking me. He killed two women after I saw them and tried to make it look like I had done it. He even stole a pen from my desk at work to leave at the scene of the second murder. I was questioned, but the cops believed me so they let me go. I was going to come clean with everything to your mum last night and throw myself at her mercy. Honestly, son, I loved her I was, just, stupid.

"I took a shower while I plucked up the courage for the confrontation. While I was in the bathroom, whoever is doing this came to the front door. When she opened it he attacked her and killed her." The tears were streaming down my face, and the words came out between sobs and taking breaths.

"I'm guessing he wanted to kill me. There is no way he would have known I would be in the shower, and I suppose he ran out of patience for the cops to arrest me. I'm sure he didn't go to the house to kill your Mum. If I hadn't taken a shower I would be dead, and I'm the one who deserves to be, never her. I'm so sorry, Jase."

He was crying too, and I heard the sound of my daughter sobbing in the background. I was obviously on speaker so they could all hear me.

Domin8

"I know it's only 7 a.m., but can you look up Tom Wilkinson's phone number? I don't know it off the top of my head. He is the company lawyer. Leave a message for him if you have to; just tell him what's happened. I'm at the city headquarters, and they are set to interview me at 9. I'm going to need his help."

"You've also met George Hallman, the Managing Director. Please call him and let him know too. Hopefully I can get out of here soon and be with you and explain everything. Please do me a favour; I think you are all safe, but you never know. There is a mad man out to hurt me. I want the three of you to stay together. Watch each other's backs. Will you do that for me?"

"OK, Dad. I'm onto it. The three of us are going to the station this morning. We are going to camp there until they let us see you. We know you wouldn't hurt Mum."

That was typical of him. He had a no-nonsense, take charge attitude, and he had put his grief aside for the moment to look after his younger brother and sister. I was never more proud of him than then.

"Thank you, son. I will get off the phone so you can make those calls. Look after Missy, she will be hurting badly, and I know this is all my fault and I understand if you all are mad at me. I deserve your anger. Please give your sister a massive hug from me, and tell her and Bryan I love you all."

Missy was the nickname for Marguerite, our youngest. When she was born, Bryan was too young to be able to pronounce her name so he called her Missy, and the nickname had stuck ever since.

I put down the phone, hung my head in my hands and let the tears flow. The urge to end my life had passed while on the phone. I had three children who would need my strength. I needed to get out of this mess. The officer could see I had finished with the phone, and he took me back to the cell. Once there, I waited for the next episode of my living nightmare to begin.

XXX

By the time they came to get me, my lawyer was waiting. I had pulled myself together and wanted to fight. No more tears, I had determined; I had replaced grief with a rage to somehow get even with the killer. I had no idea of the time as they had taken my watch from me. I was led to a room where Tom was sitting, waiting; he stood to his feet as I entered.

"Thanks for coming, Tom. I appreciate it very much. I didn't know who else to turn to."

He shook my hand shaking his head and said, "Dave, I'm so sorry to hear about your wife. This is nonsense. I'm convinced of that, but I'm not really a criminal lawyer. I'm corporate, as you know. I can help today to see what they have on you, and depending on how that goes, I know someone I can recommend. Now, sit down. We have about forty minutes before your interview. Tell me what the hell has happened."

He placed a recorder on the desk and turned it on, to save taking notes, I supposed, and I told him every sordid detail of what I had been doing.

"Dave, why didn't you contact me after the first death when the police spoke to you?"

"Because I knew I was innocent, and once I told them everything, they seemed to believe me. Apparently the timing was wrong. There was no way I could have done it—and gotten to the casino to meet my brother—without a drop of blood on me."

"And after the second homicide, why not call me then?"

"Same story. The pen incriminated me but I had noticed it missing earlier in the day. A guy had called in while I wasn't there on the pretence of leaving a note on my desk, and I'm sure he stole it. Therefore, he must be the murderer. I convinced the cops that it couldn't possibly have been me. They called Dianne to confirm what time I arrived, and again there was not enough time for me to have done it and get home without being covered in blood. I couldn't have beaten her to death without being splattered with it; it was messy and gory, apparently. Yet I was home in twenty minutes or so, and clean."

"Hmmm, you do realise the police tell lies, don't you? They may well have evidence they have not disclosed to you leading them to think you are guilty."

"Tom, there is nothing, because I didn't do it. You've known me twelve years. Do you think I could have murdered three women in three days, including my wife of twenty-six years? Is it not more plausible that someone has it in for me and has set me up? But what I can't get it, why? I have no idea."

"Dave, please understand that it doesn't matter what I think. Of course I think you are innocent, but that's not the point. It only matters what they think they can prove. There are three things they look at: they are means, motive and opportunity."

I stared back at him and replied, "All of those things are drawing a pretty long bow, Tom. The timing for the first two killings made it unlikely at best and not possible at worst. As for motive, well, why would I kill two women who were perfectly happy to have no strings attached sex with me? And Dianne, why would I kill her? I hadn't told her at the time. I got home and took a shower. While I was in the shower the killer struck. As for means, where would I get three pieces of identical scaffolding pipe? And why would I use that as a weapon? None of it makes any sense when you look at it logically."

At that moment there was a knock at the door, the duty officer stuck his head in and said "They are ready for you, would you come this way, please?"

We both stood as one, and Tom put his hand on my upper arm and squeezed it. "Try not to worry, Dave. Let me do most of the talking. We need to find out what they have. You will be asked questions. If you are not comfortable answering any of them, look at me first. Don't let them draw you into saying something you later regret. Oh and one last thing, whatever they say or do, do not—under any circumstances—lose your temper."

I nodded at him and gave a faint smile which belied how I was feeling; my heart was pounding, and I felt sick in my stomach. I followed him out of the room.

XXX

We entered the interview room, Milanski and Collins were already there looking very serious. We sat, and I waited for the axe to fall. Milanski pressed the record button and said the date and time, took a breath and added, "This is a record of interview of Mr. David Barndon. Present are his lawyer, Mr. Thomas Wilkinson, Detective Sergeant Milanski and Detective Collins. Mr. Barndon has been charged with three counts of murder, those being Ms. Patricia White, Ms. Melanie Brewster and Mrs. Dianne Barndon. Do you understand the charges Mr. Barndon?"

Domin8

"Yes." I said. Tom nodded to me, approving of saying the minimum response to questions.

"I put it to you, Mr. Barndon, that faced with the shame and embarrassment of admitting to your wife of your affairs and that you had murdered two women. You, in fact, murdered your wife rather than face her."

For just a moment I was stunned with the surreal situation. "Have you actually thought about how ridiculous you sound? Of course I didn't. Firstly, I didn't murder my two lovers, and on advice from Detective Collins I fully intended to admit my sins to my wife last night. She was murdered before I could do that."

Tom interrupted me by saying, "My client has answered your assertion. What evidence do you have of his guilt?"

Milanski was beside himself as he said, "What evidence do we have? His wife was killed while he was in the house, and he was covered in her blood. He had been having fourteen affairs in the space of six months, and we think he either told his wife and she became angry, or he killed her rather than tell her. The other possibility, of course is that he killed her because she refused to give him an alibi."

Tom nodded calmly. "So, just to be clear, Sergeant. That's all you have? No actual evidence?"

"I think that's enough, Mr. Wilkinson. He had the opportunity to kill all three victims. He admits he was there in every case."

"Hmm, so there are no fingerprints on the weapon? How do you explain that?"

He shook his head in frustration, and I noticed Sam didn't look entirely happy with things too. Clearly the interview wasn't going according to their script. "He cleaned it off and wore gloves."

"Did you find any gloves at the scene?"

"No, he must have got rid of them."

"So, it's your contention that my client took time to wipe the weapon and use gloves, which he somehow got rid of, but he didn't bother with the blood all over his clothes?"

"Yes, that is our contention."

I was fascinated watching Tom work. He had them on the back foot already.

"I see. The judge will laugh at you. You do realise that, don't you? Second point you say that my client had had fourteen affairs. I assume the other twelve are all alive? How do you explain that he chose these two and his wife, and not the others?"

"Perhaps we caught him in time."

"You caught my client because he phoned you to tell you his wife had been killed while he was in the shower. Hardly because you caught a serial killer before he could get to other victims. Isn't that so, Sergeant?"

He didn't answer, still seething, it appeared. Sam took over. "Mr. Barndon, please tell us what happened to the best of your knowledge after you got home."

Tom nodded at me, and I began to tell them my story, "I arrived home around six-twenty, my usual time. Di was in the kitchen. She was happy and appeared to be in a really good mood, maybe because we had made love that morning." I paused as the tears welled up. I blinked them away, took a deep breath and started again.

Domin8

"I told her I was going to have a shower but needed to talk to her when I finished. She said, that was fine, dinner was going to take a while. I made a scotch and went to the bathroom. I thought I heard the doorbell as I turned on the water, but I wasn't sure. I was going to come out and see if it was you guys, but— God forgive me—I didn't, as I had already undressed and thought you could wait. I finished my shower, came out, made a second drink and went to find Di."

I couldn't stop the tears as I remembered seeing her dead in the hallway.

"When I saw her, I knelt and turned her over. I was upset and distraught. All I could think of was that it was all my fault. When I saw she was dead I lost it. I hugged her to me. When I was able to, I laid her back down and called you. When the uniformed police arrived I was sitting in the hallway. It was them who lead me away and sat me down until you arrived. When you did get there, you didn't ask me any questions. You just arrested me; you wouldn't even let me call my children to tell them their mother had been murdered."

"You were in no fit state to be questioned."

I stared at Milanski, too angry to speak, especially after Tom had warned me to keep my cool no matter what they said.

"Mr. Barndon, you are the prime suspect in now three murders, you were the last person to see each of them, and in the case of your wife you were covered in her blood."

"But you know I couldn't have done the first two or at least you thought that when you spoke to me. You knew the pen was stolen from my desk, so surely, if you entertained the idea that someone was stalking me, trying to frame me, then why is it so hard to think that that stalker murdered my wife because I wasn't arrested for the first two victims?"

Stephen B. King

Tom took charge, "Gentlemen, it's not for my client to prove he is innocent. It's for you to prove he is guilty. I have not heard one thing today that offers any conclusive proof or, in fact, anything that could remotely be called evidence. Clearly the same person has committed all three murders. If you do not think my client was guilty of even one of those murders, how could you possibly think he would murder his wife? One other thing: you saw my client during the day. The clothes he was wearing—where did you find them?"

Milanski looked down at the desk, knowing he was beaten. "In the dirty washing hamper in the bathroom."

"And his towel hanging on the towel rack: was it damp, like it had been used? If so, that verifies his story, does it not?"

Milanski said, "Interview is suspended at nine forty." He turned off the recorder and then said, "We are faced with one of two scenarios, and as you have seen, this is off the record. One is you, Mr. Barndon, are a very, very clever murderer, and we will keep digging, trying to find something that proves you are just that. The second is that you have someone who is trying to punish you by setting you up for murder. Either way, arresting you while inquiries were made was the right thing to do. And in the state of mind you were in last night I saw no alternative."

"That is outrageous, Sergeant. You cannot arrest an innocent man to stop a guilty one from offending more. Last night David was in shock, and you put him in a cell." Tom was at his grandstanding angriest.

"Last night, we were faced with a horrific murder, and our prime suspect was covered in the victim's blood. I will not apologise for doing my job. If I hadn't arrested him, my boss would have fired me, and in his position I don't blame him."

Domin8

"I want to see my children. They are in shock, too; they need me as much as I need them."

"We will be releasing you on your own recognisance, Dave." Sam said. "You can call them and get them to bring you some clothes. It will take me an hour or two to organise your release, but if I were you I would stay away from them."

I knew what he was about to say, but needed to hear him say it, so asked him why.

"Let's suppose we believe you, and you are innocent, though for the moment we lack evidence to hold you so that's in the balance. You put forward the theory that this man killed your wife because he was angry the police hadn't arrested you. What do you think he might do when he knows you have been released again? Who else might he target?"

I hung my head. He was right. I could not risk their safety. I hadn't been to their homes in a while, but I had no idea how long I had been followed, days, weeks, months? He went on, "We are tracking down your other playmates Dave, the ones who are married or have partners in particular. They are going to be pretty pissed off with you, too. You are going to have a lot of people who might want to pay you a visit, and let's not forget, the killer himself is probably going to be one of them. You are in grave danger, Dave. In fact, the safest place for you right now is here: inside with us. Think about it."

"I'm not staying here just to be safe. I'd rather be out there and face the prick than live in fear, but you are right about my children. I've caused the hurt and misery that they are going through. The last thing I want is to put them in danger." I sighed, wondering when this nightmare would end.

Stephen B. King

Chapter 16 - Jason, Bryan and Missy
Pleading and Taunting

My three children came to and after I changed into clothes they brought for me. We sat in one of the interview rooms to talk. They were, as I was, still in shock, and we hugged each other and kissed. I told them I loved them and thanked them for keeping their faith in me.

Naturally, they wanted to understand. I tried my best to explain what had been going on leading up to their mother's death. They had been through a lot; they had lost their mother, heard their father had been arrested for her murder and then discovered their dad was an internet sex addict. The hardest one hit was Missy, who at one stage stood up and screamed, "How could you have done this to mum?"

She was in tears. Before I could answer, she walked out. Jason, to his credit, went after her. Ten minutes later she came back in, but she wouldn't speak another word to me. I understood her bitterness and anger towards me, and I couldn't blame her. I just had to hope that, in time, she could forgive me.

It took more than an hour for us to talk it out. There was blame, shame and recriminations, all of which I took because I rightly deserved it.

"Guys, I adored your mother. The things I did wasn't because I didn't love her, it was because, sexually I was bored and frustrated. She lost all desire for me, and I hadn't for her. I kind of slipped into a lifestyle and never really stopped to think of the consequences. I will always blame myself for what's happened, I

Domin8

would give anything to go back in time, and not taken that shower and gone to open the front door myself. It should have been me"

I think in the end they could see the love I had for their mother. I wanted to grow old with her, I told them, but before I grew too old I needed to do what I did, but I could never have imagined the outcome.

The two boys were more circumspect that their sister. Being the youngest, and only girl, she had always been closest to Dianne. Only after my sins had been thoroughly discussed did I then move on to the stalker and in my most serious tone I warned them they could be targeted themselves. At that point, even Jason become angry with me for not only being responsible for what had happened, but also for putting them in danger.

"Hate me, despise me, I can't blame you for that; I deserve whatever you throw at me. The one thing I want now is for you all to be safe and unharmed by him. You *must* be careful."

They couldn't be put in protective custody because there was no direct threat against them, but there would be patrols set up to go past their houses on a regular basis, with random visits by police officers. That was as much as Milanski could authorise. I suggested that, for the short term, if they all moved in together I would pay for a fulltime, armed security guard to move in with them. They fought me on this. They all had jobs, partners—and lives to lead—but I managed to get them to at least agree to try it for one week and review things after that.

What I didn't tell them was that, during that week, I would be deliberately putting myself in as much harm's way as I possibly could. I would become bait to try to draw the killer out. I didn't care if I lived or died: only that my children were safe.

Stephen B. King

It was a miserable situation for the four of us. They were angry, hurt and saddened deeply at their mother's brutal murder and me being the cause of it in the way that I had.

I decided it would be best to not leave with them, not knowing if I was being watched and followed, but promised to be available anytime they needed me. They elected to bunk at Bryan's place. It was the biggest and had the most parking space. I said I would have a security guard there my 5 p.m. and I made them promise to take every precaution to stay safe. We all stood and hugged, except Missy. She couldn't do it. She was still bitterly angry with me and didn't even say bye bye. At the back of my mind was one thing, I was not sure if we would see each other again. I watched them leave the room. As the door shut behind them, I felt as if it were the door slamming closed on my life.

No sooner had they gone than my possessions were returned to me, and I was asked to wait until Milanski could finalise my release. I turned my phone on and noted twenty-seven missed calls and messages. I sighed and started reading them.

Message after message were condolences from family and friends, and I texted back a short thank you to acknowledge their kind words. One was from the Managing Director, George, again offering condolences and telling me not to worry about work. They were 100% behind me and told me I should take as much time as I needed. I phoned him back personally to thank him and give him a brief run down. I didn't go into great depth, obviously, but did admit I had been targeted by a murderer who had now killed three women who were a part of my life, culminating with the death of my wife.

His main concern, naturally enough, was the company and he asked me if I thought it was a customer who felt aggrieved. I asked him to check with the service manager, as well as new and used car managers, in case there was someone upset with us who hadn't been brought to my attention. He promised he would, and I thanked him before adding, "George, you are going to hear some things about my personal life you are not going to like. If you want me to resign I will, rather than reflect badly on the business."

I was genuinely touched by his response, "Dave, you've been with the company eighteen years since you started as a salesman. I shouldn't say this but in another two you would be offered a partnership; you are very highly regarded. If you tell me you didn't do this, I believe you and the Board will stick by you. Depending on what happens we may have to review that, but for now you have the company's support."

"Thank you for that, George. You've no idea what that means to me." We hung up after I promised to stay in touch and let him know if he could help.

I called my brother back. He must have been in class, for which I was grateful. I left a message that I was fine and released, the police knew I was innocent and that I would talk to him later.

The last two messages were from women. The first one was from Jess; a playmate. She called me a bastard. The police had been by, and now her husband knew what she had been doing. She said that it was my fault I was to never contact her again, which I hadn't been intending to anyway.

The final message was from Laurel, a recent *After Dark* lover. She also said the police had been by. She had told them no way would I hurt a woman in her opinion. She offered me any help or consoling I needed and told me that I could call her any time. I messaged back a short "thank you." I added that I would keep that offer in mind. But, I had no intention of ever doing so.

Eventually Starsky and Hutch appeared. They sat down with me, and Sam spoke first. "Dave, you don't need your lawyer as we are not asking you any questions. This is all off the record, OK?"

I just nodded, weary of it all and just wanting it to be over.

"The investigation will continue, obviously. We will be looking at you still. We have to. As I'm sure you understand, no matter how unrealistic it might seem, you are still a suspect, but we acknowledge you are not the only one. There is the probability of a person at this time unknown has done this and made it appear you are guilty. What we need from you is to think, somewhere in your past if you have met this person or your paths have crossed in some way and he has focussed on you. We are looking into the partners of all of your online lovers to see if there is anyone who has become jealous of your other conquests or someone who resents you playing around with their wife, partner or lover. So far we are drawing a blank but we will keep digging and checking alibis."

I told him of the message from Jess, blaming me. He replied and said it was only to be expected, and there would probably be further fallout.

Next, it was Milanski's turn. "Dave, I know you are upset with us for arresting you, and I don't blame you for that. But I assure you, we had to. In our opinion, we had no choice with what we saw on arrival at your home last night. Our next concern is for your safety. But not only that: if this person is after you—and that seems likely—we need to protect you in such a way that it may provide an opportunity to catch him."

"So, first you arrest me, and then you want to use me as bait?" I was intending to do this myself anyway, but it was strange to hear my own idea echoed back at me.

"Basically, Dave, yes. That's it in a nutshell."

"What are you proposing?"

Domin8

"By this evening forensics will be finished at your house. I suggest that, when the police leave, one officer remains behind in secret, out of sight from the outside world. If the house is being watched—which we don't think it is at the moment, but we can never be 100% sure—then the killer will not know he is there. This officer would be armed and will keep you company when you return back to the house. We will make a press announcement that we have released you as we do not believe you can help further with our inquiries, and that you are no longer a suspect."

"You think that will draw him out for another go at me?" He didn't answer. He just stared at me but did give a small nod.

"And if he doesn't?"

"Then I would be very worried if we can't pinpoint him through our normal investigations." The unspoken implication was that if no one tried again, it would validate the theory that I was the murderer all along.

"I don't think I can stay housebound forever, not that I feel like going to work or partying, but I can't just sit around the house. Then there will be a funeral to arrange as well."

"Not for a while, there won't. I'm sorry. In a case like this is could be a while before the body is released by the medical examiner's office. Let's give it a try for three or four days. Sam here has volunteered to stay with you for that long. You can spend the time showing him how you get so many women. I think he would make a very keen apprentice."

"That's not funny. I am far from being able to laugh about things, and sex is the last thing I could think about now."

He nodded, understanding. "I apologise for my lack of sensitivity, but I do think Sam will be good company for you, for a few days anyway."

"OK, let's give it a try. Just please make sure you look after my kids. I couldn't bear it if one of them is hurt."

"I will do what I can. You have my word."

Domin8

Chapter 17 – Felix – A Room Full of Reporters
Circling Vultures

Before they let me go Milanski told me about the initial forensics report, which he had only just been given, that in effect cleared me of Dianne's murder. Information gathered from neighbours also uncovered one witness who thought she saw a tallish man wearing a black baggy hoody and jeans leaving my house about fifteen or so minutes before the sirens and flashing lights arrived.

Mrs. Huston, from number 35, opposite my house, was putting rubbish in her bin when she saw the man who was also partly obscured by the bushes in her front garden. Perhaps that was a good thing for her sake, as if the man had seen her watching him, he may have attacked her. She saw the movement and looked up; she was approximately thirty metres away, and it was evening, so visibility was not great to aid in any form of identification.

The man, she had said, walked quite normally, but quickly, down the driveway towards her but then turned right when he reached the footpath on my side of the road, then turned right again at the corner and headed off diagonally across the park on the other side of the road. My house is on a corner of a "T" junction with a park to the side.

She thought nothing of it at the time. She could not see any of his facial features, and his hands were in his hoody pockets. He just looked like any other young man. Although, being that she was in her seventies, most everyone looked young to her. The only other assistance she was able to provide was that he seemed quite slim. In the fading light and, with him wearing dark clothes, she would not have seen any blood splatters on his clothes. If nothing else it was further corroboration that I had not killed my wife, which Milanski, to his credit, pointed out.

He took me to the canteen for lunch to tell me about the forensics report. I wasn't hungry, but he forced a bacon and egg roll on me. Once I started I realised I was ravenous and finished every last crumb.

"Dave, when I saw you at the house, there were two reasons to suggest you were guilty. Are you up to talking about it as we can pretty much now discount you as a suspect?"

I breathed a quiet sigh of relief internally, and sat back, "Do you know I don't even know your first name? If I'm no longer a suspect, can we talk without me calling you 'Sergeant'?"

"Yeah, of course. I don't usually hand it out as it's a name I hate, and people tend to take the piss out of me for it. It's Felix."

I couldn't help it. I laughed for the first time in I don't know how long. It was a real laugh from deep inside and so loud everyone in the canteen looked at us, "Felix? Felix Milanski?"

All I could think of was Felix the Cat. Perhaps it was nerves, perhaps it was a release of tension, depression and the guilt I had been feeling, but I felt myself losing control into hysteria and only stopped when he said, in an angry voice, "It's not that fucking funny, Dave. If you don't stop laughing I will arrest you again."

I brought myself under control, realising he was genuinely annoyed. "Sorry, Felix. Yes, I'm fine. I'm up to talking about it. I feel anger more than anything else at the moment. I am hoping he does come for me. I'm up for it, believe me."

"OK, Dave. I will come back to the blood in a sec, but firstly your wife was facing the wrong way for her to be attacked

Domin8

from the front door. At least, that was how it appeared to us, at first."

I remembered how her bloody battered body was laying, and it dawned on me what he meant. When I turned her over she was face down with her head towards the door, so in actual fact it did look as if she had been attacked from behind, as if she was running towards the front door to escape. I nodded. It made sense that they thought I had told her about the women we argued and fought. She tried to leave, and I chased her and beat her to death before she could reach the front door.

"Yes, I see what you mean, though I didn't think of it before, Felix. What changed your mind?"

"Sure, you're up to this?" I just nodded again.

"They have recreated what they think happened. Your wife opened the front door and was punched in the face hard; there is a bruise to her left cheek, so we know the killer is right handed. Your wife staggered back but did not fall down. We found a circular bruise that matches the end of the pipe on her stomach, so after he punched her, she staggered back and he then hit her in the tummy with the end of the pipe in a jabbing motion. This made her bend forward and he then hit her on the back of the head in a downward motion which drove her face down to the floor. He then stood over her and beat her to death though she was unconscious with the first blow to the back of her head. He hit her a total of eight times, with the impact being mostly on the head."

"It should have been me, shouldn't it? He followed me to the house and parked, but by then I was in the shower. Once Dianne opened the door he had to kill her. I can see that would make sense to him. Then he would have wanted to get out of there in a hurry in case I had heard and come running."

Stephen B. King

Now it was his turn to nod, and we both thought about that for a few moments. The only comfort in a comfortless situation was that she didn't suffer past a few seconds. I blinked back tears, which welled up, yet again.

"So when we arrived, Dave, I saw your wife laying as if she as trying to get out of the house. You can see what I thought. Then of course, when you went to her you turned her over and hugged her to you, and kissed her. Your tears were on her face and her blood was all over you. You have to see how guilty you appeared at first look. Forensics now tell us that the blood on you is consistent with your story of hugging her, and that there isn't any spatter blood which there certainly would be if you had hit her with a steel pipe. Spatter is the small drops of blood which fly up and outwards from a wound like that, and without those types of stains you couldn't have hit her, unless you changed clothes afterwards. We couldn't find any clothes other than what you were wearing with blood stains so there is no possible way you could have done it. Of course we also couldn't find gloves, which again by the spatter, we know the killer wore."

"You are not a suspect in your wife's murder any longer. While it's still feasible you did the first two the timing makes it unlikely, and as the MO is exactly the same for all three, if you didn't do one, you didn't do the others. That said, there is always the possibility you had someone commit the murders on your behalf and you are a conspirator, but that doesn't hold up to scrutiny either."

Of course I had known that I was innocent all along, but it was nice for it to be formally acknowledged.

"Dave, we need to appeal for the public's help, and I'd like you to be a part of the press conference. The benefit to you is obviously that your family, friends, business contacts and so on will have no doubt that you are no longer a suspect. The downside

Domin8

is that we will be linking the three deaths. There are always leaks in any police investigation, and I suspect you are going to get asked questions you would rather not answer. The problem is, for you though, that if you don't get your version out there, they will make up their own. Either way you are not going to look good. I think as we are trying to lure the killer out of the shadows it would be best if you were very visible. But it's your choice, and I can't officially ask you to do it."

"All I care about now is my children. Whatever happens to me is no more than I deserve so I am all for it. Let the reporters do their worst."

He looked at his watch and then said, "That's good, Dave. Better gather your thoughts. It's scheduled for an hour from now. Once that's done we will get you home. Sam is already there, in hiding, waiting for you. One other thing that I haven't mentioned before: Melanie Brewster's mobile phone is missing. We know she had one by her phone bills, and we got copies of her texts between you both from the phone company. We've checked, and it's been turned off ever since her death, but if you goad him, and he contacts you using that phone, we can get his position. The carrier has been notified to watch for it. Just don't mention the phone and don't ask him to get in touch. Leave him hanging, and he will figure it out by himself. Hopefully. We have to think he will use it or else why take it?

"He must have kept it for a reason, and that reason can only be to talk to you. I'm hoping he calls to taunt you. If he does taunt him right back. Keep the call going as long as possible. If he thinks he is safe, he might leave it on. Then we have him."

I was impressed with the work they had been doing behind the scenes; while I had been the prime suspect clearly I hadn't been the only one. It was good to know they had been looking in other areas and not just at me.

Stephen B. King

XXX

There was a cacophony of noise as I entered the police media room. Behind Felix was a senior uniformed policeman who had only just been introduced to me as Assistant Commissioner Bellows. He seemed quite a cold fish as we shook hands, and his only comment to me directly was that he was sorry that the arrest that had taken place. I chose to just nod and not answer directly as there was almost zero sincerity in his tone whatsoever.

I sat on the end of the long desk alongside Felix with Bellows at the far end. We waited while microphones were set up, and the hubbub died down before the Assistant Commissioner started.

"Thank you all for coming. We are seeking any assistance from the public in our search for a man who we believe has killed three women. Firstly, Patricia White: she was killed in a motel room at the Great Eastern Lodge in Rivervale on Saturday between nine and ten in the evening. The second was Wednesday around the same time. That victim was Melanie Brewster, at Hamilton Hill Road in Hamilton Hill, and the third victim was Mrs. Dianne Barndon in her home in Applecross last night just after six-thirty. We did initially arrest Mrs. Barndon's husband, David, at the scene, but I want to categorically and unequivocally state here and now that forensic testing has completely exonerated Mr. Barndon, and he is in no way suspected of any of the three murders.

"The man we are seeking was seen leaving the scenes of two of the killings and is approximately 1.8 metres tall and of slim build. On both nights, he was wearing dark, baggy hooded clothing and dark jeans. Each murder was committed with approximately a thirty centimetre length of steel scaffolding pipe. Each time it was left behind at the scene.

"If anyone knows this person, they need to contact us. He is extremely dangerous. He may have seemed agitated after each murder and would have had blood-stained clothing. Any calls will be treated in confidence and can be made anonymously via the crime stoppers phone number.

"This is Detective Sergeant Milanski who is in charge of the investigation and will answer questions; we also have Mr. Barndon with us."

"Do you have any other suspects, Sergeant?" A woman in the front row asked. I breathed a sigh of relief as I was worried they would start in on me first. Felix answered, "We have several pieces of evidence which point towards the man we are looking for and who was seen leaving two of the scenes. This man knows we are looking for him, and if he is innocent I would urge him to come forward so we can eliminate him from our inquiries."

"Did the three victims know each other?" The voice came from the back of the room.

"No, they did not, however the two first victims were known to Mr. Barndon, and of course the third was his wife." Here it comes, I thought. This time, I was right.

"Mr. Barndon, how did you know the first two victims?"

I stayed silent for a moment or two to compose my thoughts. Then I cleared my throat and began, "I met these two women through an online dating site specialising in married people looking for affairs." You could have heard a pin drop, so I thought I would continue.

"I am not proud of my actions and deeply regret them, especially now it has resulted in the death of my wife. At some point I have become a target for a jealous, cowardly maniac.
174

Stephen B. King

Firstly, he murdered Patsy and Melanie who had done nothing wrong. Then, when I wasn't arrested for those crimes for which he had tried to implicate me, he attempted to kill me. Unfortunately, my wife answered the door to him when I was in the shower, and he brutally murdered her. Dianne was a defenceless woman whose only crime was to be married to someone like me. This man, if we can call him a man, is a gutless coward who likes to beat women with a steel pipe. I just hope he comes back for another attempt at me so I can show him how a real man handles things. But we don't think he will now. He doesn't have the guts, except to murder defenceless women. He is off somewhere hiding like the half-witted, cowardly pervert that he is. And yes, you can quote me on that."

"Will you carry on meeting women online?" Someone yelled out.

"All I am focused on at the moment is making amends to my family and children, for the loss of a beautiful woman who had a kind heart and wonderful spirit, who has been taken away from them because of my selfish actions. We have to mourn her loss, and I have to earn their forgiveness. We are all suffering in shock and grief. I deserve all I get for my sins, but my family, and the families of the first two victims, do not."

I think because I was so open, they had no sensational questions they could think to ask, but I was sure there would be more heading my way in the future.

"Are you close to an arrest, Sergeant?"

"Mr. Barndon has risen above his grief and personal feelings to be of invaluable help in helping to identify this person. Yes, it is safe to say we are close to an arrest; however, I want to reinforce we need all of the help we can get form anyone out there who knows something that can help us make an earlier arrest."

Domin8

"Mr. Barndon, has this man used the online dating scene to find his victims?"

"I have been asked not to comment specifically on operational matters, as this gutless wimp will probably run away like the scurrying rat he is. But the police will get him, of that you can be sure. As for online dating, it's a big lonely world out there and it just keeps getting lonelier. The internet is there, helping people get together. Of course people should take precautions when they want to meet someone, but I'm sure there are many, many happy couples who, if not for online dating, would still be very lonely."

"Was that your problem, Mr. Barndon? Loneliness?" I hate sarcasm, especially like that, just a cheap shot for a sensational headline.

"My problems are just that, my problems, thanks, but loneliness can take many forms and be different for different people, and I'm not the criminal here. This skulking little boy of a man with no personality to attract his own life partner likes to kill innocent woman. Because he hasn't got a hope of attracting one by himself, he is jealous of me. He's the criminal here, and it's important we stop him before he takes out his impotency, on someone else. Please help us do that, and you can all pillory me as an adulterer afterwards."

I noticed the Assistant Commissioner squirming with my relentless insulting of the unknown killer. It was not what he envisaged when he agreed to me being there, but I also saw Felix smiling. Bellows stood and said, "That will be all for now. Thank you for your support." With that he turned on his heel without waiting for us, but when we got out of the door he was waiting, red faced and angry.

Stephen B. King

"Just what the hell did you think you were doing, Mr. Barndon? If you antagonise this man, and he kills you, we will be seen to be negligent."

"If he kills me I won't give a flying fuck about how you look, will I? But at least you might then arrest the right man so it wouldn't be for nothing. You want to use me as bait. I've done all I can to hope he takes it, and trust me, I will be a lot harder to kill than my wife was."

He bit his lip. I had hit him where it hurt, and he realised that I was the victim here. A victim of my own folly, true enough, but a victim nonetheless. Slowly he calmed down and could see my point of view. "I am sorry for your loss, Mr. Barndon, you took me by surprise with your outbursts, and again, I apologise for the wrongful arrest."

With that, he turned and left, leaving me with Felix. "I know what you've done, and I know why you've done it. I hope I don't have to arrest you again for a revenge killing. Leave the police work to us, OK?" He said, still chuckling.

Domin8

Chapter 18 - Sam Collins

Day Six: The Bodyguard

A police car dropped me off at home just after six. I stood in my driveway for a few moments and looked around. The street was quiet, thankfully. Even the park across the road to my right looked quiet, unusually so for this time in the evening. I suppose a murderer loose in the neighbourhood would do that.

I used my key and entered through the front door to find Sam waiting, gun in hand. I put my hands up, and he smiled and re-holstered the pistol under his left arm.

"Hi, honey. I'm home," I said, trying to smile back. The tiled entrance hallway had been cleaned, and there was no sign of the blood from the night before.

"Did you have a tough day at the office, love?" He joked back.

I liked Sam. He seemed like a decent guy with a sense of humour, trying to do a tough job.

"Well, the press conference was fun after a rough night in a cold cell on a concrete mattress. Yeah, you could say I've had better."

"Listen, Dave, just so you know, I was totally against arresting you. It never made sense to me from the start but it wasn't my decision to make. Wiser heads than mine, etcetera. I don't even think Felix's heart was in it either, but he was concerned about the fallout. As stupid as it sounds he had to until the forensics could tell us one way or the other."

"Yeah, I know. He bought me lunch and explained it to me. I get it. I really do, even though I didn't like it. Are you on duty or do you want a beer?"

"Thought you'd never ask. One or two won't hurt, but I don't want to get too drowsy too early. I saw your performance on the early news: a 'skulking little boy of a man?' I liked that. If that doesn't flush him out, nothing will. Seriously, Dave, how are you holding up? Are you doing ok?"

I shook my head and didn't answer straight away. Instead, I walked through to the family room bar fridge and took a couple of beers out. I handed him one, and he sat at one of the bar stools. I took a sip and said, "Sam, to be honest, I don't know how I am. I don't know how I'm supposed to feel apart. From being empty inside. I miss Dianne and, of course, I blame myself for her death. I'm not frightened for myself. Basically I don't care about me because it's my actions have caused all this mess. But I am really scared for my kids. They've lost their mum, found out their dad is a prick and to cap it all off, they could be in danger themselves. Jesus, when I fuck up I do it properly."

I drank half the bottle in one go.

"Dave, there is no way you could have predicted this. People have affairs all the time, and it almost never results in someone being killed in a crime of passion. No one in the police department has ever seen anything like this before. There is no way you could have known this nutcase would focus on you in the way that he has. I'm so sorry for your loss, Dave, but you should stop blaming yourself. If you don't mind me saying: what you need to do is try to think who hates you enough to do this. You must know him. Someway, somehow, you've met him."

Domin8

"I haven't done not much else but think, but no one has ever threatened me, so if I've upset someone, they have never let on. I keep coming back to a husband or wannabe partner of one of the women I've seen, but which one? Even the woman might not know she has this guy who is a jealous nut case. It's a mystery to me, Sam and it's doing my head in. I'm sure if I had met this guy I would remember, wouldn't I? Wouldn't there be something I would remember? I just don't have the answer but I hope he reveals himself soon for everyone's sake. There's no doubt in my mind; when he came to the front door it was with the intention of killing me. That being the case it suggests a husband, or jealous lover of one of the women I've been with. But, if that were the case, why kill Patsy and Melanie? I wish it had been me, Sam, then Dianne would still be alive now. It's just not fair."

"Dave, stop right there. You don't know that. If you had opened the door, maybe your wife would have been killed right after you. I think he only panicked and ran because you didn't answer the door and he figured you would come running with the noise not knowing you were in the shower. If he got you first, he would have gone looking for her afterwards. There is no way he would have let her identify him, so either way she would have died."

I hadn't thought that before, but it did make sense. Once he got me out of the way, and Dianne came running…it didn't bear thinking about. "Time to change the subject," I thought.

"I suppose you're right. I didn't have a chance to thank you for volunteering to babysit me. I appreciate it, Sam. It's good of you to donate a few days out of your life and help try to stop this guy. Why did you do it, if you don't mind me asking?"

"Hmmm, that's a good question. My girlfriend thinks I'm mad. Who knows? Maybe I am. I haven't stopped to analyse my reasons beyond just being something I wanted to do. If I did it

Stephen B. King

would probably be a few reasons, not just one. You've never been anything but honest with us. I imagine you felt like Chicken Little with the sky falling in but you kept your head and dignity and told us the truth, and I respect that. I think thousands of men would have tried to sleaze their way out of it. You stood up like a man.

"Also, I think I'm probably just like you. I've been married once to a lovely woman, my first girlfriend from school days actually. After nine years I woke up next to her and thought, 'how did I get here? Where did it all go wrong?' And it's not like she was horrible, overweight or spending all of my money. I was just bored shitless with her and life. So, in your case, I get it. You were bored with a wonderful woman after twenty-six years, you had three great kids, none of which have been in trouble with the cops, you've been great parents and you got to fifty—and it's like, is this all there is to life? I totally get it. I think I would have done the same in the same circumstances."

It's like he was holding a mirror up to me to look into. I smiled thinly at his candour. "In different circumstances we could have been good mates," I thought.

"I appreciate that. Yeah, you're right. That just about sums it all up. I was thinking that I had been a good provider and all that stuff, but I still wanted a bit of excitement in my life, and Di didn't. I respected that she didn't. That was her choice, and I loved her, but I thought it was unfair that I had to supress my urges just because she hardly ever had any. That's just not fair. I actually think—and I'm being totally honest here—that she suspected I was getting it elsewhere, but she didn't want to know because she was happy with her life. And if my sex on the side didn't impact on her then she was cool with it. But boy, in the end, did it ever impact her. If I had any way to know that, I would have cut my cock off rather than cause the shit that I have, Sam.

Domin8

"But don't think I didn't notice you didn't actually answer the question. Why did you volunteer for this?"

"Dave, it just felt like the right thing to do. You know, most people think being a cop is like it is on a TV show: arresting bad guys, car chases and shoot outs. It's not. Most of it is just plain boring. It's a lot of interviews, paperwork and sitting in court waiting to give evidence only to be insulted by some guilty prick's lawyer. There is very little excitement to this job. So here I get a chance to actually do something. I get to spend a few days with a guy I quite like, get paid a shitload of overtime, and maybe bag this guy when he comes to teach you a lesson. That is what I signed up for."

I smiled. He really was a good guy, "Felix said it's because you want me to teach you all about online sex sites."

"Felix is a good man but a bit of a dinosaur. If you get to the point in the next few days where you want to talk about that stuff, I'm all ears, but I also understand that it's the last thing on your mind right now. Let's get this guy and maybe one day over a beer or three in the future you can show me the ropes with the other stuff. But for now, it's not part of my motivation. Trust me."

"Sounds good. Yeah I would be happy to show you around sometime, but it won't be for a while. Question though: what if this guy does come calling—which I hope he does—and you are in the shower, on the loo or asleep. Do I get a gun, too?"

"You *most definitely* do not get a gun, no. How loud can you shout? I will come running, don't worry. I do not want to be in a house with you if you are armed. You might shoot me. So, that out of the way let's run through the rules. You don't open the window or door, not even for a delivery. You do not go outside to check the mailbox—or anything else without me keeping watch. I've drawn all of the curtains. They are to stay drawn. We don't want to let this guy have any advantage. If he comes, let's get him get inside, and I will take care of him. Until then, doors and windows stay shut and locked at all times."

I could see the logic in his thinking but had to add, "Well, just so you know, there will be a very large kitchen knife under my pillow, so don't walk into my bedroom in the middle of the night without calling out first. Now, I'm going to grab a shower, then phone my kids and make sure they are OK. Then I'm going to order pizza delivery. You up for that? Help yourself to another beer. I will be back shortly."

"Pizza sounds good, Dave. Don't worry about me. I will put the TV on. Take your time."

I got my first case of the shakes when I was in the shower. I became very anxious, almost claustrophobic, so much so I had to open the clear glass door and leave it open. My hands were shaking like I was cold. It was uncontrollable. Then the tears came, yet again.

I fell to my knees under the cascading water and cried for the loss of Dianne. The realization that the last time I was in that shower my wife was being brutally murdered didn't help, and I could not stop the tears and anguish for long minutes on end.

I don't know how long I was like that, but when it did pass my knees had locked up with cramping, and it hurt to move them. I turned the water off and slowly dried. Not bothering to shave or do anything else, I put my robe on and went to lie on the bed.

I spent the next forty minutes on the phone with the kids, mostly with Jason, who answered. Then he put me on speaker phone so I could explain to them all at the same time why I was no longer a suspect. I also explained that it could be some time before their mother's body was released by the coroner. That, of course, would delay the funeral. Bearing that in mind, I proposed that they all head off to Bali or somewhere with partners for a

Domin8

week or so. I would pay. Naturally, a holiday was the last thing on their minds. They were all struggling with grief in their own ways, and a holiday did not appeal at all. I pressed on though, telling them that I would sleep better at night knowing they were safe and that I had my own armed body guard here and the trap had been set to catch the killer.

With them away I wouldn't worry about them and their safety. I understood they were hurting but to me their safety came first and I begged and pleaded for them to accept. They agreed to think about it overnight and let me know. They needed to talk to their partners and employers, but in the end I think they could see it made sense to get out of the picture while there was any kind of threat to them.

After telling them all I loved them I hung up and, once again, had tears well up in my eyes. Once that passed I went back out to order pizza and have another beer with my protector and wait together for a killer. If felt bizarre to be doing that, I'm not sure I can adequately describe my feelings; just sitting around waiting for someone to come and murder me!

When the doorbell rang, I jumped out of my skin, and Sam sprang into action. He stood gun drawn, behind and to the open side of the front door while I looked through the peephole security lens. I was both disappointed and relived to see a young guy holding an insulated pizza box holder and a Domino's delivery car in the driveway behind him. I still took a deep breath when I opened the door and imagined a steel pipe arcing through the air at my head. Fortunately, it didn't happen. I tipped the driver generously and he had no idea it was because he hadn't killed me.

"So, what's the Sam Collins story?" I asked an hour later over our third beer and a family-sized meat lovers pizza (with anchovy) sitting between us on the coffee table. Pink Floyd, one of Di's favourite albums, was playing hauntingly in the background.

"Not much to tell," he answered after finishing a mouthful. "I joined to force one year to the day after finishing school and have had a pretty unremarkable career since. I made detective three and a half years ago and been partnered with Felix ever since. I quite like the life and, as old fashioned as it sounds, I like having the chance to help people."

"You said you were married before?"

"Yeah, to Julie. We were in the same English class at school. You know something? We are better friends now that we're divorced than the last five years of sharing the same bed as a couple. We were just too young, too inexperienced, and both of us had parents who thought we should marry because we were made for each other. Let's be honest; when both sets of parents' push, it's hard not to get married at that age. At least we didn't have kids to complicate things—not that I don't want them, you understand. I'm just glad I didn't have them with her at too young an age."

At that precise moment there was the sound of breaking glass from the lounge room at the front of the house, followed by a screeching of brakes from outside. I turned to Sam. His gun was drawn. I didn't even see him move. He was that quick. He stood quickly and motioned me to stay put and took off towards the noise. "Bugger that for a joke," I thought and jumped to my feet, crossed to the bar and picked up a bottle of red wine to use as a club if Sam didn't stop the intruder.

Seconds grew into agonising minutes, and the only sound I could hear was the beating of my heart in my chest until Sam finally yelled out, "It's OK, Dave. You can come through."

Domin8

I still carried the red wine and gingerly walked in. Sam was standing in the middle of the room careful not to stand in the sparkling pieces of broken window. When he saw the wine bottle in my hand he said, "No thanks, Dave. I will stick to beer."

He then looked down at his feet and my eyes followed his. There was an old, red brick laying there with what looked like a small child's doll tied to it with string. The doll was dripping with what looked like fresh red blood, and the symbolism wasn't lost on me. The doll represented me, and the killer was coming to get me. I swallowed deeply and thought *"bring it on you fucker."*

Stephen B. King

Chapter 19 – Clinton Mooney
The Purest Evil

When a stone is tossed in the stream, ripples occur, spreading out, getting wider and wider apart, and further and further from the point of impact. Life is about cause and effect, and my selfish actions had far reaching effects, very much like those ripples hitting the banks of the stream.

XXX

Clinton Wilfred Mooney sat high, hidden from the world, up in an old Morton Bay Fig tree, thinking over and over again, "*You fucking, fucking, fucking, fucking cunt.*" A chanted mantra in his head which no sooner stopped then started again in an endless cycle of pure hatred.

Clinton wanted revenge of the purest kind. He was going to kill that David fucking Barndon for trying to steal his wife and ruining his life. That crime alone would have been bad enough, but it didn't stop there, did it? No, it was worse than that. There had been the humiliation he had to face at work: his wife of seven years being touted behind his back by people he thought were friends—well, if not friends, at least mates—as a common or garden internet slut.

Yesterday, at work, whenever he entered a room the sniggering would stop. He knew they were laughing at him, the bastards, *the fucking, fucking bastards!* Then there was the post-

Domin8

it-notes left on his desk saying things like, "Your wife called, and I spanked her for calling," or "Your wife wants to COME visit," and so on. Oh *sure*, he got that they all thought it was just *soooooo* fucking hilarious, but it *wasn't to him.*

He had been doing his job as a fork lift driver at the milk distribution warehouse for nigh on eleven years. He had thought he had always been well-liked and respected, but not anymore. Now he was the butt of every joke going: such as, "Hey, Clint, I'm going to pop round your place. When won't you be there?" or "Give my best to your wife." It just went on and on. Of course, he just had to pretend like it was all just so funny, when really it cut him to the bone. Clinton Mooney had spent a life time pretending he was like everyone else to fit in.

He had, in his own way, loved his wife and thought she loved him too, only to find out she had been some sexual slave for this car dealer bloke who she had met online.

She had wanted to leave him, probably to be with *him,* but he soon put a stop to that nonsense: just the same way his father had kept his mother inline, which he remembered from his childhood. He had been witness, many times, to the slaps, and punches delivered to her for the numerous sins committed.

She, his fucking slut of a wife, had packed her bags the day before and greeted him nervously after he had got home from work. She had the temerity to try to explain that *Dave the wife fucker,* had shown her how to be happy, how to be herself, and she wanted her freedom. That's what she had the nerve to call it: *her freedom.* He just stared her down, all the while unbuckling his belt, taking it out of the belt loops then coiling it around his hand. She tried to run of course, but he stopped her, dragged her by her ungrateful hair into the bedroom, threw her down and gave her the whipping she so richly deserved. How dare she think she could walk out on him?

188

Stephen B. King

She had cowered like the bitch she was—cried, begged and finally promised—but he didn't stop. She had to learn her place in the scheme of things. She had to be taught a lesson. She belonged to him, not some fancy car fucking dealer. When his arm tired, he wrapped the belt the other way so when he swung it was the thick plated metal buckle hit her. He was going to make sure she didn't go wandering off looking for sex ever again. This time he wanted to *really* hurt her, not only for wanting to leave, but for humiliating him at work.

When Clinton eventually stopped, completely out of breath, she was not much more than a whimpering, bleeding mess and he felt vindicated. He locked her in the bedroom and then made his own dinner. The late news was on and he watched with interest a story about a bombing in Turkey, then later slept in the spare room alone. "*She can go hungry, the fucking bitch,*" he thought with no intention of releasing her to eat dinner.

The next morning, after a really good night's sleep, the best he had had in a long while, Clinton decided that maybe he should use the spare room more often. He had gotten up and made a hearty breakfast of bacon eggs, baked beans and sausages knowing that the day might be a long one. He cleaned his plate off with slices of hand-cut bread and butter and licked his lips. His slut of a wife couldn't have cooked a better breakfast on her best day than Clinton could on his worst.

When he and his mates from their pig shooters club went on hunting camps he was always voted to cook breakfast, and was always happy to oblige. That's just the kind of guy he was. And he was sure that now, even his mates in the club would be lining up to make jokes at his, at his unfaithful wife's expense.

He contemplated cooking his wife some food, but presumed that she still needed to learn her place in the world some more. If he weakened and cooked for her now, she might

Domin8

think he was soft after all. No, the best course of action was to *really* punish her and leave her locked up for the day. Maybe, if by the time he got home later, she said sorry and meant it, *and* offered to lick his boots, she might get something to eat then. The ungrateful bitch didn't deserve a decent man like Clinton Wilfred Mooney as a husband, and it was his responsibility to teach her how lucky she was. Having watched his father discipline his mother for years, he knew she would have never, ever have dared to fuck someone while his dad was at work, earning the family's keep. Clinton realized that his father's way had been right. He had been *way* too soft on his wife.

Well, not anymore, those days were over. He had learnt his lesson, now she had to learn hers.

Clint hadn't decided yet if he would beat her some more when he got home later. He would make that decision after he told her he had shot her fancy man. If she looked at all pained, it would be more of the belt for the little slut whore.

By mid-morning the day was heating up nicely, which was perfect for a bit of hunting. He wasn't going to go to work, he had already decided. They didn't deserve a good man like him either, with all the piss taking they had been doing. They would have to manage without him. He went into the back room, opened the gun safe and took out his favourite rifle, a Winchester .22 magnum semi-automatic. Once loaded he stroked it lovingly before putting it in the car. Clinton took out a bottle of water from the fridge and an apple in case, just in case he got hungry later. Once everything was loaded into his Ford Territory Ghia, he had a brainwave. *"Just in case the bitch gets loose I'm going to load up her suitcases full of her clothes and take them with me, too. Just let her try and run away with no clothes,"* he thought to himself, snickering.

190

Stephen B. King

He stood outside and listened at the bedroom door but didn't hear a thing. "*She must be asleep still, the lazy fucking cow*," he tutted to himself. Whistling a tune, he locked up the house and climbed in his ever-reliable Territory and headed off to Applecross. The white pages phone book on line having provided the address.

By twelve forty-two Clinton had found the perfect tree, in the park which was as quiet as the grave, alongside the bastard's house. Realising he made a joke, he smiled to himself at his own sparkling wit and climbed up the western side of the very old fig tree. He nestled himself into the branches in as comfortable a position as possible. He made sure he wouldn't be seen from the ground or surrounding area and had a perfect view of the backyard and front driveway.

Through the high-powered telescopic sight, he could see the rear sliding glass door as clear as day but couldn't see inside, because the blinds were closed, as were the curtains on all of the windows he could see. "*Nothing for it but to wait*," he thought, but that was nothing new to Clinton. He was used to spending long hours in a hide. The pig shooters would wait for the wild boars to come down to the water to be picked off by them. "*This is just another pig hunt*," he thought. Once again, he smiled at his own humour.

Sooner or later Mr. David "Home Wrecker" Barndon would come out. Regardless of whether he came out the front or back door, Clinton would see him. He only needed one shot. Wild pigs were classed as vermin in the bush. This bloke was human vermin, to Clinton.

As he passed the time, Clinton thought back over the years about his marriage. All in all, he thought they were pretty good. Yes, he had to spend the first couple of years training Susan to be the wife she should be, but he always knew it was for her own

Domin8

good. His father had taken him aside after the wedding ceremony and given him instructions on how to get a compliant wife. It was a lesson well learnt.

The first thing to do, his father instructed him, was to control the purse strings, which he did by giving her an allowance to run the house and shop for groceries with, but he paid all the bills, including her clothing. If she wanted to buy clothes she would have to ask him, and he would go with her to make sure she didn't waste any of his hard-earned money. At first she complained, but she soon learnt complaining wasn't the way to live in his house. A few slaps here and there, and she soon caught on that keeping quiet was far less painful, especially once he introduced her to Mr. leather belt.

The next way to keep her in line was to give her clear instructions on what jobs she was to do that day, and that any slacking off—anything not done to his lofty standard—would also mean a slapping. She wasn't dumb and soon settled into a routine that pleased him. As for sex, her place was to make sure he was satisfied. Once again, it didn't take more than a few months to knock her into shape in the bedroom.

Sitting up in the tree, with the sun filtering down through the leaves above him, he recalled how he had taught her to enjoy the aspects of sex that he liked most. Then, in a blinding flash of realisation, he considered that maybe the lying bitch was only faking enjoying what he made her do. It was a watershed moment for him. He determined to have that little "talk" with her in more detail when he got home. He had told her time and time again— she was to do as she was told and enjoy what pleasure he permitted her to have.

That was conversation they were destined not to have, as his long suffering wife, Susan, had died around 3 a.m. earlier that morning. The bleeding in her brain, which started out as a very slight seep, got worse, and she slipped into a blessed, pain free coma, from which she would never wake up. She died all alone, battered and broken on her bed, which had been her place of misery for years, right up until she had met Dave Barndon. They had gotten together only twice, but on those two occasions he had showed her kindness and that she was a valued human being with feelings and passions that could be treasured. For only those two meetings in her life, she learnt she could, and should, orgasm. For the first time in her life, she realized it was good for her to be happy.

When everything blew up with the murder inquiry, and the police interviewed her, it had brought things home to her that she should use that time to escape her sadistic, domineering husband. Perhaps she could find happiness that had been sadly lacking in her married life. She had never discussed it with Dave. He had been too kind to her and he was happily married. She had known that. But she had hoped that if she could get free she could meet her own, single version of Dave. There was a big wide world out there. The last conscious thought she had in the midst of the pain of the beating she had endured, was a wish that she could have married Dave, rather than the pig of a man she had

Domin8

Chapter 20 – Sam (2) – Gloria Beamish – Clinton Mooney (2)
Day Six: The Consequences of a Twisted Mind

As the day wore on, the boredom was killing me, and I wasn't too sure how much longer I could put up with it without screaming. I've never been one for sitting around and doing nothing. Even on holidays I had to be doing something. That used to drive Di nuts, as she could laze around a pool in a resort and read a book all day. Not me.

A patrol car had come around after the window breaking episode the night before, and the offending brick with the macabre doll attached had been bagged up and whisked away for forensic testing. Sam said there was nothing that could have retained a fingerprint other than the doll itself, and that because it was covered in some sort of blood it might make it well-nigh impossible to lift a print. There was always the hope for a trace of DNA.

Early that morning, before breakfast, I found a board, a hammer and nails in the shed and sealed off the hole. The local glazier called out to replace the broken pane mid-morning.

I had offered to make breakfast but Sam he had brought his own muesli and almond milk. "My body is a temple," he said, and I shuddered at the mere thought of what he was eating, while enjoying my toast and peanut butter, with salt: a secret vice I had had since childhood.

Stephen B. King

By late morning, all we had accomplished was the kitchen clean up. Ten minutes after that, I was bored.

"Is the pool heated, Dave?" Sam asked.

"Yeah, it should be fine if you want to have a dip. I may go in this afternoon but not right now. I thought I might put the tennis on for a bit."

The weather was warming up nicely, but it wasn't summer's, and the US Open was in the middle stages so I thought it could be worth watching on TV. I found the remote for the pool heater in the third drawer down in the kitchen and switched it on.

"An hour or so, and it should be fine, Sam." I clicked on the tennis. The women were playing. "*Perfect timing*," I thought. I watched two incredibly fit, nubile women running around with tiny little skirts bobbing up and down over their perfect legs and panties, and tried in vain to stop thinking about sex. Maybe I was an addict, after all.

All it took was one thought about the last time I had had sex, at the sink in the kitchen with Dianne, the morning of the last day of her life, and I was over feeling horny.

"Sam, I've got to tell you: just sitting around like this is doing my head in. No offence. There is nothing wrong with your company, but I'm just used to doing things."

"None taken, I understand. Look, if you want to get out, I've got a guy on standby to go with you. He's ex-TRG, built like a brick shithouse, and is a good guy to have on your side. I think it's important I stay here, just in case a visitor comes calling, but if you want to go out and do some stuff I can get him to come and accompany you."

"What's TRG?" I queried.

Domin8

"Tactical Response Group: they are the bad boys of the police force. They are tough, fit as all fuck and armed to the teeth. They go in first when it's a hostage, terrorist threat or dangerous situation."

I was impressed. They were going out of their way to look after me and, of course, catch the killer. They also understood being housebound for long periods of time was going to drive me crazy.

"I might go into work tomorrow for a while, talk to my staff and the MD, thank them for the support and explain to them directly what's been going on. If you can arrange it for then, say late morning tomorrow, that would be good. For today, I think I will stay here and suffer."

Just then the phone rang. I picked it up immediately, hoping it would be the killer. "Hello?" I said.

"Mr. Barndon, it's Gloria Beamish, producer for "In Australia Tonight." I'm sure you've seen our show: the biggest rating current affairs show on TV. I wonder if I could have a few minutes of your time and have a chat about getting your story on air."

My heart sank. It wasn't a rabid murderer wanting to threaten me, and more media exposure could only lead to more embarrassment for me and the kids.

"I don't think I'm ready to talk about it right now Gloria. The wounds are too fresh. In case you didn't know, my life has been threatened and my wife was murdered."

"Yes, I know. I am sorry for your loss. Can I call you Dave?"

"Sure."

Stephen B. King

"Dave, let me be completely frank here. This story is going to get out, in fact it already is, and it's going to be huge. It's got everything people want: salacious sex, the internet and murder. Whether you like it or not, it's going to be all over the news. If you want my advice, it would be for you to go exclusive to one organisation that will tell your story the way you want it told. Because, Dave, if you don't give the press what you want, they will write what *they* want. You don't need me to tell you that, do you?"

"Gloria, why should I care what you guys say, or do, about me?"

"I understand how you're feeling. Anyone in your situation would be really down about it. But think of this; one day this will be over, and how you act now will dictate how you will be remembered in the future. If you want people to think the worst, so be it, but I think you have a story to tell. Deep down, I think you want to tell it."

She was right, of course. If it was all going to come out, and it would be best if I front up and be a man about it, and try to control it, rather than let them just destroy me and Dianne's memory.

"How do I know you will air my side and not your interpretation of it?"

"Dave, no one is going to give you editorial control. We are trying to make a show which informs and entertains, but I think our track record speaks for itself. We are not about doing hatchet jobs on people who give us an exclusive."

"Give me your direct number, Gloria. I will call you in the morning and give you my decision. I need to consult with my children and think about this, but I will tell you now I think what you propose will be acceptable. But the interview will be done here in my house, not in the studio. Bear in mind I have been targeted by a murderer, and your people could be in danger coming here."

She gave me her number and assured me that filming in my home would be acceptable. I wrote her number down on the pad alongside the wall phone and hung up. Sam could tell from my side of the conversation what it was about, and he raised his eyebrows at me.

"In Australia Tonight, Sam. What do you think? Do I go on TV and let them make a mockery of me?" I asked.

"If you want my honest opinion, I would do it and be strong." He leaned forward in his chair, "I hate all that shit that came out recently about sports or movie stars being unfaithful to their wives, where they claim they have a sex addiction and then go into rehab for it. What a complete load of bollocks, that is. I don't think there is anything wrong with your story, if you tell it the way it is. Most men will be on your side, and the frustrated women who are stuck in loveless and boring marriages will be too. The ones who will be against you are the holier-than-thou religious nuts or people like Felix: people who just do not entertain the idea that wedding vows are made with good intent, but can change with time and circumstances. You can use that line if you like, free of charge."

He grinned at me. I grinned back.

"Your earlier idea about a swim is a good one. I think I will go for a dip too and clear my head. Let's do it."

He disappeared into the spare bedroom while I went into the main one to change. On my way back I grabbed two towels from the linen cupboard and tossed one at him, which he caught deftly. He was sporting pale blue swimming shorts and holding his gun, which looked very James Bond. "*Jesus*," I thought. "*If I*

Stephen B. King

were gay I could go for Sam." He had a body he clearly looked after: fit, lean and strong.

I opened the blinds, unlocked the back door and slid it open. But, just as I stepped through it, the phone rang, and I turned back to answer it, "*That will be Sixty Minutes,*" I thought.

At the exact moment I was aware of a noise like a car backfiring. I was suddenly being spun around. I felt back through the doorway and sliced my arm open on the aluminium frame as I slid down it. I was disorientated and confused. What the hell had happened?

Next I felt something like a massive bee sting on my upper leg. The glass panel alongside me shattered with small shattered shards falling all over me. I lay there dazed for only a few seconds, though it seemed so much longer, as if things were happening in slow motion. Sam grabbed me under the arms and yanked me back inside, sliding my bare skin through the shattered glass.

I tried to get up, but my right leg felt like it was on fire. As I turned to my left and looked down I saw a hole in my shoulder and blood pumping out of it. Everything spun in my head, and I could hear Sam's voice coming from what sounded like miles away.

"Stay down, Dave. You've been shot."

I saw him leap over me and run out into the back garden. In a dazed wonder I watched as he ran to the side colour bond fence and jump up on the brick flower bed retaining wall so he could see over it.

"*Am I watching a movie?*" I stupidly thought and shook my head to try to clear my muddled brain. Clearly, I was in shock. I had to think straight, because if Sam went down, nothing would stop the killer coming in to finish me off. I sat up and looked

199

Domin8

around me. "*Fuck,*" I thought. There was a lot of blood around me on the tiled floor. I had left a bright red snail trail to where he had dragged me clear of the doorway.

Suddenly, I heard a series of loud gunshots, fired so quickly as to seem almost continuous: "BAM! BAM! BAM! BAM! BAM! BAM! BAM! BAM! BAM!"

The sound confused me more and was deafening and went on for what seemed like forever. I watched as Sam ejected the magazine and inserted another, slid back the slide, and then jumped over the fence. That was no small leap and showed his fitness, I marvelled. I was left alone, bleeding like a stuck pig and fearing the murderer would best Sam and come and finish the job.

There was no way I was going to let the maniac find me helpless in a puddle of blood and glistening glass shards. I had to get going. My thoughts were starting to solidify, and I looked at my leg critically to see why it hurt so much. There were two small holes either side of the fleshy part of my upper thigh, and I realised I had been shot while I had been lying on the ground. The bullet had gone straight through my leg, ricocheted off the ground and into the glass panel, which had shattered all over me.

That inspection told me there were no bones broken, just muscle damage, so there no reason I couldn't put up with some pain and stand up. My left shoulder and arm felt like lead and I had next to no movement in my arm, but I still had my right. "*Time to move,*" I thought.

I rolled over to my left, out of the worst of the glass. Then without stopping to think I pushed my right hand into the floor and felt glass cut my palm. I got up on to my knees, then onto my feet. Everything went black, and vertigo set in, but by the use of sheer willpower I refused to fall down again. I told myself that my life could depend on it. I staggered over to the breakfast bar and

Stephen B. King

leant heavily against it and waited a few seconds, or minutes—
I'm not sure—until it passed.

As soon as I was able I moved to the wall phone and
picked it up. Felix's mobile number was there. I dialled it, and he
answered on the third ring. "Felix, it's Dave Barndon. I've been
shot, and Sam has taken off after the guy. Get here quick."

I hung up because I didn't want to get bogged down
playing twenty questions and waste time. I slid the second drawer
down open and grabbed a big carving knife, then sank down
behind the cupboards to sit on the floor. I was bleeding profusely
from what seemed like a hundred places, and I thought it best to
conserve what blood I had left until help arrived.

What good a knife would do against a man with a gun I
didn't stop to think. I was past caring anyway, but I knew one
thing; if I could stab the bastard who had killed my wife, I would
do it in a heartbeat—and enjoy it.

XXX

Clinton Mooney saw the blinds move and instantly raised
the rifle to his shoulder and took a well practised aim. Through
the high power sight, he could see the mongrel that had ruined his
life as he stepped through the door he had just opened. He smiled.
The pig was about to be slaughtered.

Clinton could have brought a bigger calibre rifle and
simply obliterated him, but there was no fun in that. He had five
weapons he used for the different-sized game he hunted, but his
favourite had always been his lever action Winchester magnum.
Sure, it wouldn't bring down a pig unless he got a heart or clean
head shot, but with over 2000 feet per second muzzle velocity,
and only about a thirty to forty metre range from his tree, he could

hardly miss a full-grown man. The other deciding factor was that the .22 was significantly quieter than the others, which, he hoped, would allow him to get away without the entire neighbourhood coming to investigate.

The Ford Territory was parked behind the park furthest away from the house. Once he made the kill he intended to get down the tree and take off in the opposite direction from where the action was. Then, using the trees and bushes for cover, he would be back on the freeway heading North before anyone knew what was going on.

He was looking forward to getting home and having a good old chin wag with Susan, the slut, as he had started to think of her. He would take great delight in telling her he had shot and killed her lover boy, and that she had just better toe the line unless she wanted to go the same way.

Clinton Mooney had centred the cross hairs on the bastard's chest. "*The perfect heart shot was about to be made,*" he excitedly thought. Holding his breath, he gently squeezed the trigger, but just at that moment Clinton noticed with alarm that the bastard had turned back inside. Like a ballet dancer, Barndon had spun as the magnum shell, with all 2000 feet per second velocity, hit him in the shoulder rather than dead centre of his chest.

In one fluid motion he chambered another round and re-aimed, only to see that his victim had fallen back inside the door, out of sight, but his legs were still sticking out. Without hesitation he aimed as high up the leg as he could, hoping to hit the guy's prick, so that even if he survived he wouldn't be fucking other men's property.

He saw the impact and cloud of blood through the scope and in the same instant the glass shattered and the legs scampered back inside the house all in the time it took to chamber a third round. He cursed his bad luck and took a second or two to make a decision to go and finish him off or get away. It was no contest, really. He would get down and go over, climb the fence and finish the mongrel off. "*Fuck him,*" he thought, as he prepared to make a move.

Clinton changed position in the tree, turning and moving his right foot downwards to a lower branch. He transferred his weight onto it and levered himself up just as two bizarre things happened simultaneously.

Firstly, he realised he had been in the same position for too long, and his foot had gone to sleep. He had no feeling in it other than numbness and now he had moved it, pins and needles. As he put his weight on it he lost his balance and began to fall. He could have recovered by reaching out for a branch, were it not for the second bizarre event. There was suddenly a hail of bullets from Sam Collins' Glock hitting the branches and leaves around him, and two of them hit his body: one to his neck and the other his right hip.

As he fell down through the branches he was totally confused. How could the man he had just shot twice be shooting back? It made no sense at all.

His beloved rifle slipped from his grasp as he tried to grab a branch to halt his fall, but his reach missed. His foot that had gone to sleep snagged in the vee of two branches, so as he fell his entire weight snapped not only his ankle but the hip that had been smashed into pieces by the nine millimetre bullet. With the sudden halt in downward motion and simultaneous sideways movement, the shattered hip bone sheered the artery running through his groin.

He was stuck upside down, held only by his foot, in the middle of a God damned tree. "This is all that bitch of a wife's fault, and I'm going to give Susan, the slut, absolute hell when I get home," was his last thought as he slipped into unconsciousness.

It only took one glance from Sam Collins to see the man was dead. Sam was filled with shock and horror. He had never fired his gun before, other than at firing ranges, and his quick reaction had been purely his reflexes responding to hours and hours of training. He felt sick in his stomach and would have thrown up but for his realisation that Dave was wounded back at the house. Swallowing the bile back down, he picked up the dropped rifle and raced back across the road to the house.

Stephen B. King

Chapter 21 - Shannon – Starsky and Hutch (6) – The Kids

Day Seven: An Angel in White

I woke up with a stunningly beautiful woman, dressed in crisp white, standing over me. I thought I was dreaming or maybe I had been transported to heaven.

"Welcome back," the vision of loveliness spoke and smiled, showing her absolutely perfect teeth.

She took the thermometer out of my ear, and I groggily realised she was a nurse. I must have seemed confused because she saw the look on my face and offered some help, "They brought you into the ward from ER a few hours ago. You've lost a lot of blood, and they had to stitch you up. You have been in the wars, haven't you?"

She had a big smiley face badge on her uniform on the upper part of her right breast and the word "Shannon" was written on it in what looked like crayon. I couldn't help myself but wonder what she called her left breast, but when I opened my mouth to ask her, nothing but a croak came out. She noticed where I had been looking and gave me a slightly stern look before smiling. She picked up a glass of water with straw in it and held it to my lips and I gratefully sipped.

Old habits die hard, and as she held the glass for me I couldn't help but notice the lack of wedding ring and filed it away in my mental filing cabinet of information that might come in handy later. She was mid-to-late thirties I guessed, with her long

Domin8

brunette hair tied back in a ponytail, brown eyes with curved and long eyelashes.

"How am I doing, nurse?" I asked in a voice that, while it was now working, sounded like I was talking through a bucket of gravel.

"You'll have to wait for the doctor to do his rounds, I'm afraid, but I think you'll live. Nothing is very serious in itself, but cumulatively you will be stiff and sore for a long while yet, and they've given you quite a lot of blood."

I looked down and saw my shoulder was heavily bandaged and my arm was in an enclosed sling strapped to my body, almost like a semi-straightjacket. "*Strange,*" I thought, I didn't feel any pain. "*It must be some pretty good drugs they're feeding me through the drip plugged into my good arm.*"

"Will I be able to play the piano?" I asked quietly, and slightly less gravely. She looked immediately concerned.

"Oh, I should think so, Mr. Barndon."

"Thank God for that. I couldn't before. Call me Dave, please."

She waggled her finger at me, as if telling me off for poor taste humour before threatening me, "You know, Dave, it's up to me where I take your temperature. I have this rectal thermometer I could use."

"Promises, promises," I joked, then winked.

"I don't have to lubricate it, you know. Just saying." She was smiling too now.

"OK, I will be good, I promise. No more jokes." I felt quite euphoric. They really were good drugs, but that good mood was about to change.

Stephen B. King

"Does your wife know you're here? Would you like me to give her a call?" She must have picked from my face and changed demeanour she had said the wrong thing.

"She's dead," I said, in a very subdued voice.

"I'm sorry. Isn't that just like me to open my big mouth and put my foot right into it?"

"It's fine, don't worry. You weren't to know."

"My boss, the head bitch, is always telling me off for being too friendly with patients. Maybe she's right. Anyway, there are two serious looking cops outside waiting to speak to you; are you up to talking to them?"

"Shannon, don't you stop being friendly with patients, ok? You keep being yourself. And yes, please send in Starsky and Hutch."

She looked at me a bit blankly for a few seconds before suddenly bursting into laughter. "Oh my God, that is who they remind me of: one dark, one blonde. You're so funny." Then she stopped suddenly, "Are you some sort of criminal?"

"No, I'm a victim, though it has to be said I'm not a good man either, but I'm definitely no criminal. Please show the lads in. They are not going to arrest me, I promise."

"Press the call button if you need me to help you escape. I can have my car at the back entrance, and you can wear my ex-husbands grey raincoat as a disguise. I will show them in."

And with that she was gone. "Interesting that she made sure to tell me she had an ex-husband," I thought and I shook my head to myself. Sometimes women can be so transparent, and at other times, such a complete mystery. Perhaps it was that "bad boy" thing again; or maybe the fact that I was laid up with two

Domin8

bullet wounds and police waiting to talk to me helped her to be attracted to me? Who knew?

I admonished myself for thinking of the nurse sexually. *"What the fuck am I thinking? My wife is dead, my kids are hurt, scared and angry at me, but I'm still thinking of bedding every woman I meet? Maybe I am an addict, maybe it's the drugs or maybe I should just grow up,"* I told myself.

Quite a few minutes later Felix and Sam entered. Without preamble Felix said "What's this fucking bullshit about Starsky and Hutch?" I couldn't help it. I burst out laughing, once again in his presence, almost hysterically.

Sam joined in, but Felix maintained his grim look, and I regained my composure, "Sorry, guys, no disrespect intended, but I mentioned to Shannon that for some stupid reason you reminded me of them when I first met you at my house, and it's stuck in my head ever since."

The admission set me off again laughing, and this time even Felix smiled back before saying "Fuck me, Dave. What is it with you? You're in hospital eight hours, most of that time asleep, and one of the nurses is already throwing herself at you?"

I was in hysterics but a sudden lance of pain in my shoulder stopped me short. I winced and put my good hand up to rub it through the bandaging. When it subsided, Sam asked, "We've spoken to the doc. Have you seen him yet?"

I shook my head. I was still in pain. *"Those good drugs must be wearing off,"* I thought, grimacing.

"Well, he told us you're going to be fine. You were lucky he wasn't using hollow points. Both bullets went straight through you, the shoulder being the worst; it chipped a bone and cracked another, but glanced off, without shattering it. They removed the chips and cleaned it up. The thigh was a clean through and

Stephen B. King

through, no major muscle damage, but it's going to hurt like a bastard for a long while. Lots of minor and some not quite so minor cuts from the broken glass. You've got a couple of dozen or more stiches, but nothing significant. Knowing you, you will just use the scars to attract more women. You're going to be quite famous, I think."

"Did you get him, then?" I asked.

Sam turned just a slight shade of greyish-green, and Milanski answered for him. "Oh yes, Wild Bill Hickok here got him. Or should we call you Dirty Harry, Sam?"

Sam just shook his head. Clearly he wasn't in the mood to celebrate.

"What happened, Sam? I saw you shoot, then jump the fence, I slithered over to the phone and called Felix, but must have passed out by the time you got back."

"Just as well you had, or you would have stuck me with the carving knife I had to prise loose from your clenched hand. Not much to tell really, Dave. After I dragged you inside and ran out onto the flower bed so I could see over the fence, I saw this guy with a rifle in that Fig Tree in the park over the road. I emptied a clip into the tree and saw him stumble and fall so I knew I had hit him. Then the rifle fell out the tree so I jumped the fence. By the time I got there he was hanging upside down by his foot, dead. It wasn't a pretty sight; I can tell you." He looked green again, as if he might throw up.

Felix turned to him, "Do you want me to get nurse big tits back so she can look after you too, Sam, or do you think you can hold your lunch down?"

"Who was he?" I asked, to save Sam from further taunts, and they both got very serious.

Domin8

Felix answered, "A very, very nasty piece of work, Dave, and it's not a pretty story, I'm afraid. We had previously interviewed him at his work; he said he was on a pig shooting hunt on the Saturday in question, which was an alibi, so we didn't look much further immediately, though of course we would have in time. We now know that he could have been back in time for victim number one, as it turns out, after speaking with the guys he went with. They said he seemed agitated at the time, but thought nothing of it; he was a bit of a screwball they said. He had no alibi other than his wife for the second victim or your wife's murder, and unfortunately, we found her dead earlier today."

I felt like I was going to vomit. I knew what was about to come. I was responsible for yet another death.

"His wife was Susan Mooney, and I'm afraid she was on your list of *After Dark* contacts, we spoke to her too and she admitted to having been with you. We are waiting for post mortem results, but it looks like he whipped her with a belt and used the buckle end. Like I said, he was a very nasty piece of work. The ME thinks it was a brain haemorrhage and that she died in her sleep, locked in the bedroom where he had left her after the beating. That beating was one of the worst the ME had ever seen in a domestic violence case." Felix shook his head and continued, soberly.

"It appears he then made himself dinner and slept in the spare room before having a big cooked breakfast in the morning. Then he went gunning for you, Dave. There is evidence of a long history of abuse. It seems as if perhaps she was trying to get away from him. Her packed suitcases were in his car, and that's maybe what sent him over the edge. Don't blame yourself, Dave. I think he would have killed her anyway. We see that kind of thing quite a lot, sadly. They seem to think if they can't have their woman, no one else will. In this case he blamed you, and not his own wife-beating ways, for the breakdown of their marriage. These types of men often think they are perfect, and it's the rest of the world with the problem."

I felt so incredibly sad, "Susan was such a gentle soul though very timid. She was submissive, yes, though possibly her husband had forced her to be that way. She would have done anything for her man, I had thought at the time—that was her nature. But she didn't deserve that. This is all my fault." I wept, again. What had I done? What had I done?

Felix spoke up, sternly. "Dave, stop that right now. I don't agree with your lifestyle choices, but even my wife tells me I'm a dinosaur and stuck in my old fashioned ways. So far as I can see you didn't set out to hurt anyone. The women you've been with, who I have interviewed, all rave about how you treated them. I have no doubt in my mind whatsoever that even if you had never met Susan Mooney, her husband would have ended up killing her sooner or later along with anyone he thought he could blame for it. He was a ticking time bomb mate. It wasn't your fault."

"Thanks, Felix, I appreciate that, but the fact is that I did have an affair with Susan, and he did blame me, and he killed four women because of it, including Dianne. All of the women were totally blameless."

"Dave, I'm not going to blow smoke up your arse, but that is bullshit. Your wife, yeah, she didn't deserve it, but the others knew you were married and they did it anyway, most of them were married too. But think of this; if he didn't blame you he might have caught up with her at her work, or at a shopping centre, or at a movie theatre and killed her and a dozen others. It happens that way sometimes. You've read cases like it in the papers, I'm sure. When these type of people lose the plot they don't care who they take with the intended victim, including themselves. Life is what it is. You did what you did, and it did lead to consequences, but you didn't plan it that way. It's just life."

"Dave?" Sam interrupted, "He is right. Life is fleeting, and you made some choices to enjoy yours. It's not your fault there was a lunatic married to one of them. Stop beating yourself up and think of your three kids, who are all on their way here now, by the way. They love you and need you to be strong. It's over now, and life is for the living."

I nodded. Suddenly I was very tired. They had said some kind words, but none of it meant anything. Dianne was dead, along with three other women I had known, all because of my boredom. I just wanted to sleep for a long, long time.

"Thanks, guys, I appreciate it. And thanks especially to you, Sam, for stopping this guy. You saved my life. The drugs are wearing off now; I think I need to sleep. Let me know what else you need from me. Oh, and will they release Dianne's body now so I can arrange a funeral?"

"I will talk to the coroner and drop by tomorrow and let you know, but I would think so, yes. See you then."

Milanski nodded to me. I think he knew how I felt, and despite his words I think he still blamed me, as he should. They left and as tired as I was, I couldn't sleep for thinking of all the pain I had caused. Things just kept going around and around in my head.

First I blamed myself, but then I also wondered what could have driven this madman to kill Dianne, Patsy and Melanie. Sure, I understood his wanting to kill me and his wife, if he was that psychotic. But why the others? Why would he want to frame me for murder? Did it make sense to go to all that trouble to put me in jail? I supposed it must have made some sort of sense to him, though something about it all just didn't feel right.

Stephen B. King

It just didn't make sense no matter which way I looked at it, but then I remembered someone saying to me once that you can't use logic to understand an illogical act. I was still trying to work it all out when Nurse Shannon came back in and took my blood pressure, temperature and pulse, all without saying a word.

When she was done, she turned on her heel and was walking out when she stopped, turned and said, "I did a bad thing, and I'm sorry for it. I told those guys they reminded you of Starsky and Hutch to get back at you after they told me who you were and why you had been shot. I only asked them because I was interested, and I then told them your nickname for them because I realised what you had done while being married. I was angry at you and I had no right to feel that way. I know nothing about you. Ever since then it has been bothering me, and I'm sorry."

She was looking down at her feet, and I felt sorry for her. I was the louse, not her.

"It's absolutely none of my business what you did, or why you did it. All I can say is that my husband left me for some slag he used to have sex with in the back of his delivery van. I mean, please, how classless. And he dumped me to be with her?"

She sounded very angry, understandably so. She carried on as she seemed to have a full head of steam up, "And the thing is, I liked sex, and would have done pretty much anything with him he wanted, so he shouldn't have gotten bored with me and run off with a tart eight years younger than him. I'm sorry, Mr. Barndon, I hope the cops weren't mad at you. If you want to complain to 'the head bitch,' I wouldn't blame you. Honestly I don't know what's gotten into me, or why I'm mad at you when I have no right to be."

She looked genuinely contrite, and in that moment I knew what my life was going to be like when I got out of hospital. Everyone would have an opinion, and everyone would want a piece of me. Some would say, "See what happens when you are unfaithful?" Others would be all for extramarital sex and want to know all about my internet life. Would I ever find peace again?

"Shannon, look, it's fine honestly. And no, I'm not going to complain about you. I'm sorry you married a dickhead who didn't value you as he should have. Clearly he was the one with a problem, not you. As for me, well, my story is a bit different, but I am at fault, make no mistake and I don't run away from that. The fact is that my wife of twenty-six fantastic years lost interest in sex a long time ago, but her doing so shouldn't have given me license to go out and sleep around. I was wrong, and others have paid the ultimate price for my selfish wants. You've done nothing wrong, Shannon. I applaud you and hope you do find a man who can appreciate what a beautiful woman you are." I smiled thinly and shrugged my good shoulder, and she left, looking embarrassed. I didn't see her again for two days.

A little later the three kids all turned up, and I felt so much better when each of them hugged me in turn, even Missy, though she held herself very stiffly. I knew it was going to take a long time 'till she forgave and forgot my indiscretions—if she ever could, that was.

We spent the next hour talking about the man who had killed their mother and shot me. It may sound stupid, but I kind of got the feeling my being shot seemed to them like a karmic form of punishment, for being unfaithful to their mum. The feeling I got was that they could now forgive me, because I hadn't walked away unscathed.

They told me they were glad that they no longer had to get out of town for a while and could go back to their normal lives. But with everything being so fresh, I still felt very uneasy, though why I should was a mystery.

Stephen B. King

We spoke about the funeral, and they offered to begin preliminary arrangements. I hoped to find when Dianne's body would be released and promised to let them know as soon as I did. I also had to find out how long I would be hospitalised. By the time they left I was exhausted and in a lot of pain, not only from the shoulder and thigh but all over my back legs and buttocks from the cuts all over me. Those good drugs had worn off, for sure, and I wanted some more.

I resisted the urge to press the bell, but by the time the doctor came I was sweating profusely and shivering in pain, which he noticed immediately. He ordered a drug I'd never heard of and undid the bandaging to check my wounds.

He was a tall, thin and grey-haired man with a sever hook nose and black rimmed glasses who introduced himself in a fine Scottish accent as Dr. Dorian McLeish.

"You'll be wanting to know what the story is, no doubt." He said, and I nodded a yes, the pain making me feel so uncomfortable I didn't trust myself to speak without my voice breaking.

"Well, you'll not be needing much more than a wee bit of rest and recuperation. I've removed the bone chips from your shoulder, but sometimes bullets can leave behind some nasty infections, which we need to watch out for. You've had four bags of blood to top you up, and if all goes well you should be back home in five or six days. How does that sound?"

"What about the pain? I mumbled.

"Ach, what pain? Toughen up, laddie." He saw the look on my face and jumped in quickly, "I'm just kidding, forgive my Scottish sense of humour. We will keep you on the intravenous morphine for two more days, then the drip will come out, and you'll get some wee pills to help. Meanwhile, keep your arm as still as possible, try not to lift it over your head. You picked up a wee crack in the bone, and we want to give it a chance to knit. I will get the nurses to help you shower and move around."

He winked at me, and again I groaned. Even my doctor had heard of my reputation. "*Maybe I should join a monastery,*" I thought glumly.

Just then a different nurse entered with a syringe in a kidney shaped bowl. By the time rigmarole was done to check it was the right drug, in date and going to the right patient I was ready to climb the walls and scream at them to "*hurry the fuck up*" as the pain was getting worse and worse. I watched impatiently as he injected it into the drip line, and within minutes the pain retreated into the background. I relaxed back into my pillow, and the feeling of euphoria came creeping back, bringing bliss along with it.

"I will be back tomorrow, laddie. Remember, keep that arm still." And he was gone and within minutes I was asleep.

Chapter 22 – George – Sam (3) – Shannon (2) – Judith (2)

Day Eight: Rest and Recovery

Time dragged by, as only it can when you are stuck in hospital, especially if your movements are limited. The next morning another nurse woke me by taking my vitals, which all seemed to be fine. She was short, rather frumpy and didn't know what a smile was.

In a very short manner, she said, "I've brought you the newspaper. You are on the front page, and I thought you might like to read about yourself." She was another woman who clearly thought I was scum. There would be a long line of those, I was sure.

Dreading what I would find, I opened it to see a picture of the killer with very beady eyes, holding a rifle in a hunting pose in the centre. His photo was surrounded with four small pictures of the victims, including Di, and one of me taken from one of our sales press ads. Where the hell did they get a picture of Dianne, I wondered? The headline read, "POLICE SHOOT KILLER IN INTERNET SEX MURDER RAMPAGE."

The story was pretty accurate and was spread over three pages with the main focus being on Clinton Mooney. They focused on him owning weapons, his history of wife abuses and his jealous rages. Of course it was all supposition and full of "a family friend said this," or "an informed source said that." I was, of course, the guy who gave Mooney the motivation and was painted pretty badly, as I deserved to be.

I have to admit it was shaming to read and I stopped before the end, folded the paper and lay back in the bed. The truth had to come out, and really it was no worse than I deserved. Realistically, if the sordid story acted as any sort of deterrent to any other married men and women out there contemplating using the internet for finding playmates, then in my mind my plight had a silver lining to it.

Sam came by and told me that Dianne's body had been released and could be picked up by the funeral director of my choice. He didn't have much other news, as the investigation was winding down, with the case now closed. All he could say was that the more they found out about the man he had shot, the less they liked him. Over the eight years they had been married, Susan had been hospitalised four times for injuries, but she had never once lodged a complaint. Those injuries included a broken cheek bone, dislocated shoulder, stitches to a cut on the inside of her mouth, broken tibia and more.

To me, she had never mentioned unhappiness or the abuse when we were together, and I had never seen her bruised. Perhaps I never asked her the right questions; just one more thing to feel guilty about.

Sam suggested I should get away until the dust settled once the funeral was over. He told me the press have very short memories and within a week or so it would be old news. It was pretty good advice, but I had never run away from a fight before and I wasn't going to show the world I was a coward now. To me if I scurried away it would just shame Di's memory even more.

Stephen B. King

I told him I would just take it one day at a time and face up to my responsibilities. He nodded in understanding and added that even being in hospital would help let things quieten down.

Something had been nagging away at me, and I now remembered what it was. He had mentioned it was lucky Mooney hadn't used hollow points the day before, and I had no idea what he was talking about at the time, so I asked him about it. He explained that a hollow point shell expanded on impact to stop the bullet doing what it had: in my case, pass straight through. The downside was that, because it expanded, the damage it would have done would have been catastrophic. He said that if the one that hit my shoulder had been a hollow point, I most likely would have had my arm torn off, or my shoulder would be damaged so badly my arm would be next to useless the rest of my life. That was always assuming I lived through the trauma and blood loss. Similarly, the one which went through my leg could have badly damaged the muscle and bone, or even ruptured an artery, causing more severe blood loss or death.

He said that not many people survived being hit by a hollow point bullet in the torso, especially if it was fired from a magnum round. While he said I was lucky, I didn't feel all that lucky. I was pretty certain I was on the edge of depression, but with my kids and upcoming funeral I just kept pushing things to the back of my mind, knowing I had to confront it all at some point: just not right then.

We talked a bit more until he found an excuse to leave and was halfway out the door when he turned and said, "Oh, Dave, I almost forgot. I picked up your mobile phone for you, here." He walked back and from his right jacket pocket took my iPhone. From his other pocket he took out my charger and put them on the bedside cabinet for me, I thanked him for his thoughtfulness. He just shrugged in response and went on his way, wishing me well.

Domin8

Reluctantly, I turned it on and was amazed at all the messages and missed call tones that chirped out from the phone once it powered up. One-handed, I scrolled through the list and noted mostly names from work and family but among the most recent calls were three missed ones from Judith!

I sat there stunned as I had not heard from her in months—more than six months that I could recall, maybe even closer to a year, even. I was never very good with time frames. I decided she could wait as I had no desire to start a dialogue with her again, especially under the current circumstances. I had no doubt she was just calling to offer sympathy and condolences, having read about me in the papers or seen my face on TV.

There was also a message from George Hallman. That one I couldn't put off so I dialled his mobile. He answered after the first ring, as if he were waiting for me.

"Dave, how are you? Thanks for calling me back. Are you feeling OK?" That was typical of George to throw multiple questions at you at once, or several questions all asking the same thing.

"Hi, George, I'm doing OK, thanks. I should be out in the next five or six days they tell me. It could have been a lot worse. I've been lucky, though I don't feel very lucky. I feel pretty miserable, to be honest."

"Of course you do. Under the circumstance that's understandable, but at least it's over now. The guy is dead, and you can mourn your loss, without worrying you are a target anymore."

"Yes, George, I've a funeral to arrange now. They are releasing Di's body. I hope you are OK with me taking some personal time."

Stephen B. King

"Not a problem, Dave. In fact, I had a meeting with the board this morning after the papers came out, and we all agree you should take a month off."

I nodded silently to myself. I understood their position. If I didn't agree, the unspoken implication was obvious. No doubt Toyota themselves wouldn't want the publicity either. So far, where I worked had stayed out of the newspapers. Everyone hoped it would stay that way with me away for a month.

"George, I understand completely. If you want me to resign I can send you an email from my phone., though it will take time to type with one hand. I'm sorry everything has happened the way it has. My personal life should not impact on the business, and there will be no fuss from me if that's what you want me to do." That seemed the least I could do: to fall on my sword.

"Dave, this is a bad time for you. And no, I don't want your resignation now. A couple of the more straight-laced board members did, I will admit, but you have support from me and most of the others. What we are proposing is that you stay away for a month; I will sit in the chair for you, and let's see how this pans out. With the killer dead, things should hopefully just quieten down and be forgotten by the time you get back from leave. If things do heat up, or get too sensational, we may have to accept your resignation but hopefully it won't come to that. Is that acceptable to you?"

I completely understood their position. "Of course, George, whatever you say. The last thing I want to do is bring the company into disrepute. I appreciate you sticking by me. Please pass on my thanks and gratitude to the board," I replied. Really, what else could I say?

"Dave, if you want my advice, as soon as the funeral is over I would get away if I were you. Go to the States, or Japan or on a cruise. Just get yourself out of Perth and let things settle down."

"That's good advice, George. I will think about that. In fact, you are the second person today to suggest it. My phone will be on. If you need anything, don't hesitate to give me a call. Thanks again."

So, I was on leave for a month. I remembered back to my second day spent with Sam, when I was climbing the walls at home. I would be crazy by the time a month went by. Maybe his idea of getting away was a good one.

Next, I rang Jason and told him his mum's body could be picked up at the funeral home, which he said he would organise. He, too, had seen the papers and seemed a little more distant than he had the day before, which was understandable. I hated myself for dragging my children down into the mud with me.

The rest of the day passed uneventfully. The doctor came back. There seemed to be no deterioration and thankfully, no sign of infection so far. Nurse Frumpy Guts assisted me in the shower, which was not one of my more memorable moments, as I hurt all over from moving. Some cuts pulled against the stitches, my thigh was burning and my shoulder was agony. I questioned why they waited until I was due my next shot to shower me, rather than after I just had one. More punishment from Nurse Grumpy Tits, I was sure of it, as no doubt she had chosen when it was to be done.

The next morning Shannon was back, and I felt surprisingly glad to see her. I realised, to my horror and shame, that I liked her. Not because I wanted to seduce her, well not consciously. I was just happy to see her and wasn't thinking of her in any other way—or so I told myself after wondering, for the hundredth time, that maybe I was addicted to women and sex. Dianne wasn't even in her grave yet.

Stephen B. King

"Hello," I said. "I thought you'd got a transfer to another ward."

She looked shocked, which in turn shocked me, as she looked suddenly cross with me. "Why would you think that?" she asked.

"The way you left after our last conversation and you not being here all day yesterday, well, I thought you were upset with me and didn't want to treat me."

Her face turned just a bit pink, and then all hell broke loose as she gave me a right telling off. "Well, you are quite the egotist, aren't you? Not everything is about you, you know. For your information, Mr. Egotist, I came back to see you when I came off shift to apologise again and talk, but you were asleep so I didn't wake you. I do have patients other than you, you know. This is a hospital, and it does say on my badge that I am a nurse. Not everything revolves around you, you know. And, though it is none of your business, yesterday was my day off. I hope you don't mind that I do have a day off now and again. Most importantly of all, I am a nurse and I'm proud of what I do. I would treat anyone with professionalism regardless of my feelings for their rather seedy personal life."

"OK, OK, OK. I'm sorry, please forgive me. Calm down. I didn't mean any of it like that. If you want the truth I was disappointed I didn't see you, and umm, well I missed you. I didn't mean any disrespect to you, your feelings or your profession. My wife was a nurse. I do understand dedication to the cause."

Her face was hard to read, but I think the ice caps melted a bit. "You *missed* me? Come on, pull the other leg. It's got bells on it."

Domin8

I couldn't help it. I burst out laughing at her colourful way of speaking. She wore her heart on her sleeve. I could tell this woman would make anyone a good friend if you could put up with her total, brutal honesty. When I recovered she had just a hint of a smile, so I said "God, what is with you today? I didn't mean I was in love with you and missed you. I don't want to father your children or get into your knickers. But of all of the people I've met since being imprisoned in this place I thought you were the nicest, most honest and most fun. You telling the cops about the Starsky and Hutch thing of mine was hilarious. I really appreciated your honesty and sense of humour so shoot me for hoping you would come back. Can we be friends now?"

She stared at me for a full minute, clearly thinking about what I said. "I didn't know your wife was a nurse. I'm sorry I had a hissy fit, and I am very sorry for your loss."

"Thanks, I appreciate that. Can we both stop saying sorry now?"

"Why don't you want to get into my knickers? What's wrong with them? From what I read in the papers you aren't fussy."

Now I was stunned. Is that what people thought of me? "Oh my God, is that what you really think? Honestly? That I'm not fussy?"

She didn't answer me, and I thought how best to answer. Why did I even care what she thought? But the thing was, for some reason, I did care. Maybe this situation was a metaphor for all the people who would have an opinion of me, I didn't know, but I just felt I needed to explain.

"Shannon, please sit down. Let's just talk. Can we do that?"

Stephen B. King

"Well, I have my work to do and I'm not allowed to fraternise with patients. It's against the rules, so I can't just sit down and chat. I do have to do your vitals and take your drip out, so if you feel you want to talk to me, I can hardly stop you, can I?"

With that, she busied herself, but I did get the feeling from her that she wanted to hear what I might say.

"The day before my wife was murdered, her favourite patient died. She wasn't allowed to fraternise either, but she did because he had no family, and such was her nature she didn't want him to die alone. As it happened he did die on her day off, so he was alone, and that upset her. But, she spent hours with him the night before as she preferred to do on night shifts. I understand nursing, Shannon. Trust me, I do."

"She sounds like a wonderful woman. Why did you play around behind her back?"

"I hardly know you, but one of the things I like is your total honesty. You go straight for the jugular, don't you? I like that, I really do. How can I answer that? At the time it would have been because she had lost interest in sex with me years before, and I hadn't lost interest in her. I'm not going to dignify what I did by explaining, or bore you with trying to make my actions somehow justified. I was wrong, and people have paid for that. Oh, and, one last thing? I actually think your knickers would be pretty wonderful to get into, but I don't think you'd want me to, and I would value your friendship right now rather than being your lover. I don't think I will be capable of anything else anyway, at least not for a long time to come."

She didn't say a word. She just took my temperature and blood pressure before disconnecting my drip from my arm, but I could imagine the cogs were turning inside her head.

Domin8

"Shannon, it's OK. I get it. Your ex treated you despicably, and here am I a womaniser who has caused five deaths. Jesus, I'd be amazed if you had any interest in being a friend of mine. It's fine. Don't worry about it. Please forgive me if I've said anything that has offended you. I do think you are a woman who deserves respect. Please forget I said anything."

"Is this how you do it?"

"Do what? I don't know what you mean?"

"Charm your way into a woman's heart first—and then her knickers afterwards?"

"I don't blame you for thinking that. The fact that you had the balls to say it shows me the kind of woman you are. I really admire your forthright attitude. I think though, to be fair, if you spoke to any of the women I've known, with the exception of my wife, they would disagree with that. I didn't charm them, I met them mostly through internet sites that cater for people to meet and have sex. In particular, they were submissive women looking for a Dominant male. They weren't looking to be charmed Shannon. They were looking for something else entirely."

"So, is that what you think I need: a dominant male in my life?"

I wanted to laugh, but fortunately didn't. It wasn't that her question was funny, it was just the way she made a point by asking a question. I could see she was serious, very serious, and still more than a touch angry with me. But I couldn't get my head around why she even cared in the first place, unless of course, deep down, she just wanted to understand.

"I don't know you at all. It's not for me to tell you what you need; only you know that. All I think is that you are a good woman. You have high morals and scruples, you are dedicated to your work, you have a great sense of humour and know how to

226

have fun and you are also beautiful. You have a temper, you don't suffer fools and you gave your heart to someone who didn't deserve it and so are rightly cautious of giving it again. If things were different, I think you would be an incredible woman to know, but things aren't different. They are what they are, and you would be absolutely bonkers to want anything to do with me. But when you do try again, it will be a lucky man that gets you."

"That's right. I would be stupid, wouldn't I? I will be back in a couple of hours to shower you." And with that she was gone, leaving me alone to dread the shower, as it wouldn't have surprised me if she came back with a wire brush and Dettol to do it with.

An hour or so later my mobile rang, I looked at the display and my heart sank. It was Judith. I debated whether to answer or ignore her, but thought in the end I'd better answer. Clearly she was going to keep calling until I spoke to her.

"Hi, Judith. How are you?" I asked, trying to make my voice sound noncommittal and unfriendly.

"Dave, I've been trying to call you ever since I heard the news. Are you all right?"

"I'm recovering Judith, it will be a while till I'm fully fit, but the prognosis is good."

"Thank God for that. I've been really concerned. Can I come and visit you?"

I shook my head and wondered what was going on. How could she be serious? "Judith, thanks for your concern. I appreciate it, but I don't think that's such a good idea. Do you?"

She sighed deeply, and then in a very sad voice said, "Do you mean now, Dave? Or do you mean like forever?"

Domin8

"My wife was just murdered, Judith, because of my extramarital affairs. I've been shot, my life is all over the newspapers, and my children are in shock. The last thing I need right now is any of the people I had an affair with to show up. It's going to take time, Judith. Perhaps a long time."

There was a long silence before she spoke again, "I've been through a tough time myself, Dave, but I'm better now. Derek left me a while back. I don't blame him, really. I've been pretty tough to live with for quite a while. But I always missed you, Dave, and was sorry you lost interest in me."

"I'm sorry your husband left you, Judith. Are you OK?"

"Yeah, I'm peachy now, thanks for asking. You were always more of a man than he was. I was down for a while, but nothing like what you've been through, Dave. There is always someone worse off isn't there? Why did you stop calling me? Did I do something wrong?"

"No, not at all, I think we just ran our race. Let's face it; we were both married, we had a lot of fun, but we both moved on. At the time I thought you had lost interest in me. You seemed upset all the time."

"Yeah, I guess that was what it was like then. Will we have a chance to try again, do you think? Now we are both single again?"

I didn't know how to answer that. "Judith, I'm not even sure what day of the week it is right now, and me being with anyone in the world is honestly the last thing on my mind. Who can say what the future holds for any of us?"

"As always, Dave, you're right. But at least you didn't say no. I can live with that. You've got a lot on your plate and if you need a friend, I'm here for you. Just promise me you will call if you need someone to talk to."

Stephen B. King

"I promise, Judith."

"I'm really sorry about your wife. I'm *sure* she was a lovely woman."

"Me too, and she was. Thanks for calling. You look after yourself."

"Yes, I will, but only because you said to. You take care too, and I will see you sometime in the future."

"Yeah, OK. Thanks for the call. Bye." I shook my head to myself and felt a dull ache in my shoulder. My thoughts were interrupted by Shannon coming back in with a determined look on her face, but not much of a smile. "That's not a wire brush you're hiding there is it, Shannon?" I asked.

There was just the hint of a smile then. "Hmm, now, why didn't I think of that? Come on, Casanova, or maybe I should call you Marquis. Let's get this done."

I shook my head and smiled at her stab at humour because it was a common mistake to think that Dominants and Sadists are one and the same. Not that either of us were in the mood for me to correct that misconception.

She crossed to the bed, stood on my good side and put her arm around me to help me sit up. She smelt wonderful as she leaned in close and I felt her breast press against my chest as I lifted my arm around her and let her help me up. She then pulled the bed clothes back and helped me slide my legs around in preparation for standing up. Once on my unsteady feet she took a roll of what looked like plastic cling wrap and wound it round the bandages on my thigh, then helped me off with the sling. Any movement in my shoulder, no matter how minimal, hurt like hell. I winced.

Domin8

"It's going to hurt, I'm sorry. How's the pain in the leg, Dave?"

I replied, "So far so good, thanks."

"OK, I want you to keep your arm around me. I don't want you falling over and don't worry, and I'm stronger than I look, so lean on me."

Despite the circumstances, her using my name gave me some encouragement, and I needed that to help combat the pain I was feeling. Using her to lean on I stood up and felt a sharp stabbing pain in my wounded leg, but I was determined not to show it. Walking, or it would be better to describe it as hobbling, in agony was doable. It was very sore, yes, but the leg worked all right. It was stiff, and I felt as if my skin was pulled tightly everywhere all over my body.

I was very careful how I held on to her because I did not want her to think anything untoward was going on in my head, with my arm around her, and my hand gripped just above her hip and hers on the same place on me. But I must admit that, as she manoeuvred me into the bathroom, this whole experience was a lot less unpleasant than with Miss. Grumpy the day before.

"Can you lean against the wall so I can get your gown off? OK. What's so funny?" She had noticed me stifling a laugh and looked into my eyes questioningly, as I propped myself against the tiled wall. I felt as if I'd been caught out like a naughty schoolboy.

"I'm sorry. I'm not laughing at you, just at this weird situation. I'm about to be undressed by an incredibly beautiful woman, who I like quite a lot, and it's the most unsexy experience of my life."

"Yes, *David*, that's right. It's going to be unsexy, especially when I'm washing you, OK? I'm your nurse, not one of your floozy lovers, remember that. Oh, and stop with the compliments. You're embarrassing me."

She undid the ridiculous hospital gown and pulled it off me being very careful around my shoulder, for which I was grateful.

"Sorry, yes. I will try my best to stop calling you beautiful, even though you are, and I'm now standing buck naked in front of you. God this is so surreal." *"Funny,"* I thought, *"it didn't bother me in the slightest yesterday."*

"Try not to get your shoulder wet." She professionally ignored my comments as she turned the water on and waited until it was warm, then helped guide me under the cascading water. I leant against the wall with my good arm and kept myself turned away from her, my wounded side away from the water.

I tried. I tried really hard. I thought of football scores, angry customers with warranty complaints, sales budgets and gross profit targets and even remembered the entire colour range in Toyota by name and code. I tried anything and everything, rather than focus on the wonderful feeling of a stunningly beautiful woman washing my naked body with soapy hands in a hospital wash cloth. Much to my shock and horror, though, I failed despite my best efforts. I got an erection, and once her soapy hand got to touch me there, it was beautiful, teasing torture.

I didn't say a word and tried very hard not to moan, pant or make any sexual noises or movements while all the while I felt like I should crawl away and die. I supposed it must happen to her regularly. I'm not sure, but I got the feeling she did take longer washing that part of me, but that could just have been wishful thinking. All too soon it was over, and I was washed and rinsed, and she dried my back which didn't help my erection situation, but then she turned me round to face her. She started at the top and worked her way down until she was squatted in front of me

Domin8

drying my legs and to my absolute horror I sported an erection at her, face level.

"You must have been head of the queue when they handed these out." She actually smiled up at me.

I looked down at her gorgeous face, and shook my head, amazed that she would make a joke. She had the towel in both hands. Her right hand slowly worked my shaft while her left cupped my scrotum. She licked her lips and looked up at me. "Are you expecting me to do something about that?"

"No, Shannon, I don't want you to. It's pretty obvious how I feel right now and how much I'm attracted to you. But I think this isn't the time or the place for that. It would be disrespectful to you and your position. I'm sorry I got erect. I tried so hard not to, believe me I tried thinking of the most boring things in the world, and I failed miserably."

She stood up and let go of me but the end of it was touching her tummy as she stood in front of me not moving, perfectly aware of the touch.

"That was the correct answer, Dave, and also a compliment I will accept. Now let's a fresh gown back on and then get you back to bed." She smiled, a genuinely lovely smile, and I felt so incredibly good that I hadn't disappointed her.

Stephen B. King

Chapter 23 – Shannon (3) – Dianne (4) – Judith (3)

Day Nine to Twelve. Facing the Past

Only two things broke the monotonous humdrum of my hospital stay over the next three days. Firstly, a vase full of mixed flowers arrived from Judith with a card hoping I would get well soon and to call her anytime. I was more annoyed than pleased. After throwing the card in the bin, I asked Shannon, to find a patient in more need of the flowers than I.

The other excitement came in the form of shower time with Shannon, which was always a highlight. It always ended the same way, with me waddling back to bed with a raging erection, that took ages to go down. I'm sure she enjoyed the teasing and it seemed to me that the washing of my privates took longer and longer each time, but maybe I just imagined it.

Whenever she spent time with me we talked about lots of things. Most of it was just inconsequential chat and gossip, almost as if we both wanted to stay right away from any "dangerous" subjects. The more I spoke to her the more I realised I just loved her company. She had a wickedly direct sense of humour and on more than one occasion I couldn't understand why her husband had left her. After three days we laughed and joked together a lot, and I felt my feelings for her were reciprocated.

On my last day there I really didn't need her to help me shower as I had gotten most of my mobility back. The pain was manageable, especially after the pills kicked in, and I could walk unaided albeit slowly and gingerly. But she offered, and I couldn't refuse. She knew it was my last day, as soon as the doctor made his rounds and released me I would be gone. But he usually came late in the afternoon, and shower time with Shannon was late morning.

I noticed that she had not only closed the curtains around the bed which also obscured the bathroom door. This time she closed the door as well. The teasing and that day was more than enough and had gone on much longer than previous times, but she then looked up at me and said in a husky voice, "I've never had one this big in my hand before, let alone anywhere else in my body. God forgive me, but I am going to miss this."

I was squirming, "Shannon, you need to stop right now. Please stop," I whispered. My throat was dry and my voice croaky.

"Why?" She asked and looked up at me with a very mischievous smile on her face. "Its OK, Dave, I'm just kidding around with you."

She stepped away from me and busied herself tidying up and I thought for a moment as to what to say. "Shannon, really, you are an amazing woman. Would it be OK if I called you sometime? It's not likely to be anytime soon, but I would like to think I could one day."

"You don't have to. I didn't tease you it so you would want to call me, and I know you will have a tough time coming up with the funeral, and family stuff. I did it for me as much as for you. I may never get to handle another one as big as yours, and I'm embarrassed to say I enjoyed touching you. I'm sorry, I really shouldn't have done that."

She laughed, and I reached for her, but she stopped me firmly with a hand on my chest, and then stepped out of reach holding the same hand up in a stopping gesture. "No, you don't, mister, what I did before was bad enough. This is where I work."

Stephen B. King

I nodded, understanding. "Shannon, mentally and emotionally I'm a mess at the moment, and I don't know how I'm going to get through the next few days, weeks or even months. It's not going to be easy, but I know, no matter how bad it will be, it's no more than I deserve. When it is over, and the dust has settled, I would like to call you, and if you don't want me to, that's fine, I understand."

"David, David, David, do you really think I wouldn't want you to call me? Take your time, deal with what you need to deal with. I understand. It doesn't matter if its weeks or months. But there's one thing you must know before you ever think of picking up that phone?"

"I think I know what you are going to say, but go on."

"I'm a one-man woman, and I only want a relationship with a one-woman man. If you don't think you are capable of that, do us both a favour, and don't phone me. If you don't call, that's fine. I can live with that. Here is my number. I wrote it down for you, just in case you asked me for it."

She put a small pink piece of card into my hand. It had her name and number written on it in a purple pen, and just above her name was a small flower she had drawn. I thought that small detail summed her up perfectly.

"I swear to you; this is the truth. If and when I am capable of seeing anyone, I'd like it to be you. This has been, and will be, an ongoing nightmare I have to get through, all because of my actions, I know that. For the rest of my life I will never, ever be unfaithful again, no matter what, always assuming I find the right woman who wants to be with me, that is."

"Oh, I think you will find the right one. And your word is good enough, for now. Now get back to bed. I've got work to do."

Domin8

She got me back to bed, smiled and gave me a wave as she went back to work, and I spent the rest of the day thinking of her. I shouldn't have done that. I knew and I felt guilty for enjoying her company, but I am only human.

Later in the day the doctor called, checked my wounds and gave me a clean bill of health to go and a prescription for more painkillers. But I wouldn't leave until I had said goodbye to her, which meant waiting fully dressed in the clothes my son had brought in for me, sitting on the chair alongside the bed with the door open, so I could see her when she walked by.

She passed by half an hour later and saw me sitting there. She stuck her head in the door and said, "Most people can't wait to get out of here, but you're sitting there. Why?"

"Because I didn't want to go without saying goodbye to you, and to thank you for your care. You made this stay not only bearable, but pleasurable, and I couldn't go without telling you that."

She seemed genuinely pleased, but still felt the need to admonish me. "You daft bugger, get out of here. I was just doing my job, but thanks for the thought."

"Really, you do that for all of your patients do you?"

I smiled and winked, so she knew I was joking, and she smiled back before making a serious face. "No, Dave, I've never done anything like that before at work and probably never will again, I'm pretty sure. But don't let it go to your head. Do you want me to call you a cab? You're in no state to drive."

"My son is waiting downstairs in the car park for me. I told him I was waiting for you to say goodbye. We are going to the funeral home to talk about the service."

Stephen B. King

She looked at her watch and then said, "I'm due for a break. Let me tell the others, and I will walk you down and help find your son."

A few minutes later she walked alongside me to the elevator, and down and out into the warm afternoon sunshine where my son was waiting. I introduced them and told Jason she was my Florence Nightingale. She just laughed, shook his hand and said for him to look after me. After shaking my hand, she turned to leave and didn't look back. I smiled and waved after her. When I turned around, my son was staring at me, shaking his head.

XXX

After picking up the other two we had a meeting with the funeral director and discussed the service which was set for two days' time. Missy was very quiet; clearly she wasn't anywhere near ready to forgive me. She was at least civil to me, but distant.

Bryan offered to run me home after offering for me to stay with him for a few days until I was back on my feet. I contemplated it, but in the end just didn't feel right about it, and declined. I didn't think I was going to be terribly good company but thanked him anyway. He tried to be persistent but could see my mind was made up.

At home I felt rather nervous and anxious, but told myself it was natural having just been shot there, and I tried to relax. Sam had organised a glazier for me, the door had been repaired and the glass cleaned up. He had left a note on the table with his mobile number if I needed anything, or just felt like a chat. I was tempted to call him, but decided to hold off. I clicked the TV on for company and grabbed a beer.

Domin8

I'd no sooner sat down when my mobile rang. I had to stand back up and go to the breakfast bar where I had left it. The phone stopped ringing just as I got to it and I cursed. I checked the display and saw it was Judith, yet again, and was glad I had missed the call. *"Why is she being persistent?"* I wondered. I shrugged it off and went back to my seat.

I must have nodded off on the couch watching a John Wayne movie on the Classic channel, because the next thing I knew it was after eleven when my mobile rang again. It was Judith once more.

"Hi," I said. "Why are you calling, and why so late, Judith?"

"Oh, I was just a bit lonely and wanted to see if you were all right. I tried to call earlier, but there was no answer. I didn't catch you with another woman, did I?"

"What? Are you nuts? Another woman? Judith, seriously, no. You caught me asleep. What is the matter with you?"

"Don't be mad at me. I only wanted to make sure you were alright and I was just joking about the other woman. Did you get the flowers?"

I counted to ten slowly in my head, and then said. "As jokes go, that wasn't funny. Yes, I got the flowers thank you, but you shouldn't have done that. I'm not ready for this; it's my wife's funeral tomorrow. She was murdered because I had affairs, and right now I don't want to talk to anyone I had an affair with."

"You're mad at me, I'm sorry Dave, I was just trying to show you that you had someone out here that cared, I should have known better I suppose."

Now she was crying, and I felt bad for being so inconsiderate. "Judith, stop that." I said softly." It's nothing personal to you, and I do appreciate you cared enough to check on me. I'm sorry for being moody, but right now I'm mourning and I'm just not up to happy chats with old lovers."

"Are you saying I'm too old for you Dave? Joking, just joking. OK, I will hang up and leave you in peace, but do I have permission to get in touch in the future?"

Right then I would have agreed to anything to get her off the phone and out of my life. "Yeah, of course, we will catch up some time. Thanks for your concern. I'm sorry I was snappy; you woke me up was all. Look after yourself. Bye."

I hung up, shook my head and went to bed. Tomorrow would be another day.

XXX

The funeral was attended by over two hundred people, including family, friends and work colleagues from Di's work, as well as mine. Even Sam Collins came. They were all there, crowded into the chapel. The weather was fine, but it was without a doubt the saddest day of my life.

I was never more proud of my children than when they each spoke a eulogy about how wonderful a mother they had lost, and there was barely a dry eye in the crowd. Next was the pastor, who spoke about her life and achievements, based on things that we had all told him about her. Then, finally, it was the time I had been dreading: my turn. I limped slowly to the lectern to face the icy silence from the assembled.

I took a moment to look around. There were so many faces looking up, so many people blaming me and despising me. I could have cut the air with a knife. I took a deep breath and began, "I want to thank each and every one of you for coming today to help us celebrate Dianne's life. I know that anyone here who came in contact with her couldn't help but be touched by her kindness and spirit, and we will all miss her terribly."

"We were married twenty-six years but were together almost thirty, and we raised three incredible children together. I know most, if not all of you, think I didn't deserve her, and you would be right to think that. I didn't deserve such a wonderful woman as Dianne."

"She was, without doubt, a far better person than I could ever hope to be, and I was blessed to have had her in my life. Until the day I die I will always regret that her killer took her and not me. I think everyone knows it was my actions that led to her death, and I will suffer that burden as long as I live."

"If I could pass on any life lessons to others, it would be to take your wife, husband, lover or child, and hug them like there is no tomorrow, because sometimes, when you least expect it, there is no tomorrow."

"I will always miss Dianne and always live with the guilt of my actions, because she deserved so much better than me, and I am so, so incredibly sorry for everything. She was a beautiful woman, a spectacular mother and a very good friend."

"On the last day of her life she mourned the passing away of one of her patients who died of cancer. She had spent his last hours with him because he had no family of his own and she didn't want him to be alone when he died. Such was her heart that she would give up her time, to ease the passing of someone she barely knew. We are all so much poorer for her passing away, and she will be missed by all of us, I know."

As I looked around, I saw lots of people wiping tears away. At that moment I noticed someone at the very back of the hall. Dressed in black and holding a blood red rose was Judith. I was stunned into pausing. She noticed, gave a little wave, then left through the rear door.

"Let me finish by saying this. Dianne's nature was such that the last thing she would want is this. People crying at her passing. I have an open house for the rest of today. My children and I would like you all to come by, share a drink with us and celebrate her life, rather than mourn her death. Thank you again for coming."

I walked back to where the kids stood. Jason shook my hand, and then hugged me, followed by Bryan. Finally, even Missy hugged me. With tear-stained mascara on her cheeks, she threw her arms around me and said, "I love you, daddy, and I know mummy did too. She would have been proud of your speech. I still hate what you did behind her back, but I know you didn't mean for it to happen the way it did."

That was when I cried. I had held it in as long as I could but I sobbed hugging my daughter tightly, and didn't care who heard. I know that she didn't forgive me completely. It would be a long, long time for that, but her words touched me deeply on top of what was a very emotional day for us all.

The rest of the day passed slowly. She was buried as she was against cremation, and the service was as lovely as a service can be when it's someone you love being buried. I lost count of the people who came along to the wake but it would have been around a hundred or more. I had arranged a last minute caterer and was glad my son had suggested it.

I must admit to feeling paranoia as I kept expecting to turn around to see Judith standing there, but fortunately she didn't show. I'm not sure what I would have said to her if she had, but I'm sure I would have thrown her out on her arse, as I was already angry that she had turned up at the chapel.

Domin8

By ten that night it was only the kids and I left. The caterers had cleaned up and gone, and the four of us just sat and chatted, remembering times with their mother. The only thing I could say to them was to apologise once more and to say that we are who and what we are. I had faults, many of them, and deeply regretted the consequences of my selfishness. They didn't answer; there was nothing to say that hadn't already been said. They left by eleven and exhausted I went to bed.

On the bedside cabinet was my phone where I had left it, it was showing one message, and my heart sunk as I knew who it would be from.

Judith: I was proud of you, today ♥

I turned the phone off and put it inside my top drawer. Judith was a problem for another day. I was dead on my feet and slept for ten hours straight.

Stephen B. King

Chapter 24 - Sarah Jane – Shannon (4) – Judith (4)

Day Thirteen to Twenty-Nine. Time Away

I had cooked eggs with toast late in the morning the next day and wondered what the hell I was going to do for a month. George had spoken to me at the wake, and explained that the Board were happy things had quietened down, but were insistent I spent more time away from the dealership. I had avoided the twenty or more calls from reporters, hoping that if I ignored them, they would ignore me. I understood the Board's position and was grateful that they had kept the faith in me, and that I had a job to go back to in a month's time. *"That's all well and good,"* I thought to myself, *"but what do I do for a month?"*

My shoulder was still sore but usable, in fact I had been told to use it now and had been given exercises by the physiotherapist so that the muscles didn't shrink. I suddenly had a brain wave and called Drew Harris in Exmouth, to see if his charter boat was available.

Four years prior I had organised a fishing charter as a target based incentive for my sales people and arranged Drew and his boat to take those who achieved it. Six did and I hosted then for a four-day long weekend and had a fantastic time. It was so good it became a yearly event, and spurred the salespeople on to win a coveted spot. Drew became a good friend, and I had referred numerous other friends and acquaintances to use him for charters.

Drew said he did have a window of opportunity coming up, and I asked if we could go down the coast for a few days. I mightn't be able to fish strenuously, I explained, but I got on well with him and his deck hand Brad, and I loved being on the ocean so I knew it would be a great way to pass some time. His next charter was already due, and he was booked solid for the following ten days. He suggested fishing, snorkelling and drinking beer for six days at a cut rate which he called his 'standby' rate of five thousand dollars as soon as he got back. I immediately accepted.

In the interim I decided to fly out of Perth and get away, and The Gold Coast seemed like a good idea. The sun, surf and nightlife would help get my mind off the guilt and recriminations I was feeling. The Gold Coast and then straight up to Exmouth would be just the ticket, I felt, though I also thought it was running away. Opposing that thought was to wonder what I would do if I didn't get away, probably go quietly mad.

Exmouth sits on the Ningaloo Reef, in the northern part of Western Australia, and has some incredible black and blue marlin to catch, along with a myriad of other fish that inhabited the massive and stunningly beautiful reef. Usually, at that time of year, it enjoyed fantastic weather, but being on a peninsula, if the weather was bad there was always the other side of the gulf to find protected waters. I loved the place and the relaxed carefree attitude of the locals, and six days on a boat would be just about perfect.

During the Second World War, Exmouth had a large American base that had strategic value. These days the bases are mostly gone, though you can see where they were. It's now most famous for the whale sharks which cruise by, and the town enjoys a massive tourist influx during the season, with people wanting to swim with these massive but gentle creatures. During the season the population more than triples, and a small country town

Stephen B. King

becomes a bustling mini-metropolis full of backpackers and families on holidays.

I opened up my iPad and booked round trip flights departing that evening then called the kids to explain where I was going. They all thought it was a good idea to get some sun and relaxation away from all that had happened. Jason offered to mind the house, but I told him not to worry, the alarm would be set. As it happened, though, when I left I forgot to arm it and was halfway to the airport in the cab when I realised my mistake.

As an afterthought I called Sam and let him know where I was going in case something cropped up that he needed me for. I also mentioned the alarm. I let him know that, while I had my mobile there could well be long periods I would be out of range. He still had a key and offered to keep an eye on the house for me, and set the alarm, for which I was grateful.

Nothing of any note happened in Queensland. I relaxed, saw some sights and kept myself to myself, most days not even turning on my phone. I read two books, which was a record for me, spent time in the casino losing around three thousand for the entire trip and went to Dracula's theatre restaurant. I admit that on two or three occasions I fell into bed, alone, drunk and feeling very sad and sorry for myself.

By seven-thirty at night ten days later I was climbing aboard the Sarah Jane, in Exmouth, a fifty-five-foot game cruiser built for comfort and fishing. It was a sensational boat. No sooner was I aboard did the guys threw the ropes, and in the dying rays of the evening sun we cast off to head around to Tantabiddi, where we were going to spend the first night at a mooring.

The guys were good company, and I talked to them about what had been happening. Being men's men they understood my wandering eye and were naturally shocked at the extreme outcomes. We cooked on the barbeque at the stern of the boat,

Domin8

drank ice cold beer and talked about women, fish and how good the steaks were. The charter was costing me a lot, but I knew it would be worth every cent to get away with two good guys and relax for the week.

The weather really turned it on over the next few days, and we chased schools of tuna by spotting birds diving into the water for bait fish that they were feeding on below. I landed a smallish black marlin which gave my shoulder a workout, and I was in considerable pain by the time we put a tag in it and set it free. Luckily, I had packed the painkillers I had been given and dry swallowed two.

At the mooring that evening I took a spectacular picture on my phone of the sunset and sent it to the kids with a short note that I was OK, adding that I hoped they were too. Then, on a whim, I sent it to Shannon with a short message telling her where I was, what I was doing and that I had thought of her.

She sent back a nice reply, wishing me good luck with the fishing and thanking me for sending her such a golden sunset. She added it was currently raining in Perth, and I was a bastard for rubbing her nose in it, but she added a smiley face to let me know she was joking. I just loved her straight-forward sense of humour.

I am not into selfies but just to tease her further (after all she was the queen of tease in my book), I took a selfie with the two guys on either side of me on the stern of the boat, with the shoreline in the fading sun as a backdrop all holding beers saluting her. This one I sent her with the caption, "Wish you were here." She sent back a message saying that she wished she was too.

Drew broke out a decent bottle of red wine, and we sat around chatting. I told them about her and posed the question, with all that had happened, when was a good time to even begin to think about dating again?

Brad asked "How do you feel about her, Dave?"

I had to stop and think about that. Up until then, every time I got close to thinking about her I forced myself not to. If I was addicted to sex, as everyone thought I was, I was trying to go cold turkey.

"Brad, I just don't know. I'm torn in several different ways at once. On the one hand I don't want to be with anyone, as I still ache for Di and know it was me fucking around behind her back that got her killed. Part of me thinks I should never date again as some sort of penance to her memory. Then again, I like Shannon. She is smart and funny but also a very-strong willed woman and to be honest, I know that women like her don't come along very often. She is not the sort to be anyone's quick fuck. She's better than that, and I think she is amazing. But, when I think that, I'm angry at myself for even having that thought, this early. Does that make sense?"

"Is she good looking?" He asked as he filled up my wine glass again.

"Yeah, she is. She's stunning if you want the truth," I admitted.

Drew, a renowned "boob man," waited until I had a mouth full of wine, then asked, "Has she got good tits?"

I spat the wine out and choked at the same time with laughter. Drew was a simple man, and basically by his rules if Shannon had good tits I should go with her, but if she didn't I should wait longer in a period of mourning.

Such were the simplistic conversations we had about all sorts of things that wonderful night. They were fishermen, and no matter how complicated something could be, they helped remind me that there was always a simple way of looking at it.

The next morning it was bright and sunny again, but we were all a bit hung over and got away from the mooring later than we had intended. Twenty or so kilometres off shore we were treated to three whales, including a calf, jumping and putting on a show for us. We spent twenty minutes with them taking some photos and being in awe of such huge majestic creatures, jumping clear out of the water.

It was another beautiful day in paradise with some decent fish being caught, which would be barbequed later that evening for dinner, along with one of Brad's salads and quality alcohol.

That evening as we tied up to the mooring I turned my phone on hoping for a message from Shannon, but when the message tone did sound, my heart sank through the deck. I opened it up and read:

Judith: Why are you ignoring me now you are free? Why couldn't you love me back? Couldn't you tell how much I loved you when we were together? Even Derek knew how much I was in love with you, that's why he eventually left me. Your wife dying was fate, so we could be together but now you totally ignore me. When Derek left me I got sick, but I'm not letting them put me back in that place. I just wanted you to know that all I ever wanted was to love you. Goodbye, Dave.

"Oh my fucking God," I thought angrily. I debated whether to reply or not and decided not to. I was livid and decided that she wasn't worth it, with her persistence and a totally inappropriate timing. She had gotten completely out of control, and when I got back I would have to see her and tell her it was over a long time ago for me, and I wasn't going to start it up again—not anytime

soon anyway. And probably never, seeing how she was turning out to be.

I thought I could extricate myself from her once I explained that I had no interest in being with her now. It could be weeks or months or never that I was ready to be with another woman, I would try to explain. But once I had that thought, then I naturally thought of Shannon and realised that I did want to be with her, and possibly sooner rather than later. If she would want to be with me, that was. The problem was that as soon, as I thought that, I then admonished myself because there was no way I should even be thinking those thoughts so soon after causing the death of Dianne and the others.

One thing was for sure; I was in utter turmoil inside my head as my thoughts jumbled and stumbled around in the dark, and Judith wasn't helping one little bit. She was making my life worse, and I was going to have to tell her in no uncertain terms so she clearly understood to leave me the fuck alone.

Drew put an ice cold beer in my hand and clinked his bottle against mine. I downed half of it then put the bottle and my phone down and dove into the water off the marlin board to cool down. With the fear of sharks being ever present I didn't stay in the water long: just enough to forget about Judith's message and get over my anger.

A smaller boat approached and hailed us. It came alongside and the skipper asked if we had caught any fish. We had had a good day with three ruby snapper, some cod, a Spanish mackerel and two beautiful Mahi-mahi. They offered to swap one decent fish for a couple of crayfish and half a bucket of giant prawns they had netter earlier in the day, and we readily agreed.

We opened the first bottle of white wine while Drew and I cleaned the prawns and crayfish and Brad made a salad and three sauces: garlic butter for the crayfish, a hot spicy chilli sauce and a

Domin8

cooling aioli for the prawns. Both guys were amazing cooks, and by the time we had finished one of the best meals of my life, we had downed four bottles of wine on top of the beers earlier. I was also on painkillers. None of us were feeling any pain, and I went up to the bow and sat down to phone Shannon.

Perhaps it was the alcohol, or more likely my weak will, that made me want to speak to her. I know I shouldn't have called her, but the plain simple fact was that I missed her and wanted some part of her in my life. I knew I shouldn't want that—the guilt level was phenomenal, but I suppose at the back of my mind was the thought that if I was too slow, I might miss her to someone else.

Because I was pleasantly drunk, I made the call against the logical part of my brain telling me not to. She seemed genuinely pleased to hear from me, and we chatted for a while about the trip, the meal we just had, her work and the conversation just kind of petered into a long silence.

"What's wrong, Dave. Why did you really call?"

I paused and gathered my thoughts in my fuzzy, alcohol-fuelled brain, "Shannon, I wouldn't blame you, not one little bit if you wanted me to leave you alone. Let's face it, I'm a complete mess, with a lot of emotional baggage at the moment to work through, and if I were even half a decent man I wouldn't be calling you."

"Go on. Is this your way of saying goodbye to me, Dave?"

"Good God, no. It's actually the complete opposite. I can't stop thinking about you. But when I do a part of me screams abuse at myself because I tell myself I shouldn't be. I don't deserve to be thinking of anyone, and I should be mourning my wife of twenty-six years. Does that make sense?"

"Yes, it does. So what do you want to do?"

Stephen B. King

"I've been so dishonest for such a long time, and I don't want to do that anymore, so the short answer to your question is I want to be honest with you. I don't deserve you. I don't deserve a second chance at life with anyone, and you should be with someone a lot better than me. But I think about you all the time, and I think we have a connection. If you want my advice, you should tell me to leave you alone, and I wouldn't blame you for that."

"Are you proposing to me, Dave?" Then she laughed and added, "I'm kidding, just kidding. I do that when I'm nervous, sorry."

I loved her sense of humour and smiled, then waited patiently for her to digest things.

"I need to think about this. Is that all right? You have to admit, this situation is, well, let's just call it unusual. To be honest, I don't know if I am ready for you, yet. I thought I wouldn't hear from you for quite a while, if ever, but at the same time I'm glad you did call."

"Of course, it is all right. Take all the time you need. Right now I value your friendship, and next to my children, you are the only normal decent person in my life. One day I hope we become a bit more than friends."

"I am thirty-nine years old, which should tell you something about my feelings. Common sense tells me I should run away and hide from you, that you are dangerous. But, oh, I don't know, something is telling me to hang around, and that the ride might just be worth it."

"There is something else I want you to know, which may affect your thinking, and this will show how I have changed. I will never lie, hide or bend the truth to you, so for better or worse, you should know this."

251

Domin8

I told her about Judith, from start to finish, including the most recent message from her, and finished by reiterating she would be best if she told me to leave her alone. There was a very long silence, and I expected the worst to follow it.

Eventually she said "You are one of a kind, aren't you? I'm not into competition, Dave. I told you I'm a one-man woman, and I'm not dragging myself down ever again, because of a man. I've come to realise I'm better than that."

"I know. I like that about you. Shannon, this isn't about having sex with you, although I am sure that would be incredible. I just feel like I want some part of you in my life. If that's just as a friend, then so be it.

"When do you get back?"

"I fly back Saturday morning, around about ten."

"I'm going to think about things for a couple of days, Dave. In the meantime, don't ring me or message me. On Saturday one of two things will happen; either I won't message you or I will. If I don't it means I decided against it and would appreciate you respecting that. But if I do message it will be to give you my address. If I send you my home address you can pick me up at seven and we'll go to dinner, as friends, and talk about things. Maybe we won't like each other on a date or maybe we will. If I message you, then we will find out, won't we? One last question, and please be honest. Do I resemble your wife in some way?"

"Other than the fact you are both nurses, no, you don't. I'm not interested in a carbon copy of Dianne. I appreciate you for who you are."

"And you promise me, if I say yes, there would never, ever be any more of this internet stuff?"

Stephen B. King

"I swear to you, on my children's lives, that I will never step foot in a chatroom or dating site again while we are together. In fact, let me amend that, I will never play online in my life ever again."

There was another silence before she said, "I'm going to have a long hot bath, Dave. It was a tough day at work. I'm going to have a glass of wine, soak in the water and think about things. You may be worth the effort and trouble. I'm not sure yet. But I have always thought that everyone deserves a second chance in life. Enjoy the rest of your break and thanks for calling, bye."

She was gone, and my glass was empty. I realised the breeze, which had popped up, was chilly. Time to go below deck and sleep. I would have to try very hard not to imagine Shannon laying back naked in a long, hot bath, and I knew her well enough to know she had only mentioned that so that I would think of her. She was born a natural tease.

Domin8

Chapter 25 – Shannon (5) – Judith (7)

Day Thirty. Shadow and Light

It was a grey overcast day as the plane touched down back in Perth. The weather matched my mood because I did not see a message from Shannon when I turned my phone back on late Saturday morning. I felt saddened by that, but not heartbroken, because I understood her decision not to want to see me again. I didn't really blame her in the slightest.

It had now been almost four weeks since Dianne had been so brutally murdered, and I knew in my heart the last thing in the world I should be thinking about was another woman. But who can control their own feelings? And who could say when the right time was to be able to think of someone else. Would it be acceptable in a month, or six or a year?

All I knew was that I had hoped she would say yes, and felt sad that she hadn't. *"Oh well,"* I thought, *"life goes on."* While I was thinking that I realised I had not had any further word from Judith, thankfully. I decided I should make some sort of contact with her and determined I would do it the following day. I had washing and some long overdue housework to do, and that was the last thought I had of Judith, until later that afternoon.

I picked up my bag and polystyrene container full with over twenty kilos of frozen fish fillets, packed in dry ice to share with the kids, and made my way out to the cab rank, then home back to Applecross where I busied myself doing all the mundane things I used to take for granted that Dianne did.

Stephen B. King

By two o'clock I was kneeling, which was no mean feat with my leg still sore, yanking weeds out of the front flower bed. The clouds had disappeared, and it was bright and warm, when a shadow crossed in front of me and stopped. I first saw the white stiletto heels and white stocking clad legs, and as my eyes travelled upwards, my heart sunk. I knew who was standing in front of me long before I reached her face.

"Hi, Dave. Why didn't you reply to my messages?" Judith looked lovely in a mid-length white skirt and white shirt opened just enough to show the edge of a white bra holding her full, firm breasts. She stood with head cocked on one side, a white hat on her head and large sunglasses on her nose. The sun gave her a halo from my kneeling position.

"Hi Judith, you look lovely today. I've been away, firstly in Queensland and then in Exmouth fishing on a boat for a week and only got back today. I did get your messages and was going to give you a call tomorrow once I caught up with everything here."

"Thank you, kind sir, for saying I look nice."

She gave a little curtsey and then added, "Well, I saved you forty cents on the phone call. Did you want to talk or just fuck me?" With that she lifted her skirt up to her waist to show everything was white underneath too: suspender belt and see though lace thong.

The old Dave Barndon would have weakened, but not the new one. My anger with her had been building for days, and I lost my temper and let it fly at her, "What the fuck are you doing, Judith? This is my home, and my wife has only just been buried. I want you to fuck off and leave me alone. This is not going to work, not now, not ever."

She pulled her panty gusset to one side to show me how wet she was, "You don't mean that, Dave. I know you want some of my honey pie, and you know I can take you to the moon and back."

"You look ridiculous, Judith. Grow up. What the fuck are you doing? GO AWAY and don't ever come back. I never want to see you again. I can't be much clearer than that. LEAVE ME ALONE!"

She burst into tears and fell to her knees, hysterical. "You don't mean that Dave. Don't send me away. I'm sorry, please forgive me and give me a second chance. I missed you so much. It's been so long, and I know you love me, too."

"Love? You don't know a thing about love, Judith. If you did you wouldn't be here making yourself look like a stupid, lovelorn tramp, while I'm trying to grieve for my wife. I never loved you. I fucked you a few times, no strings attached, remember? We had an affair, some good times and memories, and it ended ages ago. We were both married and we had some great sex, but don't call it love Judith. Grow up, for fuck's sake."

"Is that all I was to you, Dave? Just a cheap fuck? Was that it? Well, it wasn't for me. My husband left me over you because he knew I loved you more than him. But because I loved you I never contacted you, I respected you were married; I suffered in silence, waiting and hoping someday we would get another chance. And then, when I was at my darkest, fate stepped in. Your wife died and now we do have a second chance."

I was enraged with her, more than I had ever been with anyone in my life. I stood up, ignoring the pain in my leg, and shouted at her, "She didn't die, you stupid fucking bitch. She was murdered, in our home, because I had had affairs including one with you. And you have the fucking nerve to turn up here lifting your skirt for the whole neighbourhood to see and tell me that *because* she was slaughtered, we have a second chance? What is wrong with you? Go away, Judith, leave me the fuck alone, and don't ever come back."

She turned from crying hysteric to ice cold and calm in a flash. She calmly stood and pulled her skirt down and smoothed out the wrinkles. Then she adjusted her sunglasses on her nose and turned away. Mid-turn, she stopped and said in a voice bereft of any feeling whatsoever, "You had your chance, Dave. You'll be sorry; I promise you that." Her voice sounded like it came from the grave.

She walked away and I watched her disappear around the corner. She must have parked her car at the park because a few seconds later I heard a car start and drive away.

I was trembling with rage. I picked up my garden tools and bucket and went back inside, dropped them by the front door and went straight to the bar and poured out a very large whisky; which disappeared in three gulps. My eyes watered and throat burned, and I slammed the glass down to fill it again. Luckily, it didn't shatter in my hand; I didn't need any more cuts on my body.

From the kitchen I heard my phone ring and raced to it. Knowing it would be Judith, I had more to say to her, and screamed into the receiver, "WILL YOU FUCKING WELL LEAVE ME ALONE!"

It wasn't her, though. It was Shannon who, in a very confused and hurt voice, said, "Dave, what's wrong? What have I done?"

"Oh God, I'm so sorry. I thought you were someone else." She immediately asked what was wrong. I could have lied. I could have told her nothing or made up an excuse, but instead I told her the truth. In doing so my voice broke with anger and pain that Judith could have been so uncaring to behave like that at my house.

Domin8

"What's your address, Dave? I'm coming over right now."

Twenty minutes later I had calmed down and opened the front door to her. She was in her nursing uniform and had parked her black Honda Civic in the driveway. She fell into my arms and hugged me. It felt so right. The hug lasted a long few minutes, and I didn't want to let her go. I led her inside not noticing the white Toyota Corolla drive by, with an angry, hysterically tearful Judith driving.

XXX

We sat in the alfresco area where I had been shot next to the pool. There were still blood stains that had seeped into the pavers, which wouldn't come out no matter how much I had scrubbed. "*I am going to have to replace them,*" I thought absently while we chatted.

We talked for quite a while about Judith. I tried to explain what had happened, which was difficult as I didn't understand it myself. When we had exhausted the subject, I asked her, "So that's enough of my problems about a disturbed woman stalking me. How come you phoned? Was it to tell me in person you decided against getting together?"

Her cheeks went pink, and she shook her head. "I hadn't made any decision, which was why I called. I had been called into work, which I don't normally do weekends, but there was a shortage of nurses, and they pleaded. We were very busy, and every time I tried to make a decision to message you or not I didn't know what to say. I still don't. So I decided to call when I finished my shift in order to listen to your voice, hoping that would guide me. Once I heard how upset you were the decision was made for me; I had to come and see you."

Stephen B. King

I reached over and put my hand over hers, "Thank you for doing that. You really are an amazing woman."

"Stop it already with the compliments. I'm here, so what shall we do?"

"Well, you are wearing your uniform, and there is something incredibly sexy about women in uniform. Oh, sorry, you meant what we shall do about the future, not right now. I'm kidding, just kidding."

She was waggling a finger at me sternly. I held my hands up and laughed and was pleased to see she laughed too.

"Do I really turn you on wearing my uniform?" She asked, and her eyes twinkled with pleasure.

Damn, the woman knew how to tease. "You could wear a hessian sack and turn me on."

"I will bear that in mind for later when you pick me up for dinner. I have a potato sack in the pantry."

"You are a very brave woman. Shall we say seven-thirty?"

She nodded and gave me her address. We stood and for the first time in a long, long time, I was uncertain what to do, even nervous for fear of making a mistake. She could tell and smiling, she leant in and kissed my cheek. It was just a peck, but it meant a lot.

"Don't be late."

"Oh, I won't." I walked her to the door and opened it for her; she turned and kissed me on the lips. I wanted to kiss her back but didn't feel she wanted that kind of kiss, but as short kisses go, it was right up there approaching the stratosphere.

I watched her get into her car and drive away and then I looked at my watch. I had to make a move and get ready.

Domin8

XXX

I took her to Lord Nelson's, which is a stunning seafood restaurant built on a jetty in the swan river, and had a wonderful dinner. The service, ambience and wine were perfect, and Shannon looked spectacular in an orange mid-length dress and a matching orange ribbon in her hair. She looked beautiful and happy, with her eyes sparkling in the dim candle light.

I wore a black suit, with a dark blue tie and a white silk shirt. Bearing in mind the tumbler of scotch I had downed earlier and wanting to enjoy a glass or three of wine with dinner to ease my nerves, I had decided not to drive. I booked a limo for four hours and had him pick me up at seven. I had ordered a bottle of Moet in a bucket of ice and two glasses in the back and felt really anxious, which, historically, was most unlike me.

The car was too big to navigate in her driveway so he stopped half on the kerb and half on the road in front of her small but very nice home. She had a manicured lawn and stunning floral displays in beds and terraces in the front garden.

When she opened the door to me she saw the limo and laughed, "So we're not being ostentatious tonight at all then? Couldn't you find a bigger limo for the two of us, Dave?"

I looked back at the car and had to agree; perhaps it was just a little over the top. I laughed, "I wanted the stretch Hummer, but it was out already."

"Thank God you didn't. That wouldn't even fit in the street. Let me get my bag and keys. Won't be a tick."

Stephen B. King

When she returned and locked the door I held my arm out. She put hers through mine, and we walked back to the car where the driver was holding the door open for us.

"OK, you win. I'm suitably impressed, and OH MY GOD you got champagne as well," she said, as she looked inside at the glowing coloured lights and plush leather interior.

We sat down, and I poured two drinks in crystal flutes, handing one to her. She shook her head at me, with a smile on her face and said, "I've never been in a stretch limo before. Just so you know, for next time, I'm more of a bring-your-own-wine Chinese restaurant kind of girl."

"I will remember that, *for next time*, but for tonight I wanted it to be something special. By the way, I'm more of a beer and barbeque kind of guy, so this won't be happening too often. You won't see me wearing a suit and tie too many more times either, so take a picture. Wearing a suit is for work, weddings and funerals, so far as I am concerned."

She sipped her champagne and asked, "So you are assuming this will happen again, are you, Dave?"

"You know one of the things I like about you is that sometimes, especially when you get flustered, you talk in questions, and when you do, you add my name at the end. It's cute."

"What do you mean by that, Dave?" When she realised she did it again she burst into laughter.

"You won't come out and say no to something. You will ask if I expect it to be a no. You are very defensive, but passive aggressive at the same time. I really like that about you. You are unique."

Domin8

"Are you taking the mickey, Dave? Oh my God, I just did it yet again, didn't I?"

We both laughed and that set the tone for the night. We had had a nice drive along the river, but we were barely halfway through the champagne by the time we arrived and she was concerned about the wastage. I reassured her that the driver was going to wait for us, and the wine would be on ice until we returned.

She was a little in awe of the restaurant, especially when she saw a TV newsreader at one table and two famous football players with their wives at another. We were shown to a table against a window looking out across the river. I ordered bourbon. She asked for a gin and tonic.

"Is this where you bring you girlfriends, Dave? I feel a bit like a fish out of water here."

I reached across the table and took her hand in mine. She was trembling ever so slightly. She looked into my eyes as I quietly said, "There is only one woman I've ever come her with, my late wife. Even that was a long time ago, for our twenty-fifth wedding anniversary. Also, let me tell you, you are so not like a fish out of water here; you are the most beautiful woman in the place. And you haven't spent four hours today having a facial, your dress isn't Christian Dior, but you are stunning. There isn't any other woman here I would rather be with."

She reached across and lightly punched my arm while biting her lip, "You are so full of shit, but it's good shit. You do know how to make a woman feel special."

"Only the ones who are special."

We spoke about our lives: where we went to school, music we liked, movies and all sorts of other things. We avoided the elephant in the room right up until dessert, when she finally asked, "Dave, it's been a lovely night, but I have to know; how did you get into that mess with all those women?"

I told her everything—no secrets—starting with the TV show that started it all, which had grown into a fascination for women who were submissive by nature. I finished at the present day.

She never interrupted, never asked a question and didn't seem shocked or horrified. She just seemed interested, "So you met Judith online?" She asked, finally.

"No, I had a short fling with her months before I got involved in that lifestyle."

She looked troubled, so I told her how we had met: that we were both married, that he knew about it all and that it was just occasional, no-strings sex.

"But, Dave, for her, obviously it was more."

"Well, I realise that now, but I certainly didn't know that then. She never told me that. She never said she loved me. Yes, she was depressed at times, more so towards the end, but I just thought she was a bit bipolar. There was also the brother. What a weird little fuck he was, and I think he was giving her grief, but she would never talk to me about it, and believe me I tried. She just never said a word about anything. She was either happy and desperate for sex, or depressed and miserable; there were never any half measures with her. We just kind of stopped seeing each other. It wasn't a plan. It just ran its course and then petered out, and that was the last I saw or heard from her until after Di was killed."

"But, now she says she always loved you, and her husband left her because of that love."

"Yes, and that bothers me, because that goes against everything she said at the time. Her hubby loved the fact that she

Domin8

slept around, according to her. He used to get off on her telling him everything we did. She said she used to masturbate him while she talked about it, and he couldn't wait to hear all the details."

Shannon shook her head and looked disgusted at that mental image. "Ugh, that's just way too much information there. And you, Dave, are you that Dominant, really?"

"No, I'm not at all. I played the part because I was fascinated by how a woman could be so submissive. I have to admit it was fun, but I was interested in two things. First, no strings sex to satisfy my wants and needs. Secondly trying to understand how these women could be so submissive, because I find it so interesting. Let me ask you a question, have you read Fifty Shades of Grey?"

She blushed and said, "Yes, it was pretty ordinary, really. It didn't do much for me, but everyone at work was yabbering about it, and so I had to find out for myself."

"And did any part of it turn you on when you were reading it?" She nodded, too embarrassed to admit it out loud.

"You see? We all have varying degrees of fascination about the subject, and I got sucked deep into it the lifestyle, to my shame and horror in the light of later events."

She looked out of the window over the river for a long time, and I watched her face, trying to read her. I feared it was going to be all too much for her, and in re-telling it, I would have understood if she agreed that it was. Eventually she turned back and said, "It must have taken a lot for you to admit all that to me. Thank you, Dave. It's a lot for me to take in, but I appreciate you opening up so much. Let's go back to your place now, can we? I think it's time for me to tell you my story, too."

I paid the bill, and then we rode in silence, holding hands, and sipping the last of the champagne, back to my place. I wanted to give her time and to let her come to grips with everything I had told her. I was glad it was out in the open. If knowing that stuff killed any future with her, then so be it. *"Better now than later,"* I thought. I didn't want there to be any secrets between us, if there could ever be an us, that was.

When we arrived back at the house she asked to use the toilet. I showed her where it was and pointed out the main bathroom alongside and went to put the coffee machine on. Within three minutes I heard her call out my name: not as a scream, but more of a loud, urgent shout. I went running.

I found her in the bathroom, and the first thing I noticed was that it was lit by several candles around the room, which I certainly had not done. Shannon was standing in the doorway, and I had to look around her to see what had upset her.

There laying in the bath, was Judith, naked. The bath was full of a combination of water and her blood, making the water pink. She had used a razor blade and slit both her wrists longways. There was blood everywhere, and one look at her glazed wide open eyes was enough to know she was dead. On the tiles above the bath, she had written in her own blood:

"WHY HER AND NOT ME?"

Domin8

Chapter 26 – Starsky and Hutch (7) Shannon (6)
Day Thirty-One. The Nightmare Returns

I put my arm around Shannon and led her away, back to the family room. Being a nurse, she had seen more blood that I ever had, but she was visibly shaken, as was I.

I phoned Felix's number, and he answered with a gruff, "This better be fucking good, Dave, I'm in bed."

"Felix, there is a woman from my past, who has broken into my home and killed herself in the bathtub."

A full thirty seconds passed in silence while he processed what I was telling him. Eventually he said, "Another one, Dave? Jesus H. fucking Christ. Are you serious, another one?"

"Yes, another one. What do you want me to do?"

"For a start, don't date any more women. Join a fucking monastery. Stay there; don't touch anything. I will be there soon. Ring Sam and tell him, too, will you? May as well fuck up his weekend as well."

He was gone. I dialled Sam's number but it went through to his message bank. I left a detailed message including that Felix was on his way, then I went and sat with Shannon. I put my arm around her shoulders and held her tightly, silently, as there seemed to be nothing I could say. In my heart, I knew this was the end between us and maybe that was just as well. I couldn't take any more deaths.

Stephen B. King

XXX

The sun was coming up when I drove Shannon back to her place, expecting her to never want anything to do with me again. Who could blame her for that? Once again my house had been swarming with police, forensics and a medical examiner, and every inch of the house was searched.

The neighbours would start a petition to get me out of the street, I was sure of that. I was also sure this would spell the end of my job when it hit the press, as it was sure to do. I just didn't care about anything anymore. I felt completely dead, except for my feelings for Shannon, and I knew she would be wondering why the hell she agreed to go out with me in the first place.

Judith had come prepared. She had brought with her candles, a bottle of wine and a crow bar to jemmy the laundry door open, and of course, a razor blade. She had undressed and folded her clothes, including her underwear, neatly on the bed I had shared for twenty-six years with Dianne. Then she had run herself the bath, poured herself a last drink and cut her wrists open, before writing me a message sometime before she passed out.

Sam, who turned up dishevelled, ten minutes after Felix, took Shannon into the dining room and took her statement, while I was questioned sitting on the family room couch. When asked what the message meant I could only explain what had happened earlier in the day and theorised that Judith had stayed in the area and seen Shannon arrive. I showed him the text messages from her and told them how she had turned up at the funeral.

"Did you have sex with her here in your home, at any time, Dave?" Felix asked me, to which I said no, only ever at her house, when her husband was away at the mine site.

Domin8

"How did she know where you lived, do you think?" And to that I had no answer. I guessed she had followed me home at some point in time.

Sam brought Shannon back into the room, and I saw them conferring in the kitchen before the both came back. Sam said, "Ms. McGuire, thank you for your help. We are sorry you have had such a shock. We are going to let you go home now. Dave, you need to vacate the house until Monday when forensics gives us the all clear."

Felix then added, "We will make some more inquiries, and we would like you both to come in at 1PM Monday and make a formal statement. This seems pretty open and shut, but we must prepare a report for the coroner's office. I'm sure you understand, in light of other recent events." He looked at me pointedly, and I nodded.

"Ms. McGuire, can I just confirm with you that you first met Dave here at the hospital after he was shot. You've never met him before?"

"Yes, I have never met Dave before he was shot, and I am not, and have never been, one of his online lovers." Her tone was cold, understandably so.

"Dave, we were intending to get in touch with you first thing Monday morning. Regardless of tonight's episode, as there are some issues still ongoing with the other three murders that we are not happy with. We had come to have serious doubts that they were committed by Clinton Money."

I sat there, open mouthed and totally confused, but I then remembered I had experienced lingering doubts myself at the time but had ignored them.

"We now believe the catalyst for Mr. Mooney's attempt to kill you occurred after your wife was killed, when we interviewed

268

him at his place of work about his wife's infidelities. His workmates, who apparently all thought he was a bit loopy anyway, took the piss out of him, which we think caused him to become enraged. He then went home, beat his wife, and then shot you the next day. We do not think he killed your wife or the other two women before her, as his alibi for the first murder was as tight as yours. There is also the issue of the doll tied to a brick and thrown through your window."

I had forgotten all about that.

"It was covered in blood you will remember—cat blood as it turns out—which also tells us it's someone pretty sick to kill a cat just to dip a doll in the blood. But the knot in the string holding the doll to the brick had bite marks in it. Clearly the person found it tricky to tie and used their teeth to hold one end, and we were able to get some DNA from it. Not enough for identification. It was far too degraded for that, but what they can tell us it was a woman's DNA."

Suddenly, everything became clear in my mind, in a warped kind of way. "Judith." I said.

"Well, Dave, none of this made much sense at all before, really. Even Mr. Mooney didn't gel completely with us. We thought we had the perfect suspect but the more we looked, the more unlikely it became. Then you bring into the mix a woman with past mental issues who became obsessed with you; then it begins to make sense. We always assumed it was a man who was the killer, as you would reasonably associate bludgeoning someone to death with a pipe with a man. We had a vague CCTV picture of what looked like a man in a hooded top in the car park of the motel, but it was so dark it could easily have been a woman. Your neighbour also thought it was a man running away from the house. But once again the person was wearing a hoody, and it is possible it was a woman. It was at a distance in very low light. On both occasions the overall impression was of a slim man, but maybe it's more likely, now, that it was a woman."

"We have a lot more inquiries to carry out, and obviously, and we don't want to jump to conclusions. But, it does seem feasible that with her saying she fell in love with you, and that she obsessed over you, the husband leaving her may have tipped her over the edge mentally. The text message she sent you infers she may have been hospitalised, and when she was released, perhaps she stalked you and discovered your, how shall we say, diverse lifestyle?"

"There's no need for delicacy. I've told Shannon everything, Felix."

"Have you now? And how are you finding honesty in a relationship? No sorry, I apologise, that was uncalled for. Dave and I have had these conversations before Ms. McGuire, haven't we, Dave?"

I nodded. Shannon stayed quiet, listening. I think she was still in shock. "Yes, we have, and I can assure you I will never do anything like that again, so long as I live."

"Well perhaps there's hope for the rest of the female population then. So, if she was following you, it suddenly explains some of the other things that didn't make sense before, such as the motel and the timing of the murders. It also makes sense why, in her mind, she killed whoever she saw as her rivals, whereas it made no sense with Clinton Mooney to have done so. It further explains why we never found the second victim's missing phone. Hopefully, it will turn up now when we search her house."

"Thank God it's finally over," I said.

All of us were dead tired, and they let us leave with the promise to make formal statements on Monday. I led Shannon though the garage, and a police car was moved so I could get out through the throng of cars in my crowded driveway.

When we pulled up at Shannon's she invited me in, and I was so tired I accepted gratefully without questioning it. I had no real plans of what I was going to do after I dropped her off. I was on auto pilot and didn't read anything into her offer.

Once inside she turned to me and said, "I don't want to have sex with you, but I do want you to sleep with me. I don't want to be alone, I feel so incredibly sad, and I just want you to hold me so I can feel safe. Is that OK?"

"That would be perfect. I feel just as sad, but also relieved it's finally over, although I thought that once before."

We went to her bedroom, and she undressed down to her panties and climbed into bed. Her body was as stunning as I imagined it would be, and once I was undressed too she coiled around me under the covers on her bed. We were both asleep within minutes.

Domin8

Chapter 27 – Shannon (7) – Starsky and Hutch (8)

Day Thirty-Two. A New Dawn Beckons

I woke up disorientated in a strange bedroom, alongside a beautiful sleeping woman, and it took long seconds to remember why and where I was. She looked peaceful in sleep, and I felt so badly that she had been drawn into my nightmare and that it had been her who had found Judith's body. I laid there for a moment or two thinking back on the death and misery my actions had caused to so many people. I realised in that moment, with absolute clarity, that I did not deserve to be in Shannon's company, let alone her bed. I made the decision to end it. It was the only right and decent thing to do.

I eased out of bed and put my shirt and pants on, grabbed my socks and shoes and crept out of her bedroom. I sat at the table and thought of what to put in a note to her to say goodbye and realised that would be the coward's way of walking away.

At fifty years old it was time to grow up and be a man and try to think of other people first. I snuck out the front door leaving it closed but not locked. I got into the car and drove quietly out of the driveway. Within a few minutes I found a bakery that was open for business.

My first dilemma was coffee. We had not got to the coffee making stage the night before so I didn't know how she took it. I ordered one with full milk, one with skinny, one black, one with caramel flavour and one cappuccino, then added another black to the order because that was how I took mine, and she may have wanted it the same.

Stephen B. King

"Then something to eat," I thought and ordered two ham and cheese croissants, and two bacon and egg muffins. "That ought to do it," I said to myself, pleased with my peace offering. They put the coffees in a cardboard tray with cut outs and the eats in a box. I paid and was back in the car with everything on the passenger side floor within minutes.

In her living room was a small table, alongside the couch, which I grabbed and put everything on, then carried that through to the bedroom and gently pushed the door open with my foot. She was still asleep and looked angelic, as I tiptoed round to her side of the bed and placed the table down next to her. Then I grabbed a black coffee and gently sat on her side at the end of the bed and softly shook her hip to wake her.

Her huge eyelashes fluttered open and she looked at me with her brown eyes, smiling. As she noticed I was dressed, her eyes went cloudy, and she said, "Are you going somewhere?"

"I've already been," I answered, and looked to her side at the table. She followed my eyes and saw the coffees and eats.

"Mmm, you're a lifesaver, aren't you? Thank you. That was very thoughtful of you"

She sat up and the bed cloths fell into her lap. All I could think of as I looked at her was Drew's question on the boat, "does she have good tits?" "*Well, Drew,*" I thought, "*the answer is yes, yes she does.*" Her breasts were full and firm. If it were a different time and place I would love to have played with them.

"I wasn't sure how you had coffee, so I brought one of everything. What would you like?"

She took the flat white with skinny milk (thank goodness I had grabbed one of those) and shook a sachet of sugar in it, stirring it with the plastic spoon. "*No expense spared,*" I thought. Maybe I was still in shock, as my mind was wandering.

Domin8

She unwrapped one of the muffins from its wrapper and bit into it. Warm egg oozed out the side of her mouth and dripped down her chin onto her breast.

"Oh dear, I don't have a napkin." She said and, being the tease she was, looked openly at me.

"We need to talk, Shannon."

She used the tip of her finger to wipe the egg off and lick it, brought her knees up to her chest without covering up and laid back against the headboard holding the cup in one hand and muffin in the other. Then, she sighed and replied, "Yes, Dave, we do need to talk, and I think you are itching to go first, aren't you? Can I just say though as I have a feeling I know what you are about to tell me, that I had a beautiful night out with you? Even the interactive horror show at the end of it hasn't altered my feelings about you or the night out we had."

I almost laughed at her attempt at humour— "the interactive horror show:" That was funny. I picked up the black coffee and took a sip to give me time to gather my thoughts, which had seemed so clear earlier and were now shrouded in self-doubt.

"For the last year or so, I've been the biggest arsehole a man could possibly be to someone I loved. I've found ways to justify it by telling myself that I thought Di suspected but didn't want to know what would hurt her, and that doing what I did kept us together. However, the truth is, all I really thought about was me; and everything else was crap. I loved Di and never really realised just how much, until she was taken from me. And let's not forget why she was taken from. I have to live with that forever more."

"Yes, you do, Dave. You did a number of wrong things, there were consequences, and you do have to live with the guilt. I totally understand and agree with that, even to the point of agreeing you deserve that guilt trip. But the fact that you acknowledge it speaks volumes. Go on, I'm sure you are getting to the bit where you dump me."

"Dump you? Is that how you see it?"

"Well, how would you like me to see it, Dave?"

She was doing it again, answering a question with a question and putting my name at the end, but this time it wasn't as cute. "That for once in my life I'm trying to do something where I don't think of myself first. I'm trying to think of you, and you don't need a rat like me in your life."

"Ah, I see. Sorry, I thought you were saying you had realised your mistakes and had learnt from them and didn't want to repeat them. I didn't realise you wanted to carry on making the same ones over and over for the rest of your life."

"You're not making this easy, are you?"

"Is that what you want, Dave? For me to make this easy for you?"

I sighed and hung my head, shaking it from side to side. This wasn't going at all how it had sounded in my thoughts earlier.

"The only thing I know for a fact, Shannon, is that you are a woman that any man would love to be with. You are kind, intelligent and loyal, not to mention gorgeous to look at. But look at me? Look at the misery I've caused a lot of people because I'm bad. I'm a horrible person, and it seems to me the one decent thing I can do in my life is not risk hurting someone else I care about."

"Dave, if you want to end it now for your reasons, then go. I won't try to stop you. But don't you dare insult me by

Domin8

pretending to do it for mine. Look at me. I'm thirty-nine years old, divorced, and I haven't been with a man for well over a year. In fact—fuck, now I think of it—it's closer to two. My best friend lives in my bedside drawer, and I use it quite a lot. He goes through a lot of batteries. I think I once told you I love sex. God help me I'm so pathetic I still fantasise about my ex-husband fucking me despite the fact he took off with a younger slut."

She took a breather; I think to slow her anger with me. "When I first met you I liked you and was very attracted to you, then I found out what a rat you had been and what you had been doing behind your wife's back. In part, because of what my bastard husband did to me, I didn't like you anymore. But then we talked, and I saw a sincerity and genuine regret for your actions. And also, I could see you were suffering, and then I liked you again. When I tried to tempt you during that first shower, I was testing you, and you surprised me when you said no. You were as hard as a rock at the time and were gagging for me to finish you off, and I respected you for not treating me like a whore. Dave, you have a lot of good qualities and character, and the fact you are trying to extricate yourself from me now shows you do care, I think. But it's your call. You have to do what feels right to you, and if that's to leave me, then so be it. I am not going to talk you out of it and argue with you. If you don't think I am worth fighting for, then maybe you should go."

I thought about what she was saying, the offer she was making, to look past all the bad things, and take a chance on me. I was stunned, quite simply stunned. "You know the old me wouldn't have gone for coffees without making love to you, and then said goodbye afterwards, but I don't want to be the old me anymore. I want to be the kind of person I should have been all along."

"Dave, let's face it. We aren't schoolkids. Forgetting all the stuff that's happened, including your dead ex-lover in your

Stephen B. King

bathtub, there still could be a hundred reasons why we don't get along together and break up. Trust is a big thing for me, and I need to be able to trust you, and time will tell if I can. But even then, you might fart in bed, squeeze the toothpaste the wrong way or pick your nose—or there could be a myriad of other reasons that might make one of us want to leave the other. And of course, you have three grown up kids to consider too, who may well hate my guts for replacing their mother. Just don't do this for the wrong reasons and don't do it because you think you are doing me a favour, because you're not. I am an adult and can make my own decision, thank you very much."

I stayed silent, thinking about what she had said and looked at her smiling back at me between her sips of coffee. I knew she was right, but still I felt I should leave: that in some way I was protecting her by leaving her. She must have sensed my indecision because she threw back the bed clothes to show her nakedness.

"Come back to bed, Dave. No promises for the future: let's just take one day at a time. Come back to bed and make love to me."

I slowly put my cup down and stood up, undressing, never losing eye contact. I watched her as she watched me. It was very erotic. I was fully erect as I unhooked myself from my underwear and slid them down to the floor, stepping out of them.

I snuggled in next to her and took her in my arms. Our lips met in a slow, sensual kiss, and then a longer, more passionate one. Her breathing was getting faster and shorter, and she gasped as my hand covered her breast.

Her hands weren't idle either as she sought to touch as much of my skin as she could. As I bit her nipple she clenched them on my back touching one of the many cuts, some with stitches still in them, causing me to flinch.

"Oh, I'm so sorry," She said, realising she had hurt me, but I was way past caring.

"It's fine. Don't worry."

"Oh my God," She moaned, as I ruthlessly attacked her, while working her panties off with her help.

Considering that it had been so long between drinks for her I wanted to make it special, and we had lots of time. I slowly licked down from her navel to just above her downy pubic hair. She was lifting her hips. She wanted me to touch her there, but I made her wait and teased her more, and not just because she had teased me in hospital. I loved the feel of her hair in my fingers and on my nose and tongue. The smell of her excitement was intoxicating.

This was what I loved the most: getting a woman turned on so her movements were automatic, so she needed stimulation and moved her body to find it. Her face contorted, her breathing ragged, I looked up along her body to her face, and our eyes met: hers pleading, mine smiling. I slowly lowered my mouth, sinking my tongue inside her, loving her taste.

"Oh, yesssss…"

I brought my hands down underneath her to hold her as I devoured her, alternating between ruthless licks and sucks to soft, gentle teases. With her fingers entwined in my hair she yelled out one long "YEESSS!" as the orgasm raced through her body, radiating out from her core.

I stopped when her movements changed to twitching, the pleasure becoming too much for her. Not wanting to spoil the afterglow I rested my head on her tummy until she recovered and got her breath back. Her fingers idly stroked my head and neck as her body continued to make small, involuntary twitches.

"Come here, Dave, hold me," she said, and as gently as I could I moved up her body to hold her in my arms. Her heart was still beating hard, but slowing, as I kissed her softly and gently.

"I haven't finished with you yet," I warned as I looked at her contented face.

"Promise?" She asked.

When we made love, it was as if we were both exorcising the demons of our pasts. It was as spectacular as it was beautiful, and we stayed joined and entwined long after we had climaxed together.

A little later, I realised something that I had forgotten from years before; that over the recent months (apart from at the sink with Di that last time) I had been having sex, but this with Shannon was *making love*, and it was infinitely much more pleasurable than just sex. At fifty years old, I had finally grown up, and this time I was determined it was for good.

Afterwards, we lay cuddling: her head on my chest, my fingers softly tracing lines up and down her back, occasionally talking but both feeling we didn't need to.

We stayed in bed all day. In the early evening she began fondling me again, she turned her head and looked at me. "I'm no expert. How could I be when I've only ever had sex with three men in my life? But I love this thing of yours in my hand, and I love what you do with it."

She lifted herself up, straddled me and guided me inside her body. I slid into her easily.

We had not put the light on and the twilight filtered through the blinds. She shook her head from side to side so her

Domin8

long brunette hair flew around her. She put her hands flat on my chest to steady herself while mine held her hips and she began to move her hips. She looked stunningly beautiful and determined as she rode me until she arched her back, which took me over the precipice.

We were going to go out to eat, until I realised I had neglected to grab some extra clothes from home, so I joined Shannon in the kitchen, wearing only my underwear and shirt. She cooked bacon and eggs on toast with coffee, which made it feel like Sunday morning, rather than the Sunday night that it was.

We talked about our plans for the following day. She, had to work, so we decided she would drive her car in and then meet me at the police station at one p.m., where we would make our statements, after which she would return to work.

I told her I should catch up with my children to see they were coping OK and explain about Judith. I hadn't seen then since returning from Exmouth and I wanted to mention I was seeing Shannon and ask them how they felt about it. I knew they wouldn't be too happy about me dating so soon, but I wasn't going to lie or hide the truth to anyone anymore. While telling them now would be bad I was sure that if I didn't tell them it would be far worse when they found out later.

In the morning I had to go and have a check-up with my Scottish Doctor and have my stitches taken out. I would be in a different area of the hospital so I wouldn't see Shannon. She told me that Doctor McLeish was very well regarded by all the nursing staff, unlike a couple of others she could name.

She had put some music on, a Coldplay compilation, and the conversation came easy. If we had been overheard by someone they would have no idea of the trauma that had caused us to come together, and it was lovely to be able to escape from that all so easily.

Sadly, that happiness and normalcy, was to be short-lived.

XXX

The doctor was only an hour and a quarter late for my 10:30 a.m. appointment, and he quickly gave me the once over and pronounced me fit enough. He got a nurse to remove my stitches, no doubt so he could try to make up some of his lost time.

I had phoned Sam earlier that morning and gotten permission to go home to change clothes. I had showered with Shannon at her house, which brought back amazing memories of our time in hospital together. This time I got to wash her body with my soapy hands, which I did slowly, as erotically as possible, to show her what it had been like for me.

Because I had to resort to putting dirty clothes back on I felt I needed a shower again and did so at home before heading to the hospital. The police had propped the laundry door closed, and I made a phone call to a maintenance company to come and repair it, but they couldn't get there before Thursday, I was told. I put a couple of screws in it so I wouldn't get broken into again.

While driving I made some calls, firstly to the kids, telling them the latest developments but didn't mention Shannon. That would happen when we were face to face, and I suggested we all catch up later that night for dinner to talk about things. I told them that the good news was the killer was now dead, albeit she chose to do it in my bathtub as a final punishment to me. I didn't tell them about the bloody note she left me, deciding to mention that at dinner, as it would lead into the necessary conversation about

Domin8

Shannon I had to have. I was no longer prepared for them to find out I was dating someone by any other means than my honesty. For better or worse I would face what they had to say about it. We agreed to meet at a hotel that was central to all and have a meal and a chat at seven-thirty that night.

My next call was to George, who also was confused at first. He, like everyone else, thought the murderer had been killed previously. I took time to explain the confusion and finished with the gruesome discovery we had made of Judith in my bathtub and the current police thinking.

That call finished as I was pulling into the hospital car park, and the next two hours dragged by until I was back in the car heading into the city for the meeting with police. The day was warm, the traffic was light and on the radio Kenny Loggins was singing about the Highway to the Danger Zone when the symbolism hit me, and I burst out laughing. I was on the freeway, not a highway, but you could argue it was heading to a danger zone.

I felt better than I had any right to feel. I even felt guilty that I felt so good. If I stopped to think of Dianne, losing her and my selfish stupidity I knew I would spiral into depression, so every time I found myself edging into that territory I jerked myself out of it by thinking of Shannon. Yes, they were ghosts I didn't want to face. Was it cowardly? You bet.

The sun glistened off the beautiful Swan River as I crossed the Narrows Bridge. "It really is a spectacular day," I thought as my phone rang via the Bluetooth connection. It was Felix.

"Hi, Felix, I'm on my way. Probably ten minutes from you. I assume that's what you're ringing for?"

"Yes, Dave, I will wait for you in the car park and take you up. Ms. McGuire has just left. She called earlier and had trouble getting out of work for one o'clock, but could make it for twelve. We have the utmost respect for nursing staff so the entire police department changed their lunchbreak to accommodate her to take her statement. She had some very nice things to say about you. I have to say, Dave, if you could bottle whatever it is makes you attractive to women you could make a fortune. See you in ten."

"See you soon, Felix," I said and hung up. I shook my head as his assessment. I didn't agree with it. Yes, to him it may seem like a lot of women, but he failed to see most of the women I met were online *looking* for men. Not me, in particular, but a certain type of man, and in most cases I wasn't the only one they found.

It wasn't as if every woman I met threw herself at me. Not at all. Were it not for the internet and my becoming obsessed with submissive woman, since meeting Dianne the number of women I had been with totalled only five, including Shannon, over a thirty year span. In my mind, that hardly made me some sort of Don Juan. Three of them were adulterous, short-term affairs. That much was true, but I still didn't consider that to match his comment about my appeal. One of them was a prostitute, for goodness sake.

Felix, I realised, was just that kind of man. His way of joking was to use sarcasm.

At the station we shook hands, and he escorted me inside and into the elevator and then into a different interview room than last time, where Sam joined us a few moments later. We shook hands too. The recorder was switched on, and off we went, again.

In my own words I told them how I met Judith, how long I had seen her and described the relationship right up to how it ended. I didn't have any idea of her instability, other than the fact that, towards the end, she seemed to be depressed at times but had never told me why. I told them about her 'open' relationship with her husband, as she described it to me, and finished with how we had drifted apart, mainly due to her bad moods, but also I felt that we were both growing out of the relationship. I thought that it had ended with a whimper rather than with any bitterness. I said I had thought she had just moved onto a new lover, and we just sort of stopped seeing each other.

I went into detail of each and every text, phone call and contact after Dianne's murder, which culminated in the discovery of her body in the bathtub. Once finished I sat back in my chair and waited for the questions to start.

"Thank you for your frank and open explanations, Dave. We have confirmed that the time of death coincides with you being at the restaurant. There is no indication of any other evidence to contradict our findings that the victim took her own life while being in an unsound state of mind. Her car was found in the car park of the park by the side of your house. Only her fingerprints were on the crow bar she used to gain access, and her prints were on the taps to turn on the water. Clearly, we think she sought to punish you by killing herself in your home because she felt you had spurned her advances in favour of Ms. McGuire."

Sam then spoke, "The only thing wrong with that scenario, as far as I can see, is that it runs contrary to her previous actions. Can you see that? Before you answer I have to say mine is the only lone voice in this doubt, in particular in light of other discoveries we have made, which we will come to."

I stopped to think what he meant and shook my head. I couldn't see it. "What do you mean?"

"The thing I keep coming back to is that, if we assume she killed the first three victims, including your wife, because she saw them as rivals and that they stopped her from getting back with you, then why did she then kill herself, rather than Ms. McGuire? That bothers me, Dave; to me it runs contrary to her previous behaviour. I think she would have killed Shannon, not herself, in the state of mind we assume her to have been in."

I nodded, deep in thought, and replayed our last encounter in my head. I remembered her skirt held high offering herself to me, and my anger and dismissal of her. Surely that was the explanation?

"Could it be, Sam, that she hadn't made contact prior to Dianne's death, so was looking to kill her rivals? But afterwards when she did make her play for me, I lost my temper with her. I yelled at her and told her to leave me alone. In fact, I told her to fuck off in no uncertain terms and told her to *never* come back. If she believed she had no chance, even if she did go on to kill Shannon, then maybe she thought she could punish me most by topping herself in my house. She told me I would be sorry."

"Yeah, I guess that does make sense in an obscure way. If she didn't drive away when you told her to leave you alone, she would have seen Ms. McGuire arrive, and put two and two together. We don't know what she did in between the time she saw you with Ms. McGuire and when she re-entered your house, something like four hours later. Is it important to know what she did? I think so, but everyone else here thinks I am worried about nothing. We found two receipts in her car, one for the bottle of wine, and the other for the candles, which suggests she didn't go home. You've acknowledged the clothes folded on the bed were the same as she was wearing earlier, so what did she do, and where did she go?"

Now it was Felix's turn. "Forgive Sam's overactive imagination, Dave; he gets like this sometimes. So far as we are concerned we are satisfied with the most likely scenario is as mentioned. Yes, not all the ends are tied up as neatly as we would like yet, but in real life that's how it is sometimes."

Domin8

"We affected a search at her house yesterday morning and unfortunately didn't find Ms. Brewster's phone, which really would have been the icing on the cake with our theory. However, we did find her husband. He had been dead for some months and buried in the vegetable patch in the back garden. We found some very large potatoes growing in the same bed. Who'd have thought?"

"So she killed Mark too? Jesus Christ she told me he left her." I was shocked. I had met some incredible liars in my time, and she had seemed so truthful and sincere. "I got the impression from her that it was him leaving her, because of her feelings for me, and that it was their breakup which sent her into some sort of depression, which is why she was hospitalised."

"Well, Dave, his head was caved in from behind with a blunt, rounded object, similar— would you believe—to a scaffolding pipe? So yes, you could say he left her, and possibly the guilt of her killing him sent her off to the funny farm. She was self-admitted to Graylands Mental Hospital, where she spent fourteen days. We have applied for her records and hope to get them in a day or two because they insist on a warrant, but to me it seems rather obvious that his death was the cause of her breakdown. Perhaps in her fucked up head she rationalised it all away as him leaving her, who can say? The initial estimated time of death is consistent with that theory."

Sam just stared back at me, not saying anything. I could tell he wasn't completely happy about things, and for some reason, because of this latest revelation, neither was I.

Felix continued, "Our report will state the following; on a date to be determined the suspect murdered her husband in a fit of rage and buried him in the back garden. We can only surmise why—perhaps an argument due to her past affair with you? She then suffered remorse and guilt and had some sort of breakdown, for which she was admitted to a mental ward for a period of two weeks. On her release she blamed you for her woes with her husband and began to stalk you over a period of time which led to her seeing you meet Patricia White in a motel. When you left she entered the room and killed her. Still stalking you she then killed Melanie Brewster in similar circumstances to Patricia White after you had left a rendezvous with her. We will never know if the attack on your wife was intentional or if it was pure chance that you didn't open the front door. Possibly after the first two women she wanted to punish you by framing you for the murders and was angry when you were released. Perhaps she was enraged that you had two women on the side, and were happily married while she was miserable. Some of these things we will never really know the truth of. Because your house is side onto a park, perhaps from a vantage point she saw you enter the bathroom and took the opportunity to kill her last rival. She then sought to make contact and when you didn't show interest, decided to take her own life in a way you would finally take notice of her. We suspect, though can't prove it was her DNA was on the string around the brick thrown through your window. And we know of no suspicious circumstances surrounding her death. Do you wish to add anything else, Dave?"

I thought long and hard for a minute or two before I said "Felix, it all sounds pat, and everything fits the facts as we know them, but I agree with Sam. Something isn't right here and for the life of me I don't know what it is. It doesn't quite fit with the Judith that I knew, but then I have to say my knowledge of psychotic women is very limited. But still, she seemed so sincere."

"We deal with liars every single day, Dave. They all sound very sincere, which is why they are good liars. Maybe in her mind she believed what she was saying, hence the sincerity. But just because she believed it didn't make it true. We didn't get to interview her, mainly because she wasn't on the list of women you told us you had seen previously. Maybe if we had spoken to her things may have ended differently."

There was definitely admonishment in his tone, and I could see his point of view.

"It wasn't like I was hiding anything, Felix. It had finished months before all of this and it didn't seem relevant. As Melanie and Patsy were from the internet, that was the only scenario I thought of. It's just one more thing for me to feel guilty over, I suppose. Jesus, there is so much blood on my hands."

"Well, water under the bridge now. We are still waiting on post mortem results and hospital notes on her. We have spoken to her children, two daughters. Both are in shock, obviously, they both knew she was troubled and were concerned their father didn't make contact with them, but they believed her story too that he had left her and wanted some time alone. There really isn't anywhere else for us to go, and other than Sam's feelings of something wrong, I don't know what else we can do at this time. I will let you know the results when they come in. One last thing: we will make our report to the Coroner's office, and I seriously doubt there will be anything further. However, that's not really for us to say. There could conceivably be an inquest, and you may need to give evidence. Again, we will let you know. Otherwise, that's it, and you are free to go. Sam will see you out. You don't mind if I say I hope I don't see you again, Dave, will you?"

I stood and shook his hand. "Thanks, Felix. Yes, I hope I don't see you either, not work related anyway. I'd like to say I've found you to be very professional and thorough, and I respect you. I don't hold any hard feelings over the arrest; I accept you did what you had to do. I also want to thank you for agreeing for Sam to stay with me and save my life from the sniper."

Stephen B. King

"Well, if you really want to thank me, just keep your dick in one woman in the future. You're a bloody menace."

That summed up the puritanical Felix, but he was right. Had I not slept around none of this would have occurred, and that couldn't be denied. I had to live with that: my cross to bear.

In the lift on the way down Sam said, "Listen, Dave, I wouldn't mind catching up with you for a quiet beer and have a chat with you, off the record. The case is all but closed now, but there are one or two things we should chat about. Are you free later?"

"I'm meeting my kids at the Queens Hotel at seven-thirty for dinner to tell them about the latest developments, but between now and then I'm free. How about we catch up there earlier, say six?"

"Yeah, that works for me, Dave. I will see you there then. You can buy me a beer."

"I will buy you a carton. I owe you, Sam, and I won't forget that."

"All part of the service mate. See you then." The doors opened and I left him there.

Knowing Shannon couldn't answer her phone at work, I sent her a lengthy message, telling her how it went and about the discovery of Judith's husband's body. I also said I hoped she was OK after making a statement and that I was sorry I hadn't been there to give her moral support. I also told her what a great time I had enjoyed with her and that I was looking forward to seeing her again.

That done I went home to do some jobs before meeting Sam at the pub a few hours later.

Domin8

Chapter 28 - Shannon (8) - Sam (4)

Day Thirty-Two, continued. Back in Black

When Shannon had arrived home after work on that fateful day she had no idea a madman was waiting for her in her bathroom.

She had been in a great mood. All day, her thoughts had been of nothing but Dave, how much she had enjoyed his company and, of course, the way he had made love to her. At thirty-nine years old she had finally found someone who seemed to care for her. He was extremely good-looking, in a Brad Pitt, distinguished kind of way, and had a confident air about himself. But the thing that had knocked her for six had been the sex. She perfectly understood why women wanted him.

She had only had two lovers before; one was her ex-husband and the other was a boyfriend she had after high school who worked in a bakery she stopped in for her lunch breaks. He took her virginity in the backseat of his car, while parked in a park one Sunday night, and they had dated on several occasions after.

It wasn't that she hadn't enjoyed sex, far from it. She loved it. But it had always seemed like she needed five more minutes than her male partner would give her. Just as her train was approaching her station, the other train was leaving. She had spent her whole life thinking that was normal, despite what some other women had said.

But that was before Dave, and two things were remarkable about him, starting with his penis. OK, she was a nurse and had seen them in all shapes and sizes, but of course when seen in
290

hospital, men are nervous, not excited, and the male member isn't impressive at times like that. Dave's was a rampant work of art when erect, and the first time she had showered him and he became aroused, she couldn't help herself from imagining it inside her. Professional ethics, of course, won out, but she remembered how it felt in her hand, and the way it throbbed. She had tried hard to stay objective and finished washing him as she had been trained, but that had not been so easy to do.

She was unused to such thoughts, other than when she let her fantasies run riot, when she used her vibrator, but her urge was almost overpowering that day in the shower. She did resist, but each successive day it was harder to ignore her desire to satisfy him.

Both her ex-husband and boyfriend hadn't compared, though they were probably average in her experience. She knew how obsessed men were with their length, and over the years she knew how precious they could be about it. She had always gone out of her way to make her man feel like he was a champion in bed, even faking orgasms at times in order to avoid the sulking.

When her ex left her for the much younger woman she had finally told him the truth that she had never climaxed with him during sex. He said that her fault, because she was a frigid bitch and that his new lover came multiple times with him in the saddle. She called him a liar.

More than anything else, it was that comment—that she was a frigid bitch—which had kept her from dating other men. She genuinely believed her ex was being honest, rather than nasty, and she had lost all self-confidence in herself. While everyone told her she was beautiful, she didn't see it that way. She thought men didn't want her, so she, in turn, decided she didn't want them.

Domin8

Then along came Dave. Part of the attraction, she admitted to herself, was his looks, and that confidant, bad boy air he had, but when they talked, she could see something deeper in him. He was honest, and even though he had shown a complete disregard for his marriage vows, that too, for some strange reason, only made him more attractive.

Then she got to feel him in her hand in the first shower. All she could do, after that first time, was think about the next time she could get to hold it again. Though she tried hard not to, she couldn't stop it.

As each day passed, they chatted and got closer, and she thought about nothing else but him, yet on his last day, she knew she would probably never see him again. She had, every night in her bed, used her vibrator numerous times, thinking about him, imagining him thrusting inside her. She had brought herself to several screaming orgasms.

To offset her excitement, she tried to let reason prevail. In the intervening days, she had deliberately been cold to him at times and seriously considered the error of his ways. But, to his credit, and her amazement, he never shirked what he had done and seemed genuinely remorseful. He seemed somewhat like a wounded animal, which only made his vulnerability more attractive to her, being a born nurturer.

It was all so complicated. She wanted him, but knew she shouldn't. His wife had been murdered, for goodness sake, so why was she so attracted to him? But want him she did, and the more she thought about him the more weak-kneed she became. She tried so hard not to have those thoughts, but to no avail. They kept coming at odd times, relentlessly. She had never felt this way about a man in her life, which made her confused and worried. Yet at the same time, she wanted him to the point that all common sense went out the window.

Stephen B. King

He had further endeared himself to her by waiting for her to say goodbye long after he could have left. Again, she realised, he was a special man. He cared.

She wanted him, wanted to feel his hardness inside her and willingly gave him her phone number, then waited like an excited schoolgirl for him to phone her. Not that she could let him know how desperate she felt. No, that would never do. But, each and every night in bed she could think of nothing else.

Then, weeks later when he returned from his time away, after an absolutely wonderful night out, the best date night she had ever had in her life, came the horror of finding the body in the bathtub. Then, the police questions and recriminations came. She could see the abject misery he so clearly felt, and the self-loathing for the consequences of his misdemeanours. Never had she felt more attracted to a man and a willingness to forgive his sins. She just wanted to hold him until his pain went away.

Then, damn him, his guilt led him to want to break up with her, and she realised more than ever that she should not let him slip through her fingers. But, how could she stop that? She couldn't let on that she had fallen for him so heavily. That would not be right, so she had to use logic to help him realise she wanted him, but only if he wanted her. And, thank God, it had worked. They the most amazing sex she could have possibly imagined. She tingled from head to toe every time she relived it in her mind.

It wasn't just his size, although that was remarkable about him. But more than that, it was all the emotion, caring and genuine interest in her pleasure. She had never orgasmed like that before—she didn't even think it was possible—and she just wanted him over and over again. She was drunk on him, and was like an alcoholic craving her next drink.

She had to give him time. She knew that it was going to be a rocky road ahead, naturally. He had lost his wife to a gruesome murderer and rightly blamed himself for it. So far, he hadn't had time to grieve her. He had probably been too busy worrying about his kids, the investigation, his career and everything else. She suspected it would hit him, if and when it did it would be hard. She had seen delayed grief before through her work. More than anything, she wanted to be there for him, to help him through it. He was worth the effort. Somehow, she just knew that.

So on the day that she went back to work after their amazing time together, she decided to work a bit later, to make up for taking time off when she went to the police station earlier that day. She knew Dave was spending time with his kids that night and that he would broach the subject of her. The thought of that scared her. She knew he would phone her when he was finished and hoped he would come and see her afterward, but she also understood that they would need to take it slowly.

She was humming a Coldplay song to herself as she turned the key in the lock of her house.

XXX

The Queens Hotel in Mount Lawley on a Monday night was pretty quiet at six o'clock. I arrived to find Sam already there, sitting at the bar. I had felt a little disappointed that I hadn't received a return message from Shannon. Perhaps she had worked later than usual, having had to take time off to go to the police station, I reasoned. I hoped that she might call me later that night, if I didn't call her first.

That feeling of disappointment that I hadn't heard from her was strange for me. It was accompanied by a longing to be with her again, which was *very* unusual. I can truthfully say I had not experienced it since Dianne and I had been dating. I also suffered the constant urge to pick up my phone to make sure I hadn't turned it to silent accidentally and missed a message from her, followed by checking it again half an hour later to see if I actually had put it on silent the time that I checked it previously. I was concerned that my thinking about her bordered on obsessive compulsive behaviour, which, again, was not like me at all.

No amount of self-admonishment would stop it, though, and finally I decided to embrace it and enjoy the ride for as long as it lasted. I liked her; I cared for her, and I looked forward to seeing her again. I did feel embarrassed, even ashamed, that I had fallen for Shannon so soon after my wife's death. I told myself I couldn't control who I cared for, or when. I assured myself with the understanding that it had just happened, and life was short—sometimes brutally short—as I had become far too aware with recent incidents.

I bought two beers, and Sam and I headed to a secluded table. Once we sat down he didn't waste any time.

"Dave, have you ever hear of a cop's gut instinct?"

"Only on TV," I replied.

He laughed and said, "Yeah, OK, stupid question. It's not like you have many cops in your inner circle of friends."

"It's not because I don't like police, Sam. I just haven't met any to have as mates. I'm interested, though. Why do you ask?"

He paused and looked very serious. He took a long draught of beer and then said, "I have always been the kind of person to follow my instincts, and they have never, not once, let me down. True it drives Felix nuts sometimes, but he has also been glad too, when I have picked something through intuition that has helped the case. Sometimes cops know when someone is guilty, even though there is no evidence. Occasionally we also know when

Domin8

someone is innocent, even though the evidence points towards them, your situation is a good case in point after Patricia White, and Melanie Brewster. Its true, there have been some famous cases over the years where cops in their belief that someone was guilty fabricated evidence to get a conviction. But I tend to think that was more laziness in the bad old days. The point is that sometimes all we have is our feelings. I always felt you were not guilty and I was right. There is something bothering me about this Judith woman, and I don't know what it is but, Dave, I think you are still very much in danger."

He paused, looking at me for a long time, and I struggled to know what to say, but before I could come up with something he said, "Dave, I know that doesn't make much sense, because the question is, if its not her, who is it?"

At those words it hit me, like a lightening bolt, and I *almost had it*, the answer was so tantalisingly close, but then he spoke again and what was within blinking distance shot out of reach for me.

"If I am right, then we are back to square one, and Felix doesn't want to be there. This case has done his head in from the very start. He is a good cop, as honest as the day is long, but what you were doing, and the consequences of doing it have seriously fucked him up, because it goes against the grain of all that he holds dear.

"Felix doesn't share your belief then, not even a niggling doubt?"

He shook his head emphatically. "No, he does not and has told me in no uncertain terms that I'm being 'fucking stupid' and jumping at shadows. But he is a man for whom the rule book is the rule book. I wouldn't say a bad word about him. But, he lacks imagination, for want of a better word. Look, he may well be

Stephen B. King

right, and I could be wrong, but this just doesn't sit right with me. How does it sit with you?"

"I don't have any experience with women with mental issues, but I would not have thought the Judith I knew to be capable of this kind of brutality. Sam, I too think there is something we are missing, scratch that, I mean that *I am* missing. The clincher for me is the murder of her husband, Mark. She only ever spoke highly of him, and he knew of her affairs. I was not her first, Sam. She told me that. She also said, that when he got back from the mines, she used to tell him what she had been up to in great detail and he got off on it. Unless something really unforeseen happened, I can't see him wanting to leave her, and I definitely can't see her murdering him. All that said, she did have that breakdown. Maybe when you find out from Graylands what that was all about it may shed some more light on it. The thing is, Sam, if I'm honest, I can't see her as being the type of person to bash a woman's head in with a steel pipe. If, in fact, she felt compelled to kill my girlfriends that's not the weapon I would have thought she would use. But again, I've never known someone who was psychotic, and her behaviour to me since Dianne was killed was bizarre to say the least. She clearly was not of sound mind."

"Dave, there is one more thing that can't be explained, and that is who was the man who stole your pen and left it at the scene of Melanie Brewster's murder? Your receptionist couldn't identify a man, but I'm sure she'd have noticed if it was a woman."

I stared back. I knew the answer was there, just over the horizon again, but just too far to see, like when you see something out of the corner of your eye, but you turn to look directly at it, it's gone. On a deep, almost subconscious, level, I knew I had the answer to it all and that it was agonisingly close, but before I could respond I felt the vibration from my pocket and heard the message tone from my phone.

"*At last,*" I thought, "*a message from Shannon!*" With schoolboy glee, I took my phone out and looked at the display to read the text. My heart sank down through my stomach to the floor below.

Melanie: Monday 6.17PM.

"Oh my God," I said. It was a message from Melanie's phone, with a picture attached. With trembling fingers, I punched in the unlock code twice to open it up, as I made a mistake on the first attempt. There, looking back at me, was a snapshot from hell.

The picture showed Shannon from the waist up, still in her nurse's uniform, which was torn to expose her white bra. There were blood spatters on her uniform and face, coming from her nose, which looked crooked as if broken. Her mouth was covered by grey packing tape. Her eyes were wide open, pleading, while a hand held a knife to her throat. She appeared to be tied to a chair but the surrounds were dark, and I couldn't tell where it was taken.

Melanie: I have your bitch. Do you want her dead or alive?

Dave: Alive. Please let her go. I will do anything you say.

Sam was looking over my shoulder, having come around to my side of the table. He put a hand on my shoulder and squeezed. "Stay calm, Dave. Keep him talking."

He dialled a number on his mobile phone, and I could vaguely hear him talking to Felix in the background.

Stephen B. King

Melanie: It's up to you. If you tell the cops, she dies. If you don't do as I say, she dies. But then again, she may die anyway. I haven't decided yet.

Dave: I will do anything you say. It's me you want. Spare her and take me.

Melanie: No. I think you're lying. You will tell the cops. I will kill her and catch up with you later. Goodbye.

Dave: Oh my God, no. Not her, please not her.

I frantically messaged back, making numerous mistakes because I was panicking. Sam was off the phone and looking over my shoulder. I tried calling the number but it rang out and went to Melanie's message bank.

"Calm down, Dave," Sam said, "take a breath. If he was going to kill her he would have already. He wants you. He just wants you rattled, trust me. Take some deep breaths."

Dave: I promise. No police. I am in East Perth I can come wherever you are now, right now. Please don't kill her, she is blameless. Everything is my fault, kill me, not her.

The seconds dragged on into minutes with no reply.

Melanie: Your bitch is dead have a nice day. ☺

"NOOOOOOOOO," I screamed loudly, and every person in the pub looked at us.

"He's lying, Dave, keep it together. He wants you panicked, don't give him what he wants."

I was typing fast, trying to save her, fearing the worst despite Sam's attempts when the phone chirped again.

Melanie: Just kidding. How did it feel to think you had lost someone you love? That's what you did to me, you prick.

Domin8

There is only one way to save her. My way. Are you paying attention?

The relief I felt was indescribable, and tears brimmed in my eyes which I blinked away so I could continue to read text messages.

Dave: Yes. Tell me what you want me to do.

Melanie: I will be watching you. I will send you to places so I can see you are not being followed. Do as you are told and she lives. Lie to me, she dies. If I see you on your phone calling the cops she dies. Remember you won't know when I'm watching. Go to McDonalds on Great Eastern Hwy Belmont. Message me when you are there. GO.

I jumped up to run outside but Sam grabbed my arm and stopped me. "Dave, if you do this he will kill you both. You know that, don't you?"

"I don't care, Sam. Let me go. I have to try. There have been too many deaths because of me. I have to go and face him."

"I'm going with you."

"No, you're not. He will see you, and I can't take the chance."

"No, Dave, I will hide in the boot of your car. He won't see me, plus if I know what's going on I can stop the cavalry. They are tracking the mobile phone. If you don't take me there is nothing I can do to stop them sending in the TRG, wherever he is, when they get the trace."

"FUCK. Alright, let's go, now. You have to keep them away."

We ran out to the car park and, after a look around to make sure we weren't being watched, I opened the boot so he could climb in and shut it on him. The trunk of a Toyota Aurion Presara

300

is big, but it wouldn't be too comfortable for him if he was in there too long. I leant in through the back door and pulled down the centre armrest so he could hear me more clearly. I started the car, put my phone in the cup holder and drove out of the car park, headed towards Belmont.

I turned the car radio off so I could hear Sam and called out to him "Are you OK in there, Sam?"

"Yeah, just try to avoid speed humps, will you? I'm calling Felix now."

I felt frantic. This wasn't fair. I pleaded with the gods to spare her. I promised them and myself I would do anything to save Shannon. I glanced down at the dash and noticed I was twenty-five kilometres over the speed limit and forced myself to slow down. There was nothing to be gained if I wrecked the car.

Fortunately, the rush hour evening traffic had eased and, in less than twenty minutes, I pulled into the McDonalds car park, got out of the car and texted.

Dave: I am here.

Melanie: Good boy. Now get to the car park by the boathouse at Garret Road Bridge within ten minutes. If you're late, she dies.

Within seconds I was back in and going, yelling to Sam what had been said.

"Dave, calm down. I have Felix on the line. They have tracked the phone to Como. He isn't at the Bridge and is giving you the run around. Stay calm."

"You don't know that. He may have an accomplice. He may have some way of re-routing the phone, and we can't take the chance. Just keep them away."

Domin8

I heard him relaying something to Felix but couldn't hear what he said through the muffling effect of the rear seat. Finally, he yelled up to me, "Felix isn't going to take any chances. He agrees with you that we can't risk her life, by assuming he hasn't got someone watching you and reporting back, but he is pretty sure he is in Como. The phone has been stationary. He is putting some discreet plainclothes people into the area so they are nearby if needed. He says for you to stay calm. We are with you and won't do anything to jeopardise her."

Listening to Sam I almost missed the turn off and had to skid around the corner, almost hitting the kerbing. Sam yelled out several expletives.

"Sorry," I yelled back and slowed down.

It was just getting dark as I pulled into the car park and looked around. I saw dog walkers, a guy pulling a canoe out of the water and another couple of guys fishing in the river, but no one looked like they were watching me. But there were a lot of bushes around that someone could easily hide in. I picked up the phone.

Dave: I'm here, now.

Melanie: Nice car, Dave. Is that a Presara or Sportivo?

Dave: Presara. Is Shannon OK?

Melanie: Come and find out. Perth Zoo, main car park, Labouchere Road. Remember: I'm watching.

Careful not to say a word until I was on the road again, in case I was being watched, I pulled out on to the road, the wheels skidding as I took off.

"Sounds like Como is right. I'm off to the zoo, and he knows what car I am in. He must be watching."

Stephen B. King

"If he has been watching you for a while, Dave, he would know what you drive, wouldn't he? It doesn't mean you are being watched now. In fact, if he was watching he wouldn't need to pretend he was by telling you what you are driving. Relax, he isn't a superman. He is just like you or me, only a lunatic."

While driving I thought about that. I agreed with Sam that by asking if it was a Presara or Sportive it did make it sound like he was trying too hard to convince me. But still I couldn't, and wouldn't, take a chance with Shannon's life. I had to save her. Nothing else mattered.

"Felix says they now have a dozen men in and around the area where the phone is located. It's a new building project, an apartment block under construction on Mill Point Road overlooking the river. There's scaffolding everywhere. He says he now knows where the pipes come from that he used as weapons."

"He mustn't move in, Sam. We know this guy is a maniac. He will kill her. I can't live with another death on my conscience. Please tell him to hold back. I have to go and face him."

A few seconds later, he yelled out again. "There are a few apartment blocks around it. The TRG are going to send a couple of snipers. You have to give them time to get into position so they can take him out if they get a clear shot."

I nodded but didn't answer. If they got there they got there, fine. My only concern was saving Shannon from him, whoever he was.

As always the traffic on Canning Highway was slow, with buses in one lane or people turning right in the other. There were always holdups.

Eventually I made it onto Labouchere Road. The zoo was in sight when my phone rang via the car Bluetooth, making me jump out of my skin. With relief I saw it was Jason calling, and I realised I had left before our dinner arrangement. Of course, they must all be back at the Queens waiting for me. I answered, "Jase, I'm really sorry I've stood you all up. I cannot tie up this phone line for long. Please listen and accept it without arguing. Don't ask questions. I have to hang up very, very soon. They haven't caught the killer. He has abducted someone I know and care for, and he will kill her if I don't do what he says. I'm with the police going to meet him to try to save her life."

"DAD. NO."

"Jase, stop it. There is no time. All this is my fault, I've caused everything. I'm the only one who can stop it. I'm so, so very sorry for everything. Please understand I must do this, I have no choice. I've caused enough death and misery. I'm not causing anymore. I love you all. Please pass that along. I love you all. Never forget that. I fucked up, and now I have to pay the piper. Stay by your phone. I will call as soon as I can, but no matter what do NOT phone back."

I hung up as I pulled into the car park and texted within seconds.

Dave; I'm here at the zoo. What now?

Melanie: Head down Mill Point Road. On the right you will see a new building under construction. It's a tower called Horizon's West. I have left the gate unlocked. Drive in and park. On the right hand side, you will see a tradesman's elevator. Come up to the roof. I am watching. I can see everything. One wrong move and I slit her throat and throw her off the roof.

I pulled out of the car park I told Sam what was happening, which he relayed to Felix.

"Felix says that TRG are probably ten or so minutes away, including getting into some sort of position to see the roof to get a clear shot. You have to slow him down, get him talking. Do whatever it takes to gain time, Dave."

"Yeah, I will do what I can. I have to get Shannon out of there. The rest, well…" I let it hang.

"When you get on the elevator, call Felix's number and put your phone in your pocket to keep the line open. That way he will be able to hear what's going on. Park in such a way so the boot of the car is in shadow of the building so I can get out. I will try to help if I can."

"OK, there is the building now coming up on the right. Jesus, it's pretty dark up there. If the snipers get there, how will they see him?"

"Don't worry, Dave. They will have night scopes. They will see him all right. Just keep him talking to gain them time."

I pulled up to the gate, which was closed, put the car in park and got out; I looked around as I unhooked the chain and pushed it open. I got back in the car and inched forward. The phone chirped.

Melanie: I'm watching you. Once you park go back and close the gate. We don't want any other visitors, do we?

I chose not to answer. What was the point? I parked as close to the building scaffolding as I could without being obvious, then went back to the gate and closed it. By the light of the nearest streetlight I navigated my way to the right hand side and looked for an elevator.

Halfway down I saw it: a cage arrangement with what looked like railway tracks going up to the roof. I gulped with fear. It was not only because I was going to go face to face with a murderer, who killed me, my wife and other women who were important to me, but also because I hated heights. At least I wasn't going up by the crane which stood idly off to my right. I unlatched the door on the cage and stepped in, then sent a message.

Dave: I am in the lift. How do I operate it?

Melanie: I left the keys in it. Look for them hanging. Above that is a lever. Push it to the right and it goes up. Remember, I am watching.

I found the keys and pushed the lever. There was a lurch, then a flashing orange light started above my head and the slow ascent began with a "clang, clang" at each level. I dialled Felix's mobile number and slipped the phone into my top pocket as instructed. Then feeling absolutely petrified, I ascended to face my destiny.

Each side of the elevator shaft was comprised of criss-cross beams with alternating horizontals, like it was some massive kid's meccano construction set. The cage shook rattled and groaned, announcing my imminent arrival. *"Sam won't be going up this way,"* I thought. There was no way he could get up here without being heard.

Once I cleared the height of the trees, I could see across the river to the Perth city lights which illuminated my way. With the help those lights as well as my eyes adjusting to the dark around me, I began to be able to pick out more detail of the surrounding buildings none of which were as high as the roof of this one. If there were snipers anywhere I couldn't see them, and I had no idea how they could get a clear shot of the roof from a lower vantage. The closer to the top I got the queasier I felt with my fear of heights, not to mention my nerves about the killer, and facing the unknown.

Suddenly the cage jerked to a halt, and I let go of the lever. The orange light stopped flashing. At this height all there was to light the roof was moonlight. I could see the immediate area around me for twenty metres or so. There wasn't a pipe wielding madman ready to pounce on me anywhere in sight.

I opened the cage door and stepped onto the concrete formwork of the top story, over the gap between the cage and the roof, which took more courage than I knew I possessed. I deliberately left the cage door open and called out "I'm here!" Trying to sound a lot more confident than I felt, I waited.

"Keep walking."

At the sound of his voice I knew who it was. The final piece of the jigsaw fell into place, and in that instant I knew how I had to handle the situation.

"No, I'm not moving. You want me and you can have me, but only when Shannon is safe."

"I will kill her, mate. How's that?"

"If you do that, I get back on this lift and go down. I know who you are and I will go to the police. You will never get to me and you will spend the rest of your life in jail. And I will be laughing at you for the rest of my life."

"You're full of shit, mate."

"Am I, Neville? Am I really? Is that how I sound to you, like I'm full of shit? Don't you want to go one on one with me? Do you have the guts, finally, or are you only good for killing women? Oh, and of course, Judith's defenceless husband: you had to kill him from behind, didn't you you gutless cunt?"

"It's all your fault, mate. You turned her head and stole her away from me. Mark and I had it all cosy, sharing her. I looked after her while he was up north. Then you came along and all of a sudden she didn't want me anymore, and you wouldn't let me join you, would you, mate? You wanted her all to yourself."

Domin8

"You mean I stole your sister away from you? Have you heard of incest, Neville? Did you know it's illegal? It was your sick obsession that drove your own sister into a mental home, you sick FUCK."

"No, mate, you did that when you dumped her. She pined for you, mate, fucking pined away, turned Mark off her completely, it did, so he was going to leave her. I couldn't let that happen, could I? I couldn't spoil the good thing we had going before you showed up with your big cock?"

"Is that your problem, Neville? You've got a small cock, have you? Is that what this is really all about?

"Shut up, mate, I'm fucking warning you. I made sure he did leave her, forever. She was to be mine, you hear me? Mine, but I was willing to share. But, because of you, she thought her life was over when you dumped her. Then when she thought Mark left her too, that's sent her to Graylands, mate, not me. I'm the one who got her out of there, back where she belonged, with me, but all she wanted to talk about was YOU."

"Are you listening to yourself, Neville? Do you know what a sick little fuck you really are? This was your sister. You had no right."

"I had every right. It was always the two of us. Even when we were kids it was her and me, our dad taught us that."

I felt my skin crawl. Their father? Could this get any sicker?

"Are you saying your father had sex with you both as children, Neville? And because of that you think it was normal for you to want your sister to yourself? Can't you see how wrong any of that is?"

"Shut up, you! You aren't fit to clean my dad's shoes."

Stephen B. King

I shook my head; you can't use logic on an illogical person, I reminded myself. "So what happened when she got out of Graylands? She talked about me?"

"She didn't just talk. She wanted to get back with you, and she came to me for help. We took turns watching you, following you to see what you were up to. We saw you meeting all those women. You broke her heart all over again, every single time you fucked one of them. She cried her eyes out. She was hysterical every single time we saw you meet up with some slut. So in the end, I decided to do something about it, to get rid of them for her. She begged me to do it. She thought that when you were free you would want her, and she promised I could still have her too."

"So she knew what you were doing? Is that what you are saying, Neville?"

"Yeah, she knew. But then, when we did help you get free, which she knew you really wanted, you broke her heart all over again by shouting at her in the street, embarrassing her like you did, mate. She had done so much for you, and you chose this nurse over her: someone who didn't deserve to wipe my sister's arse. You fuckin' chose her? You broke her heart for the last time. I tried to reach her to calm her down. She had seen your fancy woman arrive, and I followed her when she left to find out where your little nurse lived. I told her, 'Judy, don't you worry. We can just do her like the others.' But it was too late. She told me she was coming to see you and give you one last chance to choose her, but you were out with 'Nursey,' weren't you? She was all alone in your house, heartbroken, and she took her own life. YOU TOOK HER AWAY FROM ME." He screamed in demonic rage.

I had heard enough. I was trembling with anger at the demented stupidity of it all.

"Let's finish this once and for all. Send out Shannon. She can go down the lift, and you and I can dance. You've got your

Domin8

knife, and I'm sure your bit of steel pipe handy. You like hitting people with that, don't you? I've got nothing by the way, but you know what I have got, Neville? I've got guts, more guts that you could ever have. I'm going to count to thirty, and if that woman is not here in the lift by then, I'm going back down in it and getting the police. I'm tired of your sick, fucking demented games. Kill her if you want, make a decision, now."

By now my eyes had adjusted well to the dark, and I knew where his voice was coming from. He was hiding in the shadows by the main elevator shaft in the middle of the building. I looked around for anything I could use as a weapon, but couldn't see a thing. Maybe he saw to that before I arrived.

"How do I know you won't get in the lift with your slut and run out, mate?"

"Ever see the old movie with Clint Eastwood, Neville: The Good the Bad and the Ugly?"

"What if I have, mate?"

"At the end of the film, the three of them are in the centre of the graveyard, equally spaced out in a triangle, with that music playing. Shannon, she's the Good, I'm the Bad, and you're the fucking Ugly one, Neville. Bring her out so I can see you both, then you let her walk towards the lift as I walk away from it: equal distance apart, Neville. She gets in the lift and goes down leaving just the two of us, and I'm too far away to get there before you can get to me. You have a weapon, and I don't. What do you have to lose? Do you have the guts, Neville? Well do you?"

"You took everything away from me. Why shouldn't I take everything away from you and kill her, mate?"

"*FUCK! It's like dealing with a child.*" I thought for a moment and said, "Neville, she is innocent. She is the Good one in this movie, remember? She was the nurse, who looked after me when I got shot, and we went out to dinner together once. Otherwise, she means nothing to me. She did offer to put me up for the night when I couldn't stay home when Judith killed herself in my bathtub, and the cops ordered me out of the house. But that's the kind of good-hearted person she is. Sure, you could kill her, and I would be upset at that, but only because she is such a good person and didn't deserve it. Otherwise, though, I don't feel much for her either way. I am the one you want. If you come out of those shadows alone, that tells me you've killed her, and I get on the lift and I'm gone before you get to me. Then you will never get your revenge on me, and the whole world will know you killed a woman rather than face a man. It's your call mate, but make it quick. I'm getting cold."

"All right, I'm cutting her free. Give me a minute." There was silence for a few seconds, and I dared hope that I had done it; I had bargained for her freedom and life.

Suddenly his voice rang out again, "Hey, mate? I know what you see in her. She's a good fuck, ain't she?"

My blood ran cold as I realised he had raped her. Now I wanted to kill him. Soon this nightmare would all be over, and she would be safe. I heard rustling and a couple of grunts from the shadows, followed by Neville's voice telling Shannon to get up but not to make any sudden moves. After what felt like an eternity I saw them emerge, two shadows huddled together. He was obviously holding her next to him.

"Ok, Neville, I can see you both. Now let her go. Shannon, just take two steps at a time, and Neville, as she takes two steps, so will I. Shannon, walk towards where I am now and when you get here you will see the cage. Get inside, put the safety bar down and go down by pressing the lever to the left."

I took two steps away, and I saw a smaller shadow disengage from the larger as she took two steps away. It was working. I said a prayer of thanks and took two more steps, as did Shannon, and so it continued. With each step forward, she was closer to freedom, and I to my doom.

When Shannon reached the cage at I could see one of Neville's arms seemed to be much longer than the other from the angle I was now standing from. He no doubt held a length of pipe in his right hand. There didn't seem to be any other ending to this situation than my impending death, yet I was calm. If Shannon could just make her way down to Sam, that would be enough. Neville would surely kill me, but he would be caught by the police, I felt as if the ledger had been balanced. I also knew that, with this ending, my children would be safe from this madman, and if my death was the price to pay for that, so be it. I felt relaxed and took the last two steps forward.

"Go, Shannon. Go now. Thank you for all you did for me. You changed me for the better. Go now. I am so sorry for the pain and suffering I've caused you."

She stepped into the cage and pushed the lever, crying loudly, and I watched her slowly descend into safety.

I was never much of a fighter. I never even enjoyed violent movies, really, and here I was on a rooftop, alone with a madman who had a steel pipe and a knife, intent on beating me to death. What could I do?

Clearly the snipers hadn't made it in time. With the lift staying up here for Shannon to go down in, there was no way for Sam to come to my aid. My last coherent thought was, "Such is life," a quotation made famous by an old Australian bush ranger named Ned Kelly, who said that just before they hanged him.

I ran at Neville, screaming like a banshee and took him completely by surprise. I guess even though he was a killer, he wasn't used to having victims who fought back. Startled, he took a step back, then changed to run at me and then thought better of it so he was suck in no-man's-land. I saw him raise the pipe. I went for him, diving full length, arms outstretched to grab him, and my head hit him at full pelt in his stomach.

A length of steel scaffolding pipe around 35 centimetres long weighs about two kilograms. When it hits it does so with tremendous force and can smash bones, but because of its weight it is slow and unwieldy. No doubt it was the perfect weapon for unsuspecting women, but it was not quite so effective against someone who was quick. I was fighting for my life, and I took him by surprise. Neville would have done better if he had used his knife.

As I collided with him I felt the pipe hit me in the back of my head and shoulder with a sickening force, but only the base of it hit my head. I saw stars and immediately fought to stay conscious, while the momentum of my dive knocked him from his feet because he was so skinny. He couldn't hit me a second time, being off balance and falling backwards.

As we hit the ground he lost his grip on the pipe, and it rolled away. I shook the stars and fuzziness from my head and rose up and knelt above him. He was struggling to catch a breath as I punched him on the side of his face with all of the strength I could muster, but being hit by a steel pipe and struggling to stay awake, it probably wasn't my best punch. I hit him again and again, and I thought I felt his nose break on the second, but after my third blow he stabbed me in my side.

I knew what he had done as soon as it happened and realized then I was going to die. I felt a massive burning pain just under my ribs and flinched. I reached with my left hand and could feel the handle sticking out of me. I fell to the other side, and he laughed and wriggled out from under me. I lay on the concrete, feeling the cold of the surface, blood pumping out around my

Domin8

hand holding the knife handle, the blade buried deep inside me. I was desperate to stay conscious, but everything faded in and out. I knew I would be seeing Di again soon, and I hoped she would forgive me.

I saw him bend over double and spit out blood. "At least I had hurt him," I thought. But then I realized he wasn't bent over in pain. No, he was picking up the pipe, and the only thought I had as he walked back towards me was of sorrow for fucking up my life and causing misery to everyone I had cared about.

Stephen B. King

Chapter 29 – Shannon (9) – Sam Collins (5)

Embodiment of Evil and the Darkest of Times

When ripples occur from a dropped stone, spreading out and widening, a breeze can make them bigger. If the breeze turns into wind, then what started as a ripple can turn into a wave that builds momentum. The stronger the wind, the bigger the wave. Some waves become tsunamis.

XXX

When Shannon walked through her front door, her first thought was to take a long hot shower as it had been a long day. She wanted to smell nice for Dave, if he visited as she hoped that he would.

She had no other thought than of Dave as she entered her bathroom and was immediately punched in the face. She fell to the floor, dazed and in shock, aware of the blood streaming from her nose. She shook her head, trying to clear the fuzzy cloud in her brain and felt herself being manhandled so she was turned roughly onto her stomach. Her hands were taped together behind her back and then she was turned over still not understanding what had happened to her.

A scruffy thin faced man, with horrible breath put his face next to hers and said: "You wanna die, bitch? Scream or call out

Domin8

and you will. If you wanna live, keep your fucking slut mouth shut."

All of the worst fears in her life had come true: a burglar and potential rapist was in her house. She was terrified. She tasted the blood on her lips and felt the room spinning around her, but as she was about to slip into the fog, she felt her face being slapped hard, twice, and she jerked herself back to wakefulness. The man pulled her to her feet by his hand clenched on the top of her uniform. She felt and heard it tear open, and she saw his eyes light up as the intruder saw her breasts.

"Oh yeah, you want it, Nursey, don't you? Well, you're in luck; we have a bit of time to kill before we take a little trip together. Your man stole the love of my life. Now I'm gonna steal his."

The next half an hour was a nightmare for her. He pulled her uniform up, ripped her underwear off and roughly raped her from behind on her own bed. He seemed to take delight in her crying and begging for him not to hurt her. He pulled on her hair and continually slapped and punched her, as he ruthlessly rode her.

As she felt him ejaculate she was very nearly sick to her stomach. Sadly, she realised this had happened because she had fallen for Dave. The best man to come into her life had caused her the worst experience she'd ever known.

She cried tears of disgust, shame and fear as she felt him get his stinky, sweaty body off of her and heard him zip up his dirty jeans. She feared this was only the beginning of the nightmare; the madman was going to kill her.

"Stop your pathetic tears, you bitch. You loved it. You wanna see your boyfriend again? Wanna see if he cares for you or

316

Stephen B. King

not? See if he is willing to try and save you? Get up, lovey; we're going for a drive."

He grabbed her upper arm and lifted her from the bed. He turned her round and put his face within an inch of hers so she could smell his bad breath again. One hand still held her upper arm, tightly, bruising her; the other grabbed her long hair, bunched it up and pulled it, her head jolting viciously. She noticed he couldn't keep his eyes still. He continually looked from one place to the next: in her eyes, down at her tits, then to the door, down at his feet – it was making her dizzy to follow his eyes around the room.

"You got one chance to live, Lovey. Are you paying attention?" He shook her head by the bunched up handful of hair her held in his hand.

She nodded and said, "Yes, I will do anything you say. Please don't hurt me anymore."

He let go of her hair and put his hand in his front pocket of his jeans and took something out. She couldn't see what it was, but heard a light click. Then she saw what he was holding: an evil looking blade flicked out of the handle of a knife.

"I'm going to put one of your jackets over you, Lovey, so no one sees your hands are tied, and then we are going for a walk around the corner to my car. You will get in the passenger side, right? Then we are going for a drive and when we get there, well, we are going to call your lover boy who broke my sister's heart. We will ask him nicely to come and save you. If he does, you might live, but if you try to get away, call out, scream or do anything I will kill you. Understand, Lovey?"

During the long statement his eyes never stopped still for more than a few seconds. He was completely, absolutely mad, she realised.

Domin8

She nodded, too scared to speak, hoping upon hope she would live through the night, though deep down she doubted she would.

They left the house, her arms still taped behind her back, his hand holding her elbow and a coat hiding everything. She hoped someone would see her torn uniform and blood where he had punched her, but they didn't see anyone on their way to the car.

They reached a dirty, old model Ford utility. He opened the passenger door. She was amazed at how much rubbish was on the floor. It almost came spilling out as he yanked the door open. There were McDonalds and other fast food wrappers, coke cans, discarded used tissues and scrunched up shopping bags. He half helped, half pushed her inside.

Amongst the rubbish there were two lengths of grey steel pipe and some complicated looking clamps. She had to be careful where she put her feet. He reached around her and put on a seatbelt that was caked in red dust and grime. Once she was tightly buckled in, he reached up and squeezed her right breast roughly. "*God*," she thought, "*he's disgusting.*"

"Play your cards right, Lovely, and we could have a second helping while we wait for your boyfriend. You'd like that, wouldn't you?"

He laughed loudly and slammed the door, then walked around to the other side and got in. He started the engine and roared away down the street while she choked back tears and tried *really* hard not to vomit.

She didn't know how they arrived at the building site without the police stopping them or getting involved in an accident. He was a terrible driver, speeding and braking hard at traffic signs and lights while screaming obscenities at other drivers. The erratic driving was compounded by his habit of not being able to look at one thing for more than a couple of seconds at a time.

One place he did keep looking at more than any other was her legs. When stopped at a red light, he pulled her uniform up to her waist so he could see her matted pubic hair. She tried to keep her thighs tightly pressed against each other, because when he wasn't changing gears, he was touching her legs as if he owned her. He kept reaching for her crotch, trying to pry her legs apart so he could finger her.

When she didn't part her legs for him, he slapped her thigh, hard, leaving a red handprint on her. She choked back tears and gave him the access he demanded. For the rest of the trip she felt sick and ashamed as he touched her most intimate parts as if she were a common whore, or worse – his girlfriend. She felt torn between wanting to die from disgust and wanting to live.

When they pulled up at the gate, which was locked by a big chain, he turned to her, "Don't worry, Lovey. I have a key. I'm the head rigger here. I know you want me some more, and I'm ready for ya." He grabbed his crotch and squeezed it lewdly to show he was erect again. He slapped her thigh again, hard and got out to unlock the gate.

After opening it, he brought the lock and chain back with him and tossed it on the back seat. He drove through, stopped and then went back to shut the gate, but didn't relock it. He got back in the car and drove around to the rear of the building, out of sight from the road, then got out.

He walked around to her side, opened her door and dragged her out roughly. He caught her just before she landed face first into the ground. He then reached back in and grabbed a length of steel pipe. He brandished it in front of her face and said, "We need this for your boyfriend, Lovey."

They got to a red cage-like construct, which she realised was a lift on the outside of the building, and he undid another padlock, swung the gate open. He pushed her forward and they entered, then he shut the gate behind them. Then, with another key on the same ring he put it into a slot on a small consul and turned it. A red light came on, and he pushed a lever to the right. Slowly, they went up.

"Don't worry, Lovey. We will find a nice quiet spot and have some quality time before your boyfriend gets here."

Shannon was so scared, more terrified than she could ever imagine a person could be. This man was a mentally sick animal. She had no doubt her and Dave's life were in complete danger; if he came to help her, that was. Maybe he wouldn't. She hoped not. That way he might live. But if he did come, she knew in her heart they wouldn't live through the ordeal that was to come. Either way, there was no hope for her; he would kill her.

He sent the lift back down, then marched her into the shadows of the elevator housing. He put her on a plastic chair. With mounting fear, bordering on sheer panic, she watched him undo his jeans and take his filthy cock out. He was going to rape her again. Suddenly, death didn't seem too bad of an ending to the nightmare.

XXX

Sam Collins had waited until he heard the clanking of what sounded like a poorly-maintained elevator, grinding its way upwards. He inched open the boot and climbed out into the shadows of the scaffolding, listening for any sounds.

His legs had pins and needles, and he moved them to shake it off while he turned his phone off. If he was to be any help at all to Dave, he couldn't risk his phone ringing and giving away his presence.

He cursed the fact that he was unarmed. Being off duty, he had left his gun at headquarters when he had left to meet Dave. He shrugged to himself. It couldn't be helped. He looked around his feet as his eyes adjusted to the darkness and saw a piece of timber which, looked like it might do as a fairly decent club.

He searched in the gloomy haze for another way up to the roof, as the outside lift was way too noisy. Even if it came back down there was no way he could use it. The structure for the floors was in place, with some walls supporting the levels, but there were no doors or windows. There had to be stairs near the elevator shaft, he reasoned, and took off as quietly as possible to find them. He had to watch where he walked, as like all building sites he had ever seen, this one seemed to have litter and offcuts for various things all over the place. He couldn't take the chance of being heard and he didn't want to kick something accidentally and make a noise.

The further inside he got, the darker it became, but he dared not turn his phone on to use the light, for fear of tipping off his presence. After what seemed an eternity he finally found the bank of elevator shafts and concrete steps going up, and he began his climb upwards.

With three floors to go the steps ran out. They hadn't been constructed yet. Sam's heart sank. There was an aluminium ladder secured, which went up through to each next level, but aluminium ladders were noisy.

Domin8

There was nothing for it. He couldn't take his timber club with him, as he could not afford for it to accidentally hit the ladder and alert the killer he was there. He carefully put it on the ground, and then he took his shoes off. Slowly, and as quietly as possible, he climbed higher.

As he got closer to the roof, he could hear the voices yelling at each other. He felt dismayed as he realised the killer was directly above him. He could not risk going all the way up for fear he would be discovered. He had to wait. He went as high as he dared and listened to the conversation as it unfolded.

He marvelled at Dave's calmness and his goading Neville to get Shannon to safety. Sam's respect for him increased a hundredfold. It was obvious he was knowingly sacrificing his life to save hers. Even Felix would be impressed, he was sure, with Dave's bravery, knowing he was listening in on the open phone line.

Sam felt utter disgust when he heard Neville tell Dave of the incest, then even more contempt, when he said that he had raped Shannon. He barely knew her, but thought Shannon a truly beautiful woman, and she didn't deserve what had befallen her. *"Some people in this world, like Neville"* he thought, *"do not deserve to live."*

When he heard them shuffle away out of the elevator shaft area, he edged higher up the rungs, not daring to breathe out loud or make any noise that would give him away.

He was six rungs short of the roof landing as he heard Dave scream and heard the footsteps of him running towards Neville. Sam picked up the pace of his climb up, still not wanting to give his position away, but hurrying to get there as quickly as he could.

322

Stephen B. King

He heard the thud of colliding bodies as he stepped onto the roof. Inching forward, he trod on a sharp offcut piece of timber with nails sticking out of it. He had to supress a scream and bent down to pull it out. It felt as if he had turned a blowtorch onto his sole.

He bit his lower lip to help ignore the pain. By the time he got to the doorway, he saw Dave topple to the concrete holding his side in the moonlight, and the other man climb to his feet.

Sam couldn't move, as the killer was facing him, bending down and picking up the pipe, which had been dropped in the scuffle.

The man turned back to Dave and walked slowly towards him. Sam wanted to run, but he knew there was no way he could make it before Neville would cave Dave's skull in, with the pipe now held in his hand.

Neville stood over Dave, who was writhing on the roof, as Sam screamed at the top of his lungs, "STOP! ARMED POLICE! THROW DOWN THAT PIPE NOW, OR I SHOOT!" With that he took off at a run as fast as his wounded foot could, but with utter dismay heard the man say, "No way, mate. This prick dies."

Sam saw him raise his hand, which held the pipe above his head, to smash in Dave's skull. But, before he could, Dave reached up from his prone position and hit Neville on his thigh. A loud scream pierced the still of the night and Sam realised Dave had pulled the knife out of his own side to us on his attacker.

Neville screamed continuously, as he looked down at the sight of the blade sticking out of his leg. He dropped the pipe to grab his wounded thigh as a reflex. The length of scaffolding turned in freefall through the air, and the end struck Dave in the face as he lay on the roof.

Domin8

For the second time that night Neville was hit by a flying rugby tackle as Sam collided with him from behind. They rolled together as the sound of approaching sirens filled the night.

Neville, was no match for an enraged, very fit and angry Sam Collins, who had trained in mixed martial arts, even had he not been wounded. Sam hit him with his fists several times with devastating effect, breaking bones and cartilage in his face.

When the man moved no more, Sam stood up panting; his muscles tired from the adrenalin rush. He screamed at Neville to stay still, and that he was under arrest. His words fell on deaf ears; Neville was unconscious, face bloody and beaten horribly.

Stephen B. King

Afterword

Shannon had once said to me that she believed everyone deserved a second chance. I got mine, though I couldn't agree that I deserved anything good that came along after that night on the roof.

I had the strangest feeling of déjà vu when I woke up in hospital. But this time I didn't see a beautiful nurse; I saw my old Scottish Doctor frowning at me. I realised I could only see out of one eye and when I turned my good eye to look at the left, I saw bandages on the other one. Slowly my senses came back to me through the veils of drugged drowsiness and dull throbbing pains.

"I've come up with a new name for you, laddie. It's Cluedo, because you've been shot, stabbed and hit with an iron pipe. I'm just not sure if it was Professor Plum in the lounge or the Butler in the library. Welcome back to the land of the living."

It was good to hear his broad Scottish brogue, but I had to ask, "Shannon?"

"She's fine, laddie. She's been through the wringer, but I'm told she will be OK."

I closed my one good eye as a tear rolled out of it.

"Your three young'uns are waiting outside to see you, and I'm going to let them in just to see you're OK for a few minutes, but I thought you might want to know how you are first."

I nodded in gratitude, unable to stop crying. I was a complete mess emotionally.

Domin8

"Well, let's start with the concussion. You've had a hell of a blow to the back of the head and thirteen stitches to sew the gash back up. We need to watch the concussion. I don't know how you do it, laddie, but you've got a crack in your other shoulder where the pipe hit you there. What is it with you and cracking shoulder bones?"

I shrugged as best as I could, not daring to speak, as I knew my voice would break.

"You've been very lucky with the knife wound. It missed your kidney and not done any serious damage. But, you won't be going anywhere, nor doing any strenuous movement, for at least a week or two while you recover." He wagged his finger at me.

"You've broken two fingers. I've strapped them up. I think you tried to punch someone and hit some concrete instead by the look of them. You might want to have some boxing lessons for next time and learn to hit what you're aiming for."

So, I hadn't broken his nose when I punched him. I had missed and smashed my fingers on the roof. *"Some fighter I was,"* I thought.

He smiled broadly at his own humour. "You'll no be as handsome as you were, I'm sorry. There are nine stiches in your cheek. I'm told that's where the end of the steel pipe hit when it was dropped, but I'm also told some women find facial scars on men to be attractive..."

He winked at me, and I remembered him doing that once before, at an attempt of humour at my reputed attraction to women. I didn't bother correcting him. I just couldn't give a damn, really.

"That's all the good news, I'm afraid, Laddie. Then there is the wound to your eye. You've been operated on by the best eye man we have, and he has saved it, but there is corneal damage

326

which may never fully recover, only time will tell. We estimate a fifty percent loss of vision, and you'll probably need glasses or contacts to help. That pesky pipe bounced off your cheek into your eye, I'm sorry."

I shrugged again, suddenly fighting to stay awake and not really caring too much about anything, least of all my health. All I wanted was to get back to the cataract darkness of sleep; where I didn't hate myself.

"Aye, I can see you're tired and will let you go. You need your rest, laddie."

XXX

Over the next two weeks I suffered from severe depression. I had daily counselling sessions, as they believed I was suicidal, although I didn't ask for it, nor wanted it; all I wanted was to die.

Eventually, the darkness did lift. As I learnt to understand, with help from Tania, my councillor/psychologist/helper, the depression had been brought on by delayed grief and guilt. I had more guilt than anyone should have to handle, she told me. But I had one other feeling, that I dare not admit, not even to myself; I missed Shannon.

At least one of my children were with me every day and night, no matter what time. Continuously, they each told me how proud they were of me. But their words sounded so hollow to me, as I wasn't capable of feeling proud of myself.

I didn't think I would ever be able to forgive myself for the affair that had started the nightmare. There was no one to blame

Domin8

but myself. I do believe that, were it not for Tania, I would have committed suicide the first chance I had.

I think the turning point came for me several days later, when Sam and Felix came to visit and asked that my nurse tell me Starsky and Hutch asked to see me. I laughed out loud, and Bryony was pleased to see me smile for the first time since she had been taking care of me.

They knew, of course, I was battling with depression which is why they had been forbidden to see me earlier. The most important news, they told me, was that the judge had ruled Neville would not be standing trial, because he found him to be mentally incompetent. This meant that Shannon would be spared having to give evidence and suffer cross examination about the rapes she had endured at his hands.

Most likely a trial would have been useless for him anyway, as his "confession" had been recorded on the open phone line from my pocket. No doubt his lawyer, realising that, had opted for insanity instead of a trial.

It also meant that, in all probability, Neville would never see the light of day again, as he could be held indefinitely. That would save me giving evidence about my affairs and ensure that Dianne's memory wouldn't be smeared anymore. While I was past caring for myself, I was pleased the kids would be spared my dirty laundry being aired in public any more than it had already.

They told me that this would be the last episode, that's how they worded it – episode. Starsky and Hutch would be publically "aired," as not only had Sam received a commendation and would receive a medal for bravery, he had also been promoted to Sargent. As they would both be the same rank they would be separated and both gain new partners.

Stephen B. King

At that news, the tears came again for me. I did a lot of crying, no matter how hard I tried not to, but I was so pleased for Sam. He had not only saved my life twice but had believed in my innocence from the start. His promotion was well-deserved, and an award for bravery for taking on a known killer unarmed, also well-earned. He was to become a bit of a hero for the police force with the resultant publicity, and I wished him every bit of success that came his way.

They had both spoken to the press on numerous times on my behalf. The media had been hungry for details, and Felix and Sam were determined to ensure that I wasn't shown in too badly a light, for which I was very grateful. In fact, they had done such a good job, I was hailed as a hero, rather than the adulterous rat that I felt that I was.

It helped somewhat that the internet dating hadn't in fact had anything to do with unearthing a murderer. Of course, two victims were killed only because they had met me in that way, but as far as the press were concerned, that part of the story no longer captured the same sensationalist effect.

I had come to respect Felix for his straightforwardness and brutal honesty, and nothing helped me more through my dark times, than him, when he told me some home truths. Not one to pull punches he asked if I knew what redemption meant? I said, "Yes, I think so but I'm not sure. Why do you ask?"

"Dave, I might not be a good Catholic, like my wife, but I do believe in redemption. You were a self-centred, hedonistic egotist who didn't think of consequences beyond getting your rocks off. Shit happened because of your attitude to life, love and liberty but—and Dave I hope you are listening now, because this is the important bit."

Ha waited until I nodded.

Domin8

"Most men in your situation would not have gone up on that roof. They would expect us to, because that's our job. They would have waited for us or sent Sam up there, and he would have gone, unarmed. Not only did you go up there to face a killer, you then gambled your own life to save a woman who you barely knew. That is called redemption, Dave, and you have my utmost respect and admiration. You, my friend, are a genuine hero."

I couldn't speak because I was filled with gratitude and emotion, and when more tears came, somehow, they felt different.

Sam jumped in at that point, "That is what we have been pushing the press to report on. Rather than destroy your reputation for being an adulterer in the sensational internet dating world, we've pushed them to show there is a fantastic human interest story here: of a genuine heroic act done to save someone's while sacrificing your own. I agree with Felix, Dave. You did a great thing here; you deserve to stop blaming yourself. Give yourself a break, get back to normal and be a father to your children: not this depressed wounded person that you've become."

XXX

It took a lot more time, and numerous sessions with Tania, along with a lot of love and support from my children, but by the time the bandage came off my eye I felt a lot better about my place in the world. I would never see properly out of that eye again. They were right about the 50% estimate, but glasses did help. By the time I was ready to leave the hospital I felt ready to take on the world again, albeit very slowly and carefully.

The day before I left the hospital George came to see me with bad news. The board in its infinite wisdom had decided to ask me to resign, and I understood that. I had regained my balance enough by then not to tell him that I had already made that decision for myself. I did not want to go back and work there after all that had happened. I needed a fresh start though in truth I had no idea what I was going to do.

He was very sorry, of course. He told me that he was personally against it and argued my case, blah, blah, blah, but by that point in the conversation, I'd stopped listening. They wanted to make what they considered to be a very generous offer, and it was. They would transfer the car I was driving free of charge to me, and they would pay me five months' salary as a "good will" gesture for services rendered over the years, plus my outstanding leave entitlements. I thought it was very fair and accepted the offer without fuss. The money was in my bank account by the end of the week.

On my last day at the hospital, I deeply hoped Shannon would stop by, and I waited and waited in vain. Everyone was so secretive about her: as if she was a subject no one was allowed to talk about around me. I accepted that, clearly, she had chosen not to see me, and that was her right. I decided that the very least I could do was not contact her and make it that much more difficult for her. She had been to hell and back, all because of me, and I genuinely believed she was far better off without me.

Just before I left I had a visit from a senior administrator of the hospital named Elmer Lister, and because of the unusual name I was reminded of the movie Elmer Gantry about a preacher played by Burt Lancaster. He sat down in a chair by the bed and got straight to the point.

"Mr. Barndon, it has come to our attention that you have been having a 'romantic' relationship with one of our nurses Ms. Shannon McGuire. I must ask you if any form of 'romantic' occurrence happened while you were here as a patient on your last stay with us."

Domin8

"Mr. Lister, I have no idea why you are here trying to malign one of the finest nurses and most professional people I have ever had the pleasure to meet. The answer to your question is, of course, no, nothing inappropriate occurred while I was a patient here. After I was discharged I called her to ask her out, and she graciously accepted. Because of that gesture the poor woman was abducted, raped, beaten and threatened with her very life. Now as her employer you are questioning her integrity? How dare you. Has she not been through enough?"

"There is no need to take that attitude, Mr. Barndon. She has been on leave since the 'incident,' and we needed to assess her status. As you are willing to say she was totally professional while caring for you, and that nothing untoward can be attributed to her actions, we can accept it. The question had to be asked, from a liability aspect. Thank you for being so honest."

I was seething with rage. He could see that and decided to beat a hasty retreat. But at least I had found out why she hadn't visited me. She had been on sick leave herself. I worried if I should contact her or not, and in the end, despite my own feelings, I decided not to. She had suffered terribly because of me, and she deserved to be left in peace.

I would miss her terribly, but I also knew I didn't deserve any happiness with her, though Tania disagreed. I felt I should suffer for my sins, and I had accepted that was to be my lot in life going forward. Believing she would be better off without me, there was nothing to be gained by seeing her, and I thought that by trying to get over her trauma, seeing me only to say goodbye, might make things worse for her. Better to leave well enough alone and let her recover.

My children all came to help me leave what had become almost my second home. I refused their offers to stay with them. Even Missy seemed to have thawed towards me somewhat because each day when she had visited she brought me things she had baked, or cooked, though I knew she still resented me at some level for the unfaithfulness.

They understood that I wanted to be by myself, but were concerned I wasn't over my depression. I was, however, over the worst of it. I was going to keep seeing Tania for a while. I found it very comforting to talk to her about the guilt issues I still harboured, but suicide was not going to be an option for me. I had thankfully turned that corner.

I had been home eight days and had not answered the phone or door to anyone other than my children, when the doorbell rang out of the blue one warm afternoon I decided at that moment that I had been a hermit long enough, and it was time to turn my phone back on and start my life up again. I still lived in a state of permanent anxiousness and anxiety, and knowing the kids were all at work I peered through the spy hole to see who it was. There was a very well dressed business woman standing with a briefcase in her hand, who looked harmless enough. If I thought she was a reporter I would have ignored her, but she did not have that look to her so I took a deep breath and opened the door.

"Hi, Mr. Barndon, my name is Janet Glossop. Here is my card. If I may, I'd like to talk to you."

She smiled and showed perfect teeth, and I was intrigued enough to invite her in. I stood to one side for her to enter and looked at the card. She was Managing Director for Glossop, Main and Paredes, who were literary agents and publicists with offices in Melbourne, London and New York.

I took her to the alfresco overlooking the pool as it was a lovely golden day, and offered her a seat. She declined a coffee but agreed to a glass of iced water. While I got it for her she took out a thick manila folder and placed it in front of her and placed her bag on the seat beside her.

I gave her a glass and sat down, gingerly. The stab wound still hurt if I moved suddenly.

"How can I help you, Janet?" I asked, wary of what she might say.

"You could write me a book, Dave. You don't mind if I call you Dave, do you?"

I laughed and wondered who had set me up for this practical joke.

"Me? Write a book? You've got to be joking."

She opened the folder, took out a contract and a smaller piece of paper which was a cheque made out in my name for $500,000. "No, I'm not joking, Dave. I have negotiated for you an advance for a one book deal, detailing your story to be completed within four months in your own words. But, in my opinion this is only the start. From what I hear and read, this will be a movie deal, too, and will probably net you in excess of one million total. I think I can get Brad Pitt or George Clooney to play you."

She stared at me and waited for a response, but I was flabbergasted.

"One million dollars?" I thought I must have misheard her.

"I can pay you in yen, if you prefer, Dave. Now I know what you are going to say, but don't worry. You tell the story and I will have it edited for you. I just want your words, exclusively, about what happened from start to finish. Let me worry about it being written in the proper format."

"One million?"

"One million, minimum," She nodded earnestly.

Stephen B. King

"Four months?"

"Maximum. Do you always talk in shorthand, Dave?"

This was a complete and utter shock, and I sat there for minutes on end thinking, my mind racing. Could I? Should I, even?

"I just don't know that I can do it, relive it and drag it all up all over again. I'm trying to forget it all. And, there are other people to consider, my children particularly."

She nodded and opened up the folder again. She took out three small handwritten cards and laid them out on the table. The cards had the unmistakable scrawl of my children's handwriting.

"I always wanted an author for a dad. Love, Jase"

"We love you, dad. Do it. Bryan."

"You need to do this, Dad, for you. Exorcise those ghosts. Missy"

"Oh my God, what are you doing to me?" My tears, which I hoped were gone, returned with a vengeance. I wasn't up to this. No way could I go through all that again. I needed to talk to Tania. I felt like I was suffocating. This was just too much for me to take in, and I felt as if I were in a panic. I stood up and then sat back down again. I couldn't breathe.

"Dave, there is one more person I know you think of. I met with her last night, and she asked me to give you a note."

She took out a sealed pink envelope and held it out to me. There was no writing on the outside, and I dreaded what was inside. With trembling fingers, I took it and opened the letter as carefully as my shaking hands would allow.

Dear Dave,

On that roof I saw the worst, and the best, that a man can be. I was abused, beaten and raped and wanted to crawl away and die, but at the same time I desperately wanted to survive. I only survived because of you. You were willing to sacrifice your life to save mine, and I cannot imagine ever meeting another man who would care for me and protect me as much as I know you would.

I have been battling my demons, and I have heard you have been, too, so I thought it best to give you space and time, as I needed that as well.

If you will have me, I am yours, forever, even though I don't feel worthy of you. I love you, Dave, and only want to be with you.

Whether or not you want me in your life, which I hope you do when it feels right, I think you should write this book. We can't hide from what happened, so let's embrace it. I am ready for that, if you are.

Shannon

Tears brimming in my eyes, I looked up at Janet and saw the pen she held out for me. Without another word I took it and signed the contract to write this book.

The End

Stephen B. King

Stephen B. King
Perth Western Australia

Made in the USA
Charleston, SC
18 August 2016